The
Dark Lady's
Mask

ALSO BY MARY SHARRATT

Summit Avenue

The Real Minerva

The Vanishing Point

Bitch Lit (coeditor)

Daughters of the Witching Hill

Illuminations

The Dark Lady's Mask

MARY SHARRATT

Houghton Mifflin Harcourt

BOSTON   NEW YORK

2016

For information about permission to reproduce selections
from this book, write to trade.permissions@hmhco.com or to
Permissions, Houghton Mifflin Harcourt Publishing Company,
3 Park Avenue, 19th Floor, New York, New York 10016.

www.hmhco.com

Library of Congress Cataloging-in-Publication Data
Sharratt, Mary, date.
The dark lady's mask / Mary Sharratt.
pages ; cm
ISBN 978-0-544-30076-7 (hardcover) — ISBN 978-0-544-28974-1 (ebook)
1. Lanyer, Aemilia—Fiction. 2. Women poets, English—Fiction.
3. Shakespeare, William, 1564–1616—Fiction. 4. Man-woman
relationships—Fiction. I. Title.
PS3569.H3449D37 2016
813'.54—dc23   2015020514

.Book design by Rachel Newborn

Printed in the United States of America
DOC 10 9 8 7 6 5 4 3 2 1

For Joske

The myth of Aemilia Lanyer as Shakespeare's Dark Lady both testifies to our continuing cultural investment in a fantasy of a female Shakespeare, and reveals some of the anxieties about difference that haunt canonical Renaissance literature.

—Kate Chedgzoy, "Remembering Aemilia Lanyer,"
Journal of the Northern Renaissance, Issue 2, 2010

Vouchsafe to view that which is seldome seene,
A Womans writing of divinest things.

—Aemilia Lanyer, "To the Queenes most Excellent Majestie,"
Salve Deus Rex Judaeorum

PRELUDE

The Astrologer

1593

THE HUNGER TO KNOW her destiny enflamed Aemilia's heart, driving her to Billingsgate on a scorching afternoon. She hastened down Thames Street, crammed with grocers whose vegetables wilted in the heat, offering up their odors of slow decay. This parish was a gathering place of outcasts and refugees, peopled by immigrants fleeing the religious wars that raged in the Low Countries. The Dutch and Flemish paid dearly for their lodgings in once-great houses that had become tenements, rotting away like the unsold lettuces in the market stalls.

A waif darted in Aemilia's path to distract her while his accomplice attempted to snatch her purse, only to receive a swat from Winifred, her maid, who towered over Aemilia like a blond giantess. Winifred, her stalwart protectress.

"Oh, mistress, let us go home," the maid pleaded. "This is no district for a gentlewoman."

But Aemilia pressed on until she sighted the steeple of Saint Botolph's Billingsgate and beside it the Stone House, the former rectory, its chambers now let by tradesmen. Over the shadowy entrance hung the shingle she had been seeking.

DOCTOR SIMON FORMAN
MASTER ASTROLOGER & PHYSICIAN

Winifred balked, but Aemilia led the way across the threshold and up the stairs to the astrologer's consulting room. A sallow apprentice opened the door, its hinges squeaking like bats.

"The master astrologer shall see you shortly, madam."

Aemilia blinked as her eyes adjusted to the murk of this chamber with its single window. Her eyes lingered on the star charts and sigils scribed on virgin parchment and pinned to the ancient wainscoting. The room was sweltering, for a fire blazed beneath a bubbling still. The astrologer appeared absorbed in casting various herbs into the strong water, their essential oils marrying in a fragrant alchemical dance that left her reeling.

To calm her nerves, she examined Doctor Forman's bookshelf. Apart from his prominently displayed Geneva Bible, most of his texts were Latin—Alcabitius's treatise on the conjunctions of the planets and Gilbertus Anglicus's rules for testing a patient's urine. She smiled to see *Philosophia Magna* by the great Paracelsus, a book she knew well but hadn't had the opportunity to read in years. Opening the pages, she whispered the Latin words in an incantation, for Paracelsus's hermetical ideal fascinated her—nature was the macrocosm, humanity the microcosm. Everything in the universe was interdependent, like the interlocking parts inside a clock, everything moving together in divine harmony.

"Madam reads Latin?"

With a start, Aemilia turned to the astrologer, who had appeared at her side, sweating inside his black physician's robes. When he took the book from her, she couldn't resist selecting another tome, one with Hebrew letters on its spine. Though she pored through the pages, the incomprehensible letters did not yield their secrets.

"But madam does not read Hebrew," the astrologer concluded, snatching that book from her as well. "It's purported to be a kabbalist text, though I confess I can't decipher the thing. A sailor from Antwerp gave it to me in exchange for his star chart since he'd no other method of payment. Now what can I do for you, madam?"

Doctor Forman steered her away from his books and offered her a chair, then seated himself before her, far too close for her comfort, their knees almost touching. The man's fame as an astrologer was equally matched by his notoriety as a seducer of women.

Aemilia cast a glance at Winifred, who took up position beside her chair and glowered at Doctor Forman, as though prepared to brain him with one of his own specimen jars if he presumed to take liberties with her mistress. Doctor Forman cleared his throat and moved his chair a few inches back, allowing Aemilia to breathe more freely.

"Master Forman," she said. "I would have you cast two charts for me. One for my past and one for my future."

"My services do not come cheap, good mistress. What's your income?" The astrologer appeared to study her intently, as if trying to deduce her rank and station from her taffeta gown and the lace and pearls at her throat.

"Forty pounds a year," she said.

"Hardly a princely sum."

"I'm rich enough to the man who married me," she said tartly.

Her show of temper seemed to intrigue the astrologer. Perhaps he imagined that a woman with a grudge against her husband would prove an easy conquest.

"What's your name, madam?" The astrologer began to scribble notes in a small black book.

"Aemilia Bassano Lanier." She spoke her name with dignity but braced herself for the astrologer's reaction, the sly innuendo and surmising she had come to expect.

The astrologer remained bent over his notebook. "And where do you reside?"

"Longditch, Westminster."

He raised his eyebrows. "A most prestigious district. So close to court."

Aemilia said nothing.

"Now tell me how you came to receive the income of forty pounds a year. Is this your inheritance?"

She looked at the astrologer wonderingly and struggled not to laugh. Was there truly a soul left in London who didn't know her history?

I

The Magician's Daughter

I

The Liberty of Norton Folgate, 1576

PAPA WAS A MAGICIAN. No one was ever more loving or wise than he.

Seven years old, Aemilia nestled by his side in the long slanting light of a summer evening. Friday, it was, and Papa was expecting a visit from his four brothers. This was a change in custom, for previously Papa had always gone to meet them at Uncle Alvise's house in Mark Lane. *But this evening was special*, Aemilia thought, glancing at Papa's expectant face. The air seemed golden, filled with blessing, even as from outside their garden walls came the cries of the poor lunatics locked up within Bedlam Hospital. From the west came the baying of the beasts held within the City Dog House. Drunken revelers sang and howled as they spilled out of the Pye Inn just down the road. Yet none of it could touch them here within the boundaries of Papa's magic circle. Aemilia imagined his sweet enchantment rising around their family like fortress walls. This garden was his sanctuary, his own tiny replica of Italy on this cold and rainy isle.

The pair of them sat beneath an arbor of ripening grapes, planted from the vine Papa had carried all the way from Veneto. Around them, his garden bloomed in abundance. Roses, jasmine, honeysuckle, wisteria, and gillyflowers released their perfume while from within the house echoed the music of her mother singing while Aemilia's sister, Angela, played the virginals. Beyond the flower beds, Papa's kitchen garden brimmed with fennel, haricots verts, and rows of lettuce that they ate in plenty. Papa even ate the bloodred love apples, though Mother swore they were poison and she would not let her daughters near them. It was an Italian habit, Papa said. In Veneto, people prized the scarlet *pomodoro* as a delicacy.

Beyond the vegetable beds lay the orchard of apples, plums, and pears, and beyond that the chicken run and the small paddock for Bianca, the milk cow. Food in London was expensive, so what better reason to plant their own? Aemilia's family never lacked for sustenance. While Papa was away, a hired man came to look after the gardens for him.

They dwelled on the grounds of the old priory of Saint Mary Spital, outside London's city wall. The precinct was called the Liberty of Norton Folgate, Papa told her, because here they were beyond the reach of city law and enjoyed freedom from arrest. Some of their neighbors were secret Catholics, so it was rumored, who hid the thighbones of dead saints in their cellars. But Papa's secrets lay buried even deeper.

When Aemilia begged him for a *fiaba,* a fable, a fairy tale, he told her of Bassano, the city that had given him and his brothers their name. Forty miles from Venice, it nestled in the foothills below Monte Grappa. Italian words, as beautiful as music, flew off his tongue as he described the Casa dal Corno, the villa where they had dwelled that occupied a place of pride on the oldest square in Bassano. A grand fresco graced the Casa dal Corno's façade. Holding Aemilia close, Battista described the fanciful pictures of goats and apes, of stags and rams, of woodwinds and stringed instruments, and of nymphs and cherubs caught up in an eternal dance.

Aemilia turned in her father's lap to view their own house that had no fresco or any adornment at all, only ivy trained to grow along its walls. Loud black rooks nested in the overhanging elm trees.

"Why didn't you stay there?" she asked, thinking how lovely it would be to live in that villa, to be sitting there instead of here. She pictured white peacocks, like the ones she had seen in Saint James's Park, strutting beneath the peach trees in that Italian garden.

Papa smiled in sadness, plunging an arrow into her heart. "We were driven away. We had no choice."

"But *why?*" Her fingers tightened their grip on his hand. "It was so beautiful there. *Bellissima!*"

Aemilia believed that Italy was paradise, more splendid than heaven, and that Papa was all-powerful. How could he have been chased away from his home, like a tomcat from her mother's kitchen? Aemilia's father and uncles were court musicians who lived under the Queen of England's patronage. They performed for Her Majesty's delight and wore her livery. Papa was regarded as a gentleman, allowed a coat of arms. Though the Bassanos of Norton Folgate weren't rich, they had glass windows in their parlor and music room. Their house boasted two chimneys. They'd a cupboard of pewter plates and tankards, and even two goblets of Venetian glass. A fine Turkish rug in red and black draped their best table. Their kitchen was large, and they'd a buttery and larder attached, and a cellar below. Battista Bassano was eminently respectable, a man of means. How could such a fate have befallen him?

Papa cupped Aemilia's face in his hands. *"Cara mia,* you will never be driven from your home. You'll be safe always."

"When I grow up, I shall be a great lady with sacks of gold!" she told him. "I'll sail to Italy and buy back your house."

With the red-gold sun dazzling her, it seemed so simple. She would grow into a woman and right every wrong that had befallen her father.

Papa stroked her hair, dark and curling like his own. "How will you earn your fortune, then? Will you marry the richest man in England?" His voice was indulgent and teasing.

Solemnly, she shook her head. "I shall be a poet!"

"A poet, Aemilia. Truly?"

Even at that age, it was her desire to write poetry exquisite enough to make plain English sound as beautiful as her father's native tongue. Poets abounded at court, all vying for Her Majesty's favor. The Queen herself wrote poetry.

As Papa held her in his gaze, she offered him her palm. "Read my future!"

He took her hand in his, yet instead of looking at her palm, he stared into her eyes. Aemilia imagined her future unfolding before his inner vision like one of the court masques performed for the Queen. Cradling her cheek to his pounding heart, he held her with such tenderness, as though he both mourned and burned in fiercest pride when he divined what she would become.

"What do you see?" she asked him. "What will happen to me?"

Before he could answer, her uncles slipped through the back gate, which Papa had left unlatched. She watched as Uncle Alvise carefully bolted it behind them. Her uncles were usually boisterous, making the air around them explode with their noisy greetings, but this evening they were as quiet as thieves. Aemilia's heart drummed in worry. What could be wrong? Papa was old, already in his fifties, and her uncles even older, their hair thinning and gray. Giacomo, Antonio, Giovanni, and Alvise kissed her and patted her head before Papa instructed her to go inside to her mother and leave them to their business.

The child wrapped her arms around her father's waist. "No, no, no! I want to stay with you!"

The garden at this hour was at its most enchanting, with moths and fireflies emerging from the rustling leaves. She could believe that the Faery Queen might step out from behind the blossoming rowan tree, her endless train of sprites and elves swirling round her.

But there was no pleading with Papa. Stern now, he swept her up and delivered her into the candlelit music chamber. Without a word, he closed the door and left her there.

"Come here, Little Mischief." Angela held out her arms.

At sixteen, Angela was already a woman. She hoisted Aemilia into her lap and positioned Aemilia's fingers on the virginals keys. "You play the melody and I'll play counterpoint."

Papa called Aemilia his little *virtuosa*, for she was nearly as skilled in playing as her sister was. Their fingers danced across the keyboard while Mother and Angela sang in harmony, as though to cover the noise of Papa and his brothers descending into the cellar.

Mother could not read, but Papa had taught both Angela and Aemilia to read and write in English and Italian, and to scribe in a fine italic hand. Angela could play the lute and recorder. Yet Angela wasn't Papa's daughter and Mother wasn't his lawful wife. The neighbor children taunted Aemilia on account of being a bastard, something she understood to be a shameful thing. But she knew that Papa loved Mother. When Mother's husband—Angela's father—abandoned her, Papa had spent his savings to buy her this house. He had even given Angela her Italian name so everyone would think she was his.

Angela was well named. With her hair the color of spun moonlight, her sea-green eyes, and her wine-red lips, she looked as though she had swooped down from heaven. Mother was her mirror image. She was in her thirties, much younger than Papa. Angela and Mother were tall and fair, as English as elderflower posset. But Aemilia knew she took after Papa. Small and dark and foreign looking, she was wholly his.

Her thoughts flew back to him and her uncles, to what they were doing beneath the floorboards. Were they singing down there? Her sister only played louder while Mother crooned at the top of her voice. *What are they all hiding from me?* It seemed impossible to wriggle out of Angela's lap. Her arms darted across the keyboard on either side of Aemilia, pinning her in place.

As if in answer to her silent plea, a loud knock sounded on the front door. Angela's hands froze on the keys. She and Mother exchanged a long look. Usually their maid answered the door, but Papa had given her the evening free so that she could visit her parents. As the knocking continued, the men's voices arose from below, singing in another tongue. Not Italian, but something utterly alien.

Angela thrust Aemilia from her lap and made to move toward the door, but Mother shook her head.

"Keep playing," she told Angela.

All business, Mother set down her mending and marched for the front door, her face creased in worry. In their trepidation, she and Angela appeared to forget all about Aemilia. Seizing her chance, the child dashed to the kitchen and then stood above the trapdoor that led down to the cellar. Though she tugged on the ring with her entire might, it wouldn't give. The men had latched it from within.

"Master Holland!" Mother's voice came shrill with surprise.

Angela cried out in delight. Francis Holland was her suitor and Mother placed all her hopes in him, for he was a gentleman, the youngest son of a West Country knight. Even his footfalls sounded elegant as he strode the floors in his Spanish leather boots. Her sister was besotted with the man, but Aemilia despised the way he talked through his nose as though they were beneath him, the way he brayed like an ass when he laughed. Mother said his manner of speaking was a mark of quality, the way all rich men spoke.

Still hovering over the trapdoor, Aemilia considered pounding on it and begging her father and uncles to open up, to let her join them, but she knew they would refuse and even punish her for her impudence.

"What a pleasure," Mother was saying to Master Holland. "Come watch Angela whilst she plays the virginals. I'll fetch the Canary wine."

"Ah, my musical maiden, queen of all the Muses," Francis Holland drawled.

Angela giggled while she continued her arpeggios.

At the sound of approaching footsteps, Aemilia scurried beneath the kitchen table and squeezed herself into a ball as Mother fluttered in to get the wine. Her mother sang to herself like a woman already drunk, as though to cover what was happening below. Meanwhile, Angela pounded the virginals keys as if her life depended on it. But if her sister drank wine with Master Holland, Aemilia reasoned, surely she would have to lift her hands from the instrument.

"Where has that child gone?" she heard Mother ask Angela.

"I thought she was with you," said her sister.

Mother took over at the keyboard. Aemilia knew this because that unholy jangling could not have been her sister's music.

"The moon is so lovely tonight, Master Holland," Mother shouted over the jarring notes. "Why don't you and Angela step out into the garden?"

Huddled under the table, Aemilia listened to them go out the back door, Angela laughing like a Bedlamite in response to Master Holland's japes and jests. Mother waited a minute before dashing after them. Until they were formally betrothed and the wedding banns set outside Saint Botolph's church, Mother would guard Angela as though she were a diamond.

When they were finally gone, their voices swallowed in the garden's hush, the men's song arose again. Aemilia pressed her ear to the vibrating floorboards. How she yearned to unravel her father's mystery. She held her breath to hear him chant in the forbidden language he would not speak to any but his brothers.

Barukh atah Adonai m'kadeish haShabbat. Amein.

Seven years old, what could she comprehend of banishment and exile?

EVERY SUNDAY WITHOUT FAIL, the Bassanos attended church at Saint Botolph-without-Bishopsgate where Aemilia learned to stand with her spine rigid and not yawn lest Mother pinch her. The curate frowned upon organ playing, so they sang the psalms a capella. Though Aemilia adored the singing, the sermon on the torments of hell was so fiery that it raised her skin. In a panic, she gazed over to the men's side of the church where Papa stood, his face unreadable. When the service dragged to an end, she launched herself into his embrace.

"Do you fear hell?" she asked, her heart pounding sickly. How was she to know if she was part of the Elect who would be saved or merely one of the countless damned?

Papa's face crinkled as he lifted her in his arms.

"Aemilia, I will tell you a secret," he whispered in her ear. "Do you promise not to speak a word of this to anyone?"

Solemnly, she nodded.

"Hell is empty," he whispered.

As she gazed at him in astonishment, he kissed her cheek.

"All the devils live up here in plain sight."

He pointed across the road to where a gaggle of idlers loitered outside Bedlam Hospital. Their guffaws pricked the air as they pointed and jeered at the poor Toms peering back at them through the barred windows.

"Angels live amongst us, too," he whispered, turning to smile at Aemilia's sister and mother. "Look to the angels and they will look after you."

ONE SUCH ANGEL WAS their neighbor, Anne Locke. In the parlor, Aemilia read aloud from the Geneva Bible while Papa looked on and Mistress Locke listened, clearly impressed that he had taken such care to educate his daughter.

"When I was your age," Mistress Locke told Aemilia, "the mere thought of young girls reading the scriptures was heretical. Why, it was my great patroness, Catherine Willoughby, the Duchess of Suffolk, who first petitioned King Henry to read the Bible for herself. But you, my dear, are the daughter of a brave new world!"

The Widow Locke might have appeared severe to some in her plain dark gown, her hair pulled back beneath her starched white cap, but her smile was as wide as her heart. Aemilia would have turned somersaults in a tempest to please her. Anne Locke was a poet, the first to write sonnets in English. Papa said she was one of the best-educated women in the realm. During the reign of Catholic Queen Mary, Mistress Locke had fled to Geneva with John Knox and there she had published a volume of her translations of Calvin's sermons. Here in the Bassano parlor stood a great woman of letters. Mistress Locke beamed at Aemilia, as though she were her goddaughter.

Hope beat fast in Aemilia's heart. Might she not tread in Mistress Locke's own footsteps, become a poet just like her? Trembling in awe, she recited from Mistress Locke's own sonnets.

> The sweet hyssop, cleanse me, defiled wight,
> Sprinkle my soul. And when thou so hast done,
> Bedewed with drops of mercy and of grace,
> I shall be clean as cleansed of my sin.

Yet even as Aemilia uttered Mistress Locke's pious words, Papa's secret reverberated inside her. *Hell is empty.* What deeper mysteries did her father conceal? Surely in time he would reveal them to her when he judged her to be old enough.

Glowing in the warmth of his gaze, Aemilia told herself she was heir to his magic. Weren't she and Papa both born under the stars of Gemini, the Twins? This meant they had two faces, like the moon. One they showed to the world while the other remained hidden like a jewel in its case, only revealed to those they loved and trusted most.

2

APA WAS OFTEN ABSENT, his life itinerant, for court was held wherever the Queen happened to be. As royal musicians, Papa and her uncles traveled in Her Majesty's train from one palace to the next. When he returned home, Aemilia devoured his tales of the grandeur of Whitehall, Hampton Court, Greenwich, Richmond, and Saint James. Elizabeth's household moved every few weeks, Papa said, because with so many hundreds of bodies in one place even the most luxurious palace would soon stink like a cesspit if they tarried there too long.

A rare thing it was to accompany Papa to court. Aemilia was beside herself in excitement to learn that she and her sister were invited to Whitehall on New Year's Day for the annual exchange of gifts.

Mother had awoken before dawn to dress Angela and arrange her hair. In her garnet-red gown cut in the French style, her sister appeared to Aemilia as a goddess. Every garment Angela wore was borrowed, for Mother and the girls' aunts had ransacked their wardrobes in search of the most splendid things they owned. Aemilia merely wore her best Sunday gown—as a child of seven, her appearance was of lesser importance. Papa wore the red livery provided him by the Queen. But Mother, having sacrificed her finery to Angela, was obliged to stay home.

This was Angela's day of days, her chance to shine like polished crystal in the Queen's presence. Fortunes could be made at court, fates transformed in an instant. What if Angela made such an impression with her beauty and her accomplishments that the Queen took her on as one of her women? Papa made no secret of the fact that he thought Master Holland to be vain and bone idle, and that he believed Angela could do better. At court, she might catch the eye of a man Papa could respect.

As they sailed in a wherry up the Thames toward Westminster, Aemilia drank in Papa's tales of the glamor and glory they would soon behold. When Whitehall came into view, Aemilia cried out and pointed, her fingers stabbing the cold air in glee. The palace stretched nearly half a mile along the Thames. This was the Queen's principal residence, Papa explained, where her ill-starred mother had wed Old King Henry. Its grounds were vast enough to include the Queen's privy gardens where she walked daily, the royal tennis courts, bowling green, and tilting yard where her knights jousted. With more than fifteen hundred rooms, it was the largest palace in Europe.

"Your best manners today, Little Mischief," Papa told her. "Make us proud."

Aemilia nodded solemnly.

"Remember, my daughters, when the Queen smiles upon you, it's like basking in sunlight," Papa told them. "But her moods can change as swiftly as the weather. Do nothing to provoke her wrath."

Papa cradled a bulky package — their family's gift to the Queen. Mother had complained mightily about the expense. After all, Her Majesty paid Papa only thirty pounds a year, so surely she had no right to demand such an extravagant gift. But Papa insisted that the dearest thing of all was the Queen's favor. Without her patronage, they would lose everything. So Papa dipped deep into their savings to woo a woman who possessed seven palaces.

"Her Majesty speaks fluent Italian," he said, his eyes fixed on Whitehall as it loomed ever nearer. "Mind your every word. Her spies are everywhere. Her enemies' spies, too."

The guards ushered them into the Royal Presence Chamber, the biggest room Aemilia had ever seen, as though it had been built for giants. Long glassed windows flooded the space with light, and an endless banquet table ran the length of the room.

Every royal servant from the highest-born courtier to the lowliest boot boy was expected to present Her Majesty with a New Year's gift. Though the legal year began in March, the Queen celebrated New Year on the first of January according to ancient Roman tradition.

Aemilia blinked before the magnificence of the courtiers. The men were like peacocks in their silks and lace, while the ladies were more exquisite still, as though the Queen, wishing to surround herself in beauty, had selected them for their looks. The high ladies of court flaunted their velvet, forbidden by law for those of lesser rank. With their faces painted in white lead and red vermilion, they seemed creatures set apart.

"But where's the Queen?" Aemilia asked.

On the far end of the room, she saw the empty throne surmounted by its embroidered canopy.

"Her Majesty is in her Privy Chamber," Papa said, pointing to a set of great double doors flanked by guards. "Only her most trusted courtiers and advisors are allowed inside."

Aemilia's impertinence was swept aside as a gentleman in silver brocade hailed Papa. She couldn't keep herself from gawping at the man's calves, which were encased in pink silken hose. Diamonds glinted from his earlobes.

"Daughters, this is the great poet, Sir Philip Sidney. Your lordship, these are my daughters, Angela and Aemilia. Little Aemilia fancies herself a poet."

The young man seemed intrigued. "A noble vocation for a maid. My sister Mary is a poet, greatly favored by Her Majesty."

He extended his hand to the girl who appeared at his side. Mary Sidney seemed to be no older than Angela, yet already she had the bearing of a great lady of the court. Pearls gleamed in her red-gold hair and draped her velvet gown.

"A *femme savante*," her brother said. "Second only to our gracious Queen herself."

Spellbound, Aemilia swept down as gracefully as she could and her sister did the same.

"What a striking child, you are," Mary Sidney said, smiling at Aemilia, who blinked at her worshipfully. "I can just picture you in a masque as a Moorish princess. May all the Muses bless you, my little poet."

With a wink, Mary Sidney and her brother melted back into the crowd while Aemilia trembled from head to foot, giddy from their blessing.

"*Angelina mia,*" a voice cried out. "You are as lovely as the first day of spring!"

Aemilia whirled to see her uncles sweep in. They clustered around, offering their kisses. Then it was time to take their places at the banquet table.

THOUGH ANGELA ONLY PICKED at her food, no doubt terrified of staining her borrowed clothes, Aemilia happily stuffed herself, for she'd never beheld such a feast. Roasted venison there was, and veal in orange sauce, stewed kid, pheasant with sliced onions, coney in mustard sauce, and capon cooked in ale. There were pasties of fallow deer and red deer as well as tarts, fritters, and gingerbread. Servants kept filling her goblet with claret, but before she could take a swig, Papa poured most of it away and watered down what little remained. He watered his own wine as well. Too much was at stake to allow himself to become drunk.

Aemilia's eyes kept darting to the throne, which remained empty.

ONLY WHEN THE SERVANTS cleared away the empty platters did the Queen finally emerge with a trumpet fanfare. Flanking her were her most trusted advisors, William Cecil and Francis Walsingham, dressed in stark black as the sober men of government they were and setting a sharp contrast to the courtiers. The Queen set Aemilia quaking. This was no ordinary woman, but one who called herself a prince. It was impossible to judge her age, since her face was coated with so many layers of white lead. Sitting in state, high upon her throne, she was untouchable. It seemed impossible to believe that she ate and drank and used the privy pot like the rest of them.

At last the exchange of gifts began, each denizen of the court making an offering. In return, the Queen granted each royal servant gilt plate of a weight and value reflecting her subject's rank.

Some gifts were spectacular indeed. With much bowing and sighing, the Earl of Leicester presented Her Majesty with a collar of diamonds while his nephew and niece, Philip and Mary Sidney, gave her a telescope and a celestial globe—the Queen adored stargazing.

A respectful hush fell as a most impressive man made his way toward the throne. He looked to be about Papa's age and he carried himself with an austere dignity. On his arm he bore a hooded peregrine falcon, which he presented to the Queen with a deep bow.

"Henry Carey," Papa said. "The Baron Hunsdon. He put down Mary Stuart's northern rebellion against the Queen. Her Majesty rewarded him by making him her Master of Hawks. He's her first cousin on the Boleyn side. His sister, Catherine, is the Queen's most trusted lady-in-waiting."

But Angela's commentary, whispered in Aemilia's ear, was far more thrilling. "He's Old King Henry's bastard by Mary Boleyn. The Queen's half brother!"

Aemilia was awash in bewilderment, for she'd always thought a bastard birth like her own to be a mark of disgrace, yet there seemed to be no stain attached to this man. The very air he breathed seemed golden with power.

"If he had been the King's lawful son," Angela whispered, "he would be sitting on that throne. Not Elizabeth."

With a flourish, Lord Hunsdon removed the falcon's hood and untied the jesses. Aemilia gaped as, at his command, the peregrine soared over their heads to the far end of the room where it grasped in its beak a golden ring from a servant's palm before winging its way back to the throne. The Queen stood prepared, her brocade sleeve armored with a stiff leather gauntlet. *Papa is right*, Aemilia thought. *When she smiles, it's like sunlight.* Suddenly, the Queen seemed like a real woman, shining in mirth, filled with goodwill toward them all. Laughing, she offered her arm for the bird to perch upon. The falcon released the golden ring into the Queen's cupped hand while her audience cheered until they were hoarse. What a spectacle! What a magician Lord Hunsdon must be to make the Queen drop her mask, if only for a moment, and grace her subjects with the light of her joy.

AFTER THE HIGH-RANKING COURTIERS had made their offerings, the lowlier servants surrendered their gifts.

At last it was Papa's turn. Aemilia puffed in pride to watch him stride forward, bowing with fluid movements, as though he were performing a dance. But instead of a gift, he led her and Angela by the hand. Angela carried an exquisite Venetian lute.

"Your Gracious Majesty," he said, "your humble servant introduces his daughters, Angela and Aemilia Battista Bassano."

Aemilia and Angela curtsied while Papa backed discreetly into the shadows. Smiling sweetly to Her Majesty, Angela began to play the lute, and then she and Aemilia sang Italian madrigals. Madrigals were meant to be sung a cappella, but Angela displayed her virtuosity on the lute, her fingers leaping up and down the frets. The Bassano sisters' voices wove in tight harmony as they sang the music of Palestrina, Cipriano de Rore, and Orlando di Lasso. Much Italian music was forbidden, being Catholic, but the madrigal was wholly secular.

Never had Aemilia been more terrified. Papa had impressed upon her that the Queen herself could play the lute and virginals with astonishing skill.

Their last song was in English to make their homage to Her Majesty plain for everyone to hear.

> As Vesta was from Latmos hill descending
> She spied a maiden Queen the same ascending
> Attended on by all the shepherds' swain;
> To whom Diana's darlings came running down amain
> First two by two, then three by three together,
> Leaving their Goddess all alone, hasted thither;
> And mingling with the shepherds in her train,
> With mirthful tunes her presence entertain.
> Then sang the shepherds and nymphs of Diana:
> Long live fair Oriana!

After the song, Aemilia swept in a curtsy so low that her hair touched the floor. When she dared to lift her eyes, she saw Her Majesty's face soften before their tribute.

"*Brava!*" Elizabeth cried.

As the courtiers applauded, the Bassano sisters knelt before the Queen. Angela stretched out her slender arms to offer Elizabeth the Venetian lute that had cost Papa so dearly.

THE FOLLOWING MORNING, JUST as Mother was preparing to return Angela's borrowed finery, a messenger appeared at the door and asked for Papa.

"Master Bassano, the Lord Hunsdon requests an audience with you and your step daughter."

Aemilia, peering through a window, shrieked and clapped her hands. A coach waited outside their door.

Mother couldn't get Angela dressed quickly enough.

"I hope a lady will be present at the audience," Mother said, as she sewed Angela's braids into place. "Perhaps Lord Hunsdon's sister, Catherine, for surely it is she who interviews prospective ladies-in-waiting."

Having nothing to wear, Mother could not accompany Angela. Instead, she sent Aemilia, since having a child present would mean that everything was as respectable as could be. Papa's face shone in eagerness as they stepped into the coach and made their way once more to Westminster.

THE COACH DELIVERED THEM not to Whitehall but to the Royal Mews. Aemilia wrinkled her nose at the stench of bird droppings, but the creatures themselves fascinated her. Some slumbered upon their roosts while others inspected her with eyes like shiny dark beads. She was attempting to squeeze her hand through the bars of a cage, eager to stroke a hawk's soft speckled feathers, when Papa yanked her away.

"Those are no doves," he chided. "They'll rip you to shreds. Look!"

He pointed to the next cage where a particularly savage-looking bird tore at a hunk of raw meat with its talons and beak. Yet something about the bird's ravenous devouring tugged at Aemilia.

"He must be so hungry," she said, her face as close to the cage as Papa would allow.

"*She,* not he," a voice said.

They spun to face Lord Hunsdon. This day he did not appear in his velvet and gold braid but instead wore a leather doublet and high leather boots, every inch the Master of Hawks.

"All the royal hunting falcons and hawks are female," he informed Aemilia, speaking as though he were her schoolmaster and this was a lesson she must commit to her heart. "Amongst birds of prey, the female of the species is the more rapacious hunter. She's larger than the male, her flight swifter and vision keener." Aemilia turned to her father, whose eyes were fixed on the gentleman.

"My Lord Hunsdon," Papa said, bowing to him while Aemilia and Angela curtsied.

"Master Bassano," he said, "I cannot praise Angela highly enough. Truly, you have given her a most refined education. I must say the girl is well named."

Angela flushed dark pink as Lord Hunsdon bent over her hand.

"To honor your talents and accomplishments, young mistress, I thought to give you a tour of the Royal Mews—if this is agreeable, of course."

Lord Hunsdon looked to Papa, who nodded his assent.

"If you do make a career in court, you must be knowledgeable of such things," Lord Hunsdon told Angela. "After all, the Queen is as fond of hunting and hawking as she is of madrigals, and she expects her ladies to follow suit."

Aemilia watched as her sister kept looking from Lord Hunsdon to Papa, her smile radiant enough to melt snow. Angela seemed to float on air when the Master of Hawks offered her his arm and showed her the peregrines, the white gyrfalcons, and the bustards with their long slender necks and crested heads. There was even a golden eagle.

With Lord Hunsdon's attention fixed on Angela and Papa's fixed on Lord Hunsdon, Aemilia could gape at their host all she liked with no one to tell her off for it. *Old King Henry's bastard son!*

Lord Hunsdon offered Angela a leather gauntlet and then summoned a servant to bring a merlin falcon.

"This fine creature is of a suitable size and weight for a young lady such as yourself," the Master of Hawks told Angela, who stared in astonishment when the servant placed the merlin on her gloved fist.

The Master of Hawks led them out to the courtyard, where he instructed her sister how to remove the hood and loose the jesses. On cue, the merlin flew to the far end of the yard where a servant stood with a hunk of bloody meat on a plank. Seizing her prey, the merlin flew back and alighted on Angela's arm with a graceful flutter of wings. Angela stared speechlessly as the merlin dropped the meat into Lord Hunsdon's open hand.

"Is she not magnificent?" he asked, inviting them all to admire the merlin's dark brown wings and her soft plumed breast stippled with cream and palest fawn.

"She must be hungry," Aemilia blurted. "Why doesn't she eat?"

Though she had spoken out of turn, Papa didn't scold her for it.

Lord Hunsdon seemed amused. "She only eats at my command."

At that, he gave word for the servant to deliver both the merlin and the meat back to her cage where she could feed in peace.

"How do you like her?" Lord Hunsdon asked Angela, who averted her eyes from the sight of the bird ripping apart the bloody flesh.

"Marry, I like her very much," Angela said faintly.

"She is yours," Lord Hunsdon said. "She even has an Italian name — Mirabella."

Angela appeared utterly baffled and looked to Papa, who stepped forward, placing himself between his step daughter and the Master of Hawks.

"My Lord Hunsdon, you honor us with your largess," he said. "But I'm afraid Angela cannot accept such a gift. First, I would know what position she is to have in court that requires her to own such a bird. Has the Queen requested Angela's service?"

Lord Hunsdon spoke plainly. "Her Majesty has not. But under my patronage, Angela could rise far and so catch the Queen's eye, insuring her position in the court."

Papa's face hardened. "And what would my daughter do under your patronage?"

Lord Hunsdon smiled. "I think you know exactly what I offer, Master Bassano. I'm quite infatuated with the girl and wish to share her company as long as it should be mutually pleasing to us both. Surely this would be advantageous to all parties. You and the girl shall both be richer for it. Your family shall gain influence at court."

Angela turned into a statue, her mouth a frozen O. Papa's face went icy white as he clamped his lips together. Aemilia had never seen him more furious. She knew he was wrestling down his temper lest he unleash his fury and utter the words that would have him cast from his position and left without livelihood.

"My Lord Hunsdon," he said at last. "No daughter of mine shall be a courtesan. With your gracious leave, we shall now depart."

Shunning Lord Hunsdon's coach, they boarded a wherry to Billingsgate then trudged all the way across London toward Norton Folgate. Aemilia's head ached from trying to understand what she had witnessed. She had no clue what the word *courtesan* even meant.

"He was too old to marry Angela," she said, unable to keep her mouth shut, but that only made her sister cry.

"*Silenzio*," Papa said. "That man has a wife and twelve children already. It wasn't *marriage* he proposed." Then he spoke earnestly to Angela. "Henry Carey's a Boleyn through and through. I should have expected no better. Those are the games the Boleyns have always played, whoring out their daughters to pave their way to glory. But those are not our ways."

Papa sighed and wrapped his arms around Aemilia and her sister as though he could shelter them forever. Cast his magical circle to keep them safe.

3

EMILIA SOON CAME TO learn that Angela was terrified of becoming a fallen woman. As Aemilia struggled to decipher what that meant, she imagined her sister plummeting down from the sky like a hailstone. *If ever I fall, I pray Papa will catch me. Fly to me on his angel wings and raise me up again.*

A girl's reputation was like a white linen sheet that must be kept immaculate, Angela informed her. If even the slightest smudge besmirched it, the best laundress in the world wouldn't be able to get it completely clean again.

Her sister's dread of falling—falling all the way into hell—made her even more desperate for Francis Holland. She longed to become his wife as speedily as possible. Only then could she rest easy, she said, and be safe within her husband's protection. Though Papa warned her to keep her head and not rush, Mother took her side and hastened things along by dropping bolder and bolder hints to Master Holland until, as if in answer to Mother's and Angela's prayers, he presented Aemilia's sister with a golden ring.

Mother rejoiced to see Angela so respectably matched. Master Holland had read law at Balliol in Oxford and bore the title Esquire. As a youngest son, he had received only a modest bequest from his family, yet he claimed great prospects. Many an enterprising man made his fortune buying and selling London property, so Master Holland told Papa. He had purchased several tenements in Billingsgate, and he swore to provide Angela with every comfort.

Though Papa had never warmed to Master Holland, he could not put his finger on any convincing reason why Angela shouldn't marry him, especially since she was so smitten by him. How could Papa stand between the girl and her true love, particularly after blaming himself for her humiliation with Lord Hunsdon? So he swallowed his doubts and gave his reluctant blessing.

Mother saw to it that the couple wasted no time. The banns were spoken at church on three consecutive Sundays.

On a glittering February morning, Angela's wedding day dawned. With all the relations squeezed into church for the ceremony, Mother brimmed with joy, swearing that Angela was out of trouble's way forever.

"Now it's only you I need worry about," Mother whispered, stroking Aemilia's curls. "But surely Master Holland and Angela will look after you."

Aemilia smiled, sharing her mother's jubilance. Then she gazed over to Papa on the men's side of the church. Of the entire crowd, he alone remained somber.

Mother shook her head to see him so humorless. "Anyone would think he was watching a funeral."

In the Bassano parlor, packed with guests, Aemilia joined the cheers as Angela and Master Holland sipped posset from the silver-plated bridal cup.

All the Bassano kin had gathered and the Johnson relations on Mother's side as well. While her uncles played galliards and corontos, Aemilia tried to amuse her four-year-old cousin Ben by leading him in a dance.

Over the music and merriment, she heard Papa ask Mother, "Why did none of the groom's family come to the wedding?"

Mother dismissed his grumbling with a wave of her hand. "They live so far, over Bristol way. Surely they'll send gifts."

Aemilia turned her gaze to Angela, laughing and spinning in her bridegroom's arms.

Mother tugged Aemilia close and whispered, "One day you will marry and be as happy as your sister."

THEIR HOME SEEMED SO sad and silent without Angela's singing and virginals playing. How Aemilia longed for her sister, yet they heard not a word from her in the days following her wedding, and visiting her was no simple thing, for now she lived on the other end of London. Mother said they must leave Angela and Master Holland in peace for a fortnight before calling on them, that Aemilia should be happy for her sister instead of pining for her.

Angela's wedding had cost Papa deep in the purse. Not only had he paid for the festivities, but he'd also presented Master Holland with her dowry of one hundred pounds. Since it was not his way to beg his brothers for a loan, he sought to earn extra money when he wasn't at court.

As it happened, James Burbage's public theater had just opened in Shoreditch, a short walk from their home. The theater was all anyone could talk about, for it had cost Burbage seven hundred pounds, an unheard of sum, and yet he expected to turn a profit from it. A second public theater had opened in the Liberty of Blackfriars, but that was reserved for the nobility. The Shoreditch playhouse was built to pack in as many of the common rabble as could pay a penny to get in the door. Farmhands and dairymaids, brewers and draymen from the surrounding countryside streamed in. Mother complained about the noise and the many undesirables congregating in their district and relieving themselves in their hedges.

Robert Dudley's acting troupe, Leicester's Men, was putting on the very first play, and they required musicians, providing an ideal opportunity for Papa and his brothers.

"Such employment will stain our reputation," Mother said.

Their curate preached that the theater was a sinkhole of sin, no better than a bawdy house. But Papa, who looked happy for the first time in weeks, would not be dissuaded.

"The play is *Bucolia*," he said, using his most coaxing voice with Mother. "An English translation of Virgil's *Eclogues*. Virgil, the greatest of the Latin poets."

Aemilia trembled in anticipation. Papa had told her such intriguing stories of the plays and masques at court — she couldn't imagine a more wondrous spectacle.

"May I go?" She reached to clasp his hand.

"Under no circumstances," Mother said. "The playhouse is no place for a respectable girl from a good family."

A FEW DAYS LATER, when Mother was at the market, Jasper Bassano called in.

Uncle Antonio's seventh son and the youngest of her paternal first cousins, Jasper was the closest thing Aemilia had to a brother. Just a year older than she was, he seemed so much more worldly. As a boy, his future was a clearly marked path — he would become a court musician like his father. Already Jasper could play the trumpet, the viol, the recorder, the lute, the cornett, and the shawm.

"Come along with me and see the play," Jasper said.

"I'm forbidden!" Aemilia nearly spat in her frustration. "Because I'm a girl."

Jasper gave her his most conspiratorial grin. "It would be different if you were a boy."

From his satchel he pulled out a boy's doublet and a pair of breeches.

"I dare you," he said, dangling the garments before her.

"Ha!" Fire danced in her heart as she snatched the clothes from him and ran off to change.

HER HAIR STUFFED UNDER a cap, Aemilia sprinted off to the Shoreditch playhouse, racing Jasper.

Winded and panting, they each paid a penny to enter the inner court, open to the sky. Three tiers of galleries rose around it. For an extra penny, you could stand in the galleries and get a better view, Jasper told her, and for three pennies, you could even sit upon a stool. But Aemilia and Jasper were stuck with the groundlings and couldn't see a thing until they barged their way to the thrust stage where they spotted Jasper's father and the other uncles in the musicians' gallery. Only Papa was missing. Aemilia's heart drummed in fear. Was he ill?

Her uncles were too busy struggling to tune their instruments over the roar of the crowd to notice Jasper — or Aemilia in her disguise. For this she was grateful. If Mother found out, she'd surely thrash her.

Even Mistress Locke would despair of her and say she was no better than a heathen. Never had Aemilia stood so close to so many strange men, many of them reeking of spirits though it was only noon. But both Jasper's presence and her boy's clothes protected her, and she felt no fear, only a mad curiosity and impatience for the play to begin.

Her uncles began to play music so sweet that a hush fell over everyone, even the roughest quarrymen in the crowd. As the music swelled, figures appeared on the stage. Aemilia cried out in delight to see Papa with a wreath of ivy on his graying head. He carried a crook and wore a roughly woven shepherd's smock, but when he opened his mouth, poetry poured forth, as bright as sunlight dancing on a stream.

Wonderment overwhelmed Aemilia—Papa wasn't just a musician but also a player!

"The minstrel stepped in," a knowing voice behind them muttered, "because the actor was too drunk to go on stage."

"*Sh,*" Aemilia hissed.

The stage transported her to a lost and long ago place called Arcadia, peopled by shepherds who had no other labor but to sing and recite poetry of yearning and love. The place seemed as perfect as Eden in the Geneva Bible, except it was full of gods and goddesses who miraculously swooped down from a trapdoor in the stage ceiling, painted to resemble the starry heavens, and descended to the main stage upon a wire to the accompaniment of her uncles' trumpets and shawm. There was Pan, half goat and half man, playing his pipes. Pallas appeared with her helmet and spear. The dancing nymphs with their flowing blond tresses made Aemilia miss Angela all the more keenly.

"I thought girls weren't allowed on stage," she whispered to Jasper.

Her cousin laughed as though she were the biggest fool in Middlesex. "They're not *girls.* They're boys in wigs."

The illusion seemed so real. Slender and graceful with their red lips and soft hands and flowing skirts, the nymphs and naiads circled around Alexis, the fair shepherd boy, while the herdsmen praised his beauty.

"The ancients thought nothing amiss with buggery," Jasper whispered with a wicked laugh, for he liked to shock her. "They wrote poems about it!"

"What's buggery?" Aemilia asked, pitching her voice to be heard.

His face burning red, Jasper clapped his hand over her mouth while the men around them glared or even winked.

Ignoring them, Aemilia gave her entire attention to the spectacle on stage. As she stared thunderstruck at Papa, he caught her eye and gazed back with both reproach for disobeying Mother and shock at her being dressed as a boy. Then his eyes softened, and she knew he would keep her secret and never betray her. As it transpired, he replaced the stolen penny from Mother's housekeeping money before she even noticed it was missing.

THREE WEEKS HAD GONE by since Angela's wedding.

"We *must* go visit her," Aemilia clamored to Mother. She had never been separated from her sister for so long.

But that very morning, Mother opened their front door to see Francis Holland looking every inch the gentleman with his golden earring and perfumed handkerchief.

"Where's Angela?" Aemilia demanded. *Why had he come without her?*

Her brother-in-law only brushed her away while Mother blustered past to fuss over him, opening their last flask of Canary wine in his honor.

"How is our Angela?" Mother only presumed to ask this after Master Holland was seated in their best chair with the carved armrests.

"Oh, she is fine," he said. "But for one thing."

Aemilia and her mother froze.

"Might I trouble you for one small favor, Mistress Bassano? Could you lend us a few sovereigns? I'm afraid I'm in need of it. Business matters," he said ruefully. "Of course, I shall pay you back promptly. I ask for Angela's sake."

Though Aemilia glared fixedly at his face, his entire attention was on Mother who turned bright pink.

"Oh, sir! My husband is out and we haven't that much money in the house."

Rising from his chair, Master Holland loomed over Mother, who seemed to shrink inside his shadow. "Are you quite certain? I thought Master Bassano was in the habit of hiding away a few coins here and there. Is he not doing well these days, working in the theater, so I hear?"

The idea of Master Holland prying behind panels in search of Papa's hard-won savings made Aemilia seethe.

"Papa gave you one hundred pounds," she told him.

Mother's face darkened as she ordered her from the room, yet it was the glint of fury in Master Holland's eyes that frightened Aemilia. Her heart thumped in panic, but she refused to leave until she'd had the last word.

"Ten thousand mischiefs in your guts!" she screamed in her brother-in-law's face before she darted away.

HOURS LATER, WHEN PAPA returned home, her parents quarreled. Huddled in the bed she'd once shared with her sister, Aemilia couldn't have closed her ears to their shouting if she had tried.

"You promised him the virginals?" Papa's voice rang out in disbelief. "You had no right. That's for Aemilia."

"Aemilia's just a child. Angela's a married woman. She and Master Holland need—"

"He's already gone through her dowry, the wastrel. I should have forbidden the match."

"I promised him!" Mother was weeping.

Papa was silent. Aemilia could picture his face—he was too outraged to even speak.

"Can we not pawn anything?" Mother was like a dog with her teeth in meat. She would not give it up. "Surely we can give them something."

"There's nearly nothing left of our savings as it is! Would you let him bankrupt us? Let him ruin us? You think I will live forever and always be here to provide?"

Hearing her father's voice break, Aemilia began to sob. Her heart beat in terror of a world that didn't have Papa in it.

THE NEXT MORNING MASTER Holland appeared at their door, hoping perhaps to find Mother alone again. Instead Papa confronted him with a face like thunder.

"Do you think to wheedle more money from my wife?" he demanded. "I see she already gave you her housekeeping money."

Holland's mouth twisted in a sour smile. Out from behind him stepped Angela, as though emerging from her husband's shadow. She stood trembling on the threshold.

Aemilia threw herself at Angela, burying her head in her skirts. Through the worn fabric, she could feel her sister's bony hips. Angela had grown so thin, as though she hadn't eaten a morsel since her wedding feast three weeks ago. Had her sister been ill? Angela didn't hug her back but only stood there, stiff as a fence post.

"*Cara mia.*" Papa embraced her, tears in his eyes.

But Angela's eyes were empty. *This is no longer my sister,* Aemilia thought. Mother came barreling out, exclaiming how thin and pitiful Angela looked.

Aemilia scowled at Master Holland, who looked perfectly healthy and well fed while her sister was as gaunt as a starveling. No one could have mistaken her for a gentleman's wife. The only thing of quality to be found on her person was the golden ring her husband had given her, now sliding loose on her finger. Had Master Holland starved her on purpose? Aemilia's spine crawled when she remembered Lord Hunsdon telling her that his merlin falcon ate only at his command. Yet it was not Lord Hunsdon who had turned her sister into a skeleton, but her lawful husband. *Papa was wrong. Angela was wrong. She would have been happier with Lord Hunsdon. He would have made her a lady.* Aemilia imagined her mother would beat her silly if she even guessed she was thinking such thoughts.

"Let's get you some food, love." Mother held Angela as though she'd never let her go. "There's fresh baked bread. And pottage on the hob. If I'd known you were coming, I would have made you lamb-and-fennel pie."

Angela only wriggled out of her grasp and delivered her line as though she were a player at the Theater in Shoreditch.

"Poor Francis is having a dreadful time with his creditors. Papa, could you lend us anything at all?"

Papa sagged. "If your husband cannot provide, you must come back home, Angelina. We'll look after you. We always have."

"Yes!" Aemilia cried, hugging her again.

Her sister, she hoped, would sleep in their old bed again. Angela would tell her stories at night and everything would be as it was before, the house ringing with her madrigals.

"Go with your mother into the kitchen," Papa told Angela. "Let her feed you before you blow away."

Angela only stood there looking lost and miserable, as though she could no longer take a step on her own without her husband's permission. *What had he done to her?* Aemilia glared at Master Holland with pure hatred. But he ignored her the way he would a yapping dog.

"It's my grave misfortune," the man drawled, "that my creditors are as mean as Jews."

Master Holland cast a pointed stare at Papa, who went as pale as wax. Panic rose inside Aemilia's chest—why did her brother-in-law's words leave Papa so stricken?

"I've heard dark rumors indeed," said Holland, "of a secret cabal of Jews in the Liberty of Norton Folgate who convene by night in secret underground chambers."

Her heart quickened. So this was Papa's secret, what he hid from her, although Mother and Angela knew. Her father and his brothers were Jews, like the patriarchs in the Old Testament.

"What might our Queen do," Holland went on, "if she knew there were such ungodly men in her midst?"

Papa's face hardened into stone. "Get out of my house."

Aemilia trembled as her father's anger and helplessness ripped through her. If Holland betrayed him, Papa could be imprisoned or even slain. How had her brother-in-law, of all people, uncovered Papa's secret? He could have only learned this from Angela. Aemilia gaped at her sister, who looked straight ahead with blank eyes.

"Angelina," Papa said, his face softening again. "This is your home. You are welcome here always. But not that man."

Holland stood his ground, revealing his teeth with an icy smile. "Fine words coming from a Jew dog who loves his gold more than his daughter. But then Angela's not your daughter, is she? I wouldn't have sullied myself with her if she was."

Aemilia watched her father's temper rise like a storm, but Mother threw herself between the two men and shoved Master Holland out the door with such force that she knocked him backward over the threshold. He would have fallen had not Angela grabbed his arm and pulled him up again.

Aemilia gazed at her sister through her tears. How could Angela betray Papa who adored her, and all for the sake of a husband who treated her as if she were a boot scrape?

Papa and Angela exchanged one last look until Angela at last turned her back on him. Master Holland, appearing outraged for the humiliation he had suffered—bowled over by a woman!—hauled her off down the street.

"I'll flog him all the way back to Bristol," Papa said.

But Aemilia knew he was too tender to crush a fly.

"*Cara mia,*" he said, taking Mother's face in his hands, "promise me you'll never let him set foot inside this house again."

Mother's eyes flooded with tears and she made no promise at all. She looked as though she were torn apart, as though Papa and Angela each claimed half of her. If driving Master Holland out of their lives meant losing Angela, Mother would keep opening the door to him whenever Papa was out.

"She'll leave him." He gripped the back of a chair as though he might collapse without it. "We can send her away. To Italy."

Mother shook her head. "She's wed to him. She's his now."

AFTER HER PARENTS HAD sent her to bed, Aemilia crept to her chamber window and saw Papa wandering like a ghost in the moon-drenched garden. Slipping on her cloak, she stole down the stairs and out the back door. She found him sitting beneath his grape arbor, his head in his hands.

"Papa," she whispered, sidling up to him, pressing her shivering self into his warmth.

When he spoke, he sounded so undone. "Go back to bed, Little Mischief, before you catch your death in this cold."

But she clung to him with all her stubborn love until he hugged her back, wrapping her inside his cloak.

"Is that why you had to leave Italy?" she whispered in his ear. "Because you're a Jew? Uncle Alvise, Giacomo, Antonio, and Giovanni, too?"

Papa clamped his mouth shut. At first, she feared he would tell her nothing. Then he seemed to reconsider.

"It's better you should hear it from me," he said at last, "and not some hateful scoundrel like your brother-in-law."

Holding her close, speaking in a voice so soft she struggled to hear, he told her his story. The tapestry of a man forced to flee his country, to abandon any sense of belonging anywhere.

Papa and his brothers were driven from their home when the town of Bassano purged itself of its Jews. Her father was only nine years old. They fled to Venice, where they assumed the guise of Catholic conversos and sought protection under the Doge. Their music saved them. The Bassano brothers were considered the finest musicians and instrument makers in Venice, virtuosos of the cornett, crumhorn, flute, lute, recorder, shawm, sackbut, and viol. But were they truly safe there — what if the Doge proved fickle?

What was more, they were trapped in a hopeless double bind. If they lived openly as Jews, they would be forced to live within the cramped Ghetto, where the tenements were stacked eight stories tall to house all the inmates. Worse, they would no longer be allowed to earn their living as professional musicians and instrument makers. Jews, by law, were only allowed to work as moneylenders, to run pawnshops, to sell used clothing, to practice medicine, or to work the Hebrew printing press. Not very long before the Bassanos' arrival, no Jew had the legal right to reside within Venice at all, yet already people were complaining that there were too many of them for the Ghetto to contain.

But to live outside the Ghetto as a converso was to risk being unmasked as a Jew. At any moment they might be banished or sentenced to toil as galley slaves for twenty years or more. Any slip might give away their true religious loyalties — dressing too fine on a Saturday or refusing to eat pork. Papa and his brothers knew they lived in Venice on sufferance, their very survival hanging upon a thread.

Deliverance came in the person of Thomas Seymour, brother of Jane Seymour, that short-lived Queen. Italian musicians were the height of fashion, and Old King Henry coveted what he did not possess. So Sir Thomas took Aemilia's father and uncles back to England to play in the King's Musicke. On this cold island, so far from their home, her kinsmen adopted the mask of Protestants, changing their colors as deftly as any chameleon. In the early years, King Henry offered them accommodation in a former Carthusian monastery he had sacked. His Majesty loved nothing better than to float down the Thames upon his royal barge while his Italian minstrels serenaded him. Here in England, the brothers Bassano thought they could keep their secret, in this country where there had officially been no Jews since King Edward I expelled them in 1290.

Their saga of exile stretched back even further into history. Before Bassano, Papa's people had dwelled in Sicily, where they earned their bread as silk weavers until they had to flee. The mulberry tree and silk moths still graced the Bassano family coat of arms. Centuries before they arrived in Sicily, their ancestors made their home in Portugal.

Aemilia clasped his hands. "Am I a Jew then, too?"

Now that she knew, could she join Papa and her uncles in their secret prayers?

"You must stay true to the Queen's religion." He gripped her shoulders. "That's the only way to stay safe. Don't you understand, Aemilia? I came all this way so you could live in peace."

FROM THAT NIGHT ONWARD, Aemilia knew there was no pretending she was an English girl like any other, not with Papa's blood running in her veins. Like him, she would remain an outsider, heir to everything her father and his people had endured, yet she was forbidden to share in it or even to speak his religion's name.

To think Papa had left his home and traversed the continent of Europe seeking safety and refuge only to have Master Holland threaten to ruin him. Aemilia's uncles stopped visiting on Friday evenings. No more did the sound of secret singing rise from beneath the floorboards. With Holland's threat of blackmail hanging over their heads, her home became a battlefield.

Late at night, her parents' disputes raged on, providing Aemilia with a sad education. Francis Holland was a master of masks and concealment, only revealing his true face once the wedding revels had ended and his marriage to her sister was sealed. Papa discovered Master Holland was already hundreds of pounds in debt when he and Angela exchanged their vows. What money his family had given him, he had reduced to nothing, spending it on wine, fine clothes, and one failed business venture after another. Brought up in sloth, he had no head for commerce. Francis Holland shunned hard work the way Mistress Locke shunned deviltry.

4

N THE COLD MARCH twilight, Aemilia and her father walked home from Uncle Alvise's house in Mark Lane, Papa's hand enclosing hers and his head bent over his feet. How it crushed her to see him like this, the fire dimming in his eyes. He had lavished such love on Angela, only to have that love rejected. *If I was older,* Aemilia thought. *If I was a boy, I'd be able to earn my own living. Papa wouldn't have to carry this all alone.* She would be able to give Master Holland the thrashing of his life. Put the fear of God into him lest he ever dare hurt her sister or threaten her father again. But she was a girl, a millstone dragging Papa down, neither truly Italian nor truly English. She was a foreign bastard, a halfling who belonged nowhere.

PAPA WAS BROKEN AND could take no more. Seventeen years ago, he had saved Margaret Johnson, a pregnant and abandoned wife, and had raised her daughter as his own, only for that girl to marry a conniving brute who held the entire family in his thrall. Late at night, Aemilia heard Papa praying in his forbidden language. When the willow in their neglected garden burst into tender new leaves, he collapsed and took to his bed.

IN APRIL PAPA'S GARDEN was a paradise of blossom, the grass filmy with speedwell, the blackbirds trilling among blooming apple boughs. But Papa lay dying. It was just before Aemilia's eighth birthday. Her uncles gathered round his bed, weeping as openly as she did. Anne

Locke had come to pay her respects while Master Vaughan, Mistress Locke's brother, recorded Papa's last will and testament. Mother tried to drag Aemilia from the room, but the child shook her off and huddled next to Mistress Locke. Nothing could have wrenched her from Papa's bedside.

"Let Aemilia be educated," Papa said, extracting a promise from Mistress Locke. His voice broke in its urgency. "I beg you, good lady. Find her a place in Susan Bertie's household."

Aemilia had often heard Papa and Mistress Locke speak of Susan Bertie, the young Dowager Countess of Kent. The daughter of Mistress Locke's great friend Catherine Willoughby, Susan was a true humanist who believed that girls should receive the same education as boys.

"To Margaret Bassano alias Johnson, my reputed wife," Papa said, "I leave this house and property and all its effects, save the virginals, which shall be Aemilia's and kept at my brother Giacomo Bassano's house until she comes of age. My last one hundred pounds I leave to Aemilia, to be bequeathed when she turns twenty-one or upon her wedding day, whichever comes first."

This was Papa's way of keeping her inheritance — the last of his life's savings — safe from Master Holland. For all his love and care, he hadn't been able to save Angela, who was now pregnant, as good as manacled to Master Holland forever. Her beautiful sister was lost. Yet Papa would save Aemilia, sending her off to be educated by Susan Bertie, who lived at her mother's estate in Grimsthorpe, Lincolnshire. As for Mother, she had possession of the house and could take in lodgers and lead a respectable life if she could only resist Master Holland's bullying.

Papa gazed at Aemilia as though she were the most precious thing in his world. She, the only child of his blood.

PAPA MADE A SWANLIKE end, fading in music. Within his locked bedchamber, his brothers sang their prayers while Aemilia knelt outside the bolted door. Her face washed in tears, she listened as her uncles' chanting ushered Papa out of this world into the next, where his spirit rose on pure white wings, soaring in a blaze of light straight into the presence of his secret God.

5

EMILIA'S WORLD HAD BEEN a crystal globe reflecting Papa's loving intelligence. Now that orb slipped from her grasp and shattered.

At the burial, her uncles hunched together and drooped, those old men whose time might also come soon. Though it was April, the cold and damp crept up Aemilia's calves as she watched Papa's coffin lowered into the gaping earth.

She pressed her numb face against Mistress Locke's cape as the rain fell, drenching them in heaven's tears. Her soul shrank to a small black point. The last rites had only just ended when she heard Mother speak the words that turned her heart to ice.

"You and Francis must come live with us now," Mother said to Angela. "There's plenty of room and you've a baby on the way. I'll sleep with Aemilia, and you and Francis shall have the marriage bed."

Mother was inviting that devil into their home, into Papa's *bed,* and Papa was not an hour in his grave. Even Mistress Locke frowned at Mother and pursed her lips as if swallowing some rebuke.

"Come, poppet," Mother said in a too-bright voice, holding her arm out to Aemilia. "Let's go home."

Aemilia only stared at her mother. How could she ever forgive her? It was Mother who insisted that Angela wed Master Holland with all speed. Mother had invited him into their home, offered him their best wine, and would have handed over Papa's savings had she been able to find them. She was that hoodwinked. With Papa gone, there was nothing more to stop her. Master Holland would take Papa's place as master of the house. He would destroy them as he had destroyed Angela.

You will never be driven from this house, Papa had promised her, her father who had been banished from his own home at the age of nine, his beloved villa in Bassano with the fresco of apes and goats. But Aemilia knew she must flee or be ruined.

When, for the second time, Mother reached out to her, Aemilia cleaved to Mistress Locke. But she met her mother's gaze without flinching. She let her anger shine like a torch.

ASTRIDE A FAT LITTLE chestnut mare, Aemilia gazed down the long highway.

"Child, don't let your heart be broken." Anne Locke's voice was as gentle as a feather caressing Aemilia's cheek as they rode toward Lincolnshire. "Your father is with God now." The lady's voice swelled in conviction. "He is truly part of the Elect."

Papa's mask fooled even Mistress Locke, Aemilia marveled even as she splintered in grief.

The way to Grimsthorpe seemed to stretch on forever. So much open countryside with so few buildings—Aemilia felt impossibly exposed. Nowhere left to hide. She had never been so far from home. Still, she exulted to think how she had escaped living under the same roof as Master Holland.

Thomas Vaughan rode with them, as did Mistress Locke's grown son, Henry. Both men were armed with swords and rapiers in case they should meet villains on the Queen's Highway. The mere thought of that made Aemilia want to curl into a tiny ball. This was her fifth day in the saddle and every inch of her was sore.

Refined ladies rode aside, Anne Locke had explained, to look elegant while showing off their elegant gowns, which was all very well for solemn, slow processions, such as when the Queen rode in progress. But only a vain idiot, she swore, would ride long distances perched sideways in a saddle with both feet resting on a planchet and no way to properly grip the horse with the legs. Aemilia wrapped her aching calves around Bathsheba, the little mare.

"You will adore Lady Susan," Mistress Locke told her. "She has no children, poor soul, but she'll love you as though you were her own. You'll be a balm to her loneliness, just as she'll be a balm to yours. She'll teach you Latin, Greek, and French."

For the first time since Papa's death, an ember of hope flickered inside Aemilia.

"Then I can truly be a poet," she said, lifting her face to Anne Locke's. "Just like you. Madam," she added, remembering her manners.

The lady beamed like the sun. "Make your father proud, love. He's watching you from heaven."

Her words warmed Aemilia even as they made her shiver. From that moment, Papa's lingering spirit became her invisible guardian angel. She took comfort in telling herself that Papa would never truly abandon her.

Though Mistress Locke was stout and no longer young, she was nimble in the saddle. Ichabod, her tall gray gelding, seemed to worship her as fervently as Aemilia did. Mistress Locke only had to twitch her little finger down the reins to bring him down from a gallop to a halt.

As Bathsheba and Ichabod walked shoulder to shoulder, Mistress Locke smiled at Aemilia in a way that made tears of devotion prick the back of her eyes. *You are my savior!* But if she dared say that, Mistress Locke would accuse her of blasphemy.

"Mark my words," Anne Locke said. "Your sister's a fool. A pity your poor father couldn't make her see reason."

Thinking of Angela, whom she had left behind, possibly forever, made Aemilia's throat clench in pain.

"All women must marry," the lady continued, "but don't lose your head the way your sister did. A woman cannot set her sights on a husband alone. Look at me—I'm twice widowed. Yet here I am, riding to Lincolnshire! In the dark days of Queen Mary, I was forced to leave my husband and flee the country."

Papa fled his country, too, Aemilia wanted to tell her. But unlike Papa, Anne Locke had been able to return to her home.

"Though I pleaded and pleaded, my husband would not come with me," Mistress Locke went on. "He feared that if we left our property and land, the Crown would confiscate it, so he risked his very life, for his convictions were as strong as mine. But I fled with our children and Catherine Willoughby—Lady Susan's mother, my dearest friend in all the world. Both Catherine and I were with child."

A pregnant woman running away without her husband! If only Angela were so bold.

"Those were desperate times, child. Thank Providence you were not yet born. The Duchess and I both bore our babes on the Continent, and I so far from my husband. Without Catherine, I would have been a lost soul. Remember this, my dear, you must cherish your own sex."

Mistress Locke smiled as though she could hardly wait to rejoin her beloved friend, leaving Aemilia to wonder if under Susan Bertie's patronage she, too, might forge such a deep bond. If only she could befriend a girl her own age to replace the part of her heart that Angela had left so broken and empty.

"Of course, the whole affair would have been a shameful scandal had I not fled for John Knox's sake!" Mistress Locke blushed when she said his name. "He was a fiery one. Some say he hates women. Indeed, the Queen despises him because he wrote *The First Blast of the Trumpet Against the Monstrous Regimen of Women*. But he seemed to have a special fondness for me. In fact, it was he who introduced me to the great Jean Calvin and proposed that I translate his sermons."

Mistress Locke left England as a refugee and returned as a poet and translator! While Aemilia was lost in her admiration, they reached a long grassy stretch beside the highway.

"We're making good progress," Thomas Vaughan said. "Tomorrow, if the weather holds, we'll reach Grimsthorpe."

Mistress Locke turned to Aemilia. "Are you ready to spread your wings, my dear, and try a gallop? We'll take it nice and steady."

Only yesterday Aemilia would have cringed, but now she nodded, fire in her heart. She took firm hold of the reins and they were off, flying up the grassy track, Bathsheba sticking close to Ichabod's side. Her ears pricked forward in glee, the mare moved like a wave beneath Aemilia, carrying her so fast that the wind roared in her ears. On and on, Aemilia rode, aching but free.

Toward evening the following day, they reached Grims-thorpe's gatehouse. The gatekeeper's son set off at a gallop to inform their hosts of their arrival while Mistress Locke and her retinue made more leisurely progress up the Four Mile Riding that led to the castle. The avenue was shaded on both sides by ancient double-planted oak trees.

"Soon you shall see one of the greatest houses in the realm," Mistress Locke said. "Parts of it are more than three centuries old, but rest assured, you shall find every comfort there. Old King Henry once stayed here. It was he who bequeathed the estate to Catherine Willoughby's father, the Baron Willoughby de Eresby, when he married Katherine of Aragon's lady-in-waiting, a Spaniard named Maria de Salinas."

So their hostess was half foreign, Aemilia thought. *Just like me.*

"Catherine was her father's only surviving child, so she inherited Grimsthorpe. Her first husband, the Duke of Suffolk, was the widower of King Henry's younger sister, Mary. That meant her children by him were in line for the throne. Alas, both those boys died."

Aemilia's hands slackened on the reins to think how powerful this family was, so intimately connected to the Tudors. What if they didn't like her? Her heart beat in alarm when she remembered that Mistress Locke would soon ride back to London, leaving her in this household of strangers.

Bathsheba, pestered by the flies, buried her face in Ichabod's swishing tail.

"Catherine married her present husband, Richard Bertie, for love," Mistress Locke continued. "He joined her when they fled into exile. Lady Susan was only an infant, and her brother Peregrine was born on the Continent."

"Peregrine?" Aemilia tried not to laugh.

"He was born *in terra peregrina* — in a foreign land." Mistress Locke smiled. "I was there in the chamber in Wesel, Germany, holding Catherine's hand whilst she was birthing him. I gave him his first bath."

The thought of her hostess's son and heir as a naked babe in Anne Locke's arms made Aemilia less afraid.

"Lady Susan is the Earl of Kent's widow, but because they had no children, she was not allowed to live on as the mistress of her late husband's estate. She's far too young and pretty to spend the rest of her days in her mother's house, yet she dares not remarry without the Queen's leave. She also fears Her Majesty might arrange a match not to her liking."

WHEN THEY EMERGED FROM the Four Mile Riding, Aemilia cried out to see Grimsthorpe Castle gleaming golden pink in the evening sun while its countless glass windows glittered. With its towers, gables, turrets, and crenulations, it was magnificent.

The castle was ringed in gardens enclosed in yew hedges. Aemilia glimpsed roses of every hue, their perfume heavenly as they rode past gushing fountains and ornamental pools. The scent of honeysuckle and jasmine wafted toward them. Bathsheba snorted and pinned her ears back at the sight of a topiary bear.

As they approached the grand entrance of the castle, the little mare nickered and trotted forward in her eagerness. Like Mistress Locke, Bathsheba had made this journey before and she knew they had finally reached their destination. The household stood at attention to greet their guests, but Bathsheba turned her dappled rump on their august company and rushed straight into the arms of the waiting groom who would take her to her thick straw bed and give her a generous measure of oats.

Before Aemilia could blink, strong hands gripped her waist and lifted her down from the saddle. She gazed up at a grinning face haloed by auburn hair. Without a backward glance, Bathsheba clip-clopped away with the groom, leaving Aemilia gaping at a young gentleman with dazzling gray eyes.

"So you are my sister's new charge," he said, setting her on the ground. He wasn't much taller than Papa had been, but his dove gray doublet and white ruff were immaculate while her skirt and sleeves were coated in dust.

Helplessly, she looked to Anne Locke only to see her flinging her stout body into the open arms of a slender lady. The pair of them laughed and wept at once, then they kissed each other while Mistress Locke's brother and son stood on, as though not knowing what to do with themselves. Never had Aemilia thought to see English ladies behaving in such a manner. Anyone would think they were Italian.

"Here she is!" the young man sang out, taking Aemilia by the hand. "Your little *donna.*"

A young woman in rustling dark taffeta stepped forward and solemnly bent her face to hers. "You must be Aemilia. Mistress Locke says you're very clever. I hope you shall be happy here."

"My Lady Susan!" Aemilia curtsied so low that her forehead grazed the gravel.

Susan, Dowager Countess of Kent, was twenty-three years old and astonishingly beautiful. Her complexion was pearly, like the inside of a shell, but her eyes were dark hazel and her hair, the color of polished mahogany.

"I believe you've already met my brother," she said with a smile.

"My Lord Willoughby," Aemilia murmured, for that was the title by which Mistress Locke said she must address him.

Before she could launch herself into another groveling curtsy, Susan took her hand and held her upright. "We call him Perry. No need to bow and scrape and call him lord. His head is quite big enough already."

"Aemilia is far too long a name for a child," said Perry. "I'll call you Amy."

Amy. In one stroke, he made her English.

"So this is the child." Catherine Willoughby approached, her arms still entwined with Anne Locke's.

"My Lady Suffolk." Aemilia curtsied before her as though she were the Queen.

When she looked up again, she saw a kindly face etched with fine wrinkles.

"My husband sends his apologies," Catherine said. "He's abroad, buying broodmares."

"Come," Susan said. "We must show you to your room."

AEMILIA PEERED OUT THE diamond-paned window of her new bedchamber, which overlooked the ornamental herb gardens. The windows had been left open to allow the scents to waft in — aromas that brought back memories of sitting with Papa in his garden sanctuary. But before she could dissolve into tears, Anne Locke bustled into the room.

"Let's get you washed, child."

Aemilia put on a quick smile for Mistress Locke, who scrubbed her until she thought her skin would come off. Then the lady opened the saddlebag that contained Aemilia's few garments. Only her best Sunday gown, nearly outgrown, was anywhere near presentable, never mind that it was dark blue wool, far too warm and heavy for this sultry summer evening. But it would have to do.

"Susan will see to it that you get some decent clothes," Mistress Locke said. "She'll pass her older garments on and alter them to fit you. And she'll give that thing you're wearing now to the servants' children."

Aemilia smarted. This, her Sunday dress, was the best garment she'd ever owned, that Papa had worked so hard to provide, and Mistress Locke said it was just a rag, only fit for underlings to wear. Though she was no aristocrat like Catherine Willoughby, Anne Locke's father, brother, and late husband had been prosperous merchants. Born to wealth and plenty, she'd a fine gown of blue-gray lawn and slippers made of kid.

Mistress Locke whisked her down a grand flight of marble stairs. Craning her neck to gape at the paintings on the wall, Aemilia nearly lost her footing and tumbled headfirst.

"*Deport* yourself, my dear," Mistress Locke said. "You must act like a young lady. You're very lucky that they are inviting you to share their table. In most households, children your age are left to eat with the servants."

AEMILIA HAD EXPECTED TO dine in a stuffy room, seated at a long linen-draped table, but instead, owing to the weather, the Willoughby clan supped in the rose garden, their feast illumined by lanterns, torches, and the rising moon.

Servants, as silent and swift as the bats darting overhead, delivered trays of the delicacies Catherine Willoughby deemed appropriate for a late supper. Roasted pheasant and salads; a pie made of larks; crayfish and carp; breast of veal; custard tarts; strawberries and green figs; apricots and almonds. They sipped Rhenish wine as pale as the moonlight.

Mindful of Mistress Locke's admonition to act like a young lady, Aemilia struggled to ignore her ravenous hunger and follow the example of her table companions who only sampled each dish, leaving most of the food on their plates. The leftovers, she learned, would be eaten by the servants while any remaining food would be given to the poor.

Lanterns bathed the Willoughbys' faces in gold, making her hosts seem like magical beings, their laughter mingling with the night sounds of barking foxes and the wind in the oaks.

Catherine Willoughby practiced her French with Anne Locke, telling stories in that language that sent them both into spasms of laughter. While Thomas Vaughan and Henry Locke conversed with Lady Susan, Perry insisted on speaking Italian with Aemilia. Her heart exploded in joy, for she never thought to hear Papa's tongue in her new home.

She pointed to the porcelain dish of love apples set as decoration on the table. "Papa grew *pomodori* in his garden. He even ate them. I ate one once. It was delicious!"

"Don't do that here, or you'll shock my mother," said Perry, though he did not seem shocked at all. "I was your age when I first set foot on English soil. That makes me a foreigner. I feel as much at home in Europe as I do here."

"My brother speaks fluent French, Dutch, German, and Italian," Susan said, drawing the conversation back into English. "He's bound for a career in diplomacy."

"That is if I don't marry a rich heiress and live off her money while frittering away my days hunting and hawking," Perry said.

His words made Aemilia think of Francis Holland. It was as though a dead, rotting pigeon had been hurled in the middle of the lovely feast table, spoiling everything with its stench. What if Perry was no better than the brother-in-law she had fled?

"Don't look so miserable, Amy," he said, touching her wrist. "I was only joking. Do you think the great Catherine Willoughby would suffer an idle son?"

"Perry's betrothed to Mary de Vere," Susan said, "who has a tongue sharp enough to break your arm. I doubt she'll suffer any nonsense from him either."

Perry turned to Aemilia, stretching out his palms in entreaty. "Pity me, gentle Amy, for I am held captive by a tribe of Amazons!"

Ignoring her brother's jibe, Susan reached for Aemilia's hand. "Child, you mustn't take my brother too seriously."

Perry nodded. "Indeed, Susan is the serious one. Not me. The sternest and most serious school mistress you'll ever meet. You'll go blind from all the Latin and Greek she'll make you read."

Aemilia could not keep herself from gazing at Susan as though she were a goddess. She would worship her forever! Brother and sister smiled at her, their kindness warming her as tangibly as the heat from the torches that ringed the table.

Papa, this is my new life! Here she was, surrounded by learned people who had traveled the world. Here she sat with such noble company at a table strewn with rose petals while the stars blazed overhead.

6

HREE MONTHS ON, AEMILIA rose in the misty light of a September dawn and splashed water on her face. Mornings began early at Grimsthorpe with prayers in the family chapel at six, followed by her lessons at six thirty.

She gazed into the steel mirror Mistress Locke had given her before returning to London. The gift had surprised her, considering how Mistress Locke despised every form of vanity. She could still hear Mistress Locke's voice. *Let this be a mirror of your virtue.*

Tugging the comb through her hair, she smoothed her unruly curls as best she could, before tying them back with the pale violet ribbon Lady Susan had given her. How her fingertips thrilled just to touch the slippery satin. Over her new linen shift, she laced her new bodice and skirt, both gray to befit her station as a young scholar, yet Lady Susan had chosen the most delightful tone of gray that was nearly rose. A joy it was to feel the linen and lawn rustling around her as she walked. When she beheld her reflection, she could barely contain her delight.

AEMILIA PURPORTED HERSELF WITH as much dignity as she could as she descended the grand staircase to the family chapel with its stark whitewashed walls, its windows devoid of colored glass, and its single unadorned cross. Catherine Willoughby suffered no popish ornamentation. While the servants assembled on the main floor of the chapel, Aemilia took her place with the family in the balcony above. Lady Susan, Catherine Willoughby and her husband, and John Wingfield, the schoolmaster, all listened to the service with rapt attention, their eyes closed to better concentrate on the scriptures. Perry, meanwhile, looked as though he could barely stay awake. When Aemilia caught him yawning, he winked at her. His betrothed, Mary de Vere, had come to visit. As pale as alabaster with her ice-blond hair, she looked at him through her eyelashes. Lady Mary's family was rich and ancient, her brother Edward one of Her Majesty's favorites, but Aemilia thought she was nowhere near as lovely as Lady Susan.

With Mistress Locke gone, Aemilia set all her hope and affection on Susan. She had already written a poem for her but was too embarrassed to show it to her lest she deem it doggerel.

> Noble Mistress, your rare perfections shone in the Glass
> Wherein I saw my every fault.
> You the Sun's virtue, I that green grass
> That flourishes fresh by your clear virtue taught.

WHEN THE SERVICE HAD ended, Aemilia shyly took her idol's hand and walked with her to the schoolroom. Aemilia wanted to be nowhere else but here, taking her place at her desk with the tomes in Latin and Greek, with the foolscap cut into quarto size, and the quill and ink. The human skull on her schoolmaster's desk served as a reminder that life was short and all earthly existence must end. Aemilia must seize every moment to grow in wisdom and grace until she could become Susan's equal in learning if not in wealth or birth. Susan was even more learned than Anne Locke. She read Aristotle in Greek and could debate with the schoolmaster in Latin.

In truth, there was an air of loneliness in Lady Susan, though she appeared to try her best to hide it and not allow her melancholy to be a burden to others. A childless widow at twenty-three! Aemilia swore she would be a solace to her, her faithful handmaiden who would make her proud. Susan certainly seemed to love these hours in the schoolroom as much as Aemilia did, loved steeping herself in the ancient writings of Greece and Rome.

Master Wingfield was a tall and spindly young man of gentle birth but little fortune, as a third son, which explained why he had come to earn his bread as a schoolmaster. Under Lady Susan's direction, he was giving Aemilia the identical grammar-school education that a boy would receive between the ages of seven and fourteen before he was sent off to university. Of course, no girl or woman could attend university, but some, such as Lady Susan and the Queen, continued their scholarly studies throughout their lives.

John Wingfield taught Aemilia rhetoric, mathematics, French, cosmography, drawing, dancing, and continued her musical education even though he was not a virtuoso. But the heart of her studies were the classics of ancient Rome. He drilled her with English translations from the text and she replied from memory, quoting the Latin.

"We are not born, we do not live for ourselves alone," Master Wingfield prompted. "Our country, our friends, have a share in us."

Aemilia trembled in both effort and quiet pride as she uttered Cicero's original words from *De Officiis,* "*Non nobis solum nati sumus ortusque nostri partem patria vindicat, partem amici.*" *Amici,* friends, sounded so like her name, the English name Perry had given her. Amy.

"Is anyone unaware that Fortune plays a major role in both success and failure?"

"*Magnam vim esse in fortuna in utramque partem, vel secundas ad res vel adversas, quis ignorat?*" She nearly sang, for she delighted so much in the words. Latin was the grandfather of the Italian language. Every syllable brought back Papa.

"The pagan Romans believed in Fortuna," Lady Susan interjected. "But we Christians believe in Providence."

Aemilia nodded and folded her hands as Master Wingfield continued. "Of evils choose the least."

"*Primum, minima de malis.*" *Malis,* malice.

LESSONS IN THE SCHOOLROOM ended at three, at which time Susan deemed it appropriate that she and Aemilia ride out on horseback, equitation being one of the most wholesome forms of exercise.

"Every lady must learn to ride well," Susan told her, as they walked arm in arm toward the stables. "Think of what my mother and Mistress Locke endured. One never knows when one must flee."

"May Providence protect us," Master Wingfield murmured, trailing just behind them.

Perry and Mary de Vere were already mounted on fine Spanish coursers that gleamed in the sunlight, not a fleck of dirt on their white legs and oiled hooves. Lady Mary made a great show of riding aside on her saddle to show off her skirt trimmed in silver braid. She wore a hat with pheasant plumes set at a jaunty angle. But her perfect alabaster face soured at the sight of Aemilia and Master Wingfield.

"You said we would ride with your sister," she told Perry. "Not play nursemaid to a child with a schoolmaster in tow."

Aemilia burned to hear Lady Mary speak as if she and Master Wingfield were deaf and had no feelings.

"But Amy *is* my sister!" said Perry. "My little adopted sister. And Master Wingfield her celebrated mentor. Have you gone blind yet from all that Latin, little sister?"

Aemilia's heart burst with affection for Perry, for his gentle humor that set everything right.

"*Exitus acta probat,*" she told him, quoting Ovid.

Master Wingfield laughed aloud, her beloved schoolmaster whose smile made her float above the ground. Best of all, Lady Susan squeezed her hand and gave her a complicit smile. Aemilia knew that Susan had no great liking for Lady Mary either.

"The ends justify the means," Lady Susan translated. "But I think you'll find our Amy hasn't gone blind just yet."

"Amy is our Hypatia," Perry told his betrothed. "Our protégée, our laurel-crowned scholar."

"The child's head will grow enormous." Lady Mary's eyes drifted toward the horizon as though she were bored.

She and Perry rode off together, leaving the others to mount up and follow.

"I do wish he would marry someone kinder," Susan said as Master Wingfield helped her into her saddle. "Perhaps once she has a child or two, she'll grow a bit softer."

Both Susan's and Master Wingfield's horses were magnificent, for Richard Bertie only bred from the best Spanish bloodlines. The groom then led out Aemilia's mount, smaller than the coursers, with an enormous grass belly and a sunburnt pink nose. Bathsheba nickered and nuzzled Aemilia's hands to see if she carried any sweetmeats. Mistress Locke had intended to take Bathsheba back to London with her, but on the day of her departure, the little mare had gone lame and thus at Grimsthorpe she remained. Now she was sound again and needed the exercise lest she grow even more rotund. Aemilia could have begged to ride one of the Spanish purebreds, but she was stubbornly attached to the chestnut mare, who possessed in character what she lacked in breeding.

"Careful when you ride out," the groom said. "Marry, I think she's in season."

"What's that?" Aemilia asked. Bathsheba was behaving no differently than usual.

"I'm sure she'll be fine," Lady Susan said. "If the little mare can even manage to keep up with the coursers."

The three of them set out at a steady trot and soon caught up with Perry and Lady Mary. Then Perry rode alongside Master Wingfield, giving him his full attention, as though to make him feel welcome. Aemilia observed the way her schoolmaster dipped his head to Perry. What he said next took her breath away.

"As I am born to little fortune, my lord, I hope to advance myself by seeking a career in the military where a loyal man might distinguish himself."

The rest of their conversation was lost to Aemilia when Lady Susan began to speak to her. "Tonight when we gather after dinner, perhaps you can sing madrigals for Lady Mary." Susan glanced from Aemilia who rode on her left, to Lady Mary who rode on her right. "You enjoy madrigals, don't you, Lady Mary?"

As Susan went on speaking to Mary, Aemilia watched Master Wingfield and Perry conferring earnestly in hushed voices. Why would a schoolmaster wish to abandon his books for the battlefield? If he lacked wealth, surely the Willoughbys paid him handsomely enough. Who would teach her if he left? Perhaps Lady Susan, for she was every bit as learned as Master Wingfield.

Bathsheba, likewise, seemed to focus her entire attention on the men, or rather on Perry's stallion. The mare whinnied and attempted to barge forward. It was all Aemilia could do to pull her back and make her walk sedately between Lady Susan's and Lady Mary's horses.

"All this tedious conversation!" Mary cried. "Anyone would think we were sitting at your mother's table."

Lady Mary spurred her horse into a canter. Riding alongside Perry, she dared him to race her to the stream at the end of the meadow. Master Wingfield had already fallen back to join Lady Susan, but Aemilia found herself surging forward as Bathsheba leapt into a furious gallop.

"Aemilia, no!" Lady Susan shouted after her. "Make her stop!"

The wind whipping Aemilia's face brought tears to her eyes as she yanked on the reins with her entire strength, but Bathsheba had the bit in her teeth and there was no stopping her. Aemilia could only cling on helplessly as Bathsheba, whinnying and squealing, charged between Perry's stallion and Lady Mary's gelding, nearly unseating Mary who shrieked curses Aemilia never thought to hear from an earl's daughter. Screaming her apologies, Aemilia could only witness in horror as her mare tossed her head and threw little bucks as she pranced alongside the stallion. *In season.* So that was what it meant. Bathsheba wanted only to mate. *No, no, no,* Aemilia thought, panic rising in her gorge.

Master Wingfield cantered up and seized Bathsheba's bridle, yanking her to a halt. Sliding from the saddle, Aemilia collapsed in the grass and wept in humiliation.

"Feed that ill-bred creature to the hounds!" Lady Mary roared.

Is she talking about Bathsheba or me? Aemilia wondered.

Struggling to control his stallion, Perry laughed so hard he nearly came off. "Pray God, our gentle Amy has better morals than her fat little mare."

Just when Aemilia thought her heart couldn't sink any further, she saw Bathsheba squeal and hold her tail to the side, wantonly exposing her nether regions to the stallion. Perry could only force his horse around and ride for home, laughing all the way.

Lady Susan pulled Aemilia out of the grass and brushed the tears from her face. "It's my fault. I should have listened to the groom and set you on another horse."

Dazed, Aemilia could only thank her stars that Lady Susan was sweeter tempered than Lady Mary who would probably never speak to her again, no matter how many apologies Aemilia offered or how many madrigals she sang.

"Well ridden," Susan said to Master Wingfield, touching his arm. "A cavalry officer couldn't have done better."

Aemilia watched her schoolmaster's face flush to hear Susan's praise.

"Thank you, Master Wingfield," Aemilia said fervently. She didn't dare think what might have happened if he hadn't been able to bring Bathsheba under control.

Bathsheba nuzzled Aemilia's hair and the crook of her neck, as though wondering what the tears and fuss were about.

AFTER DELIVERING THE HORSES to the groom, Lady Susan and Master Wingfield returned to the house. But Aemilia, still reeling from her disgrace, retreated to the Duchess's rose garden, where she hunched on a bench and listened to the gushing fountain. From behind the great yew hedge, she heard voices. Perry and Lady Mary. She was about to creep away when she froze.

"It's not the child's fault she's an ungoverned heathen," Perry said, his voice placating. "Her father was at court most of the time, leaving her with her mother who had no more brains than a sparrow."

"It's all very well that your sister concerns herself with an unfortunate orphan, but must she join our every pastime?" Lady Mary no longer sounded angry, but cool and considered, as though choosing her words with care. "The way she preens before you to show off her Latin! Honestly, what good will Latin and Greek do for a girl like her? At least do her the mercy of reminding her of her place now and again. One day she shall have to return to her family."

"You wouldn't wish that on her," Perry said. "We receive letters from her mother, who can't even write for herself — her son-in-law writes them for her. All of them shamelessly begging for money. My mother daren't show them to the child. She burns them to spare her. Amy's life is troubled enough. Let her enjoy a few years of innocent reprieve."

Aemilia thought her heart would stop beating. A few years' reprieve — was that what Lady Susan offered? As soon as her education was finished, or as soon as Master Wingfield found an appointment in the military, would they send her back to Mother and Master Holland? But Lady Susan was so kind! Surely she wouldn't abandon her.

Yet Aemilia knew she couldn't expect to remain at Grimsthorpe Castle forever. She thought back to Master Wingfield's talk with Perry. Was her schoolmaster a fellow humble soul who hoped to use his fleeting time in this great house as a stepping stone to a better future? She, too, would have to make the most of her education, learn as much as she could in order to become a poet, a lady. Then, as a woman grown, she would return to London and drive Master Holland out of Papa's house.

"There you are!" Lady Susan appeared from beneath a bower of white roses. She sat on the stone bench beside Aemilia and touched her hot, tear-stained face. "You're not still crying over that naughty mare, are you? Think no more of it, dear."

Susan took Aemilia in her arms, a rare gesture, for the lady wasn't given to extravagant displays of affection. Leaning against her, Aemilia let herself be held, Susan's heart beating against her ear as Papa's once had.

FRESH SNOW MANTLED THE gardens and hedges in a train of diamonds. Golden shafts of winter sunlight poured into Lady Susan's room where Aemilia lingered, surrounded by her mentor's books and maps. Before the looking glass, she whirled in her new gown of rose-colored silk with brocade sleeves, a gift from Susan. She had pink and scarlet ribbons woven into her hair and a wreath of gilded rosemary crowning her brow.

Today Perry would wed Mary de Vere in the family chapel. Grimsthorpe Castle heaved with guests who had come from as far away as Oxford and Exeter. Aemilia's room had been sacrificed to accommodate such eminent persons, but the greater glory was hers, for Lady Susan had invited her to share her four-poster with the embroidered draperies.

Alone in Susan's chamber, Aemilia practiced her dance steps before the mirror. She would play the lute and sing madrigals in honor of the newlyweds. She would join the sons and daughters of earls in a masque Lady Susan and Master Wingfield had arranged. Such a day of celebration this would be! The aroma of roasting and baking wafted up from the kitchen.

Smiling into the mirror, Aemilia tried to embody the sweetness and grace Lady Susan expected of her. She spoke in dulcet tones, in her most cultivated voice. "My name is Amy."

But Angela's corpse-cold face intruded on her thoughts. Catherine Willoughby had finally broken the news that Aemilia's sister had died in childbirth. How could her beautiful sister be dead while she lived in such pomp? Did her good fortune make a mockery of all Angela had suffered? If Aemilia gave in to her grief, she feared it would devour her, that she'd start crying and never be able to stop.

She told herself she must be strong and make the most of this precious chance she had been given. Looking once more in the mirror, she said first shyly, then boldly, "Amy Willoughby."

For a long moment, she allowed herself the comfort of pretending that Susan, not Angela, was her sister. That she had been born to this manor house, titled and rich.

But she didn't look the least bit English. Even in the depths of winter, her skin remained olive in tone, no match for Susan's complexion of cream and roses. Aemilia's eyes were as black as ink with amber flecks swimming inside them. Her hair, even in high summer when exposed to the full flood of sunlight, remained dark with only a few auburn lights.

Still, she curtsied before the mirror and uttered her incantation, her prayer. "Amy Willoughby."

Then she shrieked when, like a phantom, Mary de Vere's pale face appeared in the glass behind her.

"You can preen all you want, girl," the Earl of Oxford's daughter, Perry's bride, said. "But you will never be a Willoughby."

Aemilia burned, her Bassano blood rising to the surface, beating in her ears. Before she could think what to say, Mary vanished in a swish of silk, only her carnation perfume remaining in the air.

II

Warrior Women

<h1 style="text-align:center">7</h1>

WELVE YEARS OLD, AEMILIA pored over Plutarch's *Life of Alexander,* preparing a written translation from the Greek into English. About to ask a question, she glanced at Master Wingfield, but he appeared utterly absorbed in a map of the Low Countries spread out on his desk.

"Sir, are you trying to find where Perry is now?" Aemilia asked him.

How they all missed Peregrine Bertie, who was either away on some diplomatic mission in Europe or else in Westminster with the House of Lords. Catherine Willoughby had died last year, leaving her son the barony.

Grimsthorpe Castle, Aemilia's beloved refuge, kept changing. Even Anne Locke had married for a third time and moved to Devon. Aemilia suspected she would never see Mistress Locke again.

Lady Mary was now mistress of Grimsthorpe. At this very moment, Aemilia could hear her raised voice down the corridor, berating some unfortunate servant. Marriage hadn't made Mary any milder. If anything, she had grown more brittle and bad tempered, blaming her childless state on Perry's long absences. *If I were Perry, I would sail to the East Indies to escape Mary de Vere.*

But it was the change in Lady Susan that troubled Aemilia most. Of late, Susan seemed so distracted and her health seemed likewise afflicted. This morning she had excused herself after chapel and taken to her bed, claiming troubled digestion. Even as Aemilia tried to concentrate on Plutarch's description of the Scythian warrior women, her heart squeezed in worry. What if Susan had some serious malady? Aemilia thought she wouldn't be able to bear the loss of her. Likewise, Master Wingfield seemed to mope in her absence.

"You've done enough for one day, Amy," he told her, though the clock had yet to ring three bells. "It's a fine afternoon for a ride."

"Will you ride with me, sir?" she asked.

"Not today, Amy," he said. "But I trust the groom will ride with you."

AFTER LEAVING THE SCHOOLROOM, Aemilia headed directly to Susan's door.

Her mentor lay in bed, her lustrous auburn hair fanning around her wan face.

"How were your lessons?" Susan reached to take Aemilia's hand.

"Not the same without you, my lady. May I bring you anything? Shall I ask Lady Mary to send for a physician?"

"Heavens no," Susan said, her voice uncharacteristically sharp. Then she smiled. "Don't worry yourself over me, my dear. Go out and ride. It's such a glorious day."

TWELVE YEARS OLD. AEMILIA studied herself in her steel mirror. *Almost a woman.* The servants were continually letting out her seams to accommodate the way her body kept changing. To her deep embarrassment, she already had breasts. She'd begun to bleed each month. *Will I soon be too old for the schoolroom?* she wondered. Lady Mary certainly seemed to think Aemilia had stayed at Grimsthorpe long enough. *But Lady Susan won't let her banish me. She wouldn't hear of it.*

Aemilia knew she owed Lady Susan everything. Yet when she looked inside her heart, she found a restlessness, a simmering rebellion. An aching for something she couldn't even name. How she missed her cousin Jasper, missed having a friend her own age; yet more than anything, she dreaded returning to her mother's house where Master Holland still lived. Her unknown future gaped before her like a chasm, and when her fear touched her loneliness, it tempted her to do the most reckless things that would cause even Susan to despair of her.

From the box beneath her bed she took out a white linen shirt, a doublet, a cap, and old moleskin riding breeches—Perry's old clothes that he would never miss. After checking the bolt on her door, she donned her disguise. The cap, artfully worn, hid her long hair, just as the doublet made her breasts disappear. Garments alone could make her another person.

Though Perry was short and compact for a man, his clothes were too big for her — she had to cinch the breeches to her waist with a length of cord. Still, she decided she looked no odder than her young Bassano cousins in their older brothers' handed-down clothes. She imagined Jasper daring her to wear this when she rode out today, just as he'd once dared her to dress as a boy when they'd stolen away to the Shoreditch theater five years ago. Her body shivered with the allure of it, the audacity. The look on Mary de Vere's face! But then Aemilia considered Susan, pale and weak in her bed, and how such an act would upset her. Half sick with shame, Aemilia stripped off the forbidden clothes and crammed them back inside their box.

"Is Master Wingfield riding out with you today?" the groom asked when he led out Bathsheba.

The groom was an older man who limped from a nasty fall he had taken years ago. If Aemilia rode with him, they would go slowly and carefully, and yet she knew she couldn't refuse his company, for he surely wouldn't allow her to ride out on her own.

Before she could stop herself, the lie sprang to her lips. "Master Wingfield shall be a little late. He said I could ride on ahead and practice my equitation exercises in the meadow until he can join me."

Not giving the groom a chance to object, she sprang into the saddle and trotted off.

On horseback, she was unfettered, and it no longer mattered that she was a minstrel's bastard daughter with nothing but a one-hundred-pound dowry to her name that would probably be spent paying off Mother's debts.

As soon as Aemilia was out of the groom's view, she spurred Bathsheba into a headlong gallop, letting the mare be as strong as she liked, the bit in her teeth as she bolted over hedges and ditches. The higher and more dangerous the jump, the greater the thrill that flooded Aemilia's entire body, vibrating into her fingers and toes. In truth, she was afraid of falling, but not of falling off a horse.

THE LOOK THE OLD groom gave Aemilia when she and Bathsheba returned alone was enough to make her want to shrink inside herself. In the course of her wild ride, she'd lost her hat and her hair was a disheveled mess. Slithering down from the saddle, she stroked Bathsheba's neck then slunk away.

Hoping to creep to her room without attracting attention, she slipped into the murkiest part of the gardens, the shaded walks between the yew hedges. As she rushed along, brimming with self-reproach, she found Lady Susan. Lady Susan embracing Master Wingfield, offering her flower face to his kisses.

AEMILIA WASHED AND PUT on fresh clothing. She sat on her bed, her hands folded in her lap, and waited for Susan to tell her that her school days were over. Aemilia was too frightened and confused to even cry.

Had these four years of her humanist education been a ruse for Susan's dalliance with the schoolmaster? Looking back, Aemilia recalled the smiles they had exchanged and how Master Wingfield had flushed whenever Susan praised him or touched his hand. She also remembered Anne Locke's words about Lady Susan on the journey to Grimsthorpe: *She dares not remarry without the Queen's leave. She also fears Her Majesty might arrange a match not to her liking.* Did that explain the secrecy surrounding their love affair?

When Susan finally knocked on her door and stepped inside, she looked both happy and sad.

"Sweet Amy," she said, sitting beside her on the bed. "I was waiting for the right moment to tell you. Master Wingfield and I shall be married. Perry, bless him, has found him an appointment with Her Majesty's forces in the Netherlands."

So Perry knew from the start. Aemilia remembered how Perry and Master Wingfield used to ride alongside each other discussing Master Wingfield's military ambitions.

"But, Lady Susan, won't you miss him if he goes abroad?" Aemilia almost believed that if she used the rhetorical skills Master Wingfield had taught her and came up with a sound and logical argument, she could stop time. Keep Master Wingfield in the schoolroom educating her.

Susan's smile trembled. "My darling girl, I'm going with him."

Aemilia thought her bones would no longer hold her upright. She felt herself crumbling apart.

Susan stroked her hair. "Please don't look so forlorn. Perry promised you could stay here for as long as you like."

But you're leaving me alone with Lady Mary, who hates me, Aemilia wanted to shout. One look at Susan's face silenced her.

"Be happy for me, Amy." Susan kissed her brow.

"HOW COULD YOU?" LADY Mary's voice shook the walls.

Alone in her room, Aemilia listened to the tirade taking place in the parlor below.

"Pregnant by a schoolmaster! If your mother had lived to see this, she would have died of shame. The Queen will be furious. It's just as well you and that pauper are running away to the Netherlands. You'll never be able to show your face in court again. I hope you intend to take that odious child with you."

Aemilia flung herself on the floor, her ear pressed to the boards to hear Susan's reply. What was to stop Lady Mary from turning her out? Only Susan's goodwill had kept her here this long.

"You made a solemn promise to my brother," Susan said. "Amy can stay on until an honorable marriage is arranged for her."

Marriage? Aemilia was too mortified to breathe. Then she remembered that Susan had wed the Earl of Kent at fifteen, only three years older than Aemilia was now.

"Besides," Susan continued, speaking as if she were her brother's equal as a diplomat, "she is an accomplished musician and even you have said how much you enjoy her playing and singing. Without her, there would be no more music in this house to entertain your guests."

8

OUR YEARS ON, SIXTEEN-YEAR-OLD Aemilia fever-
ishly practiced on the virginals, rehearsing her repertoire, happier than she had been in many months.
Perry was finally coming home to visit. Over her mu-
sic, she could hear Lady Mary directing the servants in their frantic
preparations.

Even Mary seemed filled with joyful anticipation. She had invited
dignitaries from across the realm. There would be feasting, toasting,
and merriment—and the music Aemilia would sing and play. Would
Perry even recognize her? When he'd last seen her, she had been an ungainly girl of fourteen, but now she was a young woman.

Nothing had come of Lady Mary's halfhearted attempts to find a
husband for her. Aemilia's paltry dowry was of no interest to the eligi-
ble men in the Willoughbys' circle, not to mention the taint of her bastard birth. Not that this stopped male guests from trying to grope her
in the corridors. She had learned to carry a bodkin up her sleeve and
lock her chamber door. But Perry's homecoming would set everything
right. Perhaps he might even find her a husband, a kind schoolmaster
who would read Latin and Greek with her.

Aemilia envisioned Perry arriving like the god Apollo in his chariot,
shining his light and mirth upon this lonely house. She lived for his and
Susan's letters. Susan and her husband lived in Bergen op Zoom with
their two little sons.

A battalion of maids now burst into the parlor, coming to polish every inch of it for their master's homecoming. Chased out of the room,

Aemilia retreated upstairs, stopping by the nursery to visit little Robert, Mary and Perry's only child.

"You're growing into a big boy," she cooed, taking the two-year-old from Nell, his nurse.

Aemilia kissed his chubby cheeks until he giggled. At least the little lad was something she and his mother could hold on to while his father traveled in foreign lands. *In terra peregrina.* Perry was so seldom home, it astonished Aemilia that he had succeeded in fathering a child.

She understood Lady Mary's secret pain that she tried to conceal beneath her haughty veneer. How could any wife not feel wounded if her husband was perpetually elsewhere? It was as though he had married Mary de Vere for her fortune and pedigree, begat a son on her, and then abandoned her to pursue his pleasures elsewhere. Aemilia had even heard it whispered among Lady Mary's own guests that Perry kept a Flemish mistress.

IN THE STABLES, AEMILIA left the aged groom and his stable boys to clean and polish tack while she saddled and bridled Bathsheba herself. She had disobeyed the groom so many times that he had at last given up insisting she be chaperoned.

While still within view of the house, she trotted along sedately, carrying herself like a lady. But once the July greenery enveloped her and she knew herself to be unobserved, she leapt from the saddle and led Bathsheba into the shelter of a thicket. Reaching into her saddlebag, she shed her skirts and donned Perry's old moleskin breeches, his shirt, and his doublet. Freedom coursed through her veins. If Lady Mary decided she could no longer suffer her, Aemilia had this. No longer a helpless young girl but a daring adventurer. Her other self. She had even given this persona a name — Emilio.

Mounting up again, she galloped away, a reckless and daring young rake, letting Bathsheba take every stone wall and thorn hedge in their path. They raced on, her heart pounding in time with her mare's hooves, until the worries that plagued her and kept her awake every night were finally beaten down — *what will become of me?*

When Bathsheba had finally had enough and stopped to drink from a stream, Aemilia gazed round, utterly disoriented. She no longer knew where she was or even if she was still on the Willoughbys' land.

The long summer day was waning. Judging from the sun's position in the sky, she guessed there was only an hour of daylight remaining. Could she trust Bathsheba to find her own way back?

Aemilia rode on, reaching a place where two dirt tracks crossed. As she tried to find her bearings, another rider approached. A gentleman on a black stallion. Bathsheba raised her head and snorted.

"Young man, you look lost," the rider said.

Aemilia was elated that her disguise had actually fooled him. Something about this stranger looked so familiar—that long slender line of his jaw—though surely they had never met. He was an older gentleman, but handsome, his gaze compelling and direct. He wore a sword and rapier, she noted. Aemilia supposed that if she was to play the part of a young man, she, too, would require arms.

"I'm riding to Grimsthorpe Castle," the man said. "Where do you ride?"

Behind him, a group of other riders appeared—Lady Mary's guests arriving days too early. Mary would be completely out of sorts, for the household had been turned upside down with all the cleaning and airing.

"Sir, please don't trouble yourself over me," she blurted out, gathering her reins. "I was just heading home."

The man gave her an incredulous smile, his green eyes piercing hers. "God's blood, you're a maid!"

Her skin burned. She cursed the girlish timbre of her voice for betraying her. Wheeling Bathsheba around, she cantered off and cleared a tall hedge, leaving the man behind.

Locked inside her room, Aemilia was scrubbing away grime and the scent of horseflesh when Lady Mary's maid banged on her door, calling her down to play the virginals in the candlelit parlor.

Aemilia's empty stomach groaned from missing supper, and the many unfamiliar faces swam before her eyes. She wore her best gown of dull blue taffeta, an old garment of Lady Mary's. The color didn't suit her and made her look jaundiced, but she molded her face into a mask of gratitude and docility.

"I hope we didn't trouble your ladyship too much with our untimely arrival," one of the guests said, his voice sending a ripple up Aemilia's spine. It was the same gentleman who had seen her in her breeches.

Keeping her back to him, she sat at the virginals.

"I must have misunderstood the date of my Lord Willoughby's homecoming," he went on. "How good of you, Lady Mary, to receive us so graciously."

Aemilia played a galliard, her music the backdrop for the guests' conversations. She willed herself to remain invisible.

"She's Italian," she heard Lady Mary say. "An orphan my sister-in-law took in. I haven't the heart to turn her out."

"How fascinating," the man said. "I've just finished reading Dante. Does this virtuosa have a name?"

Aemilia wanted to crawl behind the tapestries, but she made herself play on until Lady Mary commanded her to stand and face the tall gentleman with the green eyes.

"Her name is Amy Bassano," Lady Mary said.

"Bassano," he echoed, taking Aemilia's hand before she could sweep down in an obsequious curtsy and so hide her face. "Your people are royal musicians, are they not?"

He knew her family — did that explain why he looked so familiar? A subtle smile played on his lips as he seemed to connect her face to the rider he'd encountered a few hours earlier.

"*Amy non è un nome Italiano, signorina,*" he said, the first Italian she had heard since Perry's last visit.

"*Il mio nome è Aemilia, signore,*" she said, aware of Lady Mary's eyes on them both and how it irked Mary when her guests conversed in foreign tongues that she couldn't understand.

"Aemilia," he said, bending to kiss her hand. "A name as lovely as your music."

Would he be one of the visitors to corner her in some dim hallway? But he did not have the air of a disgusting lecher. For a man of his years, he was lean and elegant, his pale red-gold hair untouched by gray. And he was cultured. But he knew her secret and could use that to his advantage.

"Amy plays the lute and sings if it's singing you prefer," Lady Mary said in a display of breathless deference, before rounding on Aemilia with narrowed eyes. "Could you at least remember to curtsy? This is Lord Hunsdon, if you please. The Lord Chamberlain."

Aemilia felt as though she had been blasted by lightning. So that was why he seemed so familiar. Once the Master of Hawks who had tried to make Angela his mistress, he was now Lord Chamberlain. Her spine remained unbowed as she stared straight into his eyes.

"My Lord Hunsdon, do you remember my sister, Angela?" She could not keep the sting from her voice.

She expected him to bridle with arrogant denial. Instead, he gave her a long, measured look.

"I do," he said. "Ah, you were the child I met in the mews that day. Now I remember." A pensive look crossed his face. "I understand your sister's marriage was not a happy one and that your father died not long after I spoke to him that day. For that I'm truly sorry. Battista Bassano was a good man and your sister a most talented young woman."

Aemilia dropped her eyes, terrified she would dissolve into tears, for his words had reawakened her grief and loss.

"Forgive me," he said, "if I've given you cause for sadness." He spoke with such solicitude, as though her feelings truly mattered to him.

Lady Mary, who looked appalled by this entire exchange, pinched Aemilia's arm and told her to play on. Sinking back on her stool, Aemilia obeyed.

"You must pardon her insolence, my lord," Mary said.

AFTER AEMILIA HAD FINISHED her repertoire and was on her way back to her room, she heard footsteps behind her. *Lord Hunsdon?* Her heart hammering, she swung round to face him. But it was Lady Mary who had her cornered.

"What do you play at, speaking to the Lord Chamberlain like that?" Mary was looking at her in a way she never had. Her gaze was hard and sharp. Dangerous.

"I play at nothing, my lady," Aemilia said, unable to breathe until Lady Mary sighed and left her there, leaning weakly against the wall. *Oh, please let Perry come home soon.* Before his wife's nerves were stretched any thinner.

THE FOLLOWING DAY WAS stifling and airless. Lifting her eyes to the heavens, Aemilia waited for the storm to break, but the bruised clouds hung motionless in the stagnant sky.

Hoping to avoid any further cause for offense, Aemilia stayed out of Lady Mary's and her guests' way as much as possible, taking her meals in the nursery with Nell and little Robert, and only showing her face in the reception rooms when summoned. She didn't even presume to go riding, but hid herself away in the old schoolroom where she pored over Plutarch's *Life of Alexander*, the same Greek text she had been translating the day she learned the truth of what lay between Susan and the schoolmaster. Her fond memories of her mentor blurred into a hurt that had never quite healed, though she was happy that Susan was no longer lonely.

But even here, in her secret refuge where Lady Mary never set foot, the door opened and one of the guests entered on quiet feet.

"Pardon me, Mistress Bassano. I hope I'm not disturbing your studies."

Aemilia stood to wary attention at the sight of Lord Hunsdon. She tried to make her face a bland mask as he gazed down at the Greek letters in the open book.

"This is my favorite passage," he said, running his finger across the page. "When the Scythian warrior women give chase to the King of Persia, forcing him to flee their wrath." His eyes met Aemilia's. "I do believe you are cut from the same cloth as those Amazons of old, the way I saw you ride yesterday."

She tried to hide her fear. "Will you tell Lady Mary, my lord?"

He laughed. "Goodness, no. A gentleman knows how to keep a secret. But I must compliment her ladyship on your education. It's rare I meet a young woman who reads Greek. You are even more accomplished than I imagined."

"Thank you, my lord." She found herself blushing in the warmth of his praise.

How rare it was, with Susan, Perry, and Master Wingfield gone, to meet a single soul who saw her education as something to commend rather than as a ridiculous oddity for a girl of her station. Yet, despite his kindness, she didn't dare return his gaze. Stymied, she stared down at the book, for she didn't know what to say to him that wouldn't earn her some future rebuke. *What do you play at?*

"Well, I shall leave you to your reading," he said, making his retreat.

After he had closed the door behind himself, she sat down, his words still reverberating inside her.

DAY AFTER SWELTERING, WINDLESS day dragged on, the guests eating through the kitchen stores. Aemilia played and sang for them each evening. A week passed and then a fortnight, and still Perry did not come.

Lady Mary's face grew rigid from the strain. Aemilia observed what pains Mary had taken to keep up her appearance of hospitality and good cheer, but the façade grew thinner each day her husband failed to arrive.

At the beginning of the third week, Aemilia could no longer bear to mew herself up in the schoolroom. Slipping out a side door, she set off on a brisk walk. She had nearly reached the gatehouse at the end of the Four Mile Riding when she saw a messenger riding at gallop.

Her skin, clammy in the heat, suddenly chilled. She turned and rushed back, running until she was winded, walking then running again.

WHEN AEMILIA REACHED THE house, everything was in disarray, the servants muttering, the noble guests clustered in the entrance hall. She headed straight for the nursery.

"What news of my Lord Willoughby?" she asked Nell, pitching her voice to be heard above little Robert's wails.

"He's not coming." Nell grimaced as she grappled with the child and tried to spread salve on his angry red skin nettled from the heat.

Aemilia joined in to help, trying to soothe the little boy. "Surely he must come. He promised."

"Her Majesty's sent him on an urgent mission to Denmark," said Nell.

Denmark. That meant they probably wouldn't see Perry for at least another year. Why, oh why, with all his skills in diplomacy had he not persuaded the Queen to allow him a few days' leave to visit his family before he sailed abroad again? Poor Lady Mary. She must be humiliated. But at least the guests would soon be gone.

IN THE SCHOOLROOM AEMILIA found a sumptuously bound copy of Dante's *La Divina Commedia* lying on her desk. She caught her breath and opened the calfskin cover to find a message penned in a flawless italic hand.

For Aemilia Bassano, a most learned young woman
Your well-wisher always, Henry Carey, Lord Hunsdon

Her hands trembled as she held the book. Such a precious—and costly—gift. Until this moment, she had no book she could call her own. Blinking, she traced his letters on the page. *Your well-wisher always.* But why had he left it for her to find instead of giving it to her directly? Cradling the book in both hands, she carried it to her room.

AEMILIA GLANCED OUT HER bedroom window to see that some of the guests were already riding away. *Lord Hunsdon, too?* she wondered.

A fever clogged her brain. Something soon must snap. The air was full of invisible knives. *You must prepare yourself to make your own way in the world.* Without Perry or Susan to protect her, she had no true place at Grimsthorpe. *You're only a parasite, a useless dependent.*

Trying to calm herself, she put on her breeches, shirt, and doublet. Unbidden, Lord Hunsdon's words about the Scythian warrior women came back to her. Was that how he had seen her, not as a shameful hoyden but something rare and fierce? Something powerful even? Her skin tingled at the memory of the admiration in his eyes whenever he'd looked at her. Flinging herself on the bed, she allowed forbidden thoughts to dance inside her. *If I had been Angela, I would have said yes to him.*

At the sound of a sharp rap on the door, Aemilia nearly screamed.

"Open the door, if you please," came Lady Mary's crisp voice. "I wish to speak to you."

"One moment!" she called, flailing in panic.

Tearing off the men's clothes, she kicked them under the bed then donned her shift and stays, her stockings and garters and skirts as fast as she could. Her fingers fumbled as she frantically laced up her bodice.

"What are you doing in there?" Lady Mary called through the door.

"Dressing, my lady. I just had a nap."

Aemilia unlocked the door.

"Napping in the middle of the day," Lady Mary said, as she strode in. "How I envy you. I haven't slept in three weeks."

"I am so sorry to hear of my Lord Willoughby's mission to Denmark, my lady." Aemilia folded her hands and bowed her head, bracing herself for Mary's temper.

"After seven years his wife, I imagine I should be used to it." Lady Mary sat on Aemilia's bed and let out a hollow laugh. "To have relations with my lawful husband, it seems I must travel in his wake like a camp follower."

The pain in her voice undid Aemilia. It struck her that Lady Mary had no trusted confidante. But now, after nearly a month of hiding her anguish from her noble guests, Mary was baring her heart to her. For the first time, Aemilia had the inkling that they might even become friends.

"You know what it is to be left behind, Amy." Lady Mary gestured for Aemilia to sit beside her. "Peregrine and Susan are just the same. They lure us here with pretty promises. Then they run away and wash their hands of us."

Aemilia took her hand. "Will you follow him to Denmark, my lady?"

"And leave my only child behind? Or risk Robert's health by taking him along?"

"My lady," Aemilia said, wishing she could find the words to ease Mary's pain.

"It's all very well for you." Lady Mary looked away, her eyes welling, as though Aemilia's sympathy was more than she could bear. "You have your music and books for consolation." Aemilia froze to see Mary pick up the copy of Dante from the bedside table. "But shouldn't you keep them in the library and schoolroom where they belong?"

"My lady, I—" Aemilia stopped short at the sight of Lady Mary opening the book and reading Lord Hunsdon's dedication.

The look Mary gave her was enough to turn Aemilia to cinder. "So you've been accepting gifts from the Lord Chamberlain behind my back."

"My lady, he left it in the schoolroom for me to find. If you think it unseemly, pray, return it to him. I never wished to bring dishonor on your household."

"And how may I return it to him when he's already left?" Lady Mary asked, her voice scathing.

Aemilia dropped her gaze to hide her disappointment. So he had indeed gone without saying farewell. Perhaps he'd meant to say good-bye, but not finding her, had left the book behind instead.

"The book is yours to do with as you like," she told Lady Mary.

But something else had diverted Mary's attention. When she stooped to pick something off the floor, Aemilia felt her throat constrict. Lady Mary dangled the breeches in the space between them. Her face was so angry and wounded, Aemilia had to look away.

"My lady, forgive me," she began, wondering how she would explain riding out as a boy.

"These are my husband's." Lady Mary's voice rang in cold accusation.

Aemilia shook her head and held her hands out to ward herself as she divined what ugly conclusion Lady Mary must have drawn. "No, no, my lady, I swear I never—"

"Don't you dare dissemble. *Look* at me!" Lady Mary took Aemilia's chin in a bruising grip. "I've kept you fed and clothed for four long years since Susan saw the last of you. Now tell me how you came in the possession of my husband's breeches."

"I wear them for riding," Aemilia said lamely. *Ask Lord Hunsdon,* she was tempted to add, but he was no longer there.

"Liar! You're no better than the slattern who bore you."

Mary's blow knocked her sideways. When Aemilia forced herself to sit back up, her mouth was wet. She touched her lips then drew her hand away to see her fingers bright with blood.

Lady Mary was standing over her. "Peregrine never kept his promise to me, so why should I keep my promise to him?" She hurled the book and breeches at Aemilia. "By tomorrow morning, I want you gone."

AEMILIA TOLD HERSELF THAT this was her last chance, that she'd truly nothing left to lose. Her face still smarting, she dressed in her men's clothes and ran to the stables. Rushing past the groom and stable boys without looking or speaking to them, she saddled and bridled Bathsheba.

"Mistress Amy?" the groom asked, his voice rising in concern.

Before he could stop her, she sprang into the saddle and was off, tearing down the Four Mile Riding. The ancient double-planted oak trees streamed past and the wind stung her injured lip as Bathsheba raced forward, pure muscle and momentum. They swept by the gatehouse and headed south toward the highway where they continued at a steady ground-covering canter until Aemila sighted the black stallion and rider. She spurred forward, as shameless as a mare in season.

When she caught up with Lord Hunsdon, she was panting, the sweat pouring down her cheeks like tears. He looked at her in alarm, reaching out his hand.

"Mistress Bassano, what happened to your face?"

She cut him short, her voice savage. "I dare you to race me to the bridge."

Then she was off, not daring to look back to see if he followed. Lord Hunsdon, a bastard as she was, who called her father a good man.

Through her tears, she saw him galloping shoulder to shoulder with her. She kicked Bathsheba forward, letting him chase her to the bridge where, winded and spent, she slipped off her blowing mare. She thought she might collapse in the summer weeds, but instead she made herself turn to him as he leapt off his stallion. *What do you play at?*

Lord Hunsdon's face was stern. "Tell me what happened."

"Lady Mary said I must be gone by morning."

"Did she beat you?" He seemed horrified. "Because I gave you a book?"

Aemilia flinched when he touched her bloodied lip. Then her eyes locked with his. Slowly, deliberately, she tugged off his glove and kissed his hand. The strange fever held her in its thrall and now she called it by its name. Desire.

"You are a wild creature," he murmured.

He pulled off her cap and freed her hair from its bindings, letting it fall loose in his hands. Aemilia remembered when she had found Susan and Master Wingfield in the shadow of the yew hedge, Susan's face tilted to her lover's. Now Lord Hunsdon bent his face to hers. Avoiding her injured lip, he kissed her brow then her throat, his mouth like a brand. He clasped her body against his, her breasts against his chest, his groin to her belly. A shock ran through her as she felt the proof of his desire for her. Sensations she had no words for pulsed inside her. A bewildered softening.

Lord Hunsdon held her at arm's length, his eyes moving over her face. "If you're seeking deliverance from Lady Mary, you don't have to throw yourself at me, you know. But if this is truly what you want, we'll do it the proper way."

Aemilia stared, uncomprehending. It had never occurred to her that there was a correct way to do what she had just done.

He took her hand and led her to her mare. "We'll return to Grimsthorpe so that you can pack your things and ride out as a lady. I shall tell Lady Mary I'm escorting you back to your family home."

9

EMILIA THOUGHT THEY WOULD travel to London with all speed, but Lord Hunsdon seemed content to take his time. "Your poor mare has galloped quite enough. Let our pace be leisurely out of kindness to the horses if nothing else."

While she and Lord Hunsdon rode side by side with his retinue following at a distance, he practiced his Italian with her. He questioned her about her history until she told him of her family's tragedy, Master Holland's treachery, her father's death, her sister's ruin and demise, and of her education at Grimsthorpe. After they supped together at the first inn, he asked her to read Dante to him before they retired to their separate rooms. Aemilia lay rigid in the unfamiliar bed as she awaited his knock on her chamber door. But there was only the silence of the deepening night.

So their strange journey continued. Lord Hunsdon made no advances, but his eyes were on her always, intent and examining, while they rode and while they shared their meals.

Only when they reached Saffron Walden did his finger brush Aemilia's mouth when he helped her down from the saddle. "Your lip has healed."

She shivered at his touch.

At the Maypole Inn Lord Hunsdon took two rooms, as always, but these chambers were adjoining and the door between them did not possess a lock.

ALONE IN HER ROOM, Aemilia's stomach knotted. She spent an age washing her face and combing out her hair, but she could no longer put off undressing for bed. She had stepped out of her skirts and unlaced and removed her bodice when the door opened.

Lord Hunsdon entered to find her in her shift and stays. Instinctively, she reached for her discarded skirt to cover herself. It seemed particularly undignified to be caught half undressed. Could he not have waited until she was under the covers in her nightshift?

He gently pried the skirt from her and laid it over a chair.

"Now I see the young lady *en déshabillé*," he said, handing her a goblet of claret. "Not the hoyden, though both enchant me."

Aemilia lowered her face to the cup and drank deeply. A red drop spilled from her lip and ran down her throat. He caught it with his finger. Taking the goblet from her, he kissed her mouth until she kissed him back.

What am I doing? What have I brought upon myself? It's far too late to back out, she thought, as he laid her on the bed and began to unlace her stays. She took a gulp of air. He lay beside her, his eyes burning into hers.

"This arrangement will come to naught," he said softly, "unless both of us take pleasure in it. Do you understand?"

Aemilia nodded and tried to conjure Susan's bliss in the garden, losing herself in the schoolmaster's arms. But when Lord Hunsdon opened her stays and cupped her breasts through her shift, she shrank.

"Don't be afraid," he said, his mouth moving to her pounding heart. "I won't take your maidenhead until you speak to a midwife about how to keep from getting with child. Tonight I shall teach you pleasure."

He took off her stays and pulled her shift over her head so that she was naked but for her stockings and garters.

"Aren't you a jewel?" he whispered, running his hands down the length of her body.

He stroked and kissed her breasts until she lost herself beyond shame. He palmed her belly and the inside of her thighs, caressing her where she hadn't even dared to touch herself, stroking her until she throbbed against his fingers, a vehement heat rising in her belly, her cries indistinguishable from the doves in the thatch.

No daughter of mine *shall be a courtesan*. Papa's voice rang inside Aemilia as she rode toward her old home in Norton Folgate. *But Papa*, she thought, fighting back her tears. *It's you I vindicate.*

The house was so run-down, she nearly didn't recognize it. Her father's garden was a waste of weeds. The thatch roof sagged. Even the glass had been taken out of the windows—sold to pay debts, she guessed.

She remained in her saddle, as aloof as any highborn lady, while Lord Hunsdon's men drove Master Holland from her father's house. She heard them warning her brother-in-law that if ever he troubled her or her mother again, the Lord Chamberlain would see him thrown into debtors' prison.

She blinked to see a thin, frail woman watching her from the open doorway. *Mother.* Margaret Johnson, whom she had shunned at her father's funeral.

"Go to her," Lord Hunsdon said, lifting Aemilia down from the saddle. "It's a most pitiful thing for mother and daughter to be estranged."

Aemilia stepped toward the threshold where her mother hovered, ghost pale, her mouth trembling, her face wrung. Mother's beautiful blond hair had gone white. Aemilia stood before her, tried to speak, and failed.

"My darling girl." Mother's eyes filled as she touched Aemilia's cheek. "I prayed you'd come home. Marry, you've grown into such a beauty. The very image of your father."

Aemilia collapsed weeping in her mother's arms.

"Your old room is a shambles, I'll confess, but we'll clean it and make it nice again." Mother clung to her.

Aemilia had to take a deep breath before she spoke. "I shan't be living with you, Mother. I shall be staying in Westminster. But I promise you'll never lack for anything again."

Her face a question mark, Mother looked from Aemilia to Lord Hunsdon, who stood at the gate holding the reins of both their horses. Then she wept fresh tears. "Daughter, can you ever forgive me? It's because of me you—"

"Hush." Aemilia stood tall and pushed back her shoulders. "I am to join Lord Hunsdon at court." Her voice shook with the astonishment of it all. She took her mother's face in her hands and uttered the same words Susan had said to her four years ago. "Be happy for me."

EVERYTHING HAPPENED SO FAST, like a violent thunderstorm that shook earth and sky then left serene blue heavens in its wake. In a gown of dark red silk with a standing ruff of Venetian lace to frame her black hair, Aemilia swept into the Royal Presence Chamber on Lord Hunsdon's arm. She felt light-headed, as though her feet didn't touch the floor. Her lover drew her past the gawping courtiers who bowed and curtsied. He led her all the way toward the throne where the Queen sat in state.

"Your Royal Highness, may I present Aemilia Bassano."

Letting go of her lover's hand, Aemilia swooped down in the curtsy she had practiced all morning. "Your Majesty."

Rising again, she met the Queen's green eyes, nearly identical to those of her lover.

A page boy handed Aemilia a lute, and she began to play and sing the song she had composed.

> The Phoenix of her age, whose worth does bind
> All worthy minds so long as they have breath,
> In links of admiration, love, and zeal,
> To the dear Mother of our Commonweal.

The Queen's raptor-sharp gaze gentled, and she granted Aemilia the grace of her smile, her ringed hand raised in blessing. "The Lord Chamberlain does not exaggerate your talents, Mistress Bassano."

Aemilia flushed in rapture. Out of the corner of her eye, she glimpsed the pride and possessiveness on her lover's face. Slowly and reverently, she backed away from the throne and took her place again at the Lord Chamberlain's side. Then, looking past the aristocrats in their velvets and diamonds, she located the royal musicians and smiled in sheer joy at Jasper's unbelieving face.

AEMILIA COULD SCARCELY BELIEVE the company she kept. She dropped in an ecstatic curtsy before Mary Sidney Herbert, the Countess of Pembroke and the greatest woman poet in all England.

"My lady, do you recall our first meeting when I was a child with my father?" Aemilia asked, her heart beating in her throat. "I told you that I, too, aspired to write poetry."

"In truth, I do not," the Countess said. "But your verses to Her Majesty were most accomplished."

The lady's manner was benevolent, yet there remained an air of distance.

They don't dare snub me, Aemilia sensed, as Lord Hunsdon introduced her to the other high-ranking courtiers. *Yet I will never be their peer.* A mistress, not a wife, and certainly no aristocrat, she was here only because the Lord Chamberlain was so besotted with her. But she strove to hide her anxieties behind her smile.

The aging Queen surrounds herself in beauty, Lord Hunsdon had told Aemilia. *You shall be the exotic flower of her court, a dark Italian rose amongst the English lilies.*

Aemilia knew she could not help but stand out from the other ladies and that this was precisely what had first drawn Lord Hunsdon to her even before she threw herself at his mercy. Her youth, musical virtuosity, education, and Italian flair held a gleaming mirror to her lover's power and refined tastes. Aemilia knew she was Mary Sidney Herbert's equal in education, and she even surpassed her in languages. Had Susan Bertie only known that the humanist education she had given her had made Aemilia the Lord Chamberlain's perfect courtesan.

Her lover introduced her to George Clifford, the Earl of Cumberland and Her Majesty's champion of the tiltyard, and to his wife Margaret, one of the most trusted Ladies of the Bedchamber.

George Clifford gave Aemilia a look of frank appraisal before kissing her hand. He exchanged a smile with Lord Hunsdon, as though congratulating him on his choice. To conceal her discomfort, Aemilia dropped in an even deeper curtsy before his wife, laying all her respect at the lady's feet in hope that she wouldn't wish her dead.

Margaret seemed as quiet and reserved as her husband was bold and extravagant, her eyes filled with a resignation that pierced Aemilia far more deeply than arrogance or even hatred would have done. It appeared her husband's eye for other women was nothing new to Margaret Clifford.

Do these aristocratic wives view me as a traitor to womanhood? Aemilia wondered. Anne Locke's admonition haunted her—*remember this, my dear, you must cherish your own sex.* She asked herself if Anne Locke would still speak to her now that she had thrown away her virtue.

Curtsying before the Countess of Bedford, Aemilia wondered if the ladies of court were making secret bets as to how long she would last as the Lord Chamberlain's mistress before he tired of her. Even if he remained constant, he was sixty-one to her sixteen and would die long before she did. Who would want her when he was finished with her? Whenever Aemilia dropped her guard and allowed her thoughts to wander, she heard Mary de Vere's accusing voice. *Whore!* Hadn't Aemilia sold herself to the richest and most powerful man she could find?

"Why do you look so grim, my love?" Lord Hunsdon whispered. "Enchant them as you enchanted me. They will eat like doves from your hand. Let them see your beautiful smile."

Aemilia blushed to see him gaze at her like that, with undisguised adoration, as though she were a shining goddess. Unlike those miserable wives trapped in dynastic marriages, she had a fervent lover who treasured her. She lived in a fine house in Longditch, Westminster, where she entertained him by playing the virginals and lute until he led her upstairs to bed. Was this new life of hers not paradise itself, a world apart from what her sister had endured? *There are far worse fates than being a kept woman.*

At the far end of the Royal Presence Chamber, her Bassano cousins in the Queen's Musicke struck up a galliard. She could hardly wait for the opportunity to throw her arms around Jasper and reunite with her kin. But now she turned to Lord Hunsdon, who took her hand and led her in the dance.

And so she surrendered to the effervescence of court life, smiling at the ladies as though she were one of them and dancing with one earl after another, confident in the knowledge that no man would dare take liberties with the Lord Chamberlain's mistress. *Wear the mask of frivolity and charm until you become it.*

IO

HE ROYAL MUSICIANS PLAYED an oriental air as Aemilia glided to the center of the candlelit stage. Her black hair flowed loosely, crowned in a diadem of golden wire twisted into fantastical shapes. Diaphanous silks flowed around her gown. At her breast she wore an ankh. With her every sinuous step and gesture, she sought to embody Cleopatra. Flanking her were two young ladies who played Cleopatra's maids. At Aemilia's feet lay the handsome young Earl of Southampton in the role of the dead Antony.

Aemilia was by now a woman of twenty-three, Lord Hunsdon's paramour for seven years. Only one thing shadowed her happiness, but she forced it into the farthest recesses of her mind.

Through her painted mask, she gazed at her audience. There, surrounded by her courtiers, sat the Queen, her face transfixed by the spectacle on stage. Elizabeth's many jewels twinkled and glimmered as if her person encompassed all the starry heavens. At Her Majesty's right, Lord Hunsdon appeared almost as regal as the monarch in his black-velvet doublet gleaming with gold braid. As Lord Chamberlain, he was responsible for court entertainment. Nothing made him prouder than when Aemilia shone in the masque, she the moon reflecting his sun. His look of tenderness softened her belly and nearly threw her out of character. Her lover had just returned from a sojourn with his family at their country house. Aemilia tried not to think too much about that part of his life.

Aware of the many eyes on her—even the court musicians had laid down their instruments to watch the masque—Aemilia burst into her speech, framing her every word with the passion and pathos of a woman who blamed herself for her beloved's ruin.

> That I have thee betrayed, dear Antony,
> My life, my soul, my sun? I had such thought?
> That I have betrayed thee, my Lord, my King?
> That I would break my vowed faith to thee?
> Leave thee? Deceive thee? Yield thee to the rage
> Of mighty foe? I ever had that heart?
> Rather sharp lightning strike my head,
> Rather may I to deepest mischief fall,
> Rather the opened earth devour me.

This masque was drawn from Mary Sidney Herbert's translation of Robert Garnier's *Marc Antoine*. Aemilia reveled in her role, in delivering each exquisite line, only regretting that the poet and translator was not present—the Countess was away at her estate, tending to her sick child.

Beneath her mask, Aemilia's skin grew clammy. If only it wasn't so overpoweringly hot. Too many candle flames and bodies crowded into one room. Too many layers of clothing against her skin. Her stomach churned, but she made herself ignore it. Perhaps she had laced her stays too tightly.

The taste of bile flooded her mouth. The floor pitched and her world turned black.

SHE HAD FALLEN TO the bottom of a dank pit. So far down, she could no longer reach the light. Until something damp touched her face. Her eyes snapped open to see Margaret Clifford holding a wet cloth to her cheek. Aemilia wrenched her head away, unable to bear the quiet pity in Margaret's eyes.

She lay on a bed in an unfamiliar room. Her bodice and stays had been opened to expose her thin linen shift and the swollen breasts and belly she had been so determined to conceal. Ladies crowded round, murmuring as though she were still unconscious.

"She's five months on at the very least."

"Fainting in the middle of the masque! She might as well scream from the rooftops that she's heavy with Lord Hunsdon's bastard."

Their voices fell abruptly silent as Lord Hunsdon marched into the room.

"Leave us," he told them, his voice like ice.

Aemilia tried to force herself up and close her stays, but there was no time. Her lover was already standing at her bedside. He was so tall, so far above her as she lay there.

"Henry," she said, looking up through her tears.

She had never seen him so angry. It was enough to send her tumbling back down into that void.

"How long did you think to hide this from me? How could this have even happened? I thought you were taking care."

She closed her eyes. "By my troth, I was taking care."

She had been absolutely vigilant in her use of pessaries of wool soaked in vinegar to prevent conception. At the first sign of her tardy menses, she had imbibed countless decoctions of hay madder boiled in beer, to no avail. To think that Lord Hunsdon had kept her for seven years only for her own body to betray her.

"The Queen will not stand for this," he said. "A most undignified end to your time at court, I must say."

"So I am to be banished." Aemilia stared at the ceiling because she no longer dared meet his eyes. Was he so furious because this had humiliated *him*? How could her life change so completely in the course of an hour?

"Don't carry on like that," he snapped, as she began to sob. "You should count yourself fortunate. If you were a lady of high birth, the Queen would throw you in the Tower."

Though Her Majesty tolerated mistresses, the mothers of bastards were punished and ostracized. *My life is over.* Aemilia watched her lover edge away, as though thoroughly disgusted by her.

"Henry, I beg you, please don't leave." She held out her hand until he took it.

For a long moment, he sat at the edge of the bed and stroked her hair while she clung to him and wept. For a fleeting instant, he rested his hand on her belly. His lips cool against hers, he gave her his parting kiss. Then he stood and walked toward the door.

"What's to become of me, my lord?" she called after him.

He stood with his back to her. "You must be married with all speed."

AEMILIA TRIED TO REASON with herself. No one could say Lord Hunsdon had not been generous, keeping her far longer than anyone at court had thought possible. He pensioned her off with forty pounds a year and even allowed her to remain in the house in Longditch, Westminster.

It was perfectly understandable why he would want her respectably married off to a man of her own rank, a royal musician like her departed father. Perhaps Lord Hunsdon even thought he was doing her a kindness in choosing for her husband the flautist Alfonse Lanier, handsome and three years younger than she was, who shared her foreign background. The young man's father was a French Huguenot from Rouen, his stepmother none other than her own first cousin Lucrezia Bassano. Lord Hunsdon could surely be forgiven for believing he had delivered his former paramour safely into the arms of her extended family.

Except that Lucrezia Bassano had long regarded Aemilia as no better than a whore. And why would any young man cheapen himself with a hasty marriage to another man's pregnant, discarded mistress? The Willoughbys hadn't even succeeded in marrying Aemilia off when she was a beautiful young virgin.

But she was now worth forty pounds a year and rich in silk and jewels. And so she passed from one man's hands into another's, from being the Lord Chamberlain's damaged goods to Alfonse Lanier's stepping stone to wealth and advancement, her income his to spend however he desired. After everything Aemilia had gone through to escape her sister's fate, Lord Hunsdon was marrying her off to a man who only wanted her money. A man she didn't, and couldn't, love.

In October 1592, six months pregnant, Aemilia exchanged her everlasting vows with her bridegroom. She was lacerated both by the greed in Alfonse's eyes and by his father's and stepmother's contempt for her. Her own mother had passed on five years ago, and Aemilia could only be thankful the poor woman was spared from witnessing this. Her sole well-wisher was Jasper, who could hardly seem to conceal his concern for her as she walked out of the church with her avaricious new husband. To think she and Alfonse would begin their married life in the same bed where she had sported with Lord Hunsdon.

Aemilia concluded that her life hereafter would only be bearable if she thought of it as a comedy. A ludicrous marriage farce.

III

Love's Fool

II

Billingsgate, London, 1593

OR SEVEN YEARS I was the Lord Chamberlain's mistress," Aemilia told Simon Forman, the master astrologer. She spoke with pride and nostalgia. "I bore his son."

"Old Henry Tudor's bastard grandson, by my troth!" Warming to her story, Doctor Forman poured them each a glass of Malmsey. "But when you fell pregnant, you were barred from court, and the Lord Chamberlain married you off . . . to . . . to a *Frenchman*," the astrologer sputtered, as though her husband's nationality were the worst slight of all. "What would you have me reveal to you?"

"Soon my husband sails for the Azores as a privateer, seeking Spanish gold," she said, seething at the expense of it all, for Alfonse was expected to pay his own way. He would inevitably mire them both in debt. "He hopes to make his fortune or even be knighted. What shall come of this?"

"Let's cut to the chase, shall we?" The astrologer regarded her with shrewd, calculating eyes. "You wish to know if your husband shall make you a lady or no. You have fallen and you wish to rise again, like a phoenix from the ashes."

Before Aemilia could think what to say, Doctor Forman seized her hand and tugged off her glove. Though she had asked him for her star chart, he made bold to read her palm, his fingers quivering over the lines of her life and heart.

"You shall be a lady or attain some greater dignity," he said, leaning so close that his breath stirred her hair. "Your husband shall speed well on his voyage but shall get little substance. The time shall come when you will rise, madam, but hardly because of this man. And yet some good fortune shall befall you."

The astrologer's eyes seemed to dance with salacious imaginings of what this good fortune might entail and what pleasures he intended to take with her as a just reward for his services. Still clasping her hand, he yanked her toward himself.

"Master Forman, the goodwives of Westminster do not lie about your reputation." In one fluid movement, Aemilia leapt to her feet, extracted her hand, and slid her glove back on. "You are indeed a ruttish old goat."

Winifred, her maid, hurled a bag of coins on the astrologer's desk before she and her mistress sauntered toward the door.

"Italian baggage!" Master Forman yelled out after Aemilia.

But his insults were soon drowned out by his apprentice's helpless laughter.

"WHAT A HATEFUL MAN!" Winifred muttered, as she and Aemilia wound their way down the teeming street. "How could you suffer his touch? In faith, I would have screamed."

"Merely scream?" Aemilia asked her affectionately. "Winifred, you disappoint me. Marry, I think you would have toppled him and left him for dead."

Winifred did not allow this jibing to distract her from the subject at hand. "If you don't mind my saying, you should be more careful of the company you keep. All London knows Master Forman is a slavering lecher. What if Master Lanier discovers you've called in to see him?"

In truth, Winifred often despaired of Aemilia. Though she was a grown woman, a wife and mother, her mistress was far too dreamy, prone to innumerable flights of fancy.

"Peace, Winifred. I must know my destiny. So must everyone. The Queen may rely on the great Doctor Dee to read her stars, but we lesser souls must make do with lesser men."

Her mistress's dark eyes were distant. While Winifred basted in her own sweat and reeled at the stench of entrails from the hog-scalding houses in Pudding Lane, Aemilia seemed to glide along, lost in her secret world. When she was in such a state, her head in the clouds even as she trod the dung-strewn street, there was no telling what mischief she might fall into.

"Let's go home," said Winifred. Like a nursemaid taking charge of a child, she gripped Aemilia's arm.

Please God, just let her get her mistress safely back to Westminster and then Winifred could give her aching feet a good soak. Zounds, this heat was enough to melt her brains.

"I'm not yet ready to go home, Winifred." Aemilia's voice was as cold as January.

AEMILIA COULD NOT STOMACH the thought of returning to Long-ditch, where her husband awaited her. She was not prepared to stand before him like an errant child while he demanded to know where she had been.

Surely, among the minstrels deemed suitable for her, Lord Huns-don might have found some long-lashed lover of boys who would have been content to marry her for form's sake and then leave her alone. Anyone but Alfonse.

Aemilia's mind roved back to the astrologer's prediction, that she would achieve a degree of fame and importance, though not through any help from her husband. With her education, what she might have been able to achieve had she only been born a man! Were it not for her sex, she would, at the very least, be able to join her male cousins in the Queen's Musicke. But she was a woman of stained reputation who possessed neither title nor fortune. Instead, she was saddled with a re-sentful and dissolute young husband. *Let Alfonse sail. Let him be gone.*

"I am ill-suited for marriage," she told Winifred. "Better had I re-mained unwed, even with the child. In faith, I'd rather be a nun than Lanier's wife."

Winifred heaved in laughter, her flesh quaking as though she were a giant jelly. "You a nun, mistress? Oh, you slay me, you do! Ah ha ha!" As she roiled in her merriment, Winifred knocked down a stranger who hit the street with a smothered yelp.

"Oh, sir, I do beg your pardon!" cried Winifred.

Being so thick of girth, Winifred found it cumbersome to crouch down and inspect the man for damage. But Aemilia knelt at his side, her silken skirts fanning out in the filth. Winifred despaired at the scrubbing she would have to do to remove the stains.

"Sir, are you injured?" Aemilia wiped the man's face with her handkerchief. "Forgive us if you can. My maid is clumsy and forgets her own strength."

The man stared up in a daze as though struggling to get the wind back in his lungs. He looked to be in his late twenties, with soft brown hair haloing his head. But it was his clouded hazel eyes that drew her in, the eyes of a dreamer, filled with yearning intensity. This, she decided, explained why Winifred chanced to floor him—he had been too lost in the realm of his thoughts to leap out of her path.

When his bewildered gaze met hers, she drew back, embarrassed, for she'd never caught herself staring so deeply into a stranger's eyes.

With a sharp intake of breath, he heaved himself up on his elbows and staggered to his feet. Aemilia watched him brush the bits of straw and manure from his breeches and doublet. Though decent, his clothes were worn thin. Fortune, it seemed, had not been kind to him. But he could afford weaponry—at his belt hung a sheathed sword. No man of any substance walked the streets unarmed, even in daylight.

"Your hat, sir."

Aemilia handed him his flat woolen cap, which he clapped on his head with murmured thanks. He regarded her with a look of bemused inquiry, as if he didn't quite know what to make of her and her maid. But as he glanced around, as though searching for landmarks, it seemed much graver matters haunted him. The man looked so *lost*—and not just disoriented by virtue of being in an unfamiliar district. Her heart brimmed for him, an outsider like herself.

"Sir, is there something in this parish you seek?" she asked him. "That church steeple you see is Saint Botolph's Billingsgate."

"Weren't you christened in Saint Botolph's, mistress?" Winifred asked, shading her eyes from the sun's glare.

"Not this Saint Botolph's," Aemilia said. "But Saint Botolph-without-Bishopsgate, outside the city walls. Near Shoreditch."

The man's face seemed to light up at the mention of Shoreditch. Perhaps he hailed from there, though he scarcely looked familiar to her as he would have if they'd grown up in the same parish.

"Saint Botolph must have done something important to have so many churches named after him," Winifred opined. "Was he the one who was impaled on a hundred different stakes?"

"No," the man said shortly. "He wasn't a martyr but the patron of wayfarers, which is why the churches at all four city gates bear his name."

By his speech, Aemilia knew him to be an Englishman but no Londoner. He came from some far-flung county unknown to her.

"My, my," said Winifred. "Well, I suppose wayfarers do need their own patron."

"Madam," the man said, addressing Aemilia. "I seek the Stone House."

"Right over there, sir." Aemilia pointed out the way he must go.

"You're not going to that astrologer, are you?" Winifred asked him. "Sir, don't waste your money on that piss-pot prophet. You should buy a lamb pie instead. I've seen sparrows with more meat on their bones than you. Why, you are so scrawny, I could knock you flat like a bowling pin!"

"My good woman, you just *did*," the man pointed out.

"Good day to you, sir," said Aemilia. "And please accept our apologies for your mishap."

With a nod to them both, he turned and continued on his way. As he strode forward, a sheet of folded paper fell from his doublet.

"Sir, you dropped something!" Aemilia called after him. She snatched it off the street before it could be trampled.

"Is it a broadsheet?" Winifred asked, her face blazing in curiosity, for the most scandalous stories could be found on broadsheets distributed throughout the city. Blood-streaked comets foretold the Apocalypse. Women gave birth to two-headed devils. Dogs stood on their hind legs and uttered prophecies. "Mistress, what does it say?"

Aemilia's face was spellbound as her eyes scanned the inked squiggles that Winifred couldn't make head or tail of. "Our friend is a poet." She began to read softly while Winifred leaned close to listen.

Being your slave, what should I do but tend
Upon the hours and times of your desire?
I have no precious time at all to spend,

Nor services to do, till you require.
Nor dare I chide the world-without-end hour
Whilst I, my sovereign, watch the clock for you.
Nor think the bitterness of absence sour
When you have bid your servant once adieu;
Nor dare I question with my jealous thought
Where you may be, or your affairs suppose,
But, like a sad slave, stay and think of nought,
Save, where you are, how happy you make those.
So true a fool is love that in your will,
Though you do anything, he thinks no ill.

The verses cascaded through Aemilia, rendering her spellbound. Oh, to write so eloquently of the turmoil of a breaking heart and unequal love. The poet's pain pierced her, as though it were her own.

"If you please, madam."

She gave a small cry as the man, his face as red as love apples, seized back his poem. Then he turned on his heel and rushed into the entrance of the Stone House.

"Why he *is* gone to see that astrologer!" Winifred cried. "Poor sod. From the look of him, he can ill afford it."

"Indeed," Aemilia said, recovering her composure. "He might have saved his coins. I could have revealed his fate at no cost."

The man's face had shown Aemilia what ailed him, just as his sonnet had spelled out his most private yearnings.

"The man is in love," she told Winifred. "Desperately in love. He is love's fool. And his love remains unrequited."

Winifred's eyes were huge. "I wager he begs Master Forman for a love philter. Do such potions ever work, mistress?" The maid attempted to phrase the question as innocently as possible.

Aemilia shrugged. "I've never had the opportunity to find out."

AEMILIA INSERTED HER KEY into the back gate. In she and Winifred slipped, creeping like thieves. How she hated this life of tiptoeing about.

Leaving Winifred to trail behind, Aemilia picked her way through the plantings of pease and lettuce. In spring, in a fit of rare optimism, she had planted this kitchen garden, thinking that might feed them even if her husband couldn't. But she lacked her father's talent for such things. Though the servants kept the vegetable beds watered and weeded, this was nothing like Papa's lost Eden, the magical garden of her childhood home.

Aemilia stooped to pick a love apple, newly ripened, fragrant and red. Before Winifred could stop her, she devoured it, savoring every last bite, licking the sweet juice from her lips. Papa used to tell her that love apples tasted like Veneto.

"One day you'll poison yourself," her maid tutted.

A jolt ripped through Aemilia at the sound of her five-month-old son crying inside the house. Picking up her skirts, she raced to the kitchen door, only to collide with Winifred's sister Prudence, the cook.

"The master—" Prudence began.

Before Aemilia could do or say a thing, in sprang Alfonse, as though in hope of catching her in the arms of an illicit lover.

"Where were you?" he spat, her husband of eight months, as he looked her up and down. "Your skirts they are filthy. Were you rolling in the streets?"

Despite being brought up in Greenwich, Alfonse had a French accent.

"How can you call yourself a wife?" he went on, working himself up in a froth of rage. "You go wherever you please, any hour of day or night!"

Aemilia attempted to speak, but the words wouldn't come. She could only clench her fists and bite her tongue. When she looked at her husband, she felt an aversion that gripped her down to her viscera.

Why couldn't he just leave her in peace? Hadn't he already got what he wanted from this marriage—her money? She had expected a man willing to wed another man's pregnant mistress for fortune's sake to at least be worldly enough to go his own way and allow her to go hers. Why did he have to act like such an insufferable little lordling, ruled by his petty jealousies? She blamed his father and stepmother, who kept goading him to put an end to his wife's willful, wanton ways lest she make him an even bigger fool and cuckold than he already was.

Still, seeing as she was married to the boy, Aemilia supposed she might try harder to reach some accord with him. If only he could be satisfied with his lot as a royal musician instead of wasting her money on his expedition to the Azores, not to mention the way he indulged his taste for fine clothing, gambling, drinking, and—she suspected— whoring. He had already sold her lute and virginals to fund his extravagance. If he didn't begin to earn as much as he liked to spend, he would soon ruin them both.

"My good mistress took pity on a poor man who collapsed in the street, Master Lanier, sir." Winifred inserted her ample form between husband and wife. She stood with her feet splayed, her hands on her hips, taking up as much space as possible. Alfonse couldn't so much as scowl at Aemilia with Winifred towering over him. "A regular good Samaritan your wife is, sir."

Leaving Alfonse behind the bulwark that was Winifred, Aemilia darted upstairs to the bedchamber where her son still wailed, his face dark red, his little fists beating the air. She swept him from the arms of Tabitha, his wet nurse. Aemilia cooed in his ear as she paced the creaking floorboards. Her babe stopped crying at once and rested his sweet weight against her.

"Always an angel for you, he is, mistress," Tabitha said.

Aemilia smiled at the young wet nurse and thanked her stars yet again that Lord Hunsdon had seen fit to pay for her. Aemilia's own milk had dried up soon after giving birth. If not for Tabitha, her son could have died. The girl had also brought her two older sisters, Winifred and Prudence, into Aemilia's service, and now Aemilia could scarcely imagine her household without them.

Crooning in Italian, she gazed into her baby's eyes, as dark as the olives she had once tasted as a girl. She'd named him Henry after his father, but called him Enrico. Everything she did, her every scheme and forbidden act, was for him. To insure that he had a future. Sometimes she dreamed of disappearing with him into the clear blue, vanishing like smoke. But where?

"So you think to avoid me." Having somehow escaped Winifred, Alfonse strode into the bedchamber.

Tabitha exchanged glances with her mistress while Aemilia held fast to the babe. If only Alfonse would smile at her son, she might like him, but his worst flaw, even worse than his bullying and his spendthrift ways, was that he was jealous of an infant. How could she love a man who hated her baby?

"Tell me where you have gone," he said.

"To Thames Street to consult an astrologer on your voyage to the Azores." She gazed at him levely. Lord Hunsdon had once taught her how to shoot arrows. She imagined drawing the bow, keeping her eyes on the target, keeping her aim true.

"And what mischief will you get up to when I sail away?" His voice seemed to rise an octave. For a moment, Aemilia pictured him singing falsetto. She didn't know whether to laugh or scream in his face.

The floorboards shuddered as Winifred marched in. Winifred, her arms as thick as Alfonse's legs. Before Alfonse could interrogate Aemilia further, Winifred snatched the bolster off the bed and gave it a good bashing.

"You are a common bawd," Alfonse told Winifred, before he narrowed his eyes at Aemilia. "But she . . . she is a subtle whore."

Like flames scorching the inside of a chimney, Aemilia's temper surged. She handed Enrico to Winifred's safekeeping before sidling up to her husband, staring him down, eye to eye.

"Oh, you are sick of self-love! You knew what I was when you married me. No one forced you, sir. No one held a blade to your throat when you said your vows."

Her skin was on fire, her muscles twitching, her blood beating a war dance. She felt no fear, only the fury filling her, fueling the flame that blazed in her breast.

"If you are so displeased with me, I am sure Lord Hunsdon can arrange for you to sail to Virginia instead of the Azores. Or perhaps he'll send you to fight for the Queen in the next Irish uprising. Would that please you? *Husband?*"

"Shrew!" he cried. "Witch! I shall cut out your tongue."

"No matter," she said boldly, her hands on her hips. "I shall speak as much wit as you afterward."

Her words were arrows that struck their mark. Out of the room he stormed. Downstairs a door slammed. She heard his curses as he skulked off down the street. *C'est le bordel! Nom de Dieu de putain de bordel de merde!*

He would be gone for days, for he had a habit of disappearing after their quarrels, of returning to his family in Greenwich where he would lament his fate to be wed to such a faithless and hard-hearted woman.

My stars shine darkly over me. They were damned, she and Alfonse. A curse hung over their heads.

Letting out a long breath, Aemilia collapsed on the bed. The mattress heaved like the sea as Winifred flopped down beside her and gently placed Enrico in her arms. Closing her eyes, Aemilia kissed his downy head. What would she do when Lord Hunsdon died and she could no longer invoke his protection or beg his money after Alfonse went through everything she owned? *I must escape. I must.* By ingenuity or by guile, she must find a way, some other patronage, some independent income that Alfonse couldn't touch. How else could she support her son until he was old enough to support himself?

Let Alfonse call her a whore or whatever vile names he could conjure. Come nightfall, she would take matters into her own hands.

12

IGHT WAS AEMILIA'S FAVORITE time, when the cage that contained her by day sprang apart. In blessed darkness, she soared free, as in the ancient tales of village wives who left behind their sleeping husbands and flew away on the backs of beasts to some lofty mountaintop, where they cavorted like heathens until sunrise.

Clad as a young man, she galloped out of Longditch astride Bathsheba, one of her few keepsakes from her days at Grimsthorpe Castle when she was a maid as stainless as any, translating Plutarch. At twenty, the mare was a venerable age. Alfonse said the old nag was worthless and that it cost too much to feed her, but Aemilia would sooner beg in the streets than part ways with her mare. Her booted legs clung to Bathsheba's flanks as they passed the church of Saint Martin-in-the-Fields and fared forth into the pristine countryside between Westminster and London where the gentry dwelled. With the night wind singing in her ears, she was no longer Mistress Lanier but an entirely different person, her heart opening as wide as the starry sky. The full moon shone bright enough to cast skittering shadows, which sent Bathsheba leaping and snorting.

Sometimes Aemilia dreamt of remaining in this guise permanently, of making her way in the great world as a man. Let Aemilia die. Become Emilio. Such a thrill it gave her to swagger in boots and breeches instead of mincing along under heavy skirts. To boldly shoulder past the men who would otherwise leer at her.

Cattle lowed beyond hedgerows fragrant with honeysuckle and elderflower. She breathed in the scent of freshly mown hay. Her many burdens seemed to lift as she skirted the slumbering village of Saint Giles-in-the-Fields. When she arrived at the great iron gates of Southampton House, the gatekeeper let her in at once.

"Lovely evening, Master Emilio, sir. The Earl is expecting you."

Aemilia's heart thrilled, as it always did when her male guise passed muster. She swung down from the saddle and stood for a moment in the moonlight, aware that the gatekeeper was admiring the sword and rapier hanging from her belt. Pray God she looked every inch the daring young blade — a person with whom one would not wish to meddle.

Interloper though she was, she strode through the gardens with their gushing fountains and stone nymphs. The scent of night-blooming jasmine intoxicated her as she gazed at the mullioned windows radiant with candlelight. Entering the house, she caught sight of herself in a long oval looking glass. Though small of stature, she cut a dashing figure with her slender legs, well muscled from riding, and her slanting cheekbones. She appeared as a youth of seventeen summers, wavy dark hair spilling from beneath her cap.

Her host awaited her in the great parlor, its every window open to the moon-drenched garden. Huge bouquets of roses and larkspur — all the beauty this midsummer's night could offer — adorned each table.

Nineteen years old, Henry Wriothesley, the third Earl of Southampton, was as pretty as a girl, his face framed in flowing golden hair. He was arrayed with a collar of the most exquisite Venetian lace money could buy and an elaborate double earring with a pendant pearl. The color was high in his face, as if she had barged in at an inopportune moment, though she could not see anyone else in the room.

"Aemilia-Emilio," he said, stooping to kiss her hand. "How now, my master-mistress?" His blue eyes locked with hers. "The most exquisite creature in all Middlesex."

She and the Earl had befriended each other during her time at court when they had performed together in the masques. As different from her husband as a peacock was from a pigeon, Harry was as frivolous as only the wealthy could be. She had to remind herself to look behind his mask. His childhood had been wretched. His father had cast out his mother, accusing her of adultery with a commoner. Then his father died, leaving Harry with a disgraced mother—not just a presumed adulteress but also Catholic. So Lord Burghley, Master of the Court of Wards and Lord High Treasurer, had taken charge. His eye on the boy's family fortune, Burghley had arranged for Harry to marry his own staunchly Protestant granddaughter, Elizabeth de Vere, when Harry turned twenty-one.

Except, in a fit of pique, the boy declared he would never wed, that he disdained the institution of marriage, that he despised the entire female sex. But if Harry disobeyed Lord Burghley and refused to marry his granddaughter, he would have to pay Burghley the unheard-of fine of five thousand pounds. The stakes couldn't be higher. Aemilia certainly did not envy Harry the prospect of marrying into the de Vere clan.

In his rebellion against Burghley's rule, Harry had invited Aemilia to secretly visit him by night and play the virginals on the condition that she appear in breeches so no one could accuse him of giving up his hatred for her sex. For her part, Aemilia didn't care for Southampton in a romantic sense and therefore he had no power to break her heart, but she was happy enough to take his gold. Being paid to dress as a young man and visit the Earl in his mansion seemed a harmless enough way to keep herself from penury, though if Alfonse discovered that she rode out by night, he would probably have her publically flogged for adultery, never mind that the greatest liberty Harry had taken was kissing her hand.

"I hope you brought me some poetry," the Earl said, his voice both affectionate and imperious.

Bless the boy—he actually paid her for her poems. But she had been too busy of late to write any new verses for him. Humbly, she bowed her head.

"No poetry this time, my lord." As befitting their masquerade, she kept her voice in its lowest registers so that she would sound like a young man. "Instead, I bring you a song."

Then she began to sing in her natural soprano.

> Over hill, over dale,
> Through bush, through briar,
> Over park, over pale,

Through flood, through fire,
I do wander everywhere,
Swifter than the moon's sphere.
And I serve the Faery Queen
To dew her orbs upon the green.

When her song ended, she discovered that she and the young Earl were not alone. From out of a shadowy corner stepped a man who gazed at her as though her song had left him undone. A slender man with hazel eyes and soft brown hair. Her pulse quickened when she recognized the poet she had met outside the astrologer's. Though he must have been wearing his finest garments, he looked utterly out of place in this manor house. How had he earned his invitation? And why had he been hiding? Was this one of Harry's elaborate jokes? If so, then who was the laughingstock, the poet or herself? *Likely both of us,* she thought.

"Is our nightingale not enchanting?" Harry asked, glancing from the poet to her. "Aemilia-Emilio, this is my dear friend, sweet William. He writes the most enthralling sonnets just for me."

Such a gulf separated the two men in wealth, station, even age — the poet was probably a decade older than the boy. Yet Harry took his place at the poet's side, his hand on his shoulder as though claiming possession of him. How the poet quivered at Harry's touch — surely this gesture was too intimate for her eyes. Her skin flushed when she deduced what secrets they must share. Then she remembered the poet's sonnet that she had read that very morning, those verses that still held her in their thrall. *So true a fool is love that in your will, though you do anything, he thinks no ill.*

Adoration blazed in the poet's eyes. Poor besotted wretch. Aemilia tried to glance away but the poet now held her with his gaze, perhaps struggling to remember where he had seen her before. His mien then darkened, as if in jealousy. It seemed the poet truly saw her as a young man, a rival for Southampton's affections.

"Sir," she said, speaking plainly as a woman. "Do you not recognize me? We met earlier this day."

"Why this is very midsummer madness." The poet took a faltering step backward. "You sing and speak like a very young boy and yet you are grown. Are you a castrato?"

Harry collapsed on a chair and writhed in hilarity, as though she and the poet were players acting in a comedy just for his pleasure.

"In Thames Street," she said. "Outside the astrologer's."

The poet reeled, as though fearing he'd lost his senses.

"My maid knocked you down," she said, which made Harry laugh all the harder.

"Had I only been there!" Harry cried. "If only you could see your face, Will Shakespeare!"

The poet looked scalded, as though someone had tipped a boiling cauldron over his head. "This morning I saw a lady."

"And now you see a lady." She removed her cap and shook out her long black hair.

"A lady in breeches!" Harry pounded his thighs.

Aemilia remained as sober as Will. "In faith, you have never heard a trained female soprano before. We are not allowed to perform in public, sir. It's considered too vulgar. Only at court or at manor houses such as this might you hear a woman virtuosa sing."

The poet looked humiliated. She longed to take his shoulders and whisper in his ear, *No need to explain. Southampton has made us both his fools!*

She turned to Harry who struggled to make his face serious again. "More music, my lord?"

When Harry nodded, she sat at the virginals and began to play, her back to the men. In truth, she came here as much for Harry's virginals as his gold. As her fingers walked in gentle gait over the painted wooden keys, she prayed that she could lose herself in the melody and forget Southampton and his friend were even there. But it was no use —she heard every word of their ensuing spat.

"Is Master-Mistress Aemilia not a marvel?" Harry asked his friend.

"The most exquisite creature in all Middlesex?" the poet cried. "Why do you make me your ass?"

Aemilia played on, pretending that she inhabited her own universe far away from Harry's whims and jests. But her stomach dropped to hear them speak of her.

"Her people were denizens of Venice," Harry said, lolling the name of that fabled city on his tongue as though savoring a sweetmeat. "Have you heard how *inventive* Venetian courtesans are?"

She gritted her teeth to keep from striking a wrong note. Was Harry trying to convince his friend that *she* was such a courtesan who knew every lascivious trick? Big words from Harry who had never bedded a woman in all his nineteen years.

From behind her back came the sound of Harry opening a drawer.

"This," she heard him say, "is a portrait of a Venetian temptress painted in that very city."

She nearly laughed in derision. Once Harry had shown her that self-same painted miniature, his one piece of pornography, the jewel of his curiosity cabinet. She didn't need to lift her eyes from the keyboard to envision Will's befuddlement. At first glance, it resembled a staid enough picture of a richly dressed woman with an elaborate coiffure, a white handkerchief, and an ostrich feather fan. How was anyone to recognize this creature as a courtesan? However, it wasn't an ordinary miniature but a cleverly constructed novelty piece. Harry had only to lift the central panel of the lady's skirt to reveal that she wore breeches and a codpiece beneath. That the same woman could appear as a lady on the outside but conceal a codpiece under her silken skirts appeared to fascinate Harry to no end. She heard him cackling like a schoolboy to the poet whose silence was deafening.

"The Venetian ladies of pleasure are an *entirely* different class," the Earl said in his aristocratic drawl. "They are educated and quite refined."

Why couldn't Harry put that silly miniature away and talk about something sensible? The tone of conversation was starting to make her skin itch. Thankfully, the poet seemed just as eager as she was to change the subject.

"My lord, I have written a poem for you, not just a sonnet this time but an epic."

From behind her arpeggios, Aemilia could hear the rustle of paper.

"*Venus and Adonis,*" said Harry. "What a title! So saucy." His voice was gently mocking, but then his tone grew tender. "Ah, sweet William, you dedicated it to me."

"All my work is for you!" The poet couldn't hide his yearning if he tried. "The love I dedicate to your lordship is without end. What I have done is yours; what I have to do is yours, being part in all I have, devoted to you."

In her mind's eye, Aemilia saw the poet's love-struck face. How could he squander his devotion, let alone his priceless poetry, on one as inane as Harry? Passion was a treacherous game. She couldn't fathom surrendering her heart to that vain boy, even supposing he desired women in the first place.

As Harry began to read aloud, Aemilia could not help but prick her ears to drink in every word, imbibing the poetry that intoxicated her like wine. She found herself altering her rhythm so that she played in time with his verses. Yet again, the poet wrote of the anguish of unrequited love.

> Even as the sun with purple-colour'd face
> Had ta'en his last leave of the weeping morn,
> Rose-cheek'd Adonis hied him to the chase;
> Hunting he loved, but love he laugh'd to scorn;
> Sick-thoughted Venus makes amain unto him,
> And like a bold-fac'd suitor 'gins to woo him.

> "Thrice-fairer than myself," thus she began,
> "The field's chief flower, sweet above compare,
> Stain to all nymphs, more lovely than a man,
> More white and red than doves or roses are;
> Nature that made thee, with herself at strife."

"Am I then the handsome Adonis?" Harry asked. "So strenuously resisting the charms of Venus herself?"

Will replied in a voice too soft for Aemilia to hear. All went silent except for swallowed murmurs and rustlings. She burned when she guessed what must be passing between them. Surely now she must tiptoe away, give the two men their privacy. She lifted her hands from the keys only for Harry to rebuke her in a voice so haughty she longed to stuff a rag down his throat.

"What, no more music? But I *pay* you for your music, Aemilia-Emilio! If you would earn my gold, play on."

Biting her lip, she obeyed.

"Why do men seek out whores?" the Earl of Southampton asked his friend, as though making a deeply philosophical inquiry. "To seek carnal pleasures when they lack a wife to provide such delights. Or when they grow tired of their wives. Like *you*, Will!"

The poet attempted to interject only to have Harry cut him off.

"When it comes to whores, pleasure is fleeting. Our common English harlot soon bores a man of any intelligence. And why, sweet William, do men seek out the company of other men?" Harry ended on a note of wicked mirth.

The poet answered in a heartbeat. "To seek true companionship of the soul and intellect. The noblest form of love, not mere animal urges. The marriage of true minds if you will."

Aemilia decided she despised them both. Was that all women were to them, witless whores to service their beastly urges? If Southampton wished for a tête-à-tête with his poet, why had he summoned her?

The poet then had the temerity to quote the recently deceased Kit Marlowe, as though claiming those words for his own. "If the male form once defined beauty in heaven, men on earth are fairer still."

"Now imagine, if you will," said Harry, "a sensuous woman with a man's intellect and learning. Our delectable Aemilia has a humanist education. Not only does she possess male attire—she has a mind to match."

Aemilia told herself that her utter debasement was complete. That she had sunk as low as this, having to listen to Southampton gossip about her, literally behind her back, only a few yards away from where she played the virginals. Did he think she had no feelings? She certainly wouldn't give him the satisfaction of seeing her tears. If she were indeed Emilio, not Aemilia, she would have leapt from the virginals and pummeled his gut.

"Our beauty caught the eye of the Lord Chamberlain who taught her the arts of hawking as well as *amour*. But, alas, he put her aside when she revealed herself to be pregnant with his bastard—our dear Aemilia fainted and landed upon my very *person* during the masque, can you imagine the uproar? The Lord Chamberlain hastily married her off to a ridiculous French gudgeon who squanders her money. And so she is forced to fall back on her old profession."

Southampton made her life sound so tawdry, as though she were the heroine of some second-rate play penned by the likes of Thomas Middleton. Both Harry and Alfonse cast her as the eternal whore beyond redemption, even though she had only given herself to one man, Lord Hunsdon, the father of her child.

"The Lord Chamberlain must be nearly seventy," the poet said. He spoke as though listening to her tale discomfited him. As though he, for all his poverty, felt sorry for her. At least he had a heart beating in his chest. Unlike Southampton.

"Her loss is our gain," said Harry. "You should try her some time." The Earl spoke archly, as if imparting advice to a backward younger brother. "She'd be good for you, I dare say."

In her imagination, Aemilia landed a smart slap across the Earl's face. So that was Southampton's game—praising her as the paragon of whores for the sole purpose of whipping his lover into a jealous frenzy. Yet she went on playing, not missing a single note. She reminded herself that she was here in his mansion to save herself and Enrico from ruin. That was all.

When the poet spoke, his voice rasped like ice. "And you, my lord. Have you *tried* her?"

"How am I to entertain the thought of marriage if I've never even known a woman? And such a woman! The closest thing we have to the *hetairai* of ancient Athens."

The poet's silence opened as deep as a chasm.

"Ah, I forgot," the Earl said. "They never taught you Greek at your provincial grammar school. You don't even know what *hetaira* means."

"I think I must go." The poet's voice was stretched as tightly as a rope about to snap.

But Harry was already spinning away from his friend. For a moment, he hovered over Aemilia's shoulder. As she twisted on her seat to face him, he tossed a pouch into her lap.

"I give you leave to depart, Aemilia-Emilio. As charming as your services are, we shall not require them anymore this night."

While she weighed the bag of gold coins in her hand, Southampton sauntered to the far end of the room where, through the great double doors, an august company of gentlemen streamed in, arrayed like princes in their linens and silk. Soon they engulfed the young Earl.

"A midnight picnic on Midsummer's Eve! How enchanting, Southampton!"

Aemilia was about to dart from the room without further ceremony when she noticed that the poet stood as if turned to stone. How blithely his noble lord had deserted him. The pages of *Venus and Adonis* lay scattered across a table, as if those exquisite verses were of no greater worth than a soiled napkin. Aemilia went to gather them up when she heard the racket of less genteel men joining the fray at the far side of the room. Strident, common voices shouted and jibed.

"Do I spy Master Shakescene, the upstart crow?" a voice boomed. "What's he doing here? A charity case, my lord? That wretch owes me money!"

The poet seemed to jump out of his skin. As if in a blind panic, he bolted to the nearest exit—an open window. The only visible doors were on the opposite end of the room, now blocked by the intruders. Aemilia watched in horror as the poet lifted his leg over the sill. It was at least a twelve-foot drop into the garden. Dashing over, she seized his arm.

"Have you gone mad?" she hissed.

"Unhand me, woman!" he cried, his face dark red as he struggled to shake himself free.

"Never! A man of your years has no business leaping out of windows."

"A man *of my years*?"

They both jerked their heads at the sound of Harry's company advancing across the room like an invading army. Before the poet could make one final attempt to defenestrate himself, she whispered fiercely in his ear, "Come, make haste. I'll show you out the back."

Dragging him into a curtained alcove, she found the hidden door used by the servants. Gripping his hand, she led him down a warren of darkened passages and stairways. The first thing she learned in any house, great or humble, was how to escape it.

"Never fear," she told the poet. "I, too, would not wish to stay to see Southampton entertain his tribe of buffoons."

She found her way to the back corridor nearest the stables where she had left her riding cloak and her rapier and sword. The way the young Earl had toyed with them both, she fumed, using them for his amusement then turning his back on them when he tired of his little game. A poet from the provinces who had never learned Greek. A fallen woman who knew Greek and dressed as a young man. Perhaps the two of them were interchangeable as far as Harry was concerned, novelties for his curiosity cabinet, just like the miniature of the courtesan in the codpiece. *You should try her some time.* From the far end of the house, she could hear the men's laughter and hooting.

The poet wrenched his hand from her grasp. "Where's the door? I must away!"

He looked as though someone had rammed a knife into his innards. It was then she realized that his shame cut even deeper than hers. Unlike her, the poet truly loved Southampton. He had offered up his body and soul to that fickle boy. The words of his sonnet ripped through her memory. *Being your slave, what should I do but tend upon the hours and times of your desire?* Even a slave could take only so much.

Leading him down the passage, she opened a door into the blooming night garden. Something made her stand in his path, blocking his way. She could not stop herself from touching his face, wet with tears.

"You needn't be jealous on my account," she told him. "I've never so much as kissed the boy. And you mustn't take him too seriously. Aristocrats such as he might dally with the likes of you and me, but eventually they tire of us and cast us aside."

Her words only seemed to drive the poet's despair to the breaking point. Pushing past her, he fled into the garden. She called out to him, but he was gone. Only her voice remained, echoing in the midsummer night.

RIDING BACK TO WESTMINSTER, Aemilia consoled herself that this night's labors had not been in vain. Southampton's purse of gold coins hung heavy inside her doublet. These, her own earnings, she would hide from Alfonse's grasp. Yet she desperately needed to find a more reliable means of sustenance than depending on the likes of Harry.

The poet lingered in her mind. His look of utter heartbreak, how he'd reeled away when she had touched his tears. His verses had formed such an intricate counterpoint to her music, as though his art seamlessly interlocked with hers. Fancy the chance of them meeting twice on the same day—what if this was preordained in their very stars? Slowly an idea began to form inside her head. Might not the pair of them prove more formidable together than either of them on their own—his poetry combined with her education and courtly connections? Might they even become collaborators of sorts? But what man would ever agree to work with a woman, even one as learned as she? Their paths might never cross again.

Tucked inside her shirt, the precious pages of *Venus and Adonis* burned against her bound breasts. She had tried to return his poem to him, but he'd run away from her, never looking back. The night had swallowed him whole.

13

HE MISTRESS HAS BEEN creeping about in the night again," Winifred told her sisters.

The kitchen was redolent with elderflower, the scent of high summer. Winifred and Prudence pounded the filmy white blooms in crocks to make elderflower wine while Tabitha sat on a stool and nursed Enrico.

"Lucky the master hasn't returned from Greenwich yet." Tabitha wrapped her arms protectively around the baby. "What if he *knew*?"

Winifred snorted. "She thinks *we* don't know."

The three sisters gazed at the ceiling above which their mistress slept, even as the bells of Saint Margaret rang the hour of ten o'clock. From the kitchen beams hung the dried herbs Prudence had gathered. Pru knew each plant's uses and properties, in which phase of the moon to harvest it, and which planet ruled it. Winifred and Tabitha bowed to Pru's superior wisdom in such matters.

The Weir sisters hailed from deepest Essex, though they'd heard it said that their surname was Scottish and that some paternal ancestor must have wandered down from the land north of the Tweed. Folk were often surprised to discover they were sisters, for they didn't bear a strong resemblance to one another. Prudence was as thin as a broomstick while Winifred was as big as a haystack. Tabitha was as pretty as the Queen of May.

Tabby's beauty had not always been a boon. Her former master in Braintree had forced his way into her bed one night. Seven months later he threw her out without a farthing because her pregnant belly had grown too big to hide. From that moment onward, the Weir sisters had sworn a pact. Never again would they be separated. Each prospective employer must hire all three of them. Nothing good could come from separating sisters.

There was no going back to Essex. The sisters' reputations had grown too notorious. Not only was Tabitha disgraced, but Prudence was the subject of the most chilling speculations. She'd always been different from the rest, born with the caul. Even as a tot she'd seen things invisible to others. Tongues really started to wag when Tabitha's former master suffered a stroke that left him crippled and impotent, forever ending his days of raping young girls. Folk in Essex said that whoever meddled with the Weir sisters came to ruin.

After a neighbor and her two daughters were hanged for witchcraft, the Weir sisters knew it was time to flee. With pregnant Tabby in tow, they walked all the way to London. Tabitha's baby had been stillborn, drowning her heart in grief. But then Mistress Aemilia had come to their rescue, hiring Tabby as her wet nurse and giving her a new baby to love. And who would accuse Prudence of witchcraft here in the safe haven of Westminster? Yet their security seemed tenuous at best. If their good mistress was to suffer grave misfortune, they might be out on the street.

"I'm afraid for the mistress, I am." Winifred's powerful arms heaved as she pounded the elderflowers into a thick perfumed paste. "What will happen when the master discovers she rides forth by night? She can't keep her secret forever."

"Dressed as a man!" Tabitha lowered her voice. "I found the key to the coffer where she hides her men's clothes. Her sword and rapier, too."

"She could be arrested," said Winifred.

Everyone knew that cross-dressing was a crime against God and the Queen. Winifred took out her temper on the elderflowers. The kitchen table quaked under the might of her thrashing arms. Even the herbs hanging from the beams trembled.

"She's more to fear from the master than the law," said Tabitha. "Isn't that right, Pru?"

Tabby and Winifred both looked at Prudence. The eldest Weir sister had yet to voice her opinion.

"Marry, the master's bad tempered, but it's all shouting and bluster," said Pru. "Underneath it, he's soft. He's only young and he truly desires her. But he knows she despises him. So he pretends to hate her in turn."

The younger Weir sisters remained silent, digesting Prudence's words.

"He could learn how to make a woman happy," Prudence said. "All he needs is a little encouragement. He's eight months wed and never once bedded his wife."

Tabitha blushed. Winifred lowered her eyes to the crock of macerated elderflowers.

"She was six months pregnant when she married him," said Pru. "Then when Enrico was born, the midwife told her not to lie with her husband before the babe was six months old."

"If only she cared for him." Tabitha held Enrico over her shoulder, stroking his back until he burped. "If only she could be soft with him, the way she's soft with everyone else. Every beggar she passes in the street."

"If only he cherished *her* and acted a bit more kindly," said Winifred. "If only he was a good provider and stopped wasting all her money."

"If, if, if," Prudence said, rolling her eyes.

"Love!" Winifred cried, her face turning pink. "It can turn the blackest heart to light."

"If only we could *make* them fall in love!" Tabitha locked eyes with Prudence.

"I've heard of some who sell love philters," said Winifred. "Like that piss-pot astrologer in Thames Street. I'll wager he charges a fortune. Probably makes them from the bones of boiled cats." She spoke contemptuously.

"But using love charms is a crime," Tabitha said, hugging Enrico against her bosom. "A *hanging* crime." Her eyes were fearful and huge.

"Sorcery," Winifred muttered.

The younger Weir sisters stared at Prudence, who went on pounding elderflowers as though her siblings weren't even there. Flies buzzed in the kitchen. A cauldron of pottage bubbled in the hearth. A burning oak branch broke in two with a shower of golden sparks.

Finally Prudence spoke. "Why, it's no crime against God or the

Queen to make elderflower wine. Or to pray over it. Prayer is no crime."

As she spoke, the house cat wound itself around her ankle and purred.

"The old prayers." Winifred met Prudence's complicit gaze. "The country prayers."

"Why, it's a blessed and holy thing," said Tabitha, "to pray for a wedded couple's happiness."

Winifred abruptly shook her head. "Making wine takes too long. At least six weeks to ferment. God's teeth, they'll probably murder each other by then."

"*Unless* we three were to pray over that flask on the sideboard." Tabitha pointed to last year's elderflower wine that they had brought with them from Essex. It was as yet unopened.

The younger sisters turned to Prudence, who remained quiet for a long spell.

"Sure, that flask might be prayed over," said Pru. "It might be poured into a different bottle and placed on the table the next time the master and mistress dine together." She lifted her face to the herbs hanging from the beams. "Why, we might even add a few more ingredients."

All three Weir sisters gazed at the locked drawer where Prudence hid the mandrake root.

THREE DAYS LATER AEMILIA rode out at dawn. The rising sun flamed in the eastern sky, blinding her as she rode toward the parish of Saint Giles-without-Cripplegate outside London's city walls. Ben Jonson, her maternal cousin, had told her Master Shakespeare lived in that district, which was famed for its low rents.

"You'll find him in Mistress Skinner's boardinghouse behind the Whitecross Tavern," Ben had informed her. "Though *why* you should wish to seek him out is beyond my ken. I always thought he was a long-winded, sheep-biting bumpkin."

Ben didn't know, as Master Shakespeare did, that she rode out as a man. Not since her time at Grimsthorpe had she dared to appear as Emilio with the full light of day on her face. What if someone saw through her guise? Yet she would have risked even more making this journey as a woman. Saint Giles-without-Cripplegate was notorious for its thieves. Besides, she was calling on a strange man in his boardinghouse, something no respectable woman could do.

What a hellhole this was. Every sight that caught her eye was ghastly. Even at this early hour, drunkards of both sexes relieved themselves in the street. Scrawny dogs devoured refuse. In the June heat, everything festered and stank. The odorous air wafting over the city walls seemed to bring its own taint of contagion, the specter of summer fluxes that killed infants in their cradles. Her heart rattled to think of such vapors infecting Enrico. People of any wealth evacuated London and Westminster in this sultry season.

Her way took her past Cripplegate itself, which was hung with the beheaded, castrated, and eviscerated bodies of the Queen's enemies. Anyone who entered London through its western gate must pass beneath these corpses rotting in the summer swelter, drawing swarms of flies and murders of crows. Bathsheba nearly bolted from the stench. Battling her own nausea, Aemilia trotted her briskly on, but Bathsheba stopped abruptly when a beggar on crutches lurched in their path, crying out in an open-palmed lament.

"Have pity, kind sir!"

When she took out her purse and gave him a penny, half a dozen other beggars crowded round while a mob of urchins closed in from behind. In her gentleman's garb, Aemilia stood out to every pickpocket. Panic rose in her throat. How easily she could be dragged down from her horse, stripped of all possessions, including the false protection of her male garments. Gripping the reins in one hand, her sword in the other, she spurred on.

Bathsheba's hooves clattered on cobblestones when at last they entered the courtyard behind the Whitecross Tavern. The boardinghouse was a crooked, half-timbered structure with unglazed windows. What a sorry place for a poet to dwell. How could Southampton let his friend live like this—didn't he pay him for his poetry? Or was the poet too proud and high-minded to accept Southampton's money?

A woman of middle years bustled out, her hands on her hips, her eyes raking Aemilia over. Aemilia froze in the saddle. Surely another woman would see straight through her masquerade, see how her hands, too small to be a man's, trembled as she clutched the reins. But to her amazement, the woman's eyes widened and she fairly simpered.

"Good day to you, sir. Marry, I haven't seen a gentleman as handsome as you in quite some time."

The woman curtsied low enough to expose her bosom. "Nell Skinner at your service, sir." She smiled at Aemilia through her eyelashes.

Never had Aemilia contemplated what might happen if an amorous woman took her male guise to be true. She reminded herself to keep her voice in its lowest registers. "Madam, I seek a Master Shakespeare. I understand he lodges with you."

Mistress Skinner twinkled, as though delighted to be called madam. "Indeed, he does, sir. Though what a fine gentleman like you would want with the likes of him, I don't know. He's a fortnight behind on his rent. But never you mind. Come, rest your legs in my parlor whilst I fetch him down."

At first Aemilia hesitated, reluctant to turn her back on Bathsheba in this district of thugs, but Mistress Skinner insisted, showing her into another courtyard with a gate that locked. A grubby boy offered Bathsheba moldy hay, which the mare disdained in favor of the green weeds shooting up from between the broken flagstones.

In the boardinghouse parlor, Mistress Skinner made a huge fuss of seating Aemilia in her best carved chair.

"I'll just let Master Shakestaff know you've come to call. Any time you want to visit, sir, you are most welcome. My door is always open to you, sir, if you know my meaning!" The landlady spun around, giggling and lifting her skirts to flash her ankles and calves before she fluttered up the darkened stairwell.

The strain of her act left Aemilia shaking, and her heart slammed to think of the proposal she was about to make to this man, this stranger. Fumbling through her satchel, she reached for her pipe and tobacco, a habit she seldom indulged in, but she needed the strong physick to settle her nerves. Lighting the pipe from the hearth embers, she took a long draw on the sweet Virginian herb before settling back into the chair, her booted legs a-splay, as though she truly were a carefree young rake.

From up the stairwell, she heard Mistress Skinner banging on a door. "Wake up, you bugbear! There's a *gentleman* to see you!"

Moments later, Aemilia heard footsteps hurtling down the stairs. His face flushed, his hands clasped to his heart, the poet appeared before her.

"Harry!" he cried, before stopping short at the sight of her.

Enthroned in his landlady's best chair, Aemilia puffed her pipe and decided to play her part with brio. To revel in her act, as though she had been born to wear these breeches and this white linen shirt.

"Your good Mistress Skinner flirts with me in vain," she said, affecting a mimicry of Southampton's airy drawl. "For I must agree with our late, lamented Kit Marlowe. All they that love not tobacco and boys are fools."

"What are you doing here?" the poet hissed. "And what do *you* know of Kit Marlowe?"

"Why, he was a friend of my cousin's, Ben Jonson. I presume you know Master Jonson."

"I know *of* him," the poet said with much venom, making her wonder if Ben had actually called him a sheep-biting bumpkin to his face. "What can I say of a man whose greatest cause of distinction comes from dropping the *h* from his surname?"

"Why so grim, sir?" Aemilia reproved. "I think you should be glad to see me. The other night you fled with such haste that I had no chance to return *this*."

Reaching into her satchel, she handed him the scrolled pages of *Venus and Adonis*. She had devoured every line of the epic and its cadences still haunted her.

As the poet seized his manuscript and clutched it to his chest, his face seemed to unclench. For the first time, she saw him smile, which transformed his entire face. He was distractingly handsome, she noted.

"I thank you for its safe return," he said. "Has anyone else seen it?"

"Only Southampton and I."

Had he feared that Southampton's odious guests had laid hands on it?

"Sit you down, sir," she told him. "I asked your landlady to warm a lamb pie I brought for you. My maid was right — you are too thin. But I hope your lean times shall soon end. This poem will make your fortune."

"No poet can survive without a patron." He pulled up a stool. "Do you carry a message from my Lord Southampton?"

The plaintiveness in his voice made her drop her eyes. "Lord Burghley summoned him away to his country estate. He fears the boy keeps the wrong company if left to his own devices. I fear neither of us shall see Southampton for quite some time."

The poet sagged. "No matter. My London days are over."

She cocked her head. "Where do you intend to go?"

"Lancashire," he said. "To seek a teaching post with a noble family. I served them once before."

"Lancashire," she breathed. It seemed as far away as the Americas. "Is that your home?"

He laughed bleakly and shook his head. "I hail from Warwickshire."

"Do you not miss your family?" she asked him. "Your wife?" Southampton, she recalled, had mentioned Will's wife.

He stared at her for a moment before gazing down at the stale rushes on the floor. "They all see me as a failure. I'm nearly thirty, yet I've nothing to show for it. Only a few history plays performed by Lord Strange's Men. My wife earns more as a country maltster than I do in London for all my toil and ambition. I daren't return to her until I've made something of myself. I'm ashamed to show my face to my own son. But anything I do earn, I send home so he can attend grammar school." Will seemed particularly keen to make this last point.

Aemilia sensed his secret relief to be offering this confession to a stranger he thought never to see again. She could nearly taste the man's dejection. As she had, this poet had lost any sense of a true home, of belonging anywhere.

"Your wife is a maltster, you say?" she asked him.

"She brews ale," he said.

"A useful skill, indeed." Aemilia tried to imagine life as a prosperous tradeswoman, independent of the vagaries of her husband's earnings. "Why did you attempt to leap out the window at Southampton House?"

"To avoid that bleating wastrel Robert Greene." The poet let out a sigh. "He satirizes me in his pamphlets. Because I never attended university, he thinks me ignorant. He mocks me as a base-bred hayseed from the shires, a *Johannes factotum*."

"Jack of all trades and master of none," Aemilia translated.

"One night I scribe a play. The next I'm a player upon the boards. But my adventures here have ended."

"Lamb pie, good sir!" Mistress Skinner pranced in with a tray.

Her servant girl set up a table between Will and Aemilia then the landlady set down two steaming wooden trenchers. The poet fell upon his food and devoured it. When the landlady's back was turned, Aemilia took his empty trencher and passed him her own untouched portion.

"Before you leave for Lancashire, pray hear my proposal." She looked him in the eye without coyness or guile, as though she truly were another man. His equal. But what she said next made him choke. "I want to write plays with you, Master Shakespeare."

He sputtered.

"My cousin, Master Jonson, says it's not uncommon for playwrights to work with collaborators. Have you never done so before?"

"But you . . . but you . . . are a—"

"An Italian!" she said brightly, with a wink to Mistress Skinner who hovered nearby, dusting everything in sight while leaning close to eavesdrop. "And that, sir, works in your advantage. Do you think Mistress Skinner would be so kind as to fetch two goblets?"

The landlady nearly fell flat delivering her curtsy. "At once, sir!"

Aemilia returned her attention to the poet. "Master Jonson says your history plays have not made much money."

The poet's mouth twisted, as though preparing to deliver some sarcastic retort, but then he looked resigned.

"Imagine if your plays were to catch the Queen's attention." Leaning across the table, she found herself staring into his hazel eyes. She saw the face of a country man trapped on the outskirts of a heaving city that would spit him out like a broken tooth if his luck did not improve. "Her Majesty's favorite entertainments are Italian. The masque and the madrigal. Her favorite dance is la volta. And she adores commedia dell'arte. We shall write comedies, you and I. It would be scandalous for me to write under my own name, so we shall do it under yours. And evenly divide the profits."

"How shall one as lowly as I attract Her Majesty's attention?" The skepticism fairly shot from his tongue.

"Why, Southampton himself told you of my . . . my association with the Lord Chamberlain. I still have his ear. I shall persuade him to form a new theater company—the Lord Chamberlain's Men." She could not resist smiling in triumph.

Still, his suspicions were not allayed. "If you have the Lord Chamberlain at your beck and call, then surely you don't need me. Why not collaborate with your cousin, Master Jonson?"

"Because I've read your poetry, and no one writes about love the way you do." She had been in awe of his verses ever since she first laid eyes on the sonnet he had dropped in Thames Street. "Besides," she added cheerfully, "you seem rather desperate."

He shot her a cross look.

"Just imagine comedies filled with your poetry of love," she said.

"Two goblets, sir!" Mistress Skinner swept in.

"Poets may write of love," Will said in a low voice. "But poems are private things. Such sentiments are not for public display."

"Don't listen to him, sir!" Mistress Skinner interjected. "What does a provincial like Master Shakestaff know? I fancy a good love story, me. A proper romance!" She cast Aemilia a smoldering glance.

Clearing her throat, Aemilia pulled the flask from her satchel and poured pale wine into the two pewter goblets. "Drink with me, if you will, to seal the bargain," she said to the poet.

"What sort of wine is that?" Mistress Skinner asked. "Might I have a taste, sir?"

"It's nothing grand," Aemilia told her. "Just some humble elderflower wine my servants brewed in Essex."

"What are those odd bits floating in it?" the poet asked.

Aemilia shrugged. "Special herbs, no doubt. Each country wine has its own secret recipe."

"Bottom's up!" Mistress Skinner seized Will's goblet and was about to knock back the pale liquid when a caterwauling in the passageway made her wrench her head round.

"Mistress!" her maid screeched. "That lying sod Mullin is flitting off with all his goods and gear!"

The landlady slammed the untasted wine down on the table.

"Satan's toenails!" Mistress Skinner bellowed, rolling up her sleeves. "I'll have his bollocks on a plate!"

Off she thundered in pursuit of the hapless Master Mullin, whom Aemilia judged to be even further behind on his rent than the poet.

"Now we have our peace," Will said, with a smile.

They raised their goblets to each other.

"To poetry!" she cried.

"To the Muse," he said.

"I know this must seem very strange to you." With the landlady gone, Aemilia dropped her guard and spoke in her natural voice. "I have a humanist's education and yet I am forbidden to use it to earn my bread. So I am forced to wear a mask."

"And that is what you want from me," he said. "To be your mask."

He held her gaze for a second before sipping the pale wine.

She stared into her goblet. Fragrant and light on her tongue, it was clearly weak enough in alcohol content to render it harmless and completely wholesome. A child could drink it and suffer no ill. The poet drained his goblet while she sipped and savored hers.

"We shall write comedies," she said. "Full of love and Italian sunlight."

As the English sun streamed through the unglazed window, the poet seemed to warm to her proposal. Collaborating with a woman in breeches might seem an eccentric arrangement, but surely it was a more inviting prospect, she reasoned, than for the man to exile himself in Lancashire where he would surely vanish into obscurity.

"Let me give you this before I go." She passed him a small pouch of coins. "This should keep your landlady happy."

She also offered him the rest of the elderflower wine. When he shook his head, she stoppered the flask and returned it to her satchel. Their conversation concluded, she rose from her chair and headed for the door.

"Wait," he said.

She turned, glancing back at him over her shoulder.

"What is a *hetaira*?" His face shone in earnest entreaty.

She felt herself blush all the way down her neck. Damn Southampton for putting that word in the poet's head.

"It's Greek," she said quietly. "The *hetairai* were the highest class of courtesan. The Athenians kept their wives and daughters as ignorant as sheep. But the *hetairai* were as educated as the men they entertained. *Hetaira* means companion. A companion to men."

With a nod to him, she walked out, shutting the door behind her.

AEMILIA RODE HOME BY way of the shady back lanes, her hat brim pulled low over her eyes. As she approached Westminster, her heart began to hammer. What if one of her neighbors betrayed her? Even if her disguise fooled them, they might recognize her horse. She could very well finish off the day in the pillory.

Though she spurred Bathsheba on, the heat rendered the mare sluggish. The fastest gait Aemilia could push her into was a halfhearted trot.

A prayer formed on Aemilia's lips. *Please, oh please, just let us get safely home.*

She asked herself to whom she was praying—her departed father's secret God or the Queen's God who divided humanity into the Elect and the damned? On which side of that gaping divide between the saved and the condemned did she stand as a cast-off mistress, mother of a bastard, a miscreant in men's clothing? Perhaps her many sins and deceptions had cast her beyond the reach of divine grace. To think the departed Kit Marlowe had been bold enough to brag of his atheism. What did she believe or disbelieve? Papa's ghostly voice whispered, *Hell is empty. All the devils are up here.*

Aemilia swallowed a scream. His eyes red with drink, Alfonse swayed before her in the narrow lane. In a panic, she kicked the mare onward, but her husband made a drunken lurch and grabbed Bathsheba's reins. Aemilia reached for her sword then, thinking better of the idea, pulled the half-full bottle of elderflower wine from her saddle bag. Bathsheba, meanwhile, proceeded to rub her sweaty, itchy head on Alfonse's doublet, knocking him down so that his sprawled body blocked their path.

With glittering eyes, Alfonse gazed up at her. "Sir, beware of women. They will destroy you."

Something caught in her throat. Was he truly so drunk that he didn't recognize her or the horse? Bathsheba nuzzled him and started to lick his unruly hair into place, but the mare refused to step over his body. In gutter French, he railed on about the disgusting *putain,* his wife, who had bedded every man in the realm except for him, her lawful husband.

Aemilia recoiled. She must get herself home before he returned to his senses. But his inert body blocked her passage. She considered how blurred his vision must be from the drink and how tall she must appear as he lay on his back in the dust.

"Sirrah," she said, in mimicry of the poet's voice, his rustic Warwickshire vowels. "How can any woman respect you? Legless drunk at eleven in the morning. Surely you have only yourself to blame for your misery."

Alfonse gulped back a sob. From within the Lamb Inn came the voices of men calling him back inside for another round. He attempted to rise but collapsed again and curled himself in a ball, allowing Bathsheba to squeeze past him. Aemilia regarded him from her perch. She stood in her stirrups to appear even loftier.

"Don't waste your wife's money on drink." She spoke from deep in her belly. "If you must drink, take this instead."

She bent from the saddle to hand him the flask of elderflower wine. Before he could say a word, she trotted away.

"Did you see the mistress take the elderflower wine?" Prudence demanded of Winifred. "Have you any clue where she's gone?"

The Weir sisters gathered in the kitchen and stared dolefully at the empty space on the sideboard where they had placed the bottle the previous evening.

Sweat streamed down Winifred's face as she began to pace, kicking up the rushes and disturbing a mouse that darted away in panic. "She was up before the cockerel! Up and gone before dawn. She's like an airy sprite, she is, how fast she can disappear."

"Wherever she went, she took the bottle with her," said Tabitha. "Oh, what awful mischief!"

The cat pounced on the mouse. Tabitha shuddered and covered the baby's ears as the rodent squealed in its death throes.

"Good pussycat," said Prudence.

"Had we never prayed over that bottle," Winifred lamented.

"Hush!" Prudence snapped her finger to her lips.

The Weir sisters stood to attention when in tramped their mistress clad as a young gentleman for all the world to see. Her face was pale and drawn, as though she had witnessed the depths of hell. Not uttering a word, she took Enrico from Tabitha and flew up the stairs. The Weir sisters listened to the floorboards creak under her footfalls and then the thud as she bolted herself in her bedchamber.

"Awful mischief," Tabitha said again, in a strangled whisper. "At least the master didn't see her." With no baby to hug, the girl clutched her own arms and shivered.

AN HOUR OR SO later, Alfonse staggered in. His eyes were downcast, his hair a rat's nest, his clothes filthy.

"Master!" Winifred cried. "How good to see you." She pitched her voice loudly so that the mistress upstairs would hear and be warned.

Her eyes huge, Tabitha pinched Winifred's elbow and pointed to the empty flask he carried.

"How are you this fine day, Master Lanier, sir?" Prudence asked.

"Can you make the hot water for me?" The master sounded quieter and humbler than Winifred had ever heard him. "Today I shall bathe."

Thank Christ for that, Winifred thought. He stank worse than a tanner's yard.

"Right you are, sir," said Prudence. "We'll heat that water for you straight away." She sent Tabitha out to draw water and fetch firewood.

"Can you send for a barber?" The master ran his hand over the dark stubble on his chin.

"Sir, I can shave you and cut your hair at no expense to the household," said Winifred. "But first you should eat something." She turned to Pru. "Where's that lamb pie you baked yesterday?"

"Tonight I shall dine with Madame Lanier," said the master. He trembled as though this were a daunting prospect. "Have I any clean linen?"

"I'll look for you, sir," said Winifred.

"This morning I saw a gentleman." Alfonse spoke in a faraway voice. "His shirt it was immaculate. He looked like an angel."

AT THE SOUND OF her husband's voice downstairs, Aemilia made certain the bedchamber door was bolted fast. She crept as noiselessly as she could past the cradle where Enrico slept in sweet innocence. From her dressing table, she picked up the steel mirror that Anne Locke had given her so long ago. *Let this be a mirror of your virtue, my girl.*

Gazing at her reflection, she observed what an odd creature she was with her long tousled hair and her men's clothing. How had she managed to fool anyone? It seemed impossible that earlier that morning she had carried herself like a young gallant, bursting with merry wit as she persuaded her luckless poet to agree to write comedies with her. Now, like a fugitive, she cowered behind a locked door. What would Master Shakespeare think of her if he knew the truth?

Aemilia shed her doublet and breeches and her treasured linen shirt. Once she had believed this disguise would protect her as though it were magical armor. As she folded the garments carefully, her palms smoothed out every wrinkle and crease before she laid them in their coffer with her riding boots, sword, rapier, and hat. She locked the coffer, slid it under the bed, and hid the key at the bottom of the box where she kept the rags she used while menstruating—the place Alfonse was least likely to look.

Naked, she assessed herself in the mirror, eyeing herself dispassionately, as though she were looking at another person. Men, she decided, would still find this woman comely enough, but childbirth had taken its toll. Though she was as slender as ever, her belly was not as taut nor her breasts as high or firm as before her pregnancy. Her face was no longer that of a girl but of a woman who had tasted life's bitterness as well as its sweetness.

"You are a ruined woman," she told the lady in the mirror. "But fear not. It only means you answer to no one but yourself."

Perhaps Alfonse could be mollified, at least for a time, if she bedded him. But the thought of such a loveless exchange sickened her. And what if he got her with child? They could barely manage as it was.

Lord Hunsdon had done his utmost to be tender. In his way, he had truly loved her. She recalled how Master Shakespeare had asked her what *hetaira* meant. How she had sparkled in her role as Lord Hunsdon's companion. She had played the virginals for him and read poetry to him in Latin and Greek, French and Italian. They had conversed on subjects as diverse as stargazing and statesmanship. He had adored her mind as well as her body. But at the age of twenty-four, it seemed her life was finished. Even if she was the most submissive and obedient wife that ever lived, Aemilia suspected Alfonse would always hold her past over her head.

Regarding herself in the mirror, she considered how Doctor Dee, the Queen's conjuror, was said to summon spirits in his magical looking glass. Might she do the same?

"Come, you spirits that tend upon mortal thoughts," she whispered. "Unsex me now."

She closed her eyes and imagined leaving Aemilia behind. Becoming Emilio. But a woman she remained.

She dressed hastily, becoming Mistress Lanier once more. She worked her comb through her hair, ripping through the snarls until the tears came to her eyes. Beneath all the curses Alfonse heaped upon her, behind every mask she had ever worn, her true self lay hidden, and this was the one thing that could never be taken from her.

AEMILIA SAT AT THE table with her husband, her hands clamped between her knees to still their trembling. Had he truly not recognized her when he grabbed Bathsheba's reins that morning?

The young man seated opposite her seemed subdued. He was scrubbed as clean as Prudence's kitchen table, his curly hair combed back from his face. His eyes were shadowed and heavy, and his gaze seemed unfocused, as though he were seeing double, another face imposed upon hers that made him squint and shake his head. His voice seemed to be coming from beneath the waves. Aemilia put it down to the ravages of drink. His head must be splitting. Fortunately, Winifred had watered down the wine so that it tasted no stronger than cordial.

"In three days I sail," said Alfonse, staring at his plate of starling pie.

In the interests of economy, Prudence had taken to snaring birds in the garden, a trick she had learned in Essex. Aemilia lowered her eyes as she skewered a piece of sinewy fowl on her knife. For months she had prayed for Alfonse to depart. Soon she would be free of him, at least for a time — she imagined he would be gone half a year at the very least. *Perhaps this seafaring life is just what he needs*, she thought. He could direct his wrath at the Spanish instead of her, possibly even reaping his share of captured gold. If and when he returned, he might prove wiser and kinder. Or would he come back with only a heap of gambling debts?

"You shall speed well on your voyage," she said. "The astrologer said so."

"Will you miss me?" he asked, in that querulous tone she had come to despise. "Will you think of me at all?"

"Of course, I shall." But her words sounded dishonest even to herself.

"You think me beneath you," he said, shoving away his pewter plate. "You think I am nothing. What must I do to win your *tendresse?*"

His words left her reeling. She had never thought it possible that he could address her so plaintively, his naked heart bared. Could it be that in his fog of sack sherry and self-pity he harbored true feelings for her? She searched for the right words.

"Just be a good man," she said.

She reached across the table to take his hand, but before their fingers could touch, he swayed on his chair and toppled backward, hitting the floor with a bone-cracking bang. She ran to kneel beside him. Wetting her handkerchief, she pressed it gently to his brow and temples, but he only looked at her blankly as though the blow to his head had wiped away all memory of their previous conversation. When he finally revived, the familiar look of disdain was set on his face as he winced and rubbed the back of his skull.

14

EMILIA SAT AT THE dining table with paper and quill, and tried to summon words that were vibrant and piquant, some idea for a play she could pen with the poet. Perhaps a comedy of errors or mistaken identity, of an intrepid girl who dressed as a boy only to fall in love with the gentleman she served in her male guise. But when Aemilia closed her eyes and attempted to picture these characters stepping out upon the stage, she saw only Alfonse's accusing face. Yesterday he had sailed from Billingsgate, en route to Plymouth where the voyage to the Azores would officially embark. His parting words thundered inside her head: *As soon as I'm gone, one hundred men will come to your door.*

If only she could use the power of art to turn her marriage into comedy, something to bring laughter rather than tears and pain. *Surely,* she thought ruefully, *Alfonse and I could be characters in a tale of a man wed to a shrew.* The play, of course, would be set in Veneto, and the shrew would be the daughter of Battista and she would have a beautiful golden-haired sister. The shrew would possess a tongue even sharper than her own. Aemilia would give her all the best lines.

Eyes closed, Aemilia's fingers tapped the table as she imagined their innumerable quarrels: the husband's complaints and the wife's spirited retorts spoken like a true Italian.

> ALFONSO: *I say thou art a shrew.*
> AEMILIA: *That's better than a sheep.*

Winifred trundled into the chamber, interrupting Aemilia's train of thought.

"Mistress, that astrologer's at the door and says he must speak to you."

Throwing down her quill in annoyance, Aemilia stalked toward the door to see Master Forman in his black physician's gown.

"Good day to you, Mistress Lanier." Puffing like a prized cockerel, he barged past her over the threshold. "Anon I have learned that your husband has embarked for Plymouth. Surely you wish to know whether he shall distinguish himself and thereby come to any preferment during his voyage to the Azores."

Before Aemilia could reply, the astrologer thrust two star charts into her hand.

"Madam, I have drawn up charts of your past and future. As you see, you shall rise by two degrees—"

"I cannot accept these," she told him, trying to hand them back. "I can't afford to pay you, sir."

"Ah, I understand you are very needy." Master Forman wet his lips and chuckled. "Perhaps for fortune's sake, you shall offer me special tokens of gratitude. Necessity does compel! I have divined your desires."

"I do desire we may be better strangers," she said. "Please leave."

The astrologer refused to budge. "Your stars reveal that you are or shall be a harlot. Because, with your hot Italian blood, you crave the most outrageous acts of sensual pleasure." His eyes gleamed like coins as he seized her arms, his breath hot on her bosom.

"Away from me!" she snapped.

"Death and damnation!" Master Forman sprang away from her and hopped on one foot. "What manner of monstrous giant?"

Winifred loomed over him. "Did I chance to step on your foot, Master Astrologer, sir? Beg your pardon."

"Enormous cow, you have crippled me! You have broken my toe." Master Forman turned to glare at Aemilia. "You shall pay for my loss of income owing to my injury."

"Lamed by a mere maid?" Aemilia tried not to gloat. "A country girl from Essex?"

"I told you never to go near that piss-pot prophet, mistress," Winifred said.

"*Piss-pot prophet?*" Master Forman looked as though he might weep from the indignity.

"Might I interrupt?" A second man approached the open doorway.

Aemilia's heart opened like a flower. "Jasper, what a surprise!" Shoving Forman out of her way, she seized Jasper's hands. "I've hardly seen you since the wedding!" Her cursed wedding day that had been like her funeral.

The two of them kissed and embraced in the Italian fashion while Master Forman looked on, his eyes bulging like a toad's.

"Dissembling harlot," the astrologer muttered. "The day after her husband's leave-taking, she throws herself at the first strapping young man to show himself at her door."

"I'm her cousin, if you please," said Jasper. "And if you call her harlot again, I'll break your other foot."

"Indeed," said Aemilia. "More of Master Forman's conversation would infect my brain."

"This creature is your cousin?" Forman shook his head. "Mistress Lanier, may I commend you on your handsome, red-blooded, virile young *cousin.*"

But Aemilia had already turned her back on the astrologer. Taking Jasper's arm, she drew her kinsman into the house.

Meanwhile, Winifred flung the star charts at Master Forman and herded him out the door as though he were no more to her than a stray dog. Stationing herself upon the threshold, she scowled at the astrologer until at last he limped away.

AEMILIA TOOK JASPER INTO the parlor, the best chamber. Instead of costly tapestries, the walls were hung with painted cloths depicting classical goddesses. Starry-eyed Venus in her celestial chariot drawn by doves. Juno enthroned and flanked by peacocks. Diana and her hounds.

What a novelty to have a guest to entertain! She asked Prudence to bring cakes and wine then called Tabitha to come with the baby. Aemilia realized she hadn't felt this light-hearted since before she fell pregnant. Jasper brought out the best in her. Her heart brimmed to see how tenderly he held Enrico.

"I've missed you so," Aemilia told her cousin, with both fondness and reproach. "How could you stay away so long?"

Jasper smiled at her sadly. "I know how jealous Master Lanier is. That's why I waited until he sailed."

"It's so ghastly in this house," she said. "Take me somewhere amusing. Remember when we were children and ran off to the Shoreditch playhouse?"

Jasper laughed at the memory but soon sobered. "In truth, Aemilia, I wish to take you somewhere, but much farther afield than Shoreditch."

"What can you mean?" she asked.

Jasper handed the baby back to Tabitha. With a nod from her mistress, Tabby carried Enrico out of the room but left the door slightly ajar, as though to listen in. Aemilia decided it didn't matter. She and Jasper had nothing to hide.

"A letter arrived," her cousin said. "From our kin in Bassano."

"Bassano?" Aemilia felt a rush of blood behind her brow, for the very name conjured the stories Papa had told her as a girl. She could still see the picture his words had painted, as vivid as a master's oil painting. The walled city with the castle and the old covered bridge, the surrounding forests and vineyards, all nestled at the foot of Monte Grappa. On the northern horizon rose the Alps, shining white with snow. On the oldest square in Bassano, facing the ancient well, was Papa's family villa, its entire façade covered in a vast fresco.

"Our fathers' last surviving first cousin, Jacopo Bassano, writes that he has not much longer to live," Jasper said. "He wishes to make a bequest to the Bassano brothers who emigrated to England."

"Marry, they've all departed this world." Aemilia thought of the five headstones in the churchyard where Papa and her uncles lay buried.

"The bequest shall then go to the descendants. His condition is that at least one of us should travel to Italy in person to claim it. The bequest involves property and some money as well."

"You are going." Aemilia took his hand. It made perfect sense that Jasper should make the long journey for, of all her cousins, he alone remained unmarried.

"I want to take you and Enrico with me." He squeezed her fingers.

For a moment, Aemilia couldn't speak. Such an offer of deliverance seemed even beyond the power of her dreams.

"You told me your marriage was hopeless and that you hated your husband." Jasper spoke without judgment. Life at court with its countless intrigues and betrayals had rendered him unflappable and pragmatic in such matters. "Here's your chance. Alfonse has sailed and so may you."

Her head ringing, Aemilia crossed the room to close the door Tabitha had left partly open. She leaned against it, facing Jasper once more.

"What would I do in Italy?" she asked, in a voice that didn't even sound like her own.

"You might pass as a widow," he said. "They know nothing of you there. You could even remarry."

"With a husband still living?"

"How do you know Alfonse will even return?"

Aemilia stood in silence. Would an Italian husband prove any better than the one she wished to flee? Then another idea seized her, one so potent she thought her mind might explode from it. In Italy she could become Emilio. At last she might make use of her education, earn her living as a musician or a translator. Her distant kin in Bassano knew nothing of Aemilia. So why wouldn't they welcome Emilio, help him find a livelihood, a home for him and his young son? She could become Emilio and never look back. But could she? Could she truly let Aemilia die?

"You must make ready." Jasper took her hands. "Next week I'll come for you."

She nodded, her heart filled with resolve. Either as Aemilia or Emilio, she must leave this house of pain. There were so many preparations to be made. Who would look after Bathsheba? And what would she do about the poet?

"Her Majesty has already given me permission to travel," said Jasper. "She's even paying my way so that I might purchase musical instruments for the court."

"So you shall return," she said.

"England is my home. I owe the Queen my livelihood. But you, Aemilia — what ties you to this island?"

"Nothing," she breathed.

"We'll see the villa where our fathers were born. Jacopo and his sons now make it their home."

"How was Jacopo allowed to live there after our fathers were driven away?" Aemilia's heart pounded, remembering Papa's tale of loss. But not even to Jasper did she mention *why* Papa and his brothers had been banished. That was something she and her cousins never spoke of. It was as if their fathers had never crept down into the cellar on Friday nights to pray and sing. Their fathers' religion lay buried in a well of silence deeper than the men's graves.

"The Church protected Jacopo." Jasper spoke wryly.

"How can that be?"

"He's a master painter. His religious art was the pride of the Veneto churches. So they left him in peace." Jasper shrugged his shoulders at the cynical ways of the world.

Aemilia recalled how even Anne Locke had believed Papa to be an ideal Christian. Jacopo, out of necessity, must have followed a similar course. Perhaps, unlike her father, Jacopo had undergone a genuine religious conversion. Or had he simply worn his mask so well and so long that he had become the mask?

"ITALY!" TABITHA CRIED OUT, racing into the kitchen with such urgency that she caused the baby to spit up on her coif. "The mistress is off to far Italy! What if she means to take us along?"

Pru and Winifred were so stunned, they dropped the pigeons they were plucking.

In the silence that followed, the cat slunk in from the garden and dropped its kill at Prudence's feet—the biggest rat the Weir sisters had ever seen.

ON THIS, THE HOTTEST day in Aemilia's memory, she and Winifred trudged toward Charing Cross in search of a breeze and a cup of whey to cool their parched throats.

A thousand thoughts whirled through Aemilia's head. Was she indeed bold enough to leave England behind or was she a coward intent on condemning herself to her familiar hell because the journey to Bassano seemed too intimidating? Italy was no paradise, but a jumble of city-states and principalities constantly at war with one another. The Moors threatened invasion, as did the French. At least England was at peace, a fortressed isle guarded by the Queen's warships that had seen off no less a foe than the Spanish Armada.

Her jaw clenched at the very thought of the long sea voyage, enough to tax the constitution of a healthy adult. How could she put Enrico through such an ordeal? For her son's sake, should she simply swallow her pride and wild fancies, and resign herself to be Alfonse Lanier's wife?

Even Winifred was quiet for once, her head and massive shoulders drooping.

As they neared Charing Cross, a crowd blocked their path. The people's faces were drained and white, their voices a rumble of choked prayers.

Linking arms with Winifred, Aemilia wound her way to the front of the throng to see the narrow house with the red cross painted on its door. Beneath the cross were the words LORD HAVE MERCY ON US. The door was bolted from the outside and flanking it were two armed guards. The words *pest house,* echoing from the crowd, drove panic up Aemilia's gorge. She and her maid stared at each other. This was the first time she had ever seen Winifred frightened, her eyes threatening tears.

The inmates of the plague house, be they living or dead, sick or healthy, were now held prisoner, forced into quarantine. The Black Death had come to Westminster. The murmurs in the crowd seemed to indicate that London, too, was infected.

"The master of the pest house died of a bubo in his right groin," an old woman told Aemilia and Winifred. "And he'd two spots on his right thigh. The mistress, children, and servants are locked up in there."

"They're digging a pit grave near Saint Martin's," a man said, his cap clutched to his heart.

Through the upper-story window, Aemilia heard an infant wail. Her arms burned for Enrico, burned with the longing to hold him tightly against her, to escape with him as fast as she could.

WAGONS, RIDERS, AND FOLK fleeing on foot clogged the lanes, every man and woman intent on seeking refuge with kin in the countryside or some distant town. Heading against the stream of traffic pouring out of London's city gates, Aemilia rode for Saint Giles-without-Cripplegate, this time as a woman like any other. In the oxcart behind her, the Weir sisters sat atop all the worldly belongings they had managed to pack at such short notice. Enrico gurgled in Tabitha's arms. Swaddled against the sun, the baby alone seemed cheerful to ride in the cart. Winifred, who sat driving the ox, was frantic.

"Why Saint Giles, mistress?" her maid asked. "We must get to Billingsgate as quickly as we can before the ship sails."

Why indeed, Aemilia asked herself. Why was she putting all their lives at risk for the sake of a poet she hardly knew? Her bargain with him was rendered void with the theaters closed down for the duration of the plague. Perhaps he had already absconded. But she found she could not abandon him. Not without at least first offering him deliverance.

"Wait here," Aemilia told the Weir sisters, as they stopped outside the Whitecross Tavern.

Winifred, perched high in the driver's seat with Aemilia's sword and rapier strapped to her girth, was frightening enough, so her mistress hoped, to ward off the thieves who hadn't already fled.

Since speed was of the essence, Aemilia didn't bother jumping down from her horse as she entered the courtyard and yelled loudly enough to make Bathsheba jump and snort.

"William Shakespeare! If you are there, come out at once!"

Out shot Mistress Skinner.

"What do you want with him?" the landlady demanded, peering at Aemilia suspiciously. "Does he owe you money? You're out of luck, madam. God's teeth, he's skint as a mole."

The poet stepped blinking into the sunlight before staring at Aemilia as though she were a phantasm. Not since their first encounter outside the astrologer's had he seen her in feminine garb to match her true sex and station.

"The lady looks familiar," Mistress Skinner muttered, with a sidelong glance at her tenant. "Now where have I seen her before?"

"Master Shakespeare," said Aemilia. "I'm off to Italy. Will you come with me?"

"Italy?" His voice was as incredulous as if she had told him she was flying to the moon. "Why Italy?"

"Family business," she said, her every word measured and brisk. "I'm traveling with my cousin."

"Your cousin Ben Jonson?" Even in these dire circumstances, the poet could not hide his derision. Would he take the Black Death over a journey with his rival who had insulted him?

"No," Aemilia said, exasperated by his vanity. "My cousin Jasper Bassano, musician to the Queen."

"Aha!" cried Mistress Skinner. "It was your cousin who called on us a fortnight ago. A very handsome fellow, your cousin is, madam."

"Choose now," Aemilia said to Will. "Will you come or stay behind? I've no time to wait."

"But why would you take *me*?" he asked. "And how shall I pay my fare?" He lifted his empty hands to the sky. "As you well know, I'm penniless."

"That he certainly is," Mistress Skinner said.

Leaning forward in the saddle, Aemilia handed him an envelope. "I've taken the liberty of intervening on your behalf and sent word to Southampton, who has agreed to provide you with his letter of credit to pay your expenses. He's written a personal letter as well."

The poet snatched the envelope from her and cast a furtive glance round, as though he longed to dash back into the boardinghouse and read Harry's missive in the privacy of his room. Meanwhile, Mistress Skinner's eyes threatened to pop out of their sockets.

"Bless me, an earl!" she cried, fanning herself with her hand. "Since when do you receive letters from earls, Master Shakestaff? Well, what does it say?"

With a snap of her riding crop, Aemilia cut the conversation short. "You can read the letter in the cart. Come, make haste! We must away before they close the harbor."

After racing in to pack his satchel, the poet climbed aboard the cart, wedging himself between Tabitha and Prudence. With Winifred driving the ox, Aemilia rode ahead, setting a swift pace. She told herself she wouldn't look back, but it was hard to ignore Tabitha's sobbing. Aemilia glanced over her shoulder to see the poet gently take the baby from Tabby. He cradled Enrico tenderly, as if the infant were his own.

THE WIND OFF THE Thames whipped Aemilia's sweat-slick hair and threatened to sweep away her hat. Clinging to the side of the merchant ship *Bonaventure*, her heart was in her throat to see Billingsgate harbor recede from view. Her first time aboard a ship, she could not quite get used to the pitching. What would it be like once they reached the open sea? London Bridge with its traitors' heads on spikes and even the Tower were soon lost from her sight. Papa had told her she would never be banished from her home, and yet here she was, retracing his journey.

Standing beside her, the poet likewise gazed back at the world they were leaving behind. She told herself that since she was traveling with him she must start thinking of him by his name. *Will,* she thought. *William.*

Will turned, as though about to say something to her, but stopped short at the sight of Jasper approaching them. As Aemilia introduced the two men, her cousin looked Will over critically, as if inspecting a bullock at a fair.

"In faith, I don't know what you see in him," Jasper said, after Will had gone to find his berth. "You honestly mean to take him all the way to Bassano? What if he should dishonor you? You're finally shot of Alfonse only to entangle yourself with a poor scribbler?"

"Peace, cousin," Aemilia said. "I could not command him to leave this ship even if I wanted. The Earl of Southampton is paying his passage, not you or I. Whether he chooses to travel to Bassano or sail all the way to the Levant is his own choice. Besides," she added cheerfully, "I am quite safe with Master Shakespeare. He's far more enamored of his fellow man."

Jasper reddened then shook his head. "You do befriend the oddest people."

A WHILE LATER, AEMILIA found Will staring out over the water, his face pensive, Southampton's letter clutched in his hand.

"Did Harry say anything amusing?" she asked him.

"He wants me to return to him as a man of the world," Will told her. There was something bittersweet in his voice, as if he were still reeling from the young Earl's capricious treatment of him. "A model of Italian sophistication."

"And no doubt to procure for him some choice Italian pornography like that ridiculous miniature of the courtesan," she said.

To her relief, Will laughed.

"Once in Italy, I may never return," she told him. "Though you might. But whilst we are there, I shall show you the cities I know only from my father's stories. Verona, Padua, Venice." She thrilled at the magical names, yet soon they would become more than names—she would see them with her own eyes.

"But why me?" Will asked yet again, looking her directly in the eye.

With no prying landlady or cousin listening in, Aemilia could finally speak her mind.

"I think we are both lost in the world and in need of a friend. Will you be my friend?"

Her words left him speechless. *Perhaps he is shocked by my candor,* she thought. No proper lady was as blunt and reckless as she was, carelessly speaking of pornography and then offering a strange man her friendship. But he suddenly took her hand as delicately as if it were a bird and kissed it.

"Friendship," he said, "is indeed a solace in this world."

She flushed to see him so formal. How much more at ease she was when he was his sardonic self, regarding her as a brazen interloper in his male world. But then, releasing her hand, he grinned at her as though they had known each other all their lives.

"Do you still wish to write comedies with me, Aemilia-Emilio?"

"Yes!" She laughed aloud in pleasure and relief. Even as the wind blasted against the sails, she felt herself grow warm and expansive as though she were sitting in the sunlight beneath an arbor of Veneto grapes. "About a man married to a clever and quick-witted shrew. She is Italian and never lacks for repartee. I shall show you what I've already written."

They found a place to sit out of the wind where Aemilia took the scrolled pages from her case so that Will could read the beginning of the play they would finish together.

"I've lost all sight of land," Tabitha lamented, as the ship barreled down the Channel toward the Atlantic. "What's to become of us? Will we ever see England again?"

"Give me that babe," said Prudence, easing Enrico from Tabby's arms. "Marry, you'll drown the poor mite with all that weeping."

While Pru fussed over the baby, Winifred squashed Tabby in her fierce embrace.

"At least we've escaped the plague, lovey," Winifred told Tabitha. "We're still together, all three of us. Why, we're off on a great adventure."

As if in mockery of her brave words, Winifred felt a queasiness climbing up her throat. When the ship breached a huge wave, she released Tabitha and rushed to the rail where she spewed and spewed into the seething foam, her stomach wrung inside out.

"My poor Winifred!" Tabby held her shoulders.

"I'll soon be right," Winifred grumbled. "Just a bit of seasickness."

But her heart dragged like an anchor.

"Our play thus far begins with Christophero Sly." Will peered down at the pages of quarto with many smudges and crossed-out lines. "A drunkard found lying senseless outside a tavern."

Aemilia shook her head and sighed. "First of all, Christophero isn't even proper Italian, let alone Sly. It's *Christoforo*, if you please. But can we not call him Alfonso?"

She turned to Winifred, who only snorted.

Aemilia and Will worked together in the cabin she shared with Enrico and the Weir sisters. She sat on her bed, which was built into a niche in the wall, while the poet perched on the water barrel. The two of them passed Aemilia's wooden lap desk back and forth as inspiration seized them. Dosed with Prudence's seasickness remedy, Winifred remained too queasy to even do her mending. Instead, she sat green faced beside Aemilia and observed the goings-on with heavy-lidded eyes, as though on guard, even in her debilitated condition, to shield her mistress from any improprieties.

"A noble hunting party stumbles across the drunkard and decides to play a prank on him," Will continued, pitching his voice to be heard over the ship's creaking. "They drag him unconscious to the manor house, dress him in fine garments, place him in the lord's bed, and then a page boy puts on a gown and masquerades as his lady wife."

"How our Harry will relish this scene," Aemilia said.

Will narrowed his eyes at her before reading on. "Then a troupe of players arrives in the noble bedchamber and there performs the tale of the shrew." With his Warwickshire accent, he pronounced the word *shrow*. "And thus, we have a play within a play."

"Set in Padua," Aemilia said, with some satisfaction.

The Italian setting was, of course, her contribution. She had named the heroine's father Battista, a man with three daughters, two beautiful and one quarrelsome, whom he had educated in music, Latin, and Greek. But any resemblance to her own father ended there. Battista in the play wanted to be rid of his difficult eldest daughter, Caterina, as soon as he could. As for Bianca and Emelia, the beautiful and desirable daughters—he was content to auction them off to the suitors who claimed the greatest fortune.

Winifred remained unimpressed. "I don't care if it's set in Cheapside Market, mistress. It's utter nonsense if you ask me. Worthless drunkards and page boys in skirts? I thought you were writing a romance."

Aemilia had never seen her maid this short-tempered. Winifred seemed to be convinced their vessel was bound not for Italy but hell, and were it not for her loyalty to her mistress, she would have muttered her prayers and hurled herself overboard the moment they left Billingsgate harbor.

"A romance by degrees." Will exchanged a smile with Aemilia. "Have some patience, good Winifred, and it will yet unfold."

Some of their work in progress Aemilia thought very good indeed. She thrilled at the poetry Will brought to their comedy, even as the pranksters sought to fool the drunkard into believing he was a wealthy lord.

> Dost thou love hawking? Thou hast hawks will soar
> Above the morning lark. Or wilt thou hunt?
> Thy hounds shall make the welkin answer them
> And fetch shrill echoes from the hollow earth.

Only none of the poetry in this play was of love. Perhaps Will was still too wounded by Harry to write of tender things, yet he seemed happy enough to write of a man and woman sparring with words. She adored writing of a spirited shrew instead of a beautiful, limp, docile heroine, but Will's idea to write of the *taming* of her beloved shrew stuck in her craw.

"The play will only work if Caterina is Petruchio's equal in wit," she told Will.

But he was just as stubborn as she. "It only succeeds if Kate—"

"*Caterina!*" Aemilia cried. "She's an Italian lady, not a Cripplegate tavern wench."

"If *Kate* and Petruchio love each other," the poet said, with his usual dogged insistence. "Thus far you've painted Petruchio as a callous fortune hunter who marries Kate for her dowry and then starves her into submission."

"Such men exist," she said, thinking of how her brother-in-law had turned her beautiful sister into a tortured ghost. If only Angela had been a shrew, she might have stood a chance.

"Oh, that they certainly do," Winifred said darkly, agreeing with her mistress for once.

"Are we to see our hero as a rank villain?" Will argued. "That's too cynical for me. Kate's only a shrew to scare off the suitors who are after her dowry. Once she meets her true match, her barbs and prickles melt away."

Aemilia and Winifred rolled their eyes.

"You would turn my shrew into a sheep," Aemilia said. "That speech of wifely obedience poor Caterina must parrot at the end is ridiculous! Tell me true, can you imagine Mistress Shakespeare uttering such nonsense without injuring herself laughing?"

"*I* certainly can't," Winifred said.

Will's face turned stony before he threw up his hands. "Well, how would you end it, then?"

"If she makes that silly speech, she must do it with her fingers crossed behind her back for all the audience to see," Aemilia said, with a complicit glance at Winifred. "And then Emelia, her sister, must tell Polidor, her bridegroom, that a shrew is better than a sheep."

"Oh, yes, mistress!" Winifred nodded vigorously. "That's the most sensible thing I've heard you say all day."

"And *then*," Aemilia continued, "the play ends with the drunkard Alfonso—"

"Christophero Sly!" Will shot in.

"—being dragged back outside the tavern where his pranksters first found him. There he awakens in the cold dawn. The taming of the shrew was but the vain fancy of a sot who can scarcely expect his wife to respect him, much less obey him."

At that, she snatched her lap desk from Will and began to scribble furiously.

"Mistress, have a care!" cried Winifred. "You're spilling ink on the blankets."

Will cleared his throat. "And now the scene when the suitors disguise themselves as tutors to gain an audience with Battista's younger daughters. Hortensio carries a lute whilst Lucentio and Biondello bring books. However, they can scarcely conceal their desire for Bianca and Emelia."

"Our Caterina sees straight through their ruse," said Aemilia, glancing over the written page. "And knows they seek only to seduce her sisters."

Winifred looked appalled. "Why, I would never stand for such a thing! If it were me, I'd take that lute and smash it over that lying scoundrel's head! That would teach him not to take liberties with my sisters!"

Will and Aemilia's eyes locked.

"Most excellent!" Aemilia cried.

He grabbed the lap desk and began to scribe. "Iron may hold Kate," he read aloud, "but never lutes. Hortensio emerges with the broken lute over his head as though he is wearing stocks about his neck. Petruchio, upon seeing evidence of Kate's violent temper, decides he loves her all the more. Now for the dialogue when Petruchio first meets Kate."

"*Caterina!*" Aemilia cried.

Standing on the swaying floorboards as the ship pitched and tossed, Will threw himself into character and before her eyes transformed into the swaggering Petruchio.

"Come, come, you wasp," he said. "In faith, you are too angry."

The way his eyes burned into hers reminded her for an instant of how he had gazed at Harry that midsummer night in Southampton House. Her face went hot and her belly grew slack. Then she wanted to slap herself. He was a playwright and a player by profession. He was *acting.* What was worse, he was grinning in triumph because his wit had left her tongue-tied.

Gathering herself together, she leapt to her feet and responded in kind, improvising her dialogue. "If I be waspish, best beware of my sting."

"My remedy," he said, raising an eyebrow, "is to pluck it out."

"Aye," she said, beginning to enjoy playing the unrepentant shrew, "if the fool could find where it lies."

Winifred sighed as though she were locked in a cell with two Bedlamites. "Who knows not where a wasp wears his sting?"

"In his tail," Will said, his eyes glistering into Aemilia's.

"In his tongue!" she cried.

"Whose tongue?"

"Yours," she said, gazing up at him, "if you talk of tails, and so farewell."

"What, with my tongue in your tail?" he said, with such verve that she found herself blushing. "Nay, come again. Good Kate, I am a gentleman."

"What is in your crest?" she demanded, for she couldn't allow his Petruchio to best her Caterina. "A coxcomb?"

This time she made him blush. She saw that her barb reached its target, for Will did not possess a family crest or coat of arms as she did. But he soon rallied.

"A combless cock, so Kate will be my hen."

"No cock of mine. You crow too much like a craven," she said, before a wave sent her tumbling into Will. She clung to him for an instant before the next wave sent them flying apart. Will sprawled on the floor while Aemilia fell into Winifred's lap. Both of them collapsed into helpless laughter.

"My word!" said Winifred. "How the pair of you do carry on! Any more talk of cocks and I'll be wringing the fowl's neck."

"Peace, Winifred," Aemilia said fondly. "It's only a play."

IV

Pierced by the Arrows of a God

15

CROSS THE WAVES, VENICE glimmered like a dream. Aemilia hugged Enrico close then reached for Jasper's hand. Tears blurred her first glimpse of the city where their fathers once dwelled. La Serenissima, the Most Serene Republic.

Had Papa only lived to see this day. She felt the loss of him as keenly as if he had died yesterday—Enrico would never know the grandfather who would have showered him in such love and pride. Her grief subsided in a rush—here her new life would begin. Turning to Will, she found him as rapt as she, his hazel eyes gleaming.

"Our fair pilgrim has reached the hallowed shore," he told her in his teasing fashion, as if she were the heroine of a brand-new play.

His words gave her pause for thought. Perhaps she was indeed a questing pilgrim, each station on her journey bringing her closer to her father's enigma. To the mystery of who she was.

THE *BONAVENTURE* ANCHORED IN the lagoon while the passengers and cargo bound for Venice floated toward the Piazza San Marco in a convoy of smaller boats. The journey from England had been slow, the *Bonaventure* moving in fits and starts, stopping at every major port while making its cumbersome way around Iberia and the Italian peninsula. With their fleeting forays into Calais, Lisbon, Malaga, and Naples, Aemilia reckoned that she and her traveling companions had seen a goodly glimpse of the great world. But Venice defied all comparison.

It was October, an auspicious time to arrive in this watery city, so

Jasper said, when the weather was mercifully mild and the season of summer fever and marsh sickness had passed.

As their boat drew nearer, Aemilia saw a column rising into the sky, topped with the winged lion of San Marco. The piazza appeared as a vast stage crowded with characters of every description. Black-skinned, white-turbaned youths helped them dock. *No one in this city will call me dark,* she thought. Not on this piazza where she might walk shoulder to shoulder with Africans and Turks.

"Are we in the Orient?" Will asked, holding her arm to steady her as she stepped ashore with Enrico in her arms. "Nowhere in Christendom have I seen such marvels. Marry, if this is where your people came from, I cannot fathom why they'd ever want to leave."

She waited with Jasper while Will handed the Weir sisters out of the boat. They, too, seemed transfixed. Even homesick Tabitha smiled beatifically as she took the baby from Aemilia's arms and planted a kiss on his head.

Enrico's eyes drank in everything. At nine months, Aemilia's son had grown into a hearty babe. To her joy, he seemed to thrive on this life of wandering that brought new sights and another language or dialect every day to fill his ears. If she stayed in Veneto, he would grow up speaking Italian. He would have no memory of England.

San Marco's basilica gleamed with gold and gem-bright mosaics, as sumptuous as a jewel box. The jumble of domes and half domes reminded her more of a palace than a church. Beside it, the Doge's Palace, with its sculpture-graced façade and its marble-pillared arcade and loggia, made Queen Elizabeth's Whitehall resemble a stable yard. Craning her neck, Aemilia stared up at the sculpted relief of a little girl in a boat, her one hand rising to the heavens to grasp the crescent moon while another hand reached into the water to catch a crab. Such exquisite art for all the world to see, from the highest-born aristocrats to the lowest galley slaves. The Doge was no monarch but the elected ruler of a republic where the law applied impartially to all. Over the palace's pinnacled grand entrance rose the statue of Justice with her sword and scales.

Aemilia uttered a startled cry as Will pulled her out of the way of a procession. Priests waved incense thuribles and bore the banner of Saint Pelagia of Antioch.

"Take note of the saint," her friend whispered. "A reformed courtesan who disguised herself as a man and lived as a hermit in the desert, her true sex being discovered only after her death."

Sometimes Will mystified her. From the tone of his voice, she couldn't tell if he was joking or speaking in earnest. Was he trying to tell her that if a *saint* might leave her old life behind and live as a man, then so might she?

Besides, how could she hope to compete in beauty or style with the Venetian ladies who floated across the piazza in a shimmer of diamonds, rubies, sapphires, and emeralds, each woman appearing to carry a fortune in gems and gold. The men were no less opulent in their mantles of velvet and sable, their oriental brocades.

Aemilia caught Will staring open mouthed at those handsome merchants' sons.

"The gentlemen of Venice are even more beautiful than your Earl of Southampton," she said lightly. "Do you not agree?"

"I was studying their clothes," he said, somewhat huffily, before he ran his hands over his patched doublet. "To them I must appear shabbier than the most wretched pauper in Cripplegate."

But Aemilia found it impossible not to notice how their journey had transformed him. Gone was the hungry, haunted look she remembered from his London days. His English skin was now bronzed by the Mediterranean sun. *Give him a new set of clothes*, she thought, *and he could hold his own among those handsome Italian men.* A flush crept over her cheeks before she steered her thoughts to more practical matters.

"Tomorrow we shall visit the vendors of used clothing," she told Will.

Indeed, she counted the seconds before she could trade her English weeds for garments made in this city to match these people and their gentle climate. But it was not a silk gown or a lace mantle she desired. In this foreign city where no one knew her name, she would become Emilio. Become a young man, his future wide open, a blank page on which she might write anything.

As a courtier on the Queen's official business, Jasper might have secured them guest rooms in the English ambassador's palazzo. Instead, owing to the secrecy surrounding their family's past, he chose an obscure but respectable inn on the Campo Santo Stefano. They were set to stay in Venice at least a week, their onward journey to Bassano delayed until Jasper fulfilled his obligations of buying instruments for the Queen's Musicke.

After her cousin rose early to make his rounds of the instrument-makers' workshops in the Castello district, Aemilia locked herself in her narrow chamber and, for the first time since leaving England, donned her linen shirt and doublet, her boots and breeches, her sword and rapier. Rather than hiding her long hair beneath her cap, she took Winifred's sewing shears and began to cut. The finality of those sharpened blades slicing through her locks thrilled her. Here she had no husband to appease, just her new self. When she had finished, she cast her chopped-off tresses into the smoldering fire and opened the shutters to release the stink of burning hair into the morning rain. Grabbing her steel mirror, she studied herself from every angle. A short and slender young man, his wavy black hair falling fashionably to his shoulders.

Jasper would not be pleased, but what could he do? Prudence would shake her head, Winifred would berate her to high heaven, and Tabitha would sigh, but she trusted the Weir sisters would not abandon her. Her son would have no memory of her life before this moment. She could live the rest of her life in this guise and only be unmasked posthumously like the saint in Will's story.

Will would probably agree that her bold and ebullient nature was more befitting a man than the woman she was. In faith, she and the poet had grown to be friends because Will saw beyond the woman. He saw her mind equal to his own. Together they had completed the comedy of the shrew. *What more might we pen now that we have at last arrived in Venice?* she wondered. They must go to the theater, not only so they could experience the commedia dell'arte firsthand, but also so they could see female players sharing the stage with male actors.

AEMILIA STOLE DOWN THE back staircase before emerging on the Campo Santo Stefano, where she had arranged to meet Will. Spinning in a circle, she saw no sign of him. They had agreed to meet at ten bells, but when she glanced at the clock tower, she saw she was nearly half an hour late.

Scanning the *campo*, she sighted her friend vanishing into the immense brick church of Santo Stefano, perhaps to seek shelter from the rain. Sprinting across the wet cobbles, she reveled in the freedom of wearing boots and breeches again. In only seconds, she reached the church, but once she was inside, the dim silence swallowed her. The churches she knew in England were plain inside, with stark white-washed walls and no image to be seen save for the plain cross. But this was a grotto smelling of frankincense, with candles glittering at the feet of countless statues. Anne Locke and Lady Susan would have fainted at the sight of such idolatrous display. Aemilia observed the alternating red and white marble pillars dividing the aisles from the nave, then she arched her neck to view the ceiling, which resembled the keel of an upturned ship.

Monks, some in dark robes and a few in white, prowled the aisles, one giving her a long disapproving stare. She froze at the thought that he could see straight through her disguise. Or was it her sword and rapier he shunned? It occurred to her that she was completely out of her depth, that she had no clue how to behave in a Catholic church. *Have pity on a poor foreigner,* she wanted to shout. Then it struck her, like a blast of cold wind, that she was even more an alien here in the land of her father's birth than she had been back in England. *Where in this wide world do I belong?* Did she have a true home anywhere or was she doomed to be forever in exile?

Her eyes darted across the church until she finally found Will on his knees, his hands folded in prayer, gazing intently at the marble statue of the Virgin, illumined by a sea of votive candles. This act of devotion could have seen him arrested back in England. Aemilia bowed her head. So it appeared that Will was a secret Catholic, just as her father had been a secret Jew. Her friend had kept his true faith hidden. Even witnessing yesterday's procession, he had been careful not to give himself away. As she did, the poet wore a mask.

Even when he sprang to his feet, Will seemed overcome with reverence and gratitude. How easily he was being drawn into this world. Will, she decided, might make a better Italian than she.

After blinking in his surprise at seeing her as Emilio, he smiled as openly as though she were that dashing young man. His sworn friend. Her heart quickened in a burst of joy.

"I'm not especially pious," Will told her, as they walked together toward the canal. "But I am loyal. My three successive schoolmasters at Stratford Grammar School were secret Jesuits. I've rarely met men of such lofty ideals. What risks they took even setting foot in England, just to educate ordinary boys. They believed they could draw out the best in me and create something greater than anyone would expect of a glover's son."

"You follow their faith," she said quietly. "Because they had faith in you."

She thought how grateful she was to Anne Locke and Lady Susan, yet she had failed to find solace in their stern religion.

Leaning close, Will confided how the last of his teachers, John Cottam, had been betrayed and sentenced as a traitor. The man had been hanged, drawn, and quartered.

"Whenever I walked past those poor corpses spiked on Cripplegate," he said, "all I could think of was Master Cottam. What a debt I owe him. If only I could give something great to the world to vindicate him."

"Don't we all yearn to bring glory to those who believed in us," she murmured.

In a gesture of solace, she took his arm. In Italy men might walk arm in arm and no one thought ill of it. But as she gripped his sleeve and felt the warm muscle beneath the worn cloth, the thrill of the forbidden rippled through her. This was the first time she and Will had walked out alone together, an unthinkable breech of propriety for Aemilia. But as Emilio, she could do as she pleased.

When they reached the canal, she flagged down a gondola to take them to the Ghetto.

"We wish to buy clothing," she explained to the gondolier.

The best used-clothing vendors in Venice could be found in the Ghetto, so she had heard. Her heart drummed in anticipation. Soon she would arrive at the place where Papa and his brothers would have dwelled had they not elected to wear their masks.

"Two English *signori!*" the gondolier cried. "You shall not be disappointed. Our secondhand markets have richer clothes than you will find anywhere else. Soon you will be dressed like dukes!"

This young man appeared to be of Moorish ancestry, but he dressed and behaved like any other Venetian. Aemilia found his dialect nearly impenetrable until he sighed and spoke in loud, simple words, as though speaking to children.

"To reach the Ghetto, we must first pass through the Rialto, *signori*, where you shall see many beautiful *cortigiani*!"

"What's he saying?" Will asked.

"He intends to take us through the district where the courtesans ply their trade," she said archly. "Pity Harry couldn't join us."

"There is a great thick book!" the gondolier shouted, pitching his voice over the other boatmen crowding the canal. "With the names of all the *cortigiani*, their prices, their special games, and the height of their chopines, their high shoes."

Aemilia translated for Will, whose eyes widened considerably. Her friend appeared altogether too intrigued by this information for her liking.

"Might we go a different way and avoid the *cortigiani*?" she asked the gondolier. "We mustn't shock my friend. He was educated by Gesuiti."

Her plea was in vain. Soon they passed beneath the Ponte delle Tette where, despite the rain, women and girls stood with their breasts bared. Aemilia's face burned. How was she to keep up this masquerade when she wanted to clap her hands over her eyes? Here she was in Italy, embarking on her new life as Emilio, but she had never felt so much like an Englishwoman. How must those courtesans feel, exposed like that in the October chill?

"*Signore*, you lied," the gondolier observed. "It is *you*, not your friend, who is ashamed to look at the *cortigiani*. Your friend likes them very much. I can see his codpiece jumping up!"

A shock ran through Aemilia. One glimpse of Will's face revealed that he, indeed, appeared transported to the gates of paradise. She didn't dare look at him below the chin, but the swaying of the gondola kept knocking his thigh against hers. She tried to edge away only to keep sliding back into him.

Will's elbow jabbed her ribs. "Pray, gentle Emilio, why have you stopped translating?"

His gales of laughter sent the gondola rocking even harder.

"You trickster!" she hissed. "I thought you were a lover of men."

His eyes danced. "There are more things in heaven and earth, Emilio, than are dreamt of in your philosophy."

Aemilia squirmed as she remembered reassuring Jasper that she had no cause to fear anything untoward from Will. To think she could be so naïve. *God's teeth, the man sired three children!*

"How shall you hope to pass as a man in a man's world," Will asked her amiably, "if you shrink each time you see a bare-breasted courtesan?"

But I was a courtesan! The mere sight of those women and girls mirrored everything Aemilia longed to escape, all the degradation heaped upon her own sex. The way Southampton had spoken of her that night in his house, as if she were a Venetian *cortigiana* no different from those standing on the Ponte delle Tette.

"It's not enough to wear the guise," Will said, speaking now with gentle sobriety. "You must play the part and stay in character through every circumstance."

Meanwhile, the gondolier was staring at Aemilia in a way that made her stomach constrict. Had he guessed that she was a woman?

"*Signore,* our *cortigiani* are so cunning, they know a trick that will lure even one such as you. The slyest of them will put on breeches and a codpiece, then lure unsuspecting gentlemen with cultured conversation."

"What did he say?" Will asked, no longer looking at the courtesans but only at her. "Has he offended you?"

He reached for her hand, but she shoved him away.

"And the Church?" The gondolier cackled. "She allows this! For it is better that a man should sleep with a *cortigiana* in breeches than with another man."

Leaving the Rialto and its courtesans behind, the gondolier navigated the narrow canals of the Cannaregio, a poorer district with unpaved streets and taverns reeking of sour wine. They floated past workshops, their windows open to release the racket of carpenters and ironsmiths.

Turning a corner, they approached a small isle surrounded by canals and fortressed by tall scabrous walls. What doors and windows had originally been built were bricked up. Boats with armed guardsmen were on patrol.

"Is this a place of punishment?" Will asked, his face as somber as those confining walls. "Marry, even the Tower of London has windows."

"Here we arrive at the Ghetto!" the gondolier cried out, guiding his craft to the guarded entrance gate. "You recognize the Jews for they wear the red caps. Don't linger here too long, *signori*. They lock the gates at sunset."

Aemilia's heart rattled like a chain. "It looks so small. I thought the Ghetto would be bigger."

The gondolier shrugged. "It is the most crowded place in Venice. The Jews live stacked on top of one another like chickens and they still keep coming. Because our Doge is tolerant, they come from every corner of Europe, even from Turkey and the Levant. But I don't mind as long as they stay inside their Ghetto. It's the Marranos I despise."

"The Marranos," Aemilia said, her voice as flat as a plank.

"Jews who pretend they are no Jews!" The gondolier raised his hands in a gesture of disgust. "They live among us, go to our churches, marry our sisters. But they are still Jews. One was discovered in the house of a *cortigiana*, who reported him to the Inquisition. The whore knew at once he was a Jew because he was circumcised. Ha, ha!"

Aemilia clenched her jaw and hauled herself onto the landing. She waited in the open gateway, her arms tightly crossed in front of her. Even in Venice, the Inquisition could strike. Was that why her father and uncles had fled to England? Why stay in a city where the mere act of disrobing could end in tragedy? She considered her own guise, what peril she would face if her artifice was unmasked.

After paying the gondolier, Will came to stand beside her. "I still don't understand. Is this a prison?"

She explained as best she could, drawing on what she had learned from Jasper. "They may come and go as they please during the day, but at sundown they must return to the Ghetto and stay there until the bells of San Marco ring the next morning. On Church holidays and during Holy Week, the Jews are confined in these walls night and day."

As they passed through the gate and entered the crowded *campo*, she saw scores of men in red caps. Many were bearded, but some were clean shaven. One man so strongly resembled Papa, she felt her knees grow weak. The illusion was so strong, she had to beat back the urge to throw her arms around the stranger's neck.

"I've never seen a Jew before," Will whispered. "Have you? Look, some are wearing turbans."

The staccato of different tongues swirled around them. Various Italian dialects, as well as German, Portuguese, Spanish, Greek, and more exotic languages. Turkish, Aemilia guessed.

She and Will wove their way across the *campo* through the teeming mass of bodies. Thousands of souls, it seemed, lived in this confined space — this *campo* and one street beyond it with its alleyways and passageways, which she and Will reached by crossing a guarded bridge. She gazed up at the buildings, which rose so high, story upon story, with the windows facing only inward on the Ghetto.

From an upper window, she caught an achingly familiar melody that made her stop in her tracks and listen even though she couldn't understand a word of it. A sense of indescribable joy and wonder enveloped her. Suddenly, she was a little girl again, listening to Papa and her uncles singing their forbidden songs in the cellar. So these songs were not just something that had transpired in her childhood home; they were also a part of something much bigger, an entire world she now saw unfolding around her, connecting her to her lost father. *Everything I see here is a part of him — and a part of me.*

It astounded her that what appeared to be a prison on the outside could also be a precious refuge where Jews could live without artifice.

"You're so quiet," Will said. "Why are you smiling like that?"

Earlier this very day, inside the church of Santo Stefano, Will had revealed his secret Catholicism to her. She wondered if she would ever dare to reveal her secret to him. Jasper would be furious if she divulged their family's Jewish history — her cousin would regard this as an unpardonable act of betrayal.

"It's a city within a city," she told Will, trying to express her fascination without giving herself away. She waved her arm to encompass the Levantine merchants' warehouses and the women bearing baskets of almonds, grapes, and figs. "To think all this can flourish here behind such forbidding walls."

Vending stalls sold candles, wine, hats, and books. Greengrocers, butchers, barbers, tailors, and alchemists plied their trades in these narrow alleys. This would have been Papa's entire universe had he chosen to stay here and live openly as a Jew. He would have never come to England, never met Margaret Johnson. Aemilia would have never been born. Instead, he might have had another daughter, a Jewish daughter.

Reaching the dead end where the unpaved street met the boundary wall, she and Will turned and retraced their steps back to the main *campo* where dozens of Venetian Christians queued up outside the pawnshops and money lenders—the Banco Rosso, Banco Nigro, and Banco Verde. At ground level, all around the *campo*, she saw the vendors of used clothes and remembered her original intention—to purchase the garments that would transform her and Will into gentlemen, for here in this watery city they could claim to be anything as long as they looked the part.

A young man beckoned them as they approached a narrow shop front. In his sarcenet hose, he was arrayed in the height of fashion. He wore his red cap at such a jaunty angle as to make it almost stylish.

"*Signori*, you are English," he said. "I can tell because the rain doesn't bother you. And you wear *riding boots*" —he cast a pointed look at Aemilia— "in a city with no horses!"

"Then it is your task, *signore*," she said, "to clothe us in the Venetian *moda*. We have eight ducats to spend between us. What can you provide?"

The young man waved his empty hand to the sky. "Good clothes are expensive, *signore*! Many of the *cortigiani* of the Rialto do not even own their own gowns—did you know this? They must rent them from their pimps."

Aemilia translated for Will. Buying used clothing, it appeared, was a far more complicated and costly procedure than she had first envisioned. Will suggested they try their luck at another stall. But when they turned to go, the young man's father, a bearded man in black fustian, intervened.

"We can clothe you for a good price, *signori*," he said. "If my son tries to coax you to spend more, it's only because the rent and taxes we must pay to the Doge are so high. They rise every year. So we must struggle for every ducat."

With no further ado, father and son sifted through their boxes of used garments.

"First, the younger *signore*," the vendor's son said. "Look at the elegant costume I have chosen for you."

Aemilia was dazzled as he held out a shirt of whitest cambric and a doublet of dove-gray damask. To wear over the doublet, he presented a severe black jerkin, boned and padded to create a fashionably masculine silhouette. Next he held up a pair of rose-colored slops in the Venetian style, long and voluminous, that tied below the knees. Then came dove-gray nether socks and a pair of thin-soled shoes in butter-soft calfskin that would allow her to steal along as silently as an assassin.

Inspecting each garment, she found evidence of previous use—mended tears and stains that had been laundered to near invisibility. But for the price, they were more than adequate. After she was shown into the tiny changing booth with its steel mirror, the transformation astounded her. Would Jasper even recognize her?

Bursting out of the booth, she fairly swaggered before Will, whose eyebrows rose to his hairline.

"Clothes make the man," he told her, with a wink.

But beneath his banter, Aemilia caught something potent sparking in his eyes, as though these garments had truly transformed her into a young gallant—one who captured his desire. The thought left her shaking. In a rush of air, she inhaled. *Don't be ridiculous. He's your friend.*

The vendor eyed her critically.

"The slops fit well enough, but the doublet and jerkin should be taken in," he said, approaching her with his needle and thread.

Aemilia warded him off with flailing palms—how easily her secret might be revealed.

"That's quite all right, *signore*," she told him. "We English are quite fond of loose garments."

"And now for you, *signore*," the vendor said to Will.

The vendor and his son selected a linen shirt, a small ruff, a pinked doublet of olive green, hose of dark russet, black nether socks, boots that rose halfway up the calf, and a sweeping black surcoat.

When the poet emerged from the changing booth, it was as though Aemilia saw him for the first time. Styled in the very height of Venetian sophistication, his sleek new garments hugged and accentuated the slender, muscled contours of his torso and thighs. The olive-green doublet set his clouded hazel eyes darkly aglow.

"Do you like what you see, good Emilio?" Will asked, catching her in the act of staring at him stupidly, as though she were an infatuated girl. He grinned at her until her temples pounded.

"If only our dear Harry could see you now," Aemilia said drily, to hide her embarrassment.

In his few words of Italian, Will thanked the vendor profusely and was content to allow the man and his son to take in his seams until the garments were perfectly tailored.

"And your old things?" the vendor asked. "Do you wish to keep them? We couldn't offer you much for these."

Will parted from his old clothes without a second's hesitation, but Aemilia clung to hers, her beloved disguise that had been her salvation. She certainly wasn't going to part with her riding boots, for no matter where she went, she wanted to be able to make a quick escape if necessary, not trip and flounce in stylish slippers.

After Aemilia and Will had paid, the vendor and his son began to close up shop.

"Why do you close your business in the middle of the day?" she couldn't keep herself from asking.

"We are going to hear our young rabbi speak," the vendor said. "Leone da Modena. So great is his fame that bishops and foreign ambassadors come to listen to him."

"Might we come as well?" Aemilia asked, her voice rising unintentionally high, causing the vendor's son to throw her a curious look.

"Since it isn't the Shabbat, anyone may come," the vendor said. "The great rabbi speaks in Latin so that every educated visitor will understand him."

"This is our chance to hear a great rabbi," she told Will, seizing his arm and not giving him a chance to refuse.

Carrying her boots and old clothes in a cloth satchel the vendor had given her, she followed the man and his son across the *campo* toward the Scuola Grande Tedesca, distinguishable as a synagogue on the outside only by its row of five arched windows.

"For the five books in the Torah," the vendor's son explained. He kept shooting her covert glances as if he found something unaccountably strange about this young Englishman.

Trying to ignore the young man's inquisitive gaze, Aemilia followed his father up the stairs to the second floor, entering a high-ceilinged, irregularly shaped chamber, as packed as the *campo* below, with red-hatted Jews jostling with Christian visitors, including a small number of monks and priests. But as her eyes scanned the assembly, she saw not a single female.

"Are no women permitted entrance?" she hazarded to ask.

The vendor's face darkened. "What interest do you have in our women?"

She dropped her eyes to the floor in humiliation.

His son leaned over to whisper in her ear. "The women are up in the gallery. Behind the screen."

She followed his gaze to a pillared balustrade with an intricately carved screen above it, behind which shadowy figures shifted and murmured. If Papa had remained here, his Jewish daughter would be up there, peering at the men below.

Had her father ever stood in this room? The synagogue was as foreign a place as she had ever found herself in. Even in Santo Stefano, the first Catholic church she had ever set foot in, she had known how to tell the high altar from the baptismal font. Where was the altar here —on that raised platform? What was stored in that cabinet with the arched double doors on the far end of the room?

A stir went through the crowd as a man who appeared to be no older than her twenty-four years swept in and mounted the platform. Aemilia struggled to see him above the men's hatted heads. Even when she managed to catch a glimpse of the young rabbi, he appeared to her as a blur filled with frenetic energy, gesticulating as he spoke. His sermon, if that's what it was, seemed directed toward the Gentile visitors, especially the monks and priests, rather than his Jewish congregation.

"A Jew was claiming repayment for a large debt from a gentleman in Ferrara," Leone da Modena began, in an engaging tone, "which included hundreds of ducats of interest."

The crowd seemed to contemplate the enormity of such a debt and what lay at stake for both the debtor and the moneylender.

"However," the rabbi continued, "the gentleman alleged it was illegal for the Jew to take interest from a Christian. A rabbi had even written an attestation in favor of the Christian while other rabbis had written in favor of the Jew. The most illustrious cardinal then sent for me and asked me whether or not it was legitimate for a Jew to take interest from a Christian."

Aemilia glanced at Will, who seemed to listen with full concentration. She envied her friend his superior height, for he must have a clearer view of the young rabbi than she did.

"My answer," Leone da Modena said, "was 'No, your grace, and, yes, your grace.' 'Explain yourself,' said the cardinal. So I quoted Deuteronomy 23:19, which says thou shalt not lend to thy brother at interest. The Christian is our brother and can't be lent to at interest. And therefore, I said, 'No, your grace.'"

Here the rabbi paused. The room fell silent and Aemilia held her breath, awaiting his next word.

"But that is not all I told the cardinal." A touch of both humor and melancholy danced in the rabbi's voice. "I told him, 'If the Christian treated us like brothers and let us live as his citizens and subjects, and did not forbid us the familiarity in all dealings, the purchase of real estate, many trades, and in certain places such as Venice even the mechanical arts and infinite other prohibited trades, we would be equally obliged to acknowledge him as brother.'"

The word *brother* filled the air with bittersweet longing before Leone da Modena delivered his concluding salvo.

"'But if he treats us like slaves,' I told the cardinal, 'we, as slaves, would find it legitimate to lend at interest for the sake of our own survival. And therefore, I say yes.' The most illustrious cardinal, with a grave laugh, placed his hand on my shoulder and ruled in favor of the Jew.'"

Aemilia's vision blurred with tears, for in a few sentences the young rabbi had conjured all the suffering and injustice that lay at the heart of

Papa's tragedy, the loss and exile that good man was forced to endure. To think her father had intended to keep her in ignorance of his true identity, of who he most deeply was, keep her in exile from his people and their truths. At least the women behind the screen knew who they were, knew what to call themselves. What or who was she? Neither truly Christian—for Anne Locke's God left her cold—nor a real Jew, for she knew nothing about her father's religion, his secret language, or his prayers. Whether she dressed as a woman or a man, whether she called herself Aemilia or Emilio, she was just a mask with nothing behind it. An empty shell. A player in a tragicomedy uttering lines written by someone else.

"What's wrong with your friend?" she heard the vendor's son ask Will. "Why does he weep like a girl?"

"I, TOO, WAS MOVED by the rabbi's speech," said Will, his hand on Aemilia's shoulder as they walked out of the Ghetto's gate in search of a gondola that would take them back to their lodgings. "But you must learn to hide your tears lest you betray your tender female heart. The clothier's son suspected. I'll wager he was half besotted with you." There was a catch in Will's voice that confused her. He opened his mouth, as if about to say more, then ducked his head.

Wiping her eyes on her sleeve, Aemilia's throat brimmed with everything she couldn't bring herself to tell him. Since she didn't dare speak of her father, she asked Will about his.

He grimaced. "A debtor and a disgrace, John Shakespeare is. An overambitious glover who laid waste to my mother's dowry. Thanks to him, the very name Shakespeare is a thing of dishonor. Pray, let us speak of happier things."

Only when they took their seats in a gondola did his mood seem to lighten.

"What if we were to write a comedy," Will said, his eyes full of mischief, "a romance of a young Jewish clothier in the Venice Ghetto who falls in love with a girl masquerading as a boy."

Aemilia tried to smile. Then he grew more serious.

"Or a Jewish moneylender's daughter in love with a Christian," he mused.

"A romance of a Jew's daughter." Aemilia tried to picture her phantom sister, her phantom self. "Could it be a comedy or would it end in tragedy?"

"That remains to be seen." His eyes lingering on her face, Will gave her new black jerkin a tug. "The clothier was right—you need to get those seams taken in, otherwise you'll look like a boy in his father's clothes."

BACK AT THE INN on Campo Santo Stefano, Aemilia opened her chamber door to find Jasper and the Weir sisters awaiting her. Only Enrico smiled, showing off his milk teeth as he crawled across the floor to pat his podgy hands on her new thin-soled shoes.

"Mama," he said, for her guise made no difference to him at all.

Scooping her son off the floor, she buried her face in the crook of his neck to hide from Jasper's look of utter shock and disappointment.

"How could you just disappear like that, alone in a foreign city?" Her cousin's voice shook. "Have you any idea how worried we were?"

Stunned, Aemilia stared at him. Around his neck was a pendant cross she had never before seen. What would Jasper say if she told him she had spent the day in the Ghetto?

"Forgive me," she murmured, unable to take her eyes off the pendant. "But I wasn't alone. Master Shakespeare accompanied me."

At the very mention of the poet's name, Jasper's face hardened. "And was it he who encouraged you to buy those ill-fitting weeds? Aemilia, I took you here so you could finally lead a decent life with no more sneaking about."

To think her cousin would upbraid her so harshly in front of the Weir sisters. Even in Venice, in her male guise, she was subject to a man's condemnation.

"Do you not remember, Jasper, it was you who first dared me to wear your old breeches when we were children and ran off to the Shoreditch playhouse?" She yearned to coax a smile from him.

"We aren't children anymore." Jasper's eyes were stark. "You know it's a crime—you could endanger us all." He sighed. "I only wished to see you at peace."

Turning away from her, her cousin let himself out of the room.

The Weir sisters remained like statues, silent and wooden, until Winifred heaved herself to her feet.

"Mistress mine, for all we knew, you'd drowned in the lagoon."

Aemilia trembled to see the tears in her maid's eyes. Before Aemilia could say a word, Tabby took Enrico from her while Winifred and Prudence opened the sewing box, preparing to take in her seams.

16

EMILIA STOOD AT HER chamber window and watched Jasper stride across the *campo* and disappear down an alley, embarking on yet another exhaustive tour of the instrument-makers' workshops of the Castello. Though she'd suspected he would disapprove of her male guise, the dressing-down he'd given her yesterday left her wretched. Jasper had never spoken to her so harshly before. The only soul who seemed to truly understand her was Will. They had known each other a mere four months, yet he already felt like a kindred spirit.

Turning away from the window, she observed the Weir sisters, who seemed as restless as hens cooped up in too small a space.

"Why don't you go to the markets," she said, handing Winifred a small bag of coins. "Take Enrico with you."

Tabitha was already speaking enough Italian, Aemilia reasoned, to get by at the marketplace.

"If you say so, mistress." Winifred insisted on addressing her that way even when Aemilia stood before her in breeches. "I think you should get some air yourself. My stars, I've never seen you so wan."

Aemilia closed her eyes as Winifred's palm caressed her cheek. Though her new clothes now fit her like a second skin, she had the jitters about venturing forth by daylight after having come so close to giving herself away the day before, weeping in the synagogue. Venice unhinged her. Papa's presence seemed so tangible, not even a breath away. His ghost walked these narrow streets and footbridges. What if she stepped out that door only to lose her wits again, coming undone before strangers?

A soft tapping sounded on the door.

Prudence opened it. "Master Shakespeare."

"Good morning, sir," Tabitha said. She was fond of him for the way he doted on Enrico.

But Will's eyes fixed on Aemilia's downcast face.

"Is something the matter?" he asked, his voice rising in alarm. "Is the child not well?"

Aemilia was touched by his concern. "My boy is as right as rain, thank the heavens."

She watched Will swing Enrico in his arms until the little lad shrieked with delight. *How he must miss his own children,* she thought.

"Did you not say we would see the commedia dell'arte today?" he asked her.

For him, this city has no ghosts. Will's Venice, she thought, *is a treasure box and he longs to caress its every jewel.* But in order to do so, he needed her to be his translator, his interpreter, his guide through this labyrinth. Grinning for the first time that day, she swirled her cape around her shoulders. Will's dear face, alight with enthusiasm, would be her talisman against the demons that chased her.

With Will, she felt like herself again — the self she aspired to be. As they clattered down the stairs and set off across the *campo,* her spirits leapt free. Most of all, she was grateful for his lack of judgment. Whether she appeared to him as Aemilia or Emilio, he was her friend, as true a friend as she had ever had.

The temporary stage was set up at San Cassiano near the Rialto market. Though the acting troupe had yet to appear, a sizable crowd had gathered, attracting a swarm of peddlers.

A pushcart vendor, seeking to impress Will with his wares, waved a picture in the poet's face that left him doubled over with helpless laughter.

"What is it?" Aemilia stepped close to see.

"You want to buy one, *signore?*" the peddler asked her, as if anxious to salvage his self-importance while Will heaved in hilarity. "I will give you my best price!"

The peddler brandished a painted miniature of a courtesan whose skirt flap lifted to reveal breeches beneath. It was nearly identical to the curiosity piece that Southampton so coveted. Far from being a rare, priceless work of erotica, Harry's treasure was cheaply painted pornography that anyone with a few *denari* might buy.

"You don't like it?" the peddler demanded. "What about this one?"

A miniature of a nun who—when her skirt flap was lifted—proved to be a courtesan beneath her habit. Will and Aemilia shook their heads, still laughing, and prepared to turn away when the peddler lost his patience.

"You love your coins too much to spend them, *signori*? Are you Jews?"

Aemilia reeled as though the man had punched her.

Will gripped her arm. "What did he say?"

Too angry to speak, she spat on the ground where the peddler had stood. Her eyes wandered off into the crowd. Everywhere she looked she saw lovers sharing kisses. Though Italian girls from good families were not allowed out unchaperoned, young women of the servant and artisan classes might court freely as long as any babies were born within the bounds of wedlock.

The couples' love-struck faces drove a blade into Aemilia's heart. To think she had once been that young and full of hope. She shook to recall the way desire had possessed her, driving her to gallop after Lord Hunsdon. The way she had surrendered to him, dissolving in bliss as he played her body like an instrument. She had gone from being his courtesan to a sexless thing that could scarcely bear to look at courtesans—or courting lovers.

All her desire had died the moment Lord Hunsdon had so unceremoniously washed his hands of her and given her in marriage to a man she despised. She would have to spend the rest of her life paying for what to him had been a passing pleasure. The only way for a woman like her to survive in this world was by remaining dispassionate. Friendship could be her solace but never love. Never again.

Now an old woman selling card decks approached her. She pressed a pack into Aemilia's hand and allowed her to shuffle through them and examine the intricately painted images. A lady in a sumptuous gown rode a white horse and carried an unsheathed sword as though she were a female knight errant. A woman in a nun's habit sat enthroned and crowned in the papal triple tiara. The deck was old and well-worn, its edges wrinkled and nicked, its paint fading in places or smudged by fingerprints. Still, it seemed a precious thing. She passed the cards to Will, who appeared just as enchanted as she.

"Ask her how much she wants for them," he said. "I shall buy them for you."

"For me?" she asked, utterly astonished.

"Why can I not give you a gift when you have given me so much? Am I to be only the receiver?"

"They are *tarocchi* cards," the old woman said, smiling at Will while Aemilia translated. "You can play the game of *trionfi* with them, *signori*. Or you can use them to discover what Fortuna has in store."

Her gnarled hand revealed a card depicting the goddess of fate and the ever-turning wheel of fortune.

After some haggling, Aemilia and the old woman settled on a price and Will bought her the cards. Delighted, she shuffled through them until she came to a trump bearing the image of a great globe.

"Look!" she told Will. "Fortuna shall give us the world!"

A cheer exploded from the crowd, for the players had arrived and soon the show would begin. There was much shuffling and chattering behind the patched canvas curtains. Pressing her way forward, Aemilia found a space to stand at the very lip of the stage.

A man in a mask and a faded satin costume stepped from between the curtains.

"Fair citizens of Venice," he said, in a rustic dialect, "today we present to you *La Mirtilla,* a pastoral! For we've come from the countryside to bring its romance to your city."

As he spoke, a bewitchingly beautiful girl, her long blond hair streaming like a mermaid's, squeezed her way through the crowd to collect *soldi* and *denari* for the players.

"Why can't a city as rich as Venice have a proper playhouse?" Will whispered, after they had paid the girl. "This ramshackle thing looks like it might collapse in a strong wind."

"The ladies will enjoy our play, too," the man on stage said, continuing his speech. "For this play was written by a lady, the great Isabella

Andreini, who performed at the wedding of Ferdinando de Medici and Christine de Lorraine."

The women in the audience shouted their praises for La Andreini. Aemilia felt light-headed. So the commedia dell'arte not only featured female players but also female playwrights who staged their creations in the highest aristocratic circles? She had never imagined such a thing. What if her mask was unnecessary and she could write as a woman under her own name?

A boy moved through the crowd selling cups of pale Veneto wine for less money than Aemilia would have paid for milk in England. She and Will raised their cups to each other.

"Did you know that in ancient Greece, the theater was part of Dionysus's cult?" she asked him.

"The god of wine and ecstasy!" Her friend threw back his head, as if reveling in this. "No wonder the Puritans despise the theater—it's heathen to the core."

Minstrels played pipes and viols as the patched curtains opened to reveal the masked figures of Venus and her son, Amore, who lamented that mortals blamed him for their broken hearts. His mother offered her counsel.

> But you with your wings carry your followers
> to heaven, and time cannot damage
> your powers, nor can death itself,
> because you do not love fleeting beauty,
> but that beauty which is celestial and divine . . .
> You alone are the life in the life
> Of every created thing.

Aemilia cast a glance at Will, who appeared transfixed by his first glimpse of a female player, a mature woman with a deep bosom and dark golden hair. They could even smell her violet perfume. How majestic she was, speaking in her natural voice. The lisping boy actors back in England with their padded chests and rouged lips couldn't hope to compare. Will's eyes shone.

"That's what our English comedy writers forget," he whispered in her ear. "Winged Cupid is a *god*. To fall in love is to be pierced by the arrows of a god."

His words sent a shiver through her.

The *innamorati*, or young lovers, entered the stage — three shepherd boys and three nymphs. These were the only players who remained unmasked. How they suffered from the pangs of love! The nymphs Filli and Mirtilla both pined for Uranio, who desired Ardelia, who loved only herself. Iglio courted Filli in vain. Tirsi proposed to Mirtilla, but she rejected him, which only inflamed him all the more.

Though he struggled to understand the Italian, Will soon seemed to grasp the plot. "It's a pastoral like so many others I've seen," he whispered. "Save for the masks and the female players. And yet the heroines change everything."

The actresses played their roles with wit and aplomb. Far from being helpless damsels or mere objects of desire, they were fully fleshed characters, cunning and clever, giving as good as they got. Only Ardelia was as silent, chaste, and docile as a girl was supposed to be, yet she was so vain and foolish that she, like Narcissus, fell in love with her own reflection and the audience could only laugh at her.

The comedy darkened into tragicomedy when the satyr Satiro stalked the nymph Filli. The masked actor played his role with such menace that Aemilia felt her heart pound and her throat go dry.

> If she won't surrender to my will,
> I'll do her a thousand outrages!
> Neither her beauty nor her loud cries
> nor her request for mercy will help her!

But Filli, as wily as a seasoned courtesan, declared that she desired Satiro as much as he desired her and that she would do anything he wished if only he would first let her tie him to a tree. Once she had him bound, she yanked his beard and pinched him mercilessly while he bewailed his humiliation.

The courtesans and market wives in the crowd roared their approval, yelling, *"Brava!"*

Aemilia cheered herself hoarse. Never before on stage had she witnessed such a spirited heroine — neither a victim nor a scheming temptress nor even a shrew, but a resourceful young woman who knew how to survive and even triumph in a dangerous world.

Moved by the ecstasy of the moment, lifted outside of herself by the applause and the wine, Aemilia clasped Will's hand. He gazed at her, his eyes softening as she felt the heat rise in her face. She stared at their joined hands then, laughing in apology, tried to release him. But he held on for another moment, as if reluctant to let go.

The play concluded with Filli and Mirtilla saving their lovers' lives and accepting their proposals. Even Ardelia, haunted by the fear of losing her beauty and growing old alone, embraced Uranio. The three happy couples laid garlands of thanksgiving on the altar of Venus and Amore.

The play left Aemilia buoyant, as though she could float off on a cloud, and Will's happiness mirrored her own. How sparkling their own comedies would be if they could create heroines as fresh and witty as Filli.

Mirth seemed to settle on the entire crowd. Aemilia noted the camaraderie between the laughing young courtesans and the older market wives who offered the girls pears and honeyed hazelnuts. They appeared not to judge these girls but rather to acknowledge the world as it was and what a young woman must do to carve out a life for herself.

Presently, the courtesans returned to their usual commerce. Two young women sidled up to them, towering over Aemilia and standing as tall as Will in their chopines. When Will pointedly shook his head and Aemilia averted her gaze, the courtesans exploded in contempt.

"*English!*" one of them cried, glowering at Aemilia's riding boots. "They hate women! Their own Queen must remain a virgin because they only have eyes for other men."

The speaker's companion caressed Aemilia's cheek. "*Madonna mia,* aren't you a pretty boy with skin as smooth as a lady's! I bet your friend loves to bend you over and bugger you." She swiveled to address Will. "Does he have nice shapely buttocks, *signore?*"

With a most theatrical dexterity, the two courtesans proceeded to make obscene gestures concerning the carnal acts they presumed Aemilia and Will indulged in. Abruptly, the girls burst into peals of wicked laughter before racing away, their chopines smacking the cobblestones. Will swayed on his feet as though their performance had left him both speechless and deeply impressed.

"Do you require a translation?" Aemilia asked him, with a half smile. "Or was their meaning clear? By my troth, we've learned never to slight a courtesan."

She wished she could send the girls to Southampton House to give Harry a good telling off.

"*You* display an astonishing equanimity," Will said. "Unlike yesterday at the Ponte delle Tette, when I thought you were going to throw yourself overboard because you couldn't bear the sight of breasts. Which is a pity, seeing as the girls seem to prefer you over me."

She flushed in spite of herself. "At least these girls had all their clothes on."

What Aemilia hid from Will was how disturbed she truly was, not by the courtesans' bawdy insinuations, but by the accusation that she hated women. She felt sick to think how those girls had glared at her as though she were something despicable.

"What cards are these?" Tabitha asked, fingering the brightly painted deck.

"The poet gave them to the mistress," Winifred said, in a voice as dour as November.

Winifred had not been the same since they left England. Between her bouts of seasickness and the poor food aboard ship, she had lost so much weight during the voyage that her once-huge frame dwindled. Now that they were back on solid land, Tabitha had hoped her sister might regain her appetite and spirits, but Winifred was of the opinion that Venice, with its stinking canals, was the most unwholesome place she had ever seen. People here didn't eat honest food, as in England, she declared, but supped on strange spiny creatures dredged up from the lagoon. Tabby feared Winifred would soon be as thin as Prudence. Meanwhile, Tabitha bloomed.

Though Tabby had cried the hardest upon leaving England, she discovered she loved Italy more each day. She couldn't get enough of the fresh figs and pomegranates from the market, and she found swordfish and even octopus most delectable. Of her sisters, she was the quickest to learn Italian, her tongue savoring the words that sounded like angels singing. And she thrilled at the way young men gazed at her with adoring eyes as though she were an angel.

These painted cards were the latest lovely thing she had encountered in her beautiful new world. She smiled at the image of a golden-haired maiden dancing with pitchers in both hands. But she uttered a cry when she came to the card with the grinning skeleton armed with a giant bow and arrow. A shudder shot up Tabitha's spine when Prudence appeared, as though from out of nowhere, and took the card from her trembling hand.

"That would be Death," said Pru, as unflappable as if they'd never left Essex.

Tabitha wondered what Pru made of their new life in Italy. Her eldest sister was increasingly silent these days, her eyes darting everywhere, examining everything, but she rarely gave her feelings away.

"Death?" Tabitha's heart raced. Where was Enrico? She whirled around then saw him safe in Winifred's arms.

"We should fling those cursed cards in the canal," Winifred said. "What does mistress want with them anyway? They're the sort of thing that piss-pot astrologer Simon Forman would have in his rooms — if he isn't already dead of the plague!"

"Mistress says they're soothsaying cards." Pru's brow remained unruffled.

Tabitha and Winifred drew close while Prudence shuffled the deck and laid out three cards.

In the first, an old bearded man leaned upon a staff and gazed at an hourglass. In the second, a young couple clasped hands beneath a canopy while above them hovered Amore — blindfolded Cupid — about to unleash his arrows. In the third, lightning struck a tower.

"Oh, Pru," said Tabitha. "It doesn't look like good fortune to me."

Pru passed Enrico to Tabby before taking Winifred in her arms and rubbing her hair.

"I'm fine!" Winifred sniffed, swiping at her tears. "Don't fuss!"

HEARING THE KNOCK ON her chamber door, Aemilia turned, her heart lifting, for she expected Will. But it was Jasper, his face unaccountably somber.

"Aemilia," he said, for he refused to entertain her conceit of male disguise. "I've completed Her Majesty's business of buying instruments for the Queen's Musicke. Tomorrow the *Orion* sails for Southampton. I implore you to return to England with me, in a dress, if you please."

His pronouncement struck her like a blow in the gut. They had only just arrived in Venice a fortnight ago. After taking such pains to bring her here, did he truly expect her and Enrico to return to a place where the plague still raged for all they knew? Return to a husband who hated her?

"What of our business in Bassano?" she asked him.

Jasper's face twisted. "The more I think of it, the more like madness it seems. Why would a stranger leave us a bequest?"

"Jacopo is our *kinsman* and he lies dying," she said quietly. "Have we come this far only to reject his summons?"

Her cousin glanced at the servants and then back at her. "I would speak to you alone."

Aemilia's stomach pitched when she realized he didn't want the Weir sisters to hear what he had to say. After Winifred, Prudence, and Tabitha had vacated the room, taking Enrico with them, Jasper grasped Aemilia's arms and spoke in such a low, urgent voice that she strained to hear him.

"How do we know we can trust Jacopo? I can little afford to risk my good name or the Queen's patronage to accept some nebulous bequest from an old man who betrayed our fathers. What if he means us malice?"

Jasper's suspicions dumbfounded her, as had the changes Aemilia had witnessed in him since their arrival in Venice. Not only had he taken to wearing a cross around his neck, he could hardly bring himself to speak of the Ghetto without his voice going cold and distant. And now he intended to avoid Bassano altogether. But finally she understood—Jasper was as haunted by Venice and the clamoring ghosts of their fathers' past as she was. It was not that he was ashamed of their patrimony but he was terrified of losing everything if they were unmasked as the children of Marranos.

"Jasper," she murmured, wishing she could conjure the words to give him courage and comfort. "It's always been my dream to see the Casa dal Corno."

Their fathers' fabled birthplace was only fifty miles away, yet it seemed more unreal than ever, glimmering like a fata morgana, just beyond her reach.

"Don't be blinded by sentiment," he said. "Our fathers left this country for a reason. With each passing day, I better understand why they had to flee. Did you hear that in the church of Santo Stefano an old woman was reported to the Inquisition? She was a Jewish convert, as was her son, a prominent physician who donated half his money to the Church. And her crime? The senile old thing was gabbling to herself in church and they accused her of making a heretical mockery of the Mass. If they stoop to persecute some toothless crone, what might they do to us?"

Aemilia, already chilled from Jasper's story, leapt at the sound of a knock on the door. With a nod to her cousin, she went to open it. A burst of relief spread through her at seeing Will. But he appeared as solemn as Jasper.

"Your servants tell me you and your cousin are sailing for England tomorrow." Will sounded devastated, his eyes touching hers so that she caught her breath. "I've come to bid you both fond farewell."

"My cousin sails tomorrow," Aemilia told him, her heart banging, "but *I* shall continue onward to Bassano."

Resolution weighted her every word. Unlike Jasper, she had neither good name nor royal patronage at stake, but she stood to lose all happiness and freedom by returning to the life she had left behind. Staying on in Veneto promised adventure at the very least. With every fiber of her being, she longed to complete her pilgrimage to Papa's old home and meet her dying kinsman, come what may.

"You can't go alone," Jasper interjected, with an air of utter exasperation. "It's neither decent nor safe. Please listen to reason for once. What if the Inquisition arrests you for cross-dressing?"

Smarting, Aemilia wondered how he could speak to her like that in front of Will. But then she lifted her gaze to Jasper's. "Does that mean you would accompany me to Bassano if I agreed to wear a gown?"

Jasper only stared at her, as if not daring to even reply with Will in the room. As the silence between them deepened, Aemilia sensed that no words of hers could persuade Jasper to make the journey to the Casa dal Corno, just as no arguments of his could drag her back to England.

As she and Jasper stood in stalemate, Will stepped forward. "Master Bassano, if Aemilia wishes to continue her travels, I promise to escort her and guard her safety at every turn."

His loyalty kindled a flame in her heart even as she chafed under the notion that she needed his protection. He smiled at her in a way that made her swallow and blink before he turned to Jasper and held out his hand until her cousin reluctantly shook it.

Sighing, Jasper reached inside his doublet and handed her a heavy sack of coins. "This should suffice for the remainder of your journey."

Aemilia embraced her cousin and kissed his cheeks.

"YOU'RE NOT BOUND TO me, you know," Aemilia told Will. "You're free to go anywhere your heart desires."

In a canalside tavern, they sat beside a roaring fire and drank dark wine with their rabbit stew. Laughter and singing reverberated inside the packed room. There were ostensibly no respectable women here, only men and a few courtesans. Yet, as Emilio, she lounged with her legs carelessly sprawled and drank the cheap good wine and none gave her any grief for it. *Liberty,* she told herself. *This is what liberty is.*

"Do you think I would abandon my friend?" Will asked her.

She'd never seen him so expansive, so utterly at his ease. The fire's golden light played over his soft brown hair, his dark eyebrows, his cheekbones, the gentle curve of his lips.

"Besides," he said, "you promised to show me the cities of Veneto. And what about our plays?"

Our plays. A warm flush spread through her body as she raised her glass to Will, her perfect collaborator—not just in writing, but the most faithful friend to have ever graced her life. In spite of herself, Aemilia felt a welling up of regret that they could never be more than friends—even supposing he desired her, she could never again allow herself to become entangled with a married man.

"To poetry!" she said, staring into the depths of his hazel eyes.

"To the Muse!" he said, with an answering spark in his own gaze.

Clinking her glass to his, she laughed, half delirious at the freedom and adventure awaiting them both. "After Bassano, we shall see Verona and Padua."

She realized how relieved she was that Jasper had left. Nothing held her back from the journey before them.

17

UTUMN MIST CLOAKED THE Brenta River. Aemilia
stood at the prow of the *burchiello,* a boat with a small
cabin that was being towed upstream by a team of
oxen. As ever, it proved she was traveling against the
stream, in the opposite direction as everyone else. The patrician families that had summered in their riverside villas in the cool uplands now
returned to Venice, their *burchiellos* flowing easily downstream, as did
farmers' barges heaped with grapes and cheeses, wine and olive oil,
heading for the Venetian markets.

It seemed that only Aemilia and her companions were heading up-
river. With every mile, the current grew unrulier, but she would not
budge from the prow. Each painstaking mile took her closer to Papa's
lost home. His voice echoed in the chambers of her heart, telling her
of the family villa, of its walled garden of peach and pomegranate
trees. She remembered how, as a seven-year-old girl, she had solemnly
vowed to Papa that she would become a great poet and earn enough
gold to buy back his house. Closing her eyes, she stretched out her
hand to grasp his ghostly one, but her fingers enclosed warm flesh.

With a cry, she opened her eyes to see Will carrying Enrico.

"Did I startle you just now?" he asked. "You were lost in reverie."

She smiled. Back in England he had been the distracted one, lost in
a dream, but here in Veneto they had switched places. Attentive and
cheerful, he drew her back to earth.

"I wish the fog would clear so we could see the mountains," he said.
"In faith, I've longed to see the Alps from the moment I first learned

of Hannibal crossing them on his elephant. Near Bassano, I hear, they brew the most potent aqua vitae."

Aemilia's thoughts again strayed to Papa. How much of her story did she dare tell her friend? It seemed she owed him some explanation, seeing that he had accompanied her this far.

"We shall be visiting a kinsman of my late father's," she said, her eyes on the vineyards and orchards, spectral in the mists. "Jacopo Bassano knows nothing of me. I shall introduce myself as Emilio and he shall be none the wiser."

"You settle into your new role well," said Will. "Emilio Bassano has become the most accomplished player I have ever seen."

"You think I'm play-acting?"

"Are you not?" he asked her mildly. "Deceiving your own relations?"

She grew hot in the face, for up until now Will had not challenged her right to live as Emilio.

"All of us are players," she told him. "Putting on one mask or another, pretending to be what we are not. In truth, I dissemble far less as Emilio. Poor Aemilia was forever having to lie and make excuses for herself."

THE MIST CLEARED TO reveal snow-crowned Monte Grappa towering in the stark blue sky. The Brenta ran wild, foaming pale green. As the *burchiello* swept round a bend, Aemilia caught her first glimpse of the walled town of Bassano with its ruined fortress and covered wooden bridge crossing the Brenta. Beyond here, the river was practically unnavigable.

"How different this is from Venice," Will said, as they stepped ashore. "Are we even still in Italy? Look at that snowy peak. Listen to those cowbells. See those shepherdesses with their flocks on the verdant banks? This is rustic Arcadia."

A lost idyll, Aemilia reflected. Papa had always spoken of it that way.

"Why did your father leave this enchanted place?" Will asked. "Was there a war? A famine?"

Aemilia glanced down, wondering what to say, when Winifred voiced her opinion. "Bless me, this place is even more foreign than Venice, but at least it doesn't stink as much, mistress."

Aemilia gave her maid a pointed look and cleared her throat.

Winifred sighed. "I mean Master Emilio, sir." Each word sounded as if it had been dredged from her throat with a rusty meat hook.

THE TOWN WAS NOT large. Once they passed through the gates, Aemilia found her way to the Casa dal Corno in no time at all. The villa was even grander than she had imagined, its façade rising three stories. Autumn sunshine shone against the frescos her father had described with such tender remembrance. There were the stags and rams, the goats and apes, the musical instruments that had been the Bassano family's trade. The dancing nymphs were rendered larger than life in exquisite detail, as though Aemilia could practically touch their naked flesh.

Drawing a deep breath, Aemilia rapped the brass knocker. The door opened to reveal a manservant who gazed at her quizzically before glancing at Will, the Weir sisters, and the squalling child. From his puzzlement, it appeared that the residents of the Casa dal Corno were not used to receiving strange visitors at this blustery time of year.

"Salve," Aemilia said. Her mouth had gone so dry, it hurt to speak. "I am Emilio Bassano, son of Battista who was born in this house. I've sailed from England to visit your good master."

She showed the servant Jacopo's letter that Jasper had passed on to her before he departed for home. The paper was emblazoned with the Bassano coat of arms shared by both the Italian and English branches of the family—the silk moths and the mulberry tree.

A jolt seemed to pass through the servant. "The English *signori* are here!" he shouted, in a voice loud enough to reach every room in the house.

Aemilia exchanged glances with Will as the servant ushered them into the entry hall. A large crucifix on one wall faced a statue of the Madonna opposite.

"You do not arrive a day too soon!" The manservant clapped his hand on Aemilia's shoulder. "My master grows ever frailer. We fear he won't survive the winter. Oh, it is good that you have come. So good!"

Soon the entry hall was bursting with four generations of men and women, boys and girls, appearing from every corner. If the Casa dal Corno was large, it also appeared to house at least two dozen souls.

"Welcome, *signori*," a soberly attired man in his fifties said. "I am

Francesco, Jacopo's eldest son. My father has been waiting for you so long. He will be overjoyed."

The family resemblance was enough to take Aemilia's breath away. With his bottomless dark eyes, Francesco closely resembled Papa.

Francesco turned to Will. "And you must be Jasper Bassano."

"No, *signore.*" Will's Italian was improving by the day. "I am no relation, but Emilio Bassano's sworn friend."

"My cousin Jasper regrets that he had to return to England on the Queen's business," Aemilia said, wishing with all her heart that Jasper had persevered to join her in this beautiful house where she was so warmly received. "But I have come with my son, Enrico."

She gestured for Tabitha to step forward with the child in her arms. Soon her son was encircled by a swarm of women and girls who covered him in loud kisses, exclaiming how beautiful he was.

"Did you bring your wife?" Francesco asked.

Aemilia lowered her eyes. "I am a widower, *signore.*"

She had grown used to telling the same lie over and over until it became her new truth, each successive lie becoming easier.

"You must see him, see my father, as quickly as you can." Francesco was already leading her up the white marble stairway.

"But he must be famished." A plump woman, undoubtedly Francesco's wife, blocked their path. "Surely you must let the young gentlemen wash and change clothes. I shall show our guests to their chamber. I hope the two English *signori* don't mind sharing a room."

Before Aemilia could say a word, the lady delivered her and Will to a chamber that looked out on the garden of Papa's childhood. Aemilia glanced furtively at the bed she and Will would have to share. As if noting her consternation, the poet folded his arms in front of himself and appeared vastly amused. But Aemilia knew she couldn't possibly protest this arrangement.

Meanwhile the *signora* shouted for servants to carry up water, soap, and towels, along with bread and wine, cheese, olives, and pears. Other servants escorted the Weir sisters to a room on the far end of the house. Winifred shook her head at Aemilia, as though to upbraid her mistress for the web of lies she had woven that had reduced her to sharing a bed with a married man.

Everything was unfolding very fast. By the time the lady and her servants withdrew, Will fell back on the bed and roiled in silent laughter.

Aemilia narrowed her eyes at him. "A pity I'm not a blond Earl."

"Harry would find this capital sport! Shall I write a letter to him describing our new sleeping arrangement? Now just what did the courtesans say you and I got up to together?" He began making wild gesticulations.

"*Basta!*" she snapped. "Enough! Could you *at least* step out whilst I wash?"

"My good Emilio, you hiss like a snake!"

Still chuckling under his breath, Will headed for the door. But the room was so narrow, he had to squeeze past her. For a moment he stood as though rooted before her and stared at her in a way that left her slack jawed and mute. Even as his look burned her, it held her in its thrall. Wrenching her head, she pointed at the door. Quietly, he walked out. Trembling, she slid the bolt into place.

Plunging her hands into the basin, she splashed cold water against her face until her skin grew numb.

A<small>EMILIA</small> <small>FOUND</small> F<small>RANCESCO</small> <small>AND</small> his younger brother, Leandro, awaiting her in the corridor.

"Our father was troubled deep in his heart that your father and his brothers had to run away and seek refuge in a foreign land," Francesco told her. "If he can speak to you of Battista, I think he can at least die in peace."

Aemilia could think of nothing to say.

To reach Jacopo's chamber, they had to pass through his atelier with its long windows of leaded glass facing the square. Paintings, many of monumental size, hung on the walls while easels bore canvases in various stages of completion.

"You, *signori*, are master artists like your father." Aemilia studied a canvas with a scene etched in blue chalk, awaiting its first touch of paint.

"We would never claim to match our father's genius," Leandro said, with reverence. "Look at this, *signore.*"

Leandro directed her attention to a vast painting that drew her in as though the scene were unfolding before her—the figures were that lifelike. In a long pillared arcade that opened on to a view of Monte Grappa stood a lovely young woman in a gown of silver brocade. She resembled a wealthy Venetian *donna,* only her wrists were bound, her hair was uncovered, and her shoulders were hunched in shame. To her left, a fashionable young man with a falcon on his arm appeared to denounce her. Behind her gathered a throng of officious-looking men who glared at her in condemnation. But before her knelt Christ who traced Hebrew letters in the dust at her feet. The artist, Jacopo, clearly knew Hebrew.

Aemilia was familiar with the story from the Gospel of John, the tale of Christ saving the woman from being stoned as an adulteress. *Let he who is without sin cast the first stone.*

Even as she stood in the atelier of the man who had appropriated her father's home, the painting seemed to echo the biblical message. *Judge not.* How she wished she could read Hebrew. The Gospel of John didn't reveal what Jesus had written. But she wanted to know what Jacopo had written.

"One of Father's masterpieces," said Leandro. "My brother and I have painted many copies."

"Now we shall go to his room," Francesco said.

THE BEDCHAMBER WAS FLOODED in the golden light of late afternoon. Blinded by its brilliance, Aemilia had to blink before she made out the old man in his bed, his face like parchment. Francesco's wife sat at Jacopo's bedside, cajoling her father-in-law to drink from a goblet she held before him. But his eyes, as dark and compelling as Papa's, anchored upon Aemilia. He raised his right arm.

"Jasper? How good of you to come."

Aemilia had expected his voice to quaver, betraying his frailty, but he spoke with the force of a man in his prime.

"*Signore,* I am Emilio, son of Battista Bassano."

She swept into a bow then stood at attention while old Jacopo stared, as though to take her measure. His hand beckoned her near. She sat on a stool beside the bed.

"If you are truly Battista's child, tell me of him." His hand gripped hers.

So he meant to test her? She felt her skin grow clammy.

"Don't be rude, you old fool," his daughter-in-law said, her voice as fond as it was frank. "Emilio has the letter you sent to Jasper in England, only Jasper had to return." She turned to Aemilia with apologetic eyes. "Forgive the old mule, *signore*. He can be stubborn."

"Olivia, pray leave me alone with this Emilio. Francesco and Leandro, you must go as well. I will ring the bell if I need you."

Aemilia noted the brass bell propped on the bedside table.

"Stand in the full light where I may see you," the old man told her, after the others had vacated the room.

Setting her face like stone, Aemilia did as she was told.

"How am I to believe you are who you claim to be?" Jacopo asked her. "You could be some fortune seeker who murdered poor Jasper and took the letter from him in hope of gaining my bequest."

"I swear that I am indeed Battista's child." Her eyes blazed into his as though her conviction could prove it.

"Then tell me of the man."

"He and his brothers were court musicians for old King Henry of England and later for Queen Elizabeth. Papa died in the year 1577."

Jacopo stared at her steadily. "Go on."

"He was as great a musician and instrument maker as you are an artist, *signore*."

The old man waved his hand impatiently. "Any stranger might speak of Battista's public reputation. Tell me something only his child would know."

Tears stung at her eyes, but Aemilia blinked them back. "When I was a child, he told me again and again how much he loved the house he was forced to flee. The house where *you* now live, *signore*. You who interrogate me like an inquisitor."

Her bitter voice echoed so loudly through the chamber, she expected Francesco and Leandro to burst in and drag her away. But Jacopo never flinched.

"What else? What can you tell me that no one else would know?"

"My father's secret?" she asked him. "I think you know as well as I, though you pretend to have nothing to do with it."

Her voice was as cold as the tile floor beneath her thin shoes. She no longer cared whether Jacopo believed her or whether she offended him. Let him banish her just as her father had been banished. At least she could vindicate Papa in his old home, her words bearing witness to what he had suffered.

"Come closer," Jacopo said, "and tell me Battista's secret you say I know so well."

"As you will." Aemilia sat stiffly on the stool. "He and my uncles had to lock themselves in our cellar to say their Hebrew prayers. I wasn't to know. He tried to hide it even from me, but I begged him until he told me. Are you satisfied now, *signore*?"

His hand gripped hers with surprising strength.

"Did you know that Battista and I wrote to each other?" he asked.

From under the coverlet he drew a bundle of letters covered in faded ink, nearly illegible with time and wear, but she recognized her father's signature.

"So I have shown you my evidence." The old man's face was only inches from hers. "But yours is still lacking. I know you lie."

Aemilia stared at him, her throat seizing up. She attempted to pull away, but his grip was too tight.

"Emilio is an impostor. From Battista's letters, I know he had no son." The old man's face softened. "Only a daughter he loved more than the sun and moon."

Hearing his words, she cracked like glass and wept.

Jacopo stroked her cheek. "*Cara mia*, do you think an old man like me would be fooled by your disguise?"

Having lived his entire life behind a mask, he had seen straight through hers.

"Don't cry, my dear. I know you came all the way from England and it's dangerous to travel as a woman. But here you are safe with your family." He stroked her hand. "You have no more need to hide your womanhood, Aemilia Battista Bassano." He kissed her forehead the way Papa used to do. "How I wish Battista and his brothers had dared to return when I begged them, but instead Battista's beautiful daughter has come home. And you are a mother! And a widow."

Aemilia sensed he wouldn't probe any deeper. As long as she revealed herself as a woman, Battista's daughter, Jacopo would forgive her any lesser lies.

"I am so, so happy you have come, Aemilia." He gripped her hand tightly, as if he feared she might vanish as his kin had done. "Did you know your father's true name was Aaron?"

Tears in her eyes, she shook her head.

"He took the name Battista when he submitted to baptism. We all submitted. Some of us were better at burying the past than others." He let out a hollow laugh. "I never knew your father went on saying his prayers in secret. I never dared take such a risk. You must understand. We were terrified of the Inquisition."

She watched Jacopo weep even as she wept, and then she held him as though he were her father come back to life. What choices he had been forced to make, what a narrow line he had walked. She thought of his painting of Christ and the adulteress. Jacopo identified with the fallen woman—he, too, longed to be forgiven for the lies by which he had been forced to live.

SHRINKING PAST ONE OF the Casa dal Corno's maidservants, Aemilia knocked on the door of the garret room assigned to the Weir sisters.

Winifred opened up. "Yes, Master Emilio, sir?" She could not have sounded more sarcastic. But when she saw that Aemilia had been crying, she pulled her inside and held her tight. "Whatever's the matter, mistress? Did that poet take any liberties? I'll smash his head in!"

"No, Winifred." Aemilia spoke in her natural voice. "Old Jacopo has divined my true sex and wishes that I disguise myself no longer. Only I . . ." She broke off, feeling like the most wretched fool. "Only I left all my gowns behind when we left Venice. I thought I'd have no more need of them."

Winifred cackled. "Never you fear, mistress. We saved them for you."

Prudence appeared with Aemilia's best gown of claret-colored damask. It had been freshly sponged and pressed, and it smelled of lavender.

"Will this do, mistress?"

Aemilia regarded Prudence in wonder. "How in heaven's name did you know to prepare it for me?"

But the Weir sisters were already whipping off her jerkin and doublet. Winifred held the offending male garments at arm's length as though she wanted to burn them. Prudence whisked off her mistress's breeches and linen shirt.

"You can keep the slippers," Winifred remarked. "In faith, I always thought they looked like lady's shoes."

Winifred and Prudence, Aemilia decided, looked far too smug.

"Lift up your arms, mistress." With an air of great ceremony, Prudence helped her into her best chemise.

She was obliged to suck in her breath as her two servants laced her into her stays. Next came the skirt, petticoat, and bodice. She had nearly forgotten how constricting it was to dress as a woman. Prudence tied on her sleeves while Winifred ran a comb through her hair.

"Thank your stars you didn't cut it too short, mistress," Winifred said.

Prudence fitted a black velveteen snood on Aemilia's head. "Now you look a perfect lady, Mistress Lanier."

"Bassano," she said thinly. "My name is Bassano."

"Pardon my saying so," said Winifred, "but I think it best that you go as the *Widow* Lanier from now on."

Aemilia shrugged in resignation. How she had loved Emilio, and how she would miss him.

"Where's Tabitha?" she asked. "Where's Enrico?"

"In the garden," said Winifred. "With the poet."

Aemilia emerged from the Weir sisters' room only to collide with the maidservant who had been lurking in the corridor, no doubt scandalized to see the young English gentleman enter his maids' room. Now seeing Aemilia step out as a lady in a damask gown, the girl shrieked and shook her upraised hands in bewilderment before she scarpered.

"Well, look at her," Winifred said nonchalantly. "You'd think she'd never seen a lady in breeches."

WHEN AEMILIA STEPPED OUT among the peach trees and late-blooming roses, Will poked his head out over the fountain and hooted at her as though he were cheering a player upon the stage.

"But soft! What is this apparition?" he asked Enrico, lifting the child to see his mother. "'Tis none other than violet-eyed Cytherea sweeping down from her dove-drawn chariot."

The poet set down the little lad so he could scrabble toward her.

"You'll dirty your mother's fine dress!" Tabitha, her eyes enormous, picked him up but held the child close enough so he could kiss his mother and pat her face.

Aemilia glared at Will. To her irritation, he seemed to find her latest twist of fate most hilarious. But at least that awkward silence in the bedchamber had ended, swept away by his usual teasing, as though it had never happened at all.

"If you ever deign to stop laughing, sir," she said, "we need to discuss your sleeping in a separate room."

Her fine dress be damned, she took her son in her arms and planted a fierce kiss on his face.

Tabitha cleared her throat. "Pardon me, mistress, but won't these people think you're a bit odd?"

Aemilia turned to see faces popping out of every window and doorway to gape at her.

"Has fair Bassano ever known such excitement?" asked Will. "A gentleman who in a trice becomes a lady as beauteous as the Queen of Carthage? Poor Harry would be green with envy."

"So you think I am a figure of fun," she said hotly.

"No, indeed! You are the fearless heroine of a romance, a comedy of errors. I only fear that I must don a lady's gown to keep pace with your adventures, madam."

Francesco, Leandro, and Olivia now entered the garden. Handing Enrico to Tabby, Aemilia searched for the words to explain herself. Olivia, as regal as an empress, held her by the shoulders and kissed both her cheeks.

"Jacopo told us everything. It's too perilous to travel as a woman and so you disguised yourself. But why should you keep up your masquerade in front of us, your family? Did you not trust us, *signora*?"

Aemilia could only stare at the lady. Why indeed? Because she loved her guise too much? Because she pined for her boots and breeches even now? Because she had longed to cling to her liberty for as long as she could? How could she possibly tell this to her kindly hostess?

"I beg your pardon for any offense," she said. "If I appear strange to you, *signora,* it's because this has been such a long and strange journey. In faith, I can scarcely believe I've finally arrived at the Casa dal Corno, your beautiful home."

Olivia smiled in tenderness, as though to a daughter. "*Your* home, too. Welcome home, Aemilia."

18

N THE FOLLOWING WEEKS, Aemilia felt strangely light, her head abuzz with the novelty of it all. A woman once more, she no longer had to lie or lower her voice, but she still felt like an impostor, an elephant in skirts, for in her time as Emilio, she had grown accustomed to taking huge strides, to laughing aloud instead of tittering behind her hand, to speaking her mind without thought of feminine modesty. Yet Jacopo's household, far from regarding her as a monstrous specimen of womanhood, appeared to believe that her many quirks could be explained away by her Englishness.

She spent hours in Jacopo's room. Francesco and Olivia moved their daughter Giulietta's virginals to the old man's chamber so that Aemilia could play for him and sing in harmony with sweet-voiced Giulietta. The entire household crowded in to listen, and Jacopo never seemed to tire of the music.

"Sing something English," he implored her, "that I might think of the life your father and his brothers lived."

"An English song." At a loss, Aemilia turned to Will, who sat on the broad, deep windowsill with her lap desk and scribed while she played. The autumn sun shone behind him, filling his hair with red-gold light. "Can you think of one, Will?"

Her Bassano kin seemed to accept her explanation that Will was a loyal family friend who had protected her when Jasper had to return to England. But to her deep regret, the days of her easy familiarity with Will had come to an end now that she had returned to dressing as a lady. After his initial teasing had subsided, Will had become much more formal and reserved, as he would have to be with a gentlewoman in her family home. Even when they worked together on their new comedy, he remained at a cordial distance. If she had gained a family, it seemed she had lost the intimacy of their friendship. It was as though their former cameradie had been a mere illusion. Perhaps his real affection had been for Emilio, not Aemilia at all. And she, the fool, had believed in that sweet fabrication, believed they were kindred souls.

"What about that song you sang for Southampton," Will said, his eyes a world away. "About the Faery Queen."

Aemilia closed her eyes and sang, willing herself to evoke the enchantment of that moon-drenched midsummer night until she could almost smell the roses and hear Will read his impassioned poetry. *Does he still pine for his beautiful young Earl?* she wondered. *Does he still write Harry those sonnets filled with love and longing?*

When her song ended, she saw that she had lulled Jacopo to sleep. With gentle efficiency, Olivia herded them out of the room to give the old man his rest.

Aemilia found Will in the corridor, holding her lap desk with the penned pages stacked neatly on top. His eyes, she noted, were soft and unguarded as though her song had awakened his own memories of Southampton House.

"Were you writing a letter to Harry?" she asked, instantly regretting her words. What business was it of hers?

"No, I write to my son."

"Your son, not your wife?" Again the words shot out before she could stop herself. But she was indeed puzzled, for the lad couldn't be older than eight.

"Aemilia, my wife cannot read," Will said, with a stiffness she hadn't heard from him since London. "Not every woman is like you."

She stopped short, wondering what he meant by that and wondering why he could not at least write to his wife so that she could bring the letter to someone who *could* read it to her, even if it was only her young son. Did Will have so little regard for the mother of his children?

But who are you to call him a callous husband, you who abandoned your husband at the first opportunity?

Welcome distraction came in the form of thirteen-year-old Giulietta, who seized Aemilia's hands. "Mama says I may not walk out alone, but I may walk with *you*. Come, it's so close inside this house. I can't breathe!"

The girl was like a filly in her unbridled energy as she swept Aemilia along the corridor.

"Won't you join us?" Aemilia shouted to Will over her shoulder.

"Only if I can bring Enrico."

"I'VE NEVER MET A lady as brave as you!" Giulietta told Aemilia, as they crossed the square.

Both to Aemilia's pleasure and embarrassment, the girl seemed to idolize her. When her mother had learned of Aemilia's true identity and puzzled as to what room she could put her in, Giulietta had insisted that Aemilia share her room.

"Traveling so far in the guise of a man!" Giulietta went on. "You say this is an English habit? Tell me, do all English ladies wear *riding boots* under their skirts as you do, Aemilia?"

"On our native island, the sexes mimic each other," said Will, who walked alongside them, carrying Enrico on his shoulders.

If he was reserved around Aemilia, he was gallant with young Giulietta. Indeed, Aemilia was impressed at how rapidly his Italian was improving.

"I know many a boy," Will said, "who can put on a gown and pretend to be a girl, even one as winsome as you, *signorina*."

Giulietta laughed as though she were shocked and enjoyed every second of being shocked.

"Perhaps one year for Carnival, *I* shall go in pantaloons and a doublet with my face hidden behind a mask," Giulietta said, her eyes dreamy. "You are always scribbling, *signore*. You, too, Aemilia. My parents say you're uncommonly educated. What is it you write?"

"We write comedies," Aemilia said, "like Isabella Andreini."

Giulietta leapt up and clapped her hands, her face flushed pink. "I adore the commedia dell'arte! Do you write romances?"

"Yes," Aemilia and Will replied in unison.

Though Aemilia regarded their shrew play as a pale attempt at romance, their new play of a shipwrecked girl who disguised herself as a boy seemed more promising in that vein.

"Make me a promise, Aemilia." Giulietta looped her arm through hers. "When you write your next romance, you must name your heroine after me."

"At your command, *signorina*," Will said, speaking before Aemilia could get a word in. "No promise could be easier to keep."

Giulietta led the way out of the town gate and down the hill that led into the vineyards, left bare after the harvest, and the autumn forest of green pine and yellow larch. The fallow fields rested as though wrapped in a dream. But the beauty of the landscape was not all that met the eye. Aemilia understood at once why Olivia had forbidden her daughter to walk out unchaperoned—amorous couples were everywhere. Young men embraced their sweethearts with an ardor that left nothing to the imagination. Young women drew their lovers into the shadowy woods.

"Is it wise to walk here?" she asked Giulietta. "Perhaps we'd best turn back."

Will raised his eyebrows while the girl seemed to pretend not to hear.

"If you are writing a romance," Giulietta said, "you must go to Verona. I've heard a most romantic tale of a boy and girl there who died for their love of each other." Her eyes shone as though she were that enraptured heroine.

Aemilia shook her head. "It's not a comedy if the lovers *die*."

She looked at Will, expecting him to weigh in, but he was staring at the lovers with something like hunger in his eyes. The muscles in his throat twitched and he turned to gaze at her as though stricken. Her face burning, Aemilia blinked and felt a deep ache inside her.

Then, mindful of Giulietta's presence, she forced a laugh, took Enrico from Will's arms, and said they had better go back before her son caught a chill.

In Jacopo's chamber, a fire crackled in the hearth. Outside the windows, snowflakes drifted down. Propped against his pillows, the old man watched Enrico play with a carved wooden horse. Though Jacopo grew feebler, he seemed to draw renewed vitality from doting on the little boy, now the youngest resident in the Casa dal Corno.

"He looks just like my son Francesco at that age," Jacopo said, smiling at Aemilia who played Giulietta's virginals.

Aemilia and Enrico were the only ones left with Jacopo on this Sunday morning with the rest of household gone to Mass. She wondered whether Jacopo longed for them all to return, this man who seemed to relish being engulfed by the noisy bustle of his family, or if he was savoring this rare moment of stillness with just her and the child to keep him company.

"Play something cheerful," he said, when she struck a minor chord. "There will be time enough for dirges when I'm dead."

She obliged, playing the swift and lively notes of the *coronto,* a running dance that sent her fingers leaping across the wooden jacks while her body swayed. The old man nodded his head in time. Enrico giggled and made his toy horse prance along with the music.

"Have you forgiven me?" Jacopo asked her, after the vibrations of the last note faded into silence. "For usurping your father's home?"

She turned to him, silenced by the haunted look on his face.

"You see, they'd already fled," he said, "and I thought it better that I take the house than a stranger. I always prayed they would return and I would be the one to welcome them home. But I never saw them again."

The old man's face crumpled.

Aemilia sat by his bed and took his hand. "I'm sure Papa understood you never acted out of malice. When faced with hardship, we must all make bitter choices."

"I've made provisions for you after I'm gone," Jacopo said, his face serene once more. "There is a house in the hills above Verona I shall leave to you, along with a small vineyard. You and Enrico should have a decent income from the winery. Enough to lead a comfortable if modest life."

She felt like weeping all over the old man in gratitude, for now she knew she could stay in Italy forever and never return to England. Never face Alfonse again.

"You are so kind to me, Jacopo." She kissed his cheeks.

"You will love Verona," he said. "It's a beautiful city and its winters are far kinder than Bassano's. Yet you will not be too far away from your family in the Casa dal Corno. When Enrico turns twelve, he's more than welcome to join our workshop as an apprentice painter. So you see, *cara*, you've no need to worry about your future. My family shall look after you always and you'll have your own house and vineyard."

"Thank you." Her heart was too full to think of any other words.

"Will you take some advice from an interfering old man?" he asked, with a sly sideways glance. "You should think of marrying again. You're too young and beautiful to live like a nun for the rest of your life."

"Such things take their own time," she told him. "By my troth, there's no man I care for in that way, and no man who cares for me."

Jacopo's eyes pierced her. "What about your English poet? He adores you."

"My good Jacopo, you are mistaken there," she said with more vehemence than intended. "He's like a brother to me."

Or he had been like a brother, she thought sadly, *until we arrived at the Casa dal Corno and I stopped being Emilio.*

Jacopo regarded her with an indulgent smile. "First you lied to me, presenting yourself as a young man. Now you lie to yourself, Aemilia."

He had turned the tables, leaving her stunned.

"I'm a man and I know what it means when a man gazes at a woman the way Will gazes at you." The old man grinned. "He is in love. And I see the way you look at him. Do you truly have no feelings for him, *cara*? I suspect you, too, are in love."

She could no longer look Jacopo in the eye, couldn't do anything but take her seat at the virginals once more and pound out a *saltarello*, playing so fast she thought her fingers might snap off. Anything to silence the ringing in her head.

"True love is precious and rare." Jacopo raised his voice to be heard over the music. "Never turn your back on love."

But this could never be. Her collaboration with Will had hinged on her assumption that they would never desire each other, that their friendship would remain lighthearted and uncomplicated, free from the base lusts that had been her undoing as a young girl.

"Surely you can see how tender he is with Enrico," Jacopo said. "Doesn't your son deserve a loving papa?"

The old man's words left her in tears. She, who after the humiliation of being put aside by Lord Hunsdon and then forced into a hateful marriage, had commanded herself to be impervious to romance,
her heart a fortress. She was a woman of wit and reason, not some
soft creature like Angela. Will was the one who had steeped himself
in love. She would never forget his face when he stared at Harry upon
that midsummer night, his yearning writ large, not just in his sonnets
but also in the burning in his eyes.

> Being your slave, what should I do but tend
> Upon the hours and times of your desire?

She would be no man's slave.
"Aemilia, don't weep," said the old man. "There's no shame in love."
Does he guess my other secret? she wondered. *Guess I am no widow?* And
yet, as he beckoned her close, she sensed he would have given her his
blessing regardless. This dying man was calling on her to embrace life,
to allow herself to love a man who was already deeply in love with her,
who would match her devotion measure for measure. A small voice inside her whispered, *Even you deserve to know true love.*

Downstairs the door burst open. Footsteps clattered up the stairs
and down the corridors, accompanied by happy conversation. Muttering her apology to Jacopo, Aemilia grabbed Enrico and darted from
the chamber. She could not allow anyone, certainly not Will, to see her
so undone.

THE ONE ROOM WHERE she could hope to find privacy, at least on
a Sunday, was the storeroom where Francesco and Leandro kept the
rolls of canvas still waiting to be cut and stretched on frames and the
pigments from which they mixed their paints.

Enrico seemed to find the narrow chamber as amusing as any, especially when she gave him a broken piece of chalk and let him draw
upon an old slate tile. Seated on a wooden box, she opened her lap
desk and leafed through the pages of the new play she and Will were
writing. Viola, a shipwrecked maiden washed up on a strange shore,
elected to pass as a young man for both expedience and adventure. Under her new guise as Cesario, she used her considerable intelligence

and ingenuity to seek her fortune and so became the most favored servant of Duke Orsino. The duke, a romantic soul in love with love itself —Aemilia imagined him as beautiful, lazy, and vain as Southampton —sent "Cesario" to woo the beautiful Olivia on his behalf.

What, Aemilia wondered, *would the good Olivia make of her namesake in the play?* In truth, *Olivia* was a perfect anagram of *I, Viola.* They were two halves of the same woman, for even as Viola pretended to be Cesario, Olivia hid behind her veil of mourning for her dead brother. The scenes between the two heroines, with Viola courting Olivia for her master only to have Olivia fall deeply in love with her, were the most poignant in the play. Poor Olivia was enamored of an illusion while Viola was caught in a hopeless double bind, which was resolved only by the reappearance of her twin brother whom she had presumed dead. Of course, *this* fabulous contrivance was Will's doing. Was he not himself the father of a twin son and daughter?

The manuscript pages fell from her hands. How could she continue working with him if she could no longer face him? *Damn these weak tears.* Perhaps she could finish the play on her own and allow him to put his name on it just the same. Had that not been her original aim, to use him as her mask? Except the brilliance of the play emerged from the alchemy of their two minds in collaboration.

Aemilia willed herself to be dispassionate, to think only of the written word on the page. Reaching to the bottom of her lap desk, she pulled out a quarto-sized sheet, thinking it would be as blank and innocent as fallen snow. Instead, she saw his elegant hand, his letters with their flourishes. So he had written a new sonnet.

> How oft, when thou, my music, music play'st
> Upon that blessed wood whose motion sounds
> With thy sweet fingers when thou gently sway'st
> The wiry concord that mine ear confounds,
> Do I envy those jacks that nimble leap
> To kiss the tender inward of thy hand
> Whilst my poor lips, which should that harvest reap,
> At the wood's boldness by thee blushing stand!
> To be so tickled, they would change their state
> And situation with those dancing chips

O'er whom thy fingers walk with gentle gait,
Making the dead wood more blest than living lips.
Since saucy jacks so happy are in this,
Give them thy fingers, me thy lips to kiss.

His words left her quivering, as if she were the virginals frame resonant with sound. Had he written this while watching her play for Jacopo?

A thought came unbidden, plunging her into a pit of longing: *Here you are, twenty-four years old, and the only man you ever allowed to love you was old enough to be your grandsire.* The power of her desire, held at bay for so long, shook her with the force of an earthquake. Her hands clutching her face, she pictured the lovers she'd seen at the forest's edge and then the look Will had given her in the bedchamber they thought they would have to share. She imagined twining her arms around his neck and pulling his muscled body against hers. Breathing in the piney scent of his skin.

Little wonder Jasper had been so worried about leaving her alone with Will. Had she truly traveled to the far side of Europe to seek her freedom only to plunge into some doomed dalliance with a married man, a father of three? *This is madness.*

From down the hall, Giulietta and Olivia were calling for her. Soon they would serve the Sunday feast in the frescoed parlor that looked out on her father's childhood garden. What would Papa make of her predicament?

Enough of this sneaking and shrinking! A grown woman had no business hiding in a storeroom. Briskly, Aemilia dried her eyes and smoothed her hair. She couldn't hide from Will forever.

Yet, seated at the dining table, Aemilia couldn't bring herself to look at him. Such absurd torment, the buzzing in her head would not be silenced. Her hands betrayed her, shaking as she skewered a piece of roast pheasant on her knife and attempted to raise it to her mouth.

"You're so pale," said Giulietta, as guileless as she was young. "Will, too. Are you both struck by the same malady?"

"Hush, child," Olivia said to her daughter, before bowing her head close to Aemilia's and speaking softly so that no one else would hear. "If something burdens your heart, you must never be afraid to confide in me, *cara.*"

Aemilia ducked her head and stared at her plate.

AFTER HANDING ENRICO OVER to Tabitha's care, Aemilia donned her cloak and set off into the drifting snow. If she could no longer ride out alone to flee her troubles, as she'd done in England, she could at least walk, never mind that a respectable woman needed an escort. Yanking her hood over her head, she dared any denizen of Bassano to stand in her way.

But as she charged out of the city gate, she heard flying footfalls behind her. Swinging around, her fists balled, she found herself face to face with Will. Snowflakes starred his soft brown hair.

"Don't you dare creep up behind me!" she snapped. "You gave me such a fright."

"Forgive me," he said. "But I must speak to you."

"Then speak." She looked not at him but at the white mountains and the snow-dusted forest. The cold wind braced her so that she stood stiff and unbending, as though covered in armor.

"I must bid you farewell." His voice rang distant and strange. "After all, you're safe with your family and have no more need of me."

She felt a chasm open up inside her as she imagined her life without him in it, without his wit and their shared laughter, without his poetry and the thrill of their collaboration. Then again, how could she have been so naïve? Of course, their ways must eventually part. It was only that this had come much sooner than she had expected.

"You're returning to England? To your wife and children?" She tried to smile, to be glad for him. That was where he belonged, in the bosom of his family in his native land.

"In truth, I know not where." He sounded defeated.

She turned to him. "But where would you go if not back to England?" She cursed the plaintiveness in her voice.

Will gazed at her levelly. "I vowed not to return to Stratford until I had accomplished something in this world. How can I stand before my children as a failure?"

"To me, you are *most* accomplished," she said.

Allowing him to believe himself a failure was the worst thing she could do, something for which she could never forgive herself. At the very least, she had to reveal her awe of his writing.

"You have a rare gift," she said, "that will one day bring you riches and fame. As I said when we first met, no one writes of love as you do."

His face reddened like a boy's. "Did you finally discover my sonnet? I was wondering how long it would take you to happen upon it. Or if you had already read it and kept your silence because you hated it."

So Will had left that sonnet as a trap for her, and she'd fallen into it, as gullible as thirteen-year-old Giulietta. Did he think she would surrender to him for the price of a poem? Worse yet, had he nearly succeeded? Twisting away from him, she darted off, tugging her hood forward to hide her tears. But he matched her stride and kept pace with her, as speechless as she, until they reached the forest where black squirrels darted up the snow-laden boughs.

"Why did you marry in the first place if you'll not live with your wife?" Her voice was raw, ripping out of her throat with a force that hurt.

"Because I was eighteen and she was pregnant by me. What else was I to do? Why did *you* marry Lanier?"

She exploded with bitter laughter. "Because I was pregnant with the Lord Chamberlain's bastard and he arranged the marriage to cover my shame."

"Does this not make us evenly matched?" Will's voice rose like the mountain wind. Then he spoke softly. "Once I wrote a sonnet for Harry praising the marriage of true minds. In faith, it should have been written for you, for I was never better matched by any mind such as yours, Aemilia."

It was so rare that he said her name, but when he did, it sounded like a caress. She clapped her hand to her mouth and sobbed. The truth was laid bare and she could no longer deceive herself. She had loved him from the moment she first read the sonnet that had fallen from his doublet in front of Simon Forman's astrology practice in Thames Street. She had desired him ever since that midsummer night she had touched his tears. Jacopo's husky voice whispered in the snowy air, *There's no shame in love.*

The wind blew down her hood and his fingers brushed away her tears.

"Tell me," he pleaded, "one way or the other. I cannot bear to stay here and not love you."

She seized his hand and kissed his palm. Snowflakes tumbled from his hair to land on her face as he pulled her close and kissed her lips, his warmth pouring into her until she thought the snow around them would melt. She kissed him with a hunger that left her gasping.

They drew apart and stared at each other, their breath turning the air between them into smoke.

"There's so much about me you don't know," she said.

As he cradled her face to his chest, she told him about her father's secret and her sister's ruin.

"I knew you were a woman of many mysteries," he said, cupping her face in his hands. "Yet I never imagined such revelations as these. Your poor sister! Ah, that is why you painted our Petruchio as such a brute, starving his bride. And your father! I've never heard such a wrenching tale. No wonder you wept in the synagogue."

She made herself speak plainly. "Now that you know the truth about me, will you bid me farewell? I won't hold it against you."

She warded her heart with her last line of defense. *He's not mine for the taking. He belongs to another.*

His laughter was as tender as his encircling arms. "How could I tear myself from my Viola, my spirited Kate? You, my Muse and my music."

Her breath was jagged, her heart racing. What they were about to embark on was as daring and daunting as anything she'd ever done, and yet when he held her in his gaze, she felt lighter than the swirling snow.

DARKNESS DESCENDED, GLITTERING WITH the snow that kept falling, jeweling their hair and cloaks as they made their way back to the Casa dal Corno. Aemilia's feet had gone so cold, she could no longer feel her toes, yet she thrummed with the warmth radiating from her heart and Will's hand enclosing hers.

"What will we tell them?" she whispered, when he reached for the door handle.

"That we're in love," he said. As though it were that simple.

Any objection she might have raised dissolved with his kiss, his mouth covering hers.

The door sprang open.

"God's blood! We were worried sick, little Enrico bawling his eyes out for his mother." Winifred blazed like a forge, glaring at Will before she seized Aemilia's arm, her eyes searching hers.

Surely she must see it on my face, Aemilia thought. *My joy.*

"Oh, mistress." Winifred let out an enormous sigh. "Will you let him lead you into a fool's paradise?"

Aemilia could say nothing, only touch Winifred's cheek in fondness.

"Come in, come in, before you catch your death," Winifred grumbled. "Lord, what a head I have! It beats as if it would break into twenty pieces."

Tabitha beamed at Aemilia as if she could think of no happier outcome for her. Prudence merely nodded as if she had long suspected what would come to pass.

"Master Will, did you by chance ever happen to sample our elderflower wine from Essex?" Pru asked, twisting her apron string around her finger.

"Elderflower wine?" Will looked dazed, but then he glowed. "Ah, yes, back in Cripplegate. Aemilia, did you not bring a bottle of country wine that morning you visited me at the boardinghouse?"

"You visited him at his lodgings?" Winifred was incensed. "A lady should never do such a thing."

"I know, Winifred," Aemilia said brightly. "*That* was why I dressed as a man!"

"Quoting Kit Marlowe, no less," said Will, starry-eyed at the memory. "My landlady was so enamored, I was afraid to leave them alone together."

"Bring me some aqua vitae," Winifred moaned.

Aemilia savored the memory of their drinking the wine to seal their collaboration. But why Pru should want to know such a thing was quite beyond her. Ignoring the glances the Weir sisters traded among themselves, Aemilia smiled at Will, who hoisted Enrico in his arms.

The rest of the household came rushing down the stairs.

"*Madonna mia,* I thought you had lost your way in the snow!" Olivia threw up her hands. "Jacopo was beside himself."

"Forgive me," Aemilia said, her face on fire to be the object of such scrutiny.

Giulietta gaped at her and Will as if she had never seen them before. Francesco and Leandro looked at each other and then at Olivia, as if deferring to her to address this unexpected change in circumstance. A thousand thoughts seemed to cross Olivia's mind as she regarded Aemilia. All the while, Will stood rooted by her side, holding her son, as though they were a family.

Olivia took Aemilia's hand. "*Cara,* you must go to Jacopo and speak to him before he sleeps. Let him know you arrived safely home."

Shakily, Aemilia climbed the stairs, squeezing past Jacopo's kin. Will handed Enrico to Tabby before following her.

AEMILIA FOUND JACOPO IN tears. He grasped her hand.

"*Cara,* will you ever forgive a meddling old fool for causing you such grief? I—"

He fell silent when he saw Will behind her. In an instant the old man's face transformed, as though he could barely contain his glee.

"Now I can face your father in eternity," he exulted. "He will thank me at least for this. Just look at your beautiful young face! I've never seen you so happy."

Jacopo released her hand to beckon to Will. "I expect you to be loving and true, and a good father to her son."

Like a true Italian, Will kissed Jacopo on both cheeks. "*Signore,* you have my vow."

Jacopo folded his hands, his eyes gleaming. "May I trouble you, Aemilia, for a nocturne before I sleep?"

She sat at the virginals and began to play, each note reverberating in her heart.

Will leaned close and whispered in her ear, "If music be the food of love, play on."

19

EMILIA FROZE IN HER tracks as she and Will approached the Cappella di Sancta Odilia in the hills above Verona. Her eyes searched his. Did they dare? He never wavered, only kissed her. "Courage, my love. Be bold."

Head ringing, she stepped forward, past the blossoming almond trees, past the beds of blooming woodruff and Easter lilies, through the low arched door into the chapel where sunlight poured through stained glass in brilliant jewel-colored shafts. Casting a look back over her shoulder, she saw the Weir sisters following them, Tabitha carrying Enrico.

Will squeezed Aemilia's arm as the friar approached them, his hands clasped.

"*Benedicite*," the man said. "Frate Lorenzo at your service. What brings you fair strangers to my chapel?"

Aemilia cast a desperate look at Will, but it appeared that he was hunting for words as frantically as she was.

"Good friar," she stammered, "we are lately come from England. I am kinswoman to the great Jacopo Bassano, so sadly deceased."

Her voice broke in grief at the memory of Jacopo's funeral, only a fortnight ago, the way he had sighed his last breath with an expression of such yearning on his face. At Olivia's bidding, a priest had come to give him the last sacraments. At least Papa had had his brothers to sing their secret songs to send him into the world beyond. If Aemilia had known even a word of those Hebrew prayers, she would have offered them for Jacopo.

"Jacopo Bassano, the master painter!" Friar Lorenzo bowed his head in reverence. "Ah, you must be the kinswoman who inherited the vineyard."

Aemilia could still not get over her good fortune. Sometimes it pricked her conscience along with everything else. If Jacopo had not left the property to her, would it have gone instead to Giulietta as part of her dowry? Had she unwittingly robbed the girl of her inheritance?

"Indeed I am," she told the friar, gathering her wits. "And this . . . this is my betrothed." Her face feverish, she clasped Will's arm. "We are in love, Frate Lorenzo, and wish to live an honest life together."

She scarcely believed her own words, their temerity. She and Will were breaking every law.

"You see," she rattled on, "it's too close to the funeral for a big family wedding feast. And yet we wish to avoid the disgrace of living in sin."

The blood pounded in her ears as she remembered her own parents and their common-law arrangement, how Papa had made a life with another man's wife. But that was England and this was Italy. Would the friar even believe her outlandish tale? Yet what else could they do if they desired to live together and not be pariahs? As long as she and Will had dwelled in the Casa dal Corno, their love had remained unconsummated out of respect to Olivia and her family. Here in Verona their new life together would begin. And so she found herself negotiating with a friar, and she wasn't even Catholic—this was but one more mask. She glanced at Will, who reached for Enrico. The little boy was crying but quietened as soon as Will held him close.

Friar Lorenzo, observing this exchange, burst out laughing. "Signora, you ask me to marry you to this gentleman right here and now with no preparation or warning?"

He raised his palms and then, amid the beams of colored light streaming from the stained glass, a strand of gossamer from a spider's web came floating down. The friar caught it on his finger and studied it as though it were a sign sent from heaven.

"True lovers," he said, "as I see you are, can walk upon gossamer as fine as this and yet not fall, so buoyant are their hearts. And so you two can walk into my chapel, already a family with a beautiful son, and ask me to marry you, and what can I do but bow before your love and do as I am told, for the child's sake if for no other reason." He smiled. "In faith, I rarely see a love like yours. But before I can marry you, I must first shrive you of your sins."

Tongue-tied in panic, Aemilia turned to Will.

"Goodness me," she heard Winifred mutter in English. "If she's to confess all her sins, we'll be here past midnight."

"So be it, good friar." Will handed Enrico back to Tabitha. "Let me be first."

In a daze, Aemilia watched Will kneel at the shriving bench and fold his hands in prayer.

"Forgive me, Father, I have sinned," he told the friar. "I've yielded to temptation of the flesh, and so begat a child without benefit of holy wedlock."

She trembled to hear the contrition in his voice, as though he had been longing for years to receive absolution for getting Anne Hathaway with child and so binding them both in an unhappy marriage. Yet he was ingenious enough to speak the truth of his past in such a way as to lead the friar to believe he was speaking about Aemilia and fathering her child.

When it was her turn, Aemilia followed Will's lead and knelt at the shriving bench. "Forgive me, Father. Without benefit of wedlock, I too have succumbed to wicked temptation and so gave birth to my son, the fruit of my sin."

"This man?" The friar's mild eyes met hers. "Do you truly love him?"

"Yes." She felt such a welling up of relief to speak the truth without subterfuge. "I love him with all my heart, Frate Lorenzo."

As the friar uttered the words of absolution, Aemilia's head spun. Here she was, a Jew's daughter, educated by high-minded Puritans, participating in this papist rite in order to seal a doubly bigamous marriage. She could almost see dead Anne Locke rise from her grave to look on in horror. What Catholic hell would she and Will burn in for this deception of theirs, and would that be more gruesome than the fire and brimstone Anne Locke had described when translating Calvin's sermons? She imagined Jacopo shaking his head at her in wry admiration.

As the friar went to fetch his missal, Will raised her to her feet.

"*Fiat,*" he whispered, kissing her.

When the friar returned, Will took her hand.

"My good women," Frate Lorenzo said, addressing the Weir sisters, "I presume there is no reason why this man and woman may not be lawfully wed?"

Aemilia glanced back at them, her heart in her throat. Prudence's face was inscrutable. Winifred looked as though she had swallowed a gargoyle. But Tabitha, who spoke the best Italian, lifted her gaze to the friar.

"Good Father, there is no reason why they should not marry with every blessing!" With the child in her arms, Tabitha looked as beautiful and innocent as the painted Madonna on the wall.

"Very well," said the friar. "We shall proceed."

Aemilia distinctly thought she heard Prudence whisper to her sisters, "The spell is full wound." But when she looked back, Prudence only smiled.

AEMILIA'S KNEES WERE STILL knocking when Will led her back into the daylight. The path undulating between the vineyard and olive groves, now her property, led to their new home, a crumbling old villa covered in blooming wisteria. It glimmered like a dream and yet it was real.

"What if the friar had refused us?" she whispered, still not believing they had got away with such a liberty.

He laughed and hugged her close. "Why, then we would have had to live together as two gentlemen, of course. Do you not miss your breeches?"

"LOVE IS A SMOKE raised with a fume of sighs," Will said, his voice throaty as she straddled his lean body. Beneath her closed eyelids, stars exploded.

"Being purged," he gasped, "a fire sparking in lover's eyes."

She threw back her head, flame igniting her loins. She thought her naked flesh must glow like a lamp lit from within. *Now I know.* Know what it meant to be truly in love, abandoning all restraint to surrender to a passion that left her breathless.

"A madness most discreet," she murmured, while together they rocked and churned until at last they cried out in one voice, "I die! I die!"

Seized by ecstasy, her soul lifted out of her body to entwine with his. When she collapsed panting at his side, he raised himself on one elbow to trace her flesh bathed golden in the afternoon sun.

"My beautiful love," he said. "The sun never saw her match since the world first began."

"You turn everything into a poem." She nestled against him.

"Because I am a poet in love."

His heart pounded against her ear when he reached for her hand and played with the golden ring he had given her, turning it round and round on her finger. They were criminals—bigamists!—who had broken every rule, as star-crossed lovers will do. But love must triumph—the friar had said so himself. Eros was their god who would redeem their every sin. And how were they harming their spouses who, as sure as spring rain, would be happier without them? The old Will and Aemilia had died to be reborn as lovers in this villa in the hills above Verona, their past wiped clean, as though no vows had ever bound them to Alfonse Lanier or Anne Hathaway.

"You are my true husband," she whispered. "Had I only met you before I met Lord Hunsdon. And had you only met me before Anne."

"Then you would have been young indeed for I married at eighteen," he said. "That would make you as young as Giulietta, a maid of thirteen."

"If I could only be a girl again. Turn back time."

"Our love *shall* turn back time. You are my first true love." His hand cupped her belly. "I want to have a child with you."

"A daughter," she said, her eyes moistening to imagine his babe quickening in her womb. "A sister for Enrico."

"We'll name her Odilia after the chapel where we plighted our troth," he said. "Odilia, the patroness of good eyesight. Our daughter shall never be shortsighted!"

Aemilia laughed and reached for her shift while Will reached for his shirt, but instead of dressing and rising from bed, they settled back against the bolster, shared a cup of wine, and plotted their next play.

"It will make Giulietta happy if we write the romance of Giuletta of Verona," she said. "The tale of the two famous lovers."

Luigi da Porto's tale, *Giulietta e Romeo,* was drawn from two ill-fated young lovers who had lived in fourteenth-century Verona, children of rival families, the Capuleti and Montecchi.

"You wish to turn from comedy to tragedy?" Will asked her. "You know how the tale ends. He poisons himself. She kills herself with his dagger."

"We shall make the tale our own," she said. "We shall give them their happy ending."

"Can we truly?"

"Two poets in love." She kissed him fervently. "We might do anything."

Will summed up the story in a sentence. "Star-crossed lovers fight cruel time to make their love last forever."

"And so shall they succeed! For true lovers may stride upon gossamer and yet not fall."

With Paolo, the wine grower, and Antonio, his son, looking after the vineyard and olive groves, the warm spring days passed in bliss, the new play growing and flourishing like the young grapes. Most of the writing transpired in bed, in their chamber overlooking the green vines and the chapel where they had exchanged vows. Lying atop the coverlet, the sun warm on their bare tangled limbs, *tarocchi* cards scattered around them, they penned scene after scene filled with their poetry.

How Aemilia delighted in their creation, this testament of their love. Here were the youthful *innamorati,* here the masked ball where Giulietta and Romeo fell in love at first sight, plunging straight into their passion without the tedious formalities of courtship. Here was the sympathetic friar who married them in secret, and here was cynical Mercutio, possessive of Romeo and as mercurial as his name — a sly portrait of Southampton. Mercutio viewed love as a feat of conquest. Only Giulietta and Romeo understood the true sacred mystery of love, unstained and eternal.

As Aemilia read the lines of thirteen-year-old Giulietta, the burden of her own twenty-five years fell away, rendering her as pure as that virginal girl on the tender cusp of womanhood.

"Come, gentle night," she recited, "come, loving black-browed night."

She trembled as Will traced her own black eyebrows. "Go on," he whispered.

"Give me my Romeo; and when he shall die —"

She stopped short, unable to hide her smile, for *die* meant not just physical death but surrendering to the heights of sensual ecstasy. She shivered as Will traced her breasts through the thin fabric of her shift.

"Take him," she continued, her eyes locked with Will's, "and cut him out in little stars, and he will make the face of heaven so fine that all the world will be in love with night and pay no worship to the garish sun. Oh, I have bought a mansion of a love, but not possessed it —"

The pages flew from her hand as she pounced upon Will and took possession of him. She laughed and caught her fingers in his hair.

"My dark lady," he said. "You hang like a jewel on the cheek of night."

Together they writhed and then died in each other's arms.

"Such happiness," she whispered. "My life before I loved you was but a dream."

His hand found her belly, still flat and taut, though for how much longer she could not say, given the vigor of their lovemaking.

"We'll have a family as big as Jacopo's," he said. "A whole brood of children, each of them as beautiful as their mother."

20

O YOU EVER MISS England?" Aemilia asked Will, one glittering June morning as they walked arm in arm down the path between the vineyard and olive groves. She smiled to think that they had known each other for a full year. How quickly their love had blossomed, leading them to this paradise.

"Last night I dreamt of the Forest of Arden," Will said. "But I found it full of cypress trees. The Faery Queen appeared in the moonlight as an Italian lady with long black hair." He spun her in his arms and kissed her. "So you see, my love, Italy has conquered even my dreams. What can compare with this?"

They gazed down at Verona nestled below in the bend of the Adige River. The cathedral, the basilica, the old Roman forum and amphitheater, and the *castello* glowed hazy pink in the early morning light. Set within massive fortified walls, this was the largest city in mainland Veneto and nearly as rich as Venice, for it lay at the crossroads of the great trade routes. German and Dutch merchants passed by on their way south to Rome and Naples while French and Spanish traveled through en route to Venice and Trieste.

Scattered around Verona lay farms, orchards, and vineyards, some large and some as modest as Aemilia's own small holding. But all of them prospered, thanks to the Turkish trade embargo blocking the importing of wine from Greece and the Levant. The Veneto wine growers made their fortunes shipping off barrel after barrel to satisfy the Venetian market.

At this fresh hour of morning, before the baking heat of midday, Verona and its environs seemed like lost Arcadia come to life. Aemilia squeezed Will's hand, scarcely believing how fortune had blessed them.

"Is this not the perfect setting for our romance of Giulietta and Romeo?" she asked him.

"Ah, if there is one thing I do miss, it's the chance to see our plays performed at the Rose Theater," he said.

"What, have our tender Giulietta played by a boy in a wig?" She enjoyed teasing him. "Let's translate them into Italian and see them performed right here in Verona."

He shook his head. "All my wordcraft would be lost. No, when we're finished, I shall send our plays to Harry."

When Will spoke of his former love, she detected neither longing nor bitterness, only a fondness he might reserve for an old friend. Still, she was secretly glad that Harry was not yet in possession of *Giulietta and Romeo.*

"I fear he would make us twist our romance into a tragedy," she said. "People like him seem to put great store in maidens stabbing themselves and bleeding all over the stage."

None of Isabella Andreini's heroines would have killed themselves, she thought.

"The original tale *is* a tragedy," Will pointed out. "How could it not be in such a clannish place?"

Verona, like many an Italian city, was riven by feuding families competing for power and wealth, each plotting the others' downfall. Aemilia was grateful to live up in the hills, far removed from such intrigue.

"Think for a moment—is not tragedy more profound?" Will asked. "For tragedy is high art, not mere entertainment. It touches the deepest places inside us."

Aemilia rolled her eyes to hear him expound on Aristotle when he had never learned Greek. But she took care not to remind him of that fact or that she, a woman, had received a more thorough education. Instead, she used reason.

"How could any tragedy ever written, even by the ancients, be a finer work of art than Dante's *Divine Comedy?*" she asked him. "For comedy *is* at its essence divine. What could touch the spirit more profoundly than the triumph of love and goodness over hatred, violence, and greed?"

Comedy in its true, classical sense, she reflected, did not refer to humorous, lighthearted entertainment but to the belief in a just universe that orders all things to their ultimate good, just as Dante's pilgrim progresses from the inferno to the heights of heaven.

Will stared at the city below as if to read his answer in that labyrinth of streets and piazzas.

"We have written four comedies in the Italian style," he said. "The romance of the shrew. Viola's tale of adventure. Rosalind's tale. The romance of Benedick and Beatrice."

Aemilia warmed to hear him list their creations, their strong-willed heroines.

"Might we not have *one* tragedy?" he asked her. "If only to prove we are masters of the entire range of drama, not just comedy."

When he was being stubborn, his Warwickshire accent grew stronger. She tried not to laugh lest he think she was mocking him. Instead, she considered his boyhood in Stratford, apprenticed to his glover father who had expected him to live a humdrum existence in a backwater town. Will's stubbornness had preserved him, raising him to loftier aspirations. If he had not been such a willful, contrary soul, he would have never come to London to carve out his life as a poet. She would have never met him, never fallen so deeply in love. Instead, the stars had conspired to bring them to this vine-clad slope high above Verona. *How lucky we are! How lucky!*

"Let us think on it," she said gently.

They turned and walked back up the path where they came across Prudence gathering herbs in the long shady grass of the peach orchard. Singing under her breath, Pru was trailed by a procession of goats and geese, as if the creatures were in her thrall.

"There's something of the witch in your Weir sisters," Will remarked. "Particularly that one. I heard Lucetta muttering that Prudence dabbles in love potions."

Lucetta was Paolo the winemaker's wife, and she and the Weir sisters were currently engaged in a fraught battle over supremacy of the kitchen.

"Don't be ridiculous," Aemilia said. "Lucetta's only vexed that her son is so besotted with Tabitha, as if a pretty girl like her had any need of a love philter. Look there! Romance transpiring before our eyes."

She pointed to Tabitha trading pleasantries with Antonio, who was as handsome as Apollo. Tabitha appeared as Venus herself, her golden hair gleaming even brighter in the sun. Now that Aemilia was in love, every single person and thing seemed to shimmer with a deeper radiance. And why should Tabitha not be blessed with romance, have a child of her own now that Enrico was weaned?

Even Winifred seemed back to her old self. Her hand clasping Enrico's, Winifred inspected the plump young lambs, as if trying to decide which one she would pick for her lamb pie. Here in the countryside, Winifred's girth had expanded once more to its full magnificence.

"Papa!" Enrico broke free from Winifred to toddle toward Will, not content until he rode in grandeur on his idol's shoulders.

It brought tears to Aemilia's eyes to hear Enrico call Will papa, to see how Will treasured him. Truly, they were a family and soon there might be another child on the way. Even as the thought danced inside her head, she felt a twinge inside her, a slight dizziness as the day grew hotter. But she wouldn't breathe a word to Will until she was certain.

His eyes traveled over her face. "You've gone pale. Go inside, love. Out of the sun."

"Not just yet," she said, jingling her chatelaine with the keys to the wine cave, storerooms, and cellars. "Duty first."

At that, she set off to find Paolo. Meanwhile, Will was careful to carry Enrico out of the sun before it scorched him.

Paolo was weaving his way among the vines, inspecting them for pests. Everything Aemilia knew about wine growing she had learned from him. He saw to the husbandry and harvest, the winemaking and oil pressing, while she saw to the accounts and the shipping of the wine and olive oil to Bassano and Venice.

Their small holding produced three different red wines. The first was a young, fresh-tasting table wine that slaked the thirst on a dusty summer day. One could drink a glass or two and not be drunk. The second, the *ripasso*, was stronger with fermented grape pomace added to create a more robust flavor. But their finest vintage was the *amarone*, made in the Greek style with grapes dried for three to four months before fermentation began. Then the wine was aged in oak barrels in their cave for at least three years. The *amarone* was heady and potent. Half a jug could render a strong man legless.

Paolo, Aemilia concluded, *is an artist as gifted as Jacopo had been, an artist of wine.*

"Will it be a good year?" she asked him.

The man's sunburnt face creased into a smile. "The best year in memory, *signora.* If this weather holds. If God spares us from hailstorms and heavy autumn rain."

Lifting his eyes to the heavens, Paolo crossed himself. Aemilia bowed her head. Again the mask constricted her. What must Paolo and the farmworkers think of their new mistress, this foreigner, so hastily married? She who attended Mass as infrequently as possible.

"There's a matter I must discuss with you," Paolo said. As the sun glared down, the edges of his face seemed to blur. "It's only gossip, *signora,* and you know how foolish folk are, but I've heard it murmured that your Prudenza is a *strega,* a witch."

Aemilia's temples pounded in the heat. "You would use kitchen gossip to condemn my faithful servant? She's an herb wife, to be sure, but there's no wickedness in her. I trust her with my own son."

If she had only known Prudence during her time with Lord Hunsdon, Aemilia had no doubt that Pru's remedies would have prevented her from falling pregnant, unlike the useless decoctions of that midwife Lord Hunsdon had bade her use.

"I just thought you should know what people are saying," Paolo said. "The neighbor's washerwoman told my wife that she saw Prudenza at the marketplace and your Prudenza gave her the evil eye. Later that same day, the poor woman suffered a miscarriage."

A wave of dizziness seized Aemilia, forcing her to kneel in the black earth.

"*Signora,* are you not well?" Paolo helped her to her feet.

"Dear God," she said. "Many a woman miscarries. But surely this has nothing to do with Prudence. Tell me, Paolo, have there been recent witch trials in Verona?"

Unlike in England, where supposed witches were hanged, here the Inquisition had the authority to torture the accused and burn them at the stake. Aemilia couldn't bear to think of such a fate befalling Prudence.

"Not in many years, *signora*," Paolo said. "I pray we will be spared such an event."

"Mistress!"

Aemilia turned to see Tabitha come sprinting, cheeks flushed and eyes shining. Truly this girl had no clue what was being said about her sister.

"Mistress," Tabitha panted. "Olivia and Giulietta have come to visit all the way from Bassano!"

Close at Tabitha's heels came Giulietta. The girl flung her arms around Aemilia, nearly knocking her over.

"How I've missed you, Aemilia! It's so *dull* without you," the girl said breathlessly. "Have you and Will finished your romance of Giulietta and Romeo?"

"Nearly." Aemilia kissed her cheeks. "Today our lovely heroine has come to Verona."

"I'm so glad *I'm* not a character in one of your plays!" Olivia had finally caught up with her daughter. "I'd find it rather embarrassing."

Aemilia and Giulietta shared a secret glance, for Aemilia had shown the girl the play of Viola and Olivia. But the girl made an earnest face for her mother.

"Giulietta in the play is not *me*, Mama, but a young lady who lived in the time of Dante Alighieri." The girl's eyes were dreamy. "She lost her heart to Romeo, secretly married him, and then died for love when she was only thirteen!"

Olivia cringed. "I would never let you marry so young, *carissima*. Not a day before you turn sixteen. Don't speak of this nonsense of dying for love! Love is meant to make us happy."

"You both must be hot and dusty from your journey." Aemilia linked arms with her kinswomen. "Let me take you to the loggia. It's cool and breezy there."

"First show us around the property before it gets too hot, *cara*," said Olivia. "I came here once when I first married Francesco, but that was many years ago."

Just a few minutes with Giulietta and Olivia had lightened Aemilia's heart. Her guests chatted of Bassano and of Francesco and Leandro's paintings as she led them through the olive and almond groves and the orchards of peach, apricot, apple, and pear. Giulietta admired the goats and sheep that wandered freely, their presence announced by the trilling bells tied to their necks.

"You've done well with the kitchen garden," Olivia said approvingly. "You are truly self-sufficient. The only thing you need buy is meal to bake bread. Francesco once said that if he was in charge of this property he would plant mulberry trees to raise silkworms. You might consider this, *cara,* for some years the wine harvest fails."

Aemilia pictured the mulberry tree and three silk moths in the Bassano family coat of arms. Then she thought of Papa's ancestors who had raised silkworms in Sicily until they were driven away. Yet something told her not to mention this buried history to Olivia. Apart from the late Jacopo, it seemed her kin in the Casa dal Corno thought the past was best left to lie.

"Where's Will?" Giulietta asked.

"He took Enrico inside." Aemilia gazed at the villa dripping with wisteria, its shutters closed to keep out the heat.

"Ah, speaking of Will, I have a letter for him." Olivia drew an envelope from the brocade purse that hung at her waist. "It arrived only a few days ago."

Taking the letter from Olivia, Aemilia saw the Earl of Southampton's coat of arms on the wax seal. As she stepped out of the shade, intent on showing her guests the olive press, the heat closed in with a force that sent her stumbling. The letter fell from her slack hand.

"It's only the heat," she said, when Olivia took her arm. "I swear I'll be fine."

"*I* think it's hot, too," Giulietta declared. "It's *far* hotter here than in Bassano."

The girl bent down to pick up the fallen letter and handed it back to Aemilia.

"Come, let's away," said Aemilia. "Out of the sun."

IN THE COOL REFUGE of the loggia, the midday feast awaited them. Winifred poured wine, still cool from the cellar. Tabitha carried out Enrico so the guests could fuss over him while Prudence and Lucetta bustled back and forth from the kitchen carrying out dish after dish of freshly baked bread, soft white cheeses made from the milk of their goats and sheep, peaches and apricots, almonds and olives, a stew of lentils, and *bigoli*, homemade buckwheat noodles, and *fagioli* seasoned with rosemary, raisins, and pine nuts. When Lucetta appeared with the platter of braised rabbit in *amarone* sauce, the sight and smell made Aemilia's stomach curdle. Staggering from the table, she heaved over the rail into Prudence's herb garden.

"She *is* ill!" Giulietta cried.

Olivia laughed and supported Aemilia's shoulders. "I think I know the sickness she suffers and it's a very happy sickness for married ladies." She wiped Aemilia's mouth with her handkerchief. "Does Will know, *cara?*"

"Not yet," Aemilia said.

Olivia took her back to the table. "Come, have a glass of watered wine and some bread. You need something in your stomach."

Winifred hovered over Aemilia protectively. "Never you worry, mistress. From now on, we'll make proper *English* food. Let me take this evil-smelling rodent away."

With a pointed look at Lucetta, Winifred carried the offending rabbit back to the kitchen.

"Why hasn't Will come to the table?" Giulietta asked.

"He must be upstairs writing," Aemilia said. "When he writes, he loses all sense of time."

She imagined him in their shuttered bedchamber, mewed up like a molting hawk, scribbling his heart out. Perhaps he was so immersed in his inner world, he hadn't even realized guests had arrived.

"Shall I fetch him down, mistress?" Tabitha asked.

But just then Will appeared, his face animated and cheerful as he took his seat beside Aemilia.

"At last!" Giulietta clapped her hands. "Were you truly writing up there?"

"Indeed," he said. "I was hard at work on the play of your Veronese *innamorati*. This is the scene I've just written." Flushed with excitement, he turned to Aemilia. "Romeo is peaceable and yet he is fated to live in feuding Verona. Thus, he's drawn into a duel to avenge the death of his friend Mercutio who died fighting to save Romeo from attack." Here Will had to pause for breath. "And so Romeo kills Giulietta's cousin. This sets everything else in motion. From this scene onward, comedy turns to tragedy."

He gazed expectantly at the women, who viewed him with uncomprehending stares.

"Fighting duels." Giulietta made a face. "What about the *romance?*"

"So it's Mercutio who comes between the lovers and spoils their happiness," Aemilia said in a hollow voice, as flies buzzed around her head.

At the corner of the table lay Harry's letter, which Will had evidently not yet noticed.

"Will, we far prefer to hear your poetry of love," Olivia said.

For a moment, Will looked crestfallen. Then he shrugged, his eyes darting up and down the table. "What, there's no meat for our guests?"

Olivia offered Aemilia a complicit smile. "Meat spoils quickly in this heat. Have some cheese instead."

Will turned to Aemilia. "You're so quiet. This is very unlike you."

Olivia smothered a giggle.

Will raised his hands in exasperation. "So what is this secret you ladies are hiding from me?"

"That's what *I'd* like to know!" Giulietta shot her mother an indignant glance.

Aemilia took his hand and felt her face flame even hotter. Though it seemed awkward to tell him in front of their guests, there seemed little point in keeping her condition a mystery.

"I'm with child," she told him. "I hope it's a little girl this time."

"*Oh,*" said Giulietta, turning to her mother in amazement.

Tabitha cried out in delight and clapped her hands. Prudence grinned.

"Such a blessing," said Will, kissing Aemilia before them all. "Such happy news."

Aemilia blinked back her tears, her heart pounding in joy. She imagined a daughter with Will's hazel eyes flitting like a dryad through the olive groves.

"Here comes a cooling breeze, mistress," Prudence said in English, too softly for Will to hear. She spoke as though the weather itself obeyed her command. "Eat in peace, sweet mistress. Your troubles shall soon pass."

Pru's eyes locked with Aemilia's as the wind swept Harry's letter off the table. Meanwhile, Will, Olivia, and Giulietta were too engrossed in their happy chatter to notice. Prudence smiled to her mistress, as though to seal a pact.

IN THE COOL OF early evening, Will escorted their guests down into Verona to show them the sights while Aemilia sat in the loggia and read the scene he had penned. By killing Giulietta's cousin, Romeo made himself a wanted man, an outlaw forced to flee Verona. Even with the aid of their sympathetic friar, the story had evolved so that it could only end in tragedy. The sole way Giulietta and Romeo could preserve their love was by dying together in a double suicide. *Might we not have one tragedy?*

Leaving the pages on the table, Aemilia stood at the rail of the loggia and looked down at the city glowing in the evening sun. Soon Will and their guests would be back. It was only twenty minutes to Verona by foot, down the cobbled cart track, perhaps slightly longer for the return up the steep hill. She would hear their laughter echoing through the olive trees before she saw them. Then it would be time to light the candles and watch the moon rise. Winifred and Prudence would bring out a simple supper and a jug of wine. As there was neither virginals nor lute in her new household, she would entertain her guests by singing madrigals. Giulietta might join in, their voices weaving in harmony.

Aemilia's eyes caught sight of something tangled in the wisteria vines. Harry's letter. She stooped to extricate it from the greenery and then held it in both her hands. It shamed her to think she could be tempted into such dishonesty, allowing Will's letter to be lost, even though Prudence had offered the perfect excuse — blown away in the wind!

In the searing heat of midday, she had felt sick and had not been herself, but now with a clear head and a settled stomach, she would do what was right. How could she betray Will's trust? Surely their love must be strong enough to withstand a letter scrawled in Harry's careless hand.

She placed the letter atop Will's newly written pages then carried the sheaf of papers upstairs and placed them in their lap desk.

With the shutters closed, their bedchamber was stifling and oppressively dark. Singing a lullaby under her breath for the tiny new life stirring inside her, Aemilia opened the shutters wide, allowing fresh air to pour into every corner.

AFTERWARD, AEMILIA'S HEART RESTED easy and unburdened. Even if their play lurched into tragedy, their love would endure, and in their long life together, they could write many more comedies ending in perfect bliss. Leaning back in her chair, she sipped watered wine while listening to Giulietta praise Verona's silk market as though it were paradise on earth.

"Tomorrow we *must* go back and buy that apricot brocade with the silver threads!"

"We certainly won't," said her mother. "The price the vendor quoted was outrageous. Because we are visitors from Bassano, he thinks we are fools."

"But he was so handsome," Giulietta said. "I think I shall marry a Veronese silk merchant."

"Say no more," said Will. "We shall burn *Giulietta and Romeo* and instead write *Giulietta and the Silk Vendor of Verona.*"

The girl's eyes widened. "If you write another romance with a heroine named Giulietta, she must fall in love with someone of the highest nobility."

"Your imagination!" Her mother sighed. "You'll probably marry a painter like your father."

"Before I forget," Aemilia said to Will, "Olivia brought a letter for you from Bassano. From the Earl of Southampton."

She gave Harry his full title for Giulietta's benefit. The girl sat bolt upright.

"An English Earl! Is he good-looking?"

"As handsome as he is young and dashing," Will said, with a wink to Aemilia. "And as full of self-regard and hot wind."

Aemilia laughed to hear Will's gentle mockery of his friend. Her belly eased and warmed.

"Still, it will be amusing to see what he has to say," said Will. "Perhaps he writes to rebuke me for not sending certain . . . *artwork* his way."

Aemilia grinned to catch Will's surreptitious reference to Harry's fondness for pornography. Giulietta only looked mystified.

"Even when you two speak Italian," the girl said, "it's as if you have your own secret language just for each other."

"Perhaps we do, indeed," Aemilia said, smiling at Will.

"At that," said Will, "I shall excuse myself." He kissed her and whispered in her ear, "Don't be too long, love."

AEMILIA LINGERED A SHORT while to sing madrigals with Giulietta while Olivia listened. They sang a cappella, their only accompaniment the night birds and the wind in the trees. She thought she heard some pitiful creature howl in the darkness, but still she sang, never falling out of harmony. Moths fluttered around the candle flames. How she hated to see them burn like Icarus. Finally, out of pity for them, she blew out the candles. Tabitha appeared with a lantern to show Giulietta to her guest room.

"I will be up soon," Olivia told her daughter.

When the girl had gone, Olivia took Aemilia's hands. "It's good to see you so happy. I only wish you had told me the truth from the beginning. Why would you ever wish to lie to me?"

"The truth?" Aemilia's mind was a blank. Which of her many falsehoods had tripped her up this time? Had Olivia divined that her and Will's marriage was a sham?

"I heard Enrico calling Will papa," Olivia said. "You should have told us from the start that he's your son's father. We are your family, *cara*. You must speak the truth to us."

"Forgive me," Aemilia murmured.

She felt like an even worse liar for not daring to correct Olivia's false assumption, which was far more pleasant and less complicated than the facts. That she had no business living with Will as his wife and bearing his child. If Olivia knew, would she shun her completely? Forbid her innocent daughter from coming near her?

Olivia hugged Aemilia. "I'm so relieved you're finally married. Now everything shall turn out well for you, *cara*. God smiles upon true lovers."

Warmth welled up in Aemilia's heart. She imagined Will and herself as *innamorati* in Arcadia, laying garlands of thanksgiving upon the altar of Eros.

SHAFTS OF MOONLIGHT POURED through the windows to illuminate Aemilia's path up the stairs. Her palm found their bedchamber door.

Back in Westminster, when she first married Alfonse while six months pregnant with Lord Hunsdon's child, the midwife had warned her not to lie with her husband until six months after the baby was born. But Aemilia no longer believed in such prohibitions. No, she would make love with Will for as long as her body allowed her to do so. Her desire pulsed like a flame of pure-white heat.

Their chamber was lit by a single guttering candle throwing shadows on the walls. Will stood at the open window, his back to her.

"Such an enchanting moon," she said, taking her place beside him, twining her arm around his. "Soon it will be full. You better not stare at it too long, love, or the servants shall murmur that you're bewitched."

Her gentle teasing brought no smile to his face. He only stared out into that night, his face immobile. His flesh felt as cold as marble to her touch.

"What is it, my love?" she asked.

She raised his chilly fingers to her lips and kissed them, but he seemed listless and numb, as though his soul had been stolen away. The moon bleached all color from his skin. Only when she touched his face did she feel his tears. But his eyes were frozen wide open. For a moment, he reminded her of a corpse. Even as she shoved that image from her mind, her chest seized up.

"Speak to me, love."

"The beautiful boy," he said faintly.

"Harry?" she asked. "How does he fare?"

Will only barked out a laugh that frightened her more than his tears.

She felt herself lurch, as though the floor could no longer support her. "Look at me, I beg you."

When he finally turned to her, she thought she stood face-to-face with his effigy. Not the living man. In one hand, he clutched the letter. As she gazed at those folded pages, his hand began to shake as though he'd no more control of it than he had of the stars in the heavens. The letter fell to the floor.

What had Harry written to leave Will in such a state? Had Prudence been right—should she have simply allowed the cursed thing to float away on the wind?

"You have to tell me what happened."

"I have no words." He looked past her into the darkness. "No feeble words of mine could ever . . ."

He broke off into jagged weeping, covering his eyes with one hand. Though she held him in the circle of her arms, his heart banging against her ear, she couldn't reach him.

"The letter," she murmured. "May I read it?"

Uttering no protest, he stared at the moon as if to lose himself in that pale inconstant orb.

Kneeling on the floor, she picked up the two leaves of paper. The first page was of fine heavy stock and emblazoned with the Southampton coat of arms.

My dear friend,

Let not your heart despise me for passing on this news from your wife, though it possesses the most terrible weight a soul can bear. My thoughts abide with you. Please make use of my letter of credit should you wish to return to Stratford.

Ever your loving Harry

The heaviness Harry described now pressed down on her. So Anne Shakespeare, her beloved's true and lawful wife, who could neither read nor write, had managed to send her straying husband a message so grave that it had humbled even Harry.

The second page was of much cheaper paper, the letter written by the curate of Holy Trinity Church in Stratford, who had taken illiterate Anne's dictation. *How humiliating,* Aemilia thought, *for Anne to be forced to channel her letter through a clergyman and then through Harry.*

My dear husband,

Some months ago you wrote to us from far Italy. I can scarce picture such a place. I know not where you are now, so I send this

letter in care of the Earl of Southampton and pray that it reaches
your hand.

    It is with a broken heart I must tell you that our son Hamnet has
taken ill and died. He now lies buried in Holy Trinity churchyard.
Your parents, and Hamnet and Judith Sadler, his godparents, attended
the funeral in your stead.

    Thank merciful Heaven our daughters Susanna and Judith are
well but are sorely grieving their poor dead brother.

    Your faithful wife Anne

Anne's words, scrawled in the curate's ungainly hand, left Aemilia drowning in shame. *What have we done?* She imagined the woman weeping at her son's grave, and beside her an empty place where her husband should have stood. Will, had he only known, would have returned to Stratford with all speed. But Aemilia had lured him away to the far side of Europe and written sunny Italian comedies with him while his son lay dying.

"I am so, so sorry," she began.

She wanted to say more but found she couldn't go on. Her tongue had frozen. Will was right. No words existed to match this loss. While he had been living with her in their beautiful idyll, his only son had died and the funeral had gone on without him.

As she tried to hold Will, he was seized by a fit of silent weeping. *The beautiful boy.*

Will's grief filled their chamber with his dead son.

In the morning Aemilia awakened alone. She found Will sitting in the shadowiest corner of the loggia.

"My love," she said.

Their guests had not yet come down, but Tabitha now appeared with Enrico. Upon seeing Will, the little boy launched himself at him.

"Papa, Papa!" Enrico hugged Will's knees, begging to be lifted into his lap.

Her hand on her mouth, Aemilia watched Will tremble uncontrollably as he had done the night before when he could no longer even hold Anne's letter. It seemed he could not bear the touch of those little hands. Tabitha was too dumbfounded to react as Enrico wailed in confusion, his cries piercing the morning stillness. Aemilia swooped down to take him away.

"Your papa is tired today," she heard herself say in a too-bright voice. "You must let him rest. Shall we go see the donkeys?"

As Will walked off in the direction of the olive groves, a spell of dizziness forced Aemilia to sink onto the bench he had vacated. Black spots danced before her eyes while her son squirmed in her arms, still calling out for his papa.

"*Cara,* are you so sick in the morning that you can't even smile?" Olivia's face swam before her. "Why do you look so sad? It's not good for the little babe you're growing."

Aemilia could hardly face her guests in their blameless good cheer. But Olivia was already taking charge, lifting the crying child from Aemilia's lap, hefting him on her hip and covering him in kisses. She summoned Winifred to bring her mistress bread and warm milk with honey.

"What happened to Will?" Giulietta asked. "Why is he wandering about the groves at this hour?"

"He's not himself," Aemilia said. "The letter brought sad tidings from England. His beloved young kinsman has died."

"How very sad!" Olivia's eyes brimmed in sympathy. "Ah, then we must cut our visit short as not to burden him. Grief takes its own course. But don't let him grieve too long, *cara.* Though losing a loved one is always terrible, his thoughts should be on you and the new baby."

Aemilia was too choked to speak.

"A new life to replace a death." Olivia laid a tender hand on Aemilia's belly.

IN THE PRISTINE COOLNESS of the following morning, Aemilia bade farewell to her guests but not before lading their packhorses with casks of *amarone* and olive oil, a bushel of apricots, and a pot of honey.

"Give my love to Francesco and Leandro," she told Olivia, who clasped her like a mother. Aemilia imagined trading places with Giulietta, becoming a blameless young girl with her whole life before her. Not the woman she had become, shackled with too many lies.

21

N THE FULL GLARE of the noontide sun, Aemilia found Will hacking at weeds in the kitchen garden with a fury that took her breath away. Clods of earth flew everywhere. A salamander's skull landed at her feet. Caked in dirt and sweat, he reminded her of a grave digger.

What shall we do now? All the questions she burned to ask him stuck in her throat. In the face of his anguish, she became a tiptoeing shadow, terrified of saying or doing anything to worsen his pain. What hurt her most was how his grief made him turn away from her, not toward her. Why couldn't he let her comfort him? Did he blame this entire conundrum on her? Was she the author of his tragedy?

As the heat rose in shimmering waves, she forced herself to speak. "Will you return to Stratford?" She braced herself for his answer.

"How can I go there now?" he asked her bitterly. "How can I ever face them again? I am fortune's fool. To think I didn't want to return until I had accomplished something. I was wandering the world while my son died."

HE WAS SOUL SICK, her beloved. Grief was a fortress and inside those dank walls he now dwelled. She was locked outside, calling out to him in vain. Though they shared the same table and bed, he was lost to her, utterly irretrievable.

She bade herself be patient. As Olivia had said, grief took its own course, and she could hardly abandon him to his pain. *But don't let him grieve too long,* cara. *His thoughts should be on you and the new baby.* In another five months, she would hold that child in her arms. Would his melancholy be healed by then? Would he be able to share her joy, fall in love with the new life they had created together?

AUGUST FLAMED LIKE A furnace, and Paolo muttered of drought. They hadn't seen a drop of rain since June. The laborers and their children trudged back and forth carrying buckets from the spring to water the vines, but the spring threatened to run dry.

"Will this spoil the harvest?" Aemilia asked Paolo.

The grim lines set in the winegrower's face gave her little cause for hope.

"If the spring dries up and there's no rain, we'll have to drag up water from the Adige," he said, mopping the sweat from his face with the cloth she handed him. "But even if we break our backs hauling water up that slope, the grapes might be scorched."

Aemilia squinted down at the baking valley where the river ran low in its banks.

"But still we have the olives, do we not?" she asked. "Olive trees require far less water than grapevines, so I understand."

"If the drought is harsh enough, we will lose most of the olives as well. We must pray for rain."

She nodded soberly and was about to excuse herself when Paolo gave her a long grave look. "We haven't seen a drought like this in years, *signora*. It could ruin us."

"What can we do?" She felt a kick inside, as though even her unborn child were succumbing to panic.

Paolo took off his dusty straw hat and lowered his voice to a whisper. "I beg you, *signora,* send your Prudenza back to Bassano. For her own safety if nothing else."

The hot wind blew up dust that stung Aemilia's eyes. "Why should my servant have to fear for her safety, Paolo?" But she sensed his answer even before he spoke.

"Already before the drought, people whispered that she was a *strega*. Now, when we must pray for our very survival, the neighbors will take justice into their own hands. I won't be able to stop them and neither will you, *signora*."

"Surely it takes more than gossip to try someone for witchcraft," she said.

"There is no time to wait for a trial," he said darkly. "If the drought lasts much longer, they will try to summon the rains by swimming the witch."

The sweat dripping down Aemilia's back ran cold.

"What do you mean?" Her voice shook in terror.

"They will bind her right thumb to her left big toe, tie a rope around her waist, and throw her into the Adige. If she sinks, she is innocent and they will pull her out, by the grace of God, before she drowns. If she floats, it proves she's a witch, *signora.*"

The heat beat down on Aemilia's head like an anvil. *Swimming the witch.* She had heard of such barbarities taking place in England, the usual outcome being death by drowning for the accused woman, but this was the first she'd heard of such a brutal act being used to bring rain during drought.

When her father was nine years old, he and his brothers were driven out of Bassano because they were Jews. Now that she had finally arrived at what was meant to be her lasting refuge and home, might she, too, be banished because a mob of peasants believed her maid to be a witch? Paolo, of course, was only asking her to send Prudence away. But if the drought continued even after her maid's absence, who might they blame then?

"I will speak to you about this later," she told Paolo.

Hurrying up the path toward the cellars, she came upon Winifred hanging laundry on the bushes to dry.

"Did I ask you to do the laundry?" Aemilia snapped, she who never raised her voice to her servants.

Seeing Winifred's face go white in the face of her temper, Aemilia lowered her head in contrition. "No more washing, please, until this drought ends."

"Mistress, pardon my saying so, but you look like death." Winifred's eyes probed hers. "Go inside now, if you please. A woman in your condition—"

Aemilia held up her palm to cut Winifred short.

"They are saying the darkest things about Prudence." Her voice broke like a child's. "Rain." She closed her eyes, hardly believing her own words as they left her throat. "If indeed she has any . . . influence over such things, tell her we need rain."

In the cellars, Aemilia tallied the casks of olive oil and wine they could sell. If worse came to worst, she could sell the smallholding, although that would sorely disappoint her family in Bassano. But what else was she to do—return to them a pauper with a babe in arms? There must be a way.

The time had come to discuss this with Will. No matter how bleak his mood, they must speak. She had bowed to his grief, but the strained silence between them had lasted far too long. Even he had to recognize how dire things might become if they did not act to protect Prudence and salvage what they could of the harvest.

Aemilia found Will in the dark cavern of their bedchamber, the shutters bolted against the sun and heat. He crouched on the floor with her emptied lap desk. Spread in neat piles around him were the plays.

The plays. Could they be their salvation if the harvest failed? And did Will's renewed interest in them mean that at last his melancholy was lifting? She hadn't seen him pick up a quill since the day Anne's letter arrived two months ago.

"We should write something new," she said, a warm rush in her heart.

To her joy, he stood and turned to her. But his face was somber.

"How can I go on writing your comedies when I've lost all my mirth?"

"Then write poetry," she said.

If they sparred, so be it. At least he was speaking to her.

"Oh, God," he said. "How stale the world seems. And you speak of poetry."

His hostility left her scalded.

"Then why, pray, did you empty the contents of our desk if not to think of writing?" Her hands on her hips, she was determined to keep him engaged, to not let him sink back into apathy. But something in him had already changed—she noted a new resolve in his eyes as he faced her squarely.

"I must return to England," he said.

Seconds passed before Aemilia could speak. "So you're going back to Stratford?" She forced herself to spill it out.

Back to his lawful wife. How could she stand in his way of doing what was right by his family?

"Aye, I shall visit Stratford to pay my respects to my son's grave and see my daughters before death snatches them away." His voice rang cold and distant. "But then I must return to London. God willing, I might see my work performed on the Southwark stage."

Her head pounded in bewilderment. So he wasn't returning to Anne, after all, the prodigal husband making his amends. Then why leave *her*? She sensed something steely and determined rising in him, as though grief had withered his love and now what ruled him was restless ambition.

"Where will you find the funds to rent the stage?" she asked him. "How shall you pay the players?"

He said nothing, only glanced away from her.

"You're running back to Harry!" she cried, unable to disguise her spite.

"Not to Harry." His gaze was blistering. "To being my own master. Don't you understand? My son is dead and I'm wasting my life here. If I'd wanted to live off a woman in some backwater, I would have stayed in Stratford."

Aemilia opened her mouth then closed it.

In her stymied silence, he spoke. "I'm of little use to you here in the vineyard, but Paolo will be steadfast and your family in Bassano—"

"Did you ever truly love me at all?" How she hated herself for sounding like a spurned mistress in a melodrama.

"I did love you once." He could not meet her eyes.

"You certainly led me to believe so."

Before her anger could spiral out of control, she made herself take a deep breath. Perhaps he didn't mean what he said. This heat was enough to turn any reasonable person into a fiend. Hadn't she shouted at poor Winifred?

Aemilia clasped Will's hands and made herself speak from the tender depths of her heart. "My love, I am so sorry that you lost your Hamnet. Such a loss would madden any soul. But how can you turn against *me*?"

She pressed his right palm to the swell of her belly.

"What of *our* child?" she asked him. "You wanted this child."

She stared into the depths of his clouded hazel eyes that reminded her of English country hedgerows.

His face seemed to soften. "The pleasures we shared were as lovely as Arcadia."

Her heart galloped in hope.

"And just as unreal," he said, blinking as though to hold back his tears. "A false paradise."

To think she had come up with every single excuse for him rather than face the truth that he no longer loved her. There was no more looking away.

"You would abandon a pregnant woman," Aemilia said. *Had he not done so before?*

Will's jaw began to tremble as though he were fighting his own yearning. But when at last he spoke, his voice was cool and measured.

"I will send you money."

White-hot rage exploded inside her skull.

"Those plays are *ours*!" Her voice tore out of her throat. "Whatever money they earn is not yours to dole out as *you* deem fit! Have you forgotten our agreement?"

He backed away from her as though she had turned into a demon. *Hell is empty, all the devils are up here.*

"Who do you think you are?" she demanded, throbbing in fury. "When I met you, you were a penniless nobody."

His face hardened. "And you thought I was yours for the taking. Your creature whom you could bind with a bottle of country wine, some potion brewed by your weird sisters."

His accusation left her too stunned to speak. Her hands clutching her mouth, she watched as he walked away, not even bothering to close the door behind him.

Aemilia's entire strength drained from her. She collapsed on the floor as though she'd no bones left in her body.

To think he'd accused her of using witchcraft to ensnare him! Her thoughts raced in panic—what if it was true that Prudence meddled with spells and Aemilia had unwittingly shared some sort of potion with Will when she brought him the bottle of elderflower wine? If Will told anyone else of his suspicions, would she, too, be condemned as a *strega*? Tied up and cast into the Adige along with Prudence and left to drown? This was her punishment for daring to open her heart to a man.

If Will's passion for her had indeed been the mere fabrication of some enchantment, did that explain how his love for her could be so irrevocably shattered, his overpowering grief and regret rendering the spell void? How seamlessly love could twist into contempt. When Frate Lorenzo had joined them in their illusionary marriage, the friar said that true lovers could walk upon gossamer and yet not fall. But when their love turned bitter, she and Will had come crashing down to earth.

This past year had taken her on an odyssey from England to her father's boyhood home in Bassano and then to this new life in Verona. From trying to live as a man to surrendering to a man's love, opening the barricades of her fortressed heart. To think it had come to such an inglorious end. She was pregnant and Will wanted rid of her, just like Lord Hunsdon before him.

As Aemilia sobbed on the floor like the most wretched of souls, heavy footfalls sent the boards beneath her quivering. Had Will come to take it all back, beg her forgiveness? She lifted her head to see Winifred stooping over her. Her maid raised her up and cradled her, rocking and crooning while Aemilia wept until she thought her eyes would run dry.

"Oh, my sweet lady." Winifred was crying along with her. "I thought you had better sense than to take up with him. He left one wife behind. What made you think he wouldn't leave you?"

"And now I carry his child!"

"If you wish it wasn't so," Winifred whispered, "our Prudence has a store of herbs."

"No," Aemilia said. "I couldn't do that."

If everything else had been taken from her, she would not sacrifice her unborn child, the flowering of the lost sweetness of her love.

Winifred opened the shutters, allowing the cool air of dusk to waft into the stifling chamber.

"Look, mistress. A new moon."

Neither of them made a move to light a candle or lamp, for that would only attract mosquitoes. Instead, they sat on the bed and contemplated the evening sky.

"How shall I go on?" Aemilia rested her head on her maid's massive shoulder. "Oh, Winifred, how?"

Winifred smoothed her mistress's rumpled hair. "You know you can't stay here and suffer the things they'll say about you once he's gone and you're left behind with a big belly. If you want my honest advice, we'd best return to England."

"What, go back to Alfonse?" Aemilia recoiled. "Bassano would be a far kinder refuge."

Even as she spoke, she asked herself how she could face Olivia again after telling her so many lies. She imagined the dear woman's incredulous face. Cara, *I thought I knew you, but I never knew you at all. Who are you?*

"But, mistress, there's that horrible talk of our Prudence being a witch." Fear gripped Winifred's voice. "What if the rumors follow us to Bassano? In God's name, we should flee Italy as quickly as we can."

A shiver rippled through both women as the word *witch* hung in the air.

WHEN WILL DID NOT return, Winifred spent the night with her mistress, reluctant to leave her alone.

Sleep eluded Aemilia. Her shift billowed in the breeze wafting through the window as she paced the chamber, setting the boards beneath her creaking and groaning. The wind scattered the pages of the plays across the floor like autumn leaves.

"Sleep, mistress," Winifred begged her. "At least lie down and close your eyes for a spell."

Aemilia stood at the window and stared out into the gloom. The moon had set hours ago and even the stars faded one by one.

"If only things could go back to the way they were before. Perhaps I can talk some sense into him. When he comes back in the morning, he might be of a better mind, mightn't he, Winifred?"

Aemilia's heart leapt in hope as she turned the golden ring Will had given her round and round on her finger.

"Mistress mine, it's morning already. Did you not just hear the lark?"

Aemilia shook her head as her tears fell. "Surely that was the nightingale, not the lark."

The maid lumbered over to join her at the window. "You can little afford to be love's fool any longer. If you're set on having this babe, your thoughts should be on the child, not the man."

Miserable from lack of sleep, Aemilia stared at her reflection in her steel mirror and saw a woman with swollen red eyes, a nest of tangled hair, and a crumpled nightshift. Drooping with shame, she was the adulteress in Jacopo's painting, condemned to be stoned. Yet Jacopo knelt before her and traced Hebrew letters in the dust at her feet. *Judge not.* Of all her Bassano kin, only Jacopo had truly understood her.

At last the cold clarity gripped her. *Here you are, pregnant and on the verge of abandonment.* The stark truth pierced her like a bodkin. If Will was determined to leave her, she could do nothing to stop him.

Setting down her mirror, she glanced across the bedchamber. Her eyes came to rest on her open lap desk and the written pages lying about the floor in wild disarray.

"Winifred, bolt the chamber door! Quickly, before he returns!"

Though her maid looked puzzled, she rushed to do her bidding while Aemilia scrambled to collect the pages. Frantically, she read over each leaf until, at last, the five plays she and Will had written together were accounted for and restored to their proper order. The comedy of the shrew. The tale of shipwrecked Viola. The merry romance of Beatrice and Benedick. The pastoral of Orlando and Rosalind, yet another heroine who disguised herself as a young man. And the unfinished *Giulietta and Romeo*. With trembling hands, Aemilia stacked them back inside her lap desk—*hers!*—and clutched it to her breast as though it were a chest of gold. And so it might prove to be.

She could not prevent Will from forsaking her, but she could and would stop him from absconding with their plays and reaping the glory and profit from the work they had done together. Soon enough she would have two children to feed.

Once more she turned to the window that framed the fragile morning sky. A cockerel's crow shattered the stillness. She expected him to return at any moment in search of the plays.

Aemilia placed her lap desk in her maid's powerful arms. "Winifred, pray pack this along with our other things." She spoke with a finality that surprised even herself. "We must away this very morning before any harm comes to Prudence. Let us return to England. I shan't chase after Will. If he wants the plays so badly, he shall have to seek us out."

"Right you are, good lady." Winifred beamed, as though delighted to see her mistress back in full possession of her senses.

"But how shall I face Alfonse?" she asked, her spirits sinking at the thought of returning to her lawful husband in order to grant her unborn baby the veneer of respectability. "Pregnant with another man's child?"

Winifred cleared her throat. "If you recall, you were pregnant with another man's child when he married you. With any luck, he'll get used to it."

HER DECISION MADE, AEMILIA wasted no time. As soon as she had washed and dressed, she rushed off to tell Paolo.

"I've taken your words to heart," she said. "I shall leave with Prudence and her sisters today. But first you and I must go down into Verona to sell the wine in the cellar. Never fear—I shall leave enough funds with you to insure the laborers and servants have enough to tide them over should the harvest fail."

The worry lines on Paolo's face eased into the first smile she had seen on him in days. "This is a wise decision, *signora*. Please know that you can place your faith in me. I have stewarded this property for your family for twenty years, and so shall I continue, even if you need to spend some months in the Casa dal Corno."

Paolo, of course, assumed that she was heading back to Bassano and that she would return to the vineyard—preferably without Prudence—once the drought had ended. She said nothing to correct his assumption.

THAT BRIGHT MORNING UNFOLDED like a dream with Paolo and Antonio loading the wine casks onto the wagon. They set off down the steep cobbled track toward the city with its churches and *palazzi* gleaming in the sun. When they arrived at the wine merchant's, part of Aemilia stood outside herself, watching like a witness as she and Paolo haggled to get the best profit. The drought and predicted poor harvest were driving up the prices, with wine merchants scrabbling to buy up good *amarone* while they could still get it. *At least this small mercy.*

Could Paolo see the difference in her, she pondered, as she weighed the sack of gold and silver in her hands. Could he tell from her puffy eyelids that she had spent the entire night waking and weeping? Had he heard from Lucetta that Will had not returned the night before, or did Paolo blame her distress on the rumors of witchcraft?

Once they had returned to the villa, she was relieved to see that the Weir sisters had already saddled the mules and loaded the pack donkeys for the overland journey. After safely stowing her coins, Aemilia leapt into the saddle. Under her skirts she wore her riding boots.

"Farewell, good Paolo. Be of good hope. Perhaps the harvest shan't be as bad as they say."

Despite her sleepless night, she felt more alert than she had in months, her senses honed and blazing.

Paolo looked troubled. "Where's your husband? Is he not riding with you? *Signora,* you know it's not safe for women to travel alone."

His words threw Aemilia off balance. Where was Will, indeed?

Meanwhile, Tabitha was in tears, her eyes locked on her infatuated Antonio. Aemilia reckoned that the young man would have given anything to accompany his beloved, but Lucetta would have sooner disowned him than let him take up with a foreigner whose sister was a suspected *strega. Tabitha and Antonio are the true star-crossed lovers,* Aemilia concluded, opening her heart to their plight if only to distract herself from her own despair.

But even Tabby and Antonio parted gazes at the sight of Will trudging down from the hills. His hair was disheveled, his clothing rumpled, as though he had spent the night wandering like a ghost. His eyes froze on Aemilia as she perched in the saddle about to ride away from him. Of course, she had expected him to appear any minute that morning, if only to demand to know what she'd done with the plays. Everything stood still as they stared at each other.

It would take so little, she thought. Just a single look of regret. Will only had to speak her name or ask where she was riding in such haste. If he revealed his heart in any way. Her own heart was pounding hard enough to knock her out of the saddle.

Paolo glanced from Will to her then hung his head, as if silenced. The Weir sisters remained motionless.

Even now Aemilia longed to smooth Will's hair with her fingers, to caress the stubble on his chin and tease him about growing a beard. True love could turn back time. They had never quarreled. He had never scorned her. That single moment of waiting, not daring to breathe, seemed to stretch into eternity.

Until Will blinked and looked away, as if unable to hold her yearning gaze. His shoulders stiffened, as though to shield himself from her love. His remorse over his son had poisoned his heart, and he could not lay down his bitterness, and now, in his mind, Aemilia seemed to be tangled up inextricably with his darkest sense of guilt. Only severance could heal that. Perhaps that was what they both needed to keep themselves from going mad.

Aemilia kicked the mule's flanks and set off at a jarring trot, leaving Will behind so he wouldn't see the tears streaming down her face. It felt like an age since she had last sat in the saddle. *This is what freedom feels like. Don't you remember?* She didn't know whether to laugh or howl. A masterless pregnant woman riding across Europe, just as Anne Locke had done when fleeing to Geneva with pregnant Catherine Willoughby.

Will's only power was in leaving, she told herself. Leaving Anne and his three children. Running away from Harry's midnight revels rather than stay and be mocked by the Earl's friends. Now he was bent on leaving her, except she had beaten him at his own game. Let him discover how it felt to be the one left behind.

Though Aemilia wouldn't allow herself to look back, she slowed her mule to a walk and pricked her ears. If he called out to her, if he came running, she would have stopped. She would have hurled herself into his arms.

A TOMBLIKE HOLLOW FILLED Aemilia's chest where her heart used to be. By noon, they were within view of the Lago di Garda where her party and their animals would travel by ferry to the northern end of that long lake. On the other side, they would begin their trek across the Alps, before selling the mules and sailing up the Rhine and its tributaries until they reached the English Channel. They would follow the same route as the overland traders—Aemilia had the maps in her saddlebag. She was determined to arrive back in England before Will did. He wouldn't be able to stage the merest outline of one of the plays without her knowledge.

While Winifred and Prudence remained silent, Tabitha couldn't seem to shut her mouth. The young woman was both tearful and querulous. "How can you just abandon the vineyard, mistress? What will happen to it now?"

"Let it be sweet Giulietta's dowry," Aemilia said. "Perhaps she will find happiness there."

"Are we truly going to cross the mountains on muleback? Paolo said it wasn't safe to travel without a man." Wide-eyed as a hare, Tabitha traded glances with her sisters.

Even Winifred looked as though she were having second thoughts.

"You shall have your man," Aemilia said.

Tabby was speechless as her mistress slipped from the saddle and stripped off her skirt to reveal the breeches she was wearing beneath. *Just like the courtesan in Harry's favorite piece of pornography.* She removed her bodice and replaced it with her boned and padded doublet that would hide her pregnancy for a few more months if she was lucky. Finally, she strapped her sword and rapier around her waist.

She looked up to see Enrico in Tabby's arms. Her son was staring at her in confusion. Mounting up again, she rode alongside Tabitha and took Enrico in her arms, balancing him in front of her on the saddle, singing to him until he relaxed, his weight settling against her.

"Henry," Aemilia said, calling her son by his English name.

Leaning back in the saddle, she rode the sure-footed mule downhill toward the shining lake. Beyond it, the snowcapped Dolomites rose like a crown. Once she passed those peaks, she would never see Italy again.

V

Unblind Your Eyes

22

HE OCTOBER SKY LASHED down rain as if to drown the whole world. Huddled under the wherry's canvas canopy, Aemilia braced her body against the cold and damp. Squeezed around Aemilia's skirts, young Henry and the Weir sisters sagged and shivered while the wherryman struggled to row up the Thames toward Westminster.

Over eight weeks had passed since they left Italy. It seemed impossible for Aemilia to believe that she had ever known drought and searing heat, or that she had once been so blissfully in love. Yet the evidence traveled with her in her swelling belly that made a mockery of any attempt at male disguise. One hand on her womb, Aemilia felt the patter of her child's limbs as though the unborn babe were trying to converse with her. What kind of future could she give her child? Such were the questions that had once sent her to Simon Forman the astrologer.

With numb fingers, she opened the fustian pouch and spilled out the *tarocchi* cards Will had bought for her in Venice — which seemed a lifetime ago. Her tears fell upon the gilded pictures of female knights riding into battle, of the female pope with her triple tiara. Such images of power and authority sent her sinking even deeper into the void of uncertainty. She clutched at La Stella, the card of the golden-haired maiden reaching to cup a star in her palm.

Never had Aemilia felt more alone, ashamed to show her face to Jasper. In two and a half months, she would give birth. That meant she had about ten weeks to locate Alfonse and reconcile with him — assuming he had returned from his sea voyage. If Alfonse had hated her before, how would he treat her now?

Aemilia's hands shook as she stuffed the *tarocchi* cards back into their pouch. *You have the plays,* she reminded herself. Let the stars be kind for once. Let the plays provide her children's future fortune.

THE WEIR SISTERS HARDLY lifted their gaze from the rain-swollen Thames while Aemilia paid the wherryman. Only young Henry gaped with huge eyes at this drenched world with its dripping buildings of gray stone.

Aemilia carried her son while slinging a satchel over one arm.

Stepping off the Westminster landing, she set her jaw and led the way up the muddy street. The Weir sisters hefted the bags and boxes that contained their own and their mistress's worldly belongings. Tabitha muttered quietly, as though she were praying.

"Cold," Henry said, his teeth chattering. "I want to go home."

"This is your home," Aemilia told him. "You are an Englishman born. The grandson of a King."

Trudging up the Westminster streets toward Longditch, Aemilia flinched under the eyes of old neighbors, familiar grocers, and market women who would spread the gossip that Mistress Lanier had returned from God-knows-where with a huge belly. She yanked up her hood to hide her face.

WHEN THEY REACHED THE back gate of the house Aemilia thought she had left behind forever, it was unlocked. With a sharp inhalation, she entered her neglected wasteland of a garden that was overrun by weeds. The wisteria-clad vineyard villa shimmered in her memory to taunt her with everything she had lost.

"Look, mistress." Winifred pointed at the thin sputter of smoke rising from the chimney. "The master must be home."

Aemilia passed Henry to Tabitha before she moved forward. What could she possibly tell Alfonse? The two of them had barely managed to restrain themselves from murdering each other even before she had run away to Italy. How could they possibly live under the same roof now that she was pregnant with her second bastard?

She wrenched open the door and stumbled into her kitchen only to find a doxy with carmine-smeared cheeks straddling a fat, bald man. The man was not Alfonse. His eyes lit on Aemilia and the Weir sisters.

"Hey ho, what sport!" he cried. "More wenches come to join in!"

Aemilia covered her son's eyes and prepared to flee, but Winifred charged past her with a bucket of cold rain water from the garden. With a bellow that split the air, Winifred doused the rutting couple. Doxy and swain fell apart, sprawling ingloriously on the filthy rushes. Their curses flew like arrows.

"I'll show you sport, I will," Winifred said, looming over the man who groped to hide his now piteously shriveled member. She aimed her booted foot at his privates. "Out of my mistress's kitchen before I geld you, sirrah!"

Gibbering, he scrambled to his feet and scarpered out the door as if his feet were on fire.

"What about my payment?" the doxy screamed after him. "You promised me five shillings!"

"Five shillings? For the likes of you?" Winifred threw back her head and roared.

Smiling thinly, the doxy took her time lacing up her bodice. "And who might you lot be?"

Aemilia stepped forward. "I am Mistress Lanier." She attempted to speak with some semblance of authority. "This is my house. You aren't welcome here. Now go."

"Ooh, so it's Mistress Laa-nee-yay," the doxy said, drawing out the syllables in a singsong. "So you decided to return to your miserable waste of a husband after all. You're welcome to that French dung-hill, you are, madam." She minced her way smartly across the littered floor to gather up various baskets containing her belongings — she had clearly been staying for a while. "Good riddance to the both of you. Frankly speaking," she said, snorting at the sight of Aemilia's pregnant belly, "I'd say you deserve each other."

Grabbing her cloak from the hook by the door, she turned to Winifred.

"See you in hell, fat sow!" the doxy spat, dashing away before Winifred could clout her.

"Just look at our kitchen!" Tabitha wailed, kicking at the gnawed bones and soiled rags strewn among the rushes.

Winifred grabbed a broom and started sweeping the foul rushes into the fire. "Some work it will take to get this house in order."

"Bless me, my herbs are still here!" Prudence smiled up at the dried leaves and flowers hanging from the beams.

Before Aemilia could shut the door, the old gray cat burst in and launched itself at Prudence, rubbing its head into her skirts and purring.

"Graymalkin!" Pru reached down to stroke it.

Then, from above the herb-hung beams, Aemilia heard a drawn-out groan. *Alfonse?* She and Winifred locked eyes. Aemilia led the way up the stairs followed by Winifred and Prudence while Tabitha stayed in the kitchen with little Henry.

Aemila's heart thudded sickly as she forced herself down the corridor. The bedchamber door was ajar, but even before she reached it, the stench broadsided her. The sight awaiting her was even worse than the smell.

There, in her marriage bed, tangled in a piss-stinking blanket, lay Alfonse, his eyes glazed in fever, his emaciated body so full of boils that he couldn't stir from the bed. Lesions and crusts covered his face, his palms, and his soles. Her heart split to see him lying naked in his own excrement as though he were an animal left to die all alone. A skeleton coated in pustules, he resembled some creature from Anne Locke's most horrific vision of hell.

Her husband gazed up at her as though she were an apparition. As though he were already halfway down that passage between life and death.

"Dear God," Aemilia said. "Just look at you."

She couldn't keep herself from weeping as she reached to take his hand, but Prudence grabbed her wrists. "You mustn't touch him, mistress, or you'll infect yourself and the baby."

Aemilia shook her head in bewilderment. "I see no buboes."

"Mistress, it's the great pox," said Pru. "That strumpet — or one like her — gave him the disease."

Aemilia stared at her husband in disbelief. As though racked in shame, Alfonse raised his arms to hide his face.

"But we can't just leave him to lie in his own filth." Aemilia ached to comfort him even as Prudence and Winifred held her back. "Is there nothing we can do?"

"We'll make him as comfortable as we can," said Prudence. "I can't cure his pox, but I can try to break the fever. He'll need broth and clean linens. We'll have to burn these bedclothes and the mattress as well."

"When was the last time that disgusting creature fed you?" Aemilia asked her husband.

Uncovering his eyes, Alfonse seemed to regard her in a state of shock, as though not trusting his senses. "Have you truly returned?"

"Aye, and I'll look after you and nurse you as best I can," she said. "But, by God, don't ever ask me to share your bed."

AEMILIA SANK ON THE kitchen bench and held her head in her hands. Now, besides having a son to feed and another child on the way, she had a husband with the great pox. At least they'd had a reconciliation of sorts. In the haze of his illness, Alfonse seemed to have not even noticed her pregnancy.

Prudence had taken his care upon herself, not letting Aemilia or her sisters near him. If, through Prudence's potions and poultices, Alfonse recovered from his fever and crippling pains, if the boils themselves shrank and healed, would he be able to work again or would Aemilia have to turn to his family in Greenwich for help? Alfonse's stepmother, Aemilia's own cousin, Lucrezia Bassano, would probably accuse *her* of infecting her husband. Aemilia's head throbbed.

Even the plays were no use to her until she had the funds to rent a playhouse and pay the actors. Only one person could help her. Though she was huge with child, she would have to squeeze herself into her best gown and swallow her pride.

She rummaged through the boxes until she found her lap desk. After cutting a fresh quill, she set ink to paper and wrote her beseeching letter. When the ink had dried, she sealed the missive with wax and pressed it into Winifred's huge hand.

"Deliver this to Somerset House, if you please."

Somerset House, Lord Hunsdon's palace on the Strand.

With Prudence upstairs tending Alfonse, Aemilia helped Tabitha and Winifred turn the house upside down, scouring away any traces of the cursed doxy and her men. Winifred lifted the floorboards, revealing where the Weir sisters had safely stowed the pewter, iron cooking pots, and rolled-up wall hangings before their exodus to Italy.

"Our Pru had an inkling we'd be back," Winifred said smugly, as she shook out the rolls of painted cloth and hung them back up in the scrubbed-down parlor.

When the house was in order, they laundered Aemilia's best gown then let out the seams and sewed in new panels to accommodate her belly. By this time, a fortnight had passed and Aemilia had still heard no word from Lord Hunsdon. Just as she began to fear he wouldn't deign to reply at all, a letter arrived saying he would visit the following day.

"I'm as huge as a whalefish," Aemilia lamented, while Winifred laced her into her gown.

"At least you finally have some cleavage," Winifred commented, while arranging her mistress's freshly washed hair.

Tabitha handed Aemilia the near-empty vial of attar of roses so that she might perfume her breasts and neck. She hung Aemilia's pearls around her throat.

Tabby and Winifred stepped back to appraise her.

"From the bosom up, you do look a picture," said Winifred, pinching Aemilia's cheeks for good measure. "Try to smile. Act blithe and bonny for Lord Hunsdon."

Aemilia thought of the screaming doxy and wondered if she were any less the whore, having to preen like this to seek the favor of her former lover. What would Lord Hunsdon do when confronted with her pregnancy? This very house was his property. If she fell from his good graces, he had the power to turn her out on the street.

Aemilia paced the parlor, her heart pounding out a *saltarello*. She clasped her trembling hands.

"My Lord Hunsdon," she heard herself say when Winifred showed her former lover into the room.

Not daring at first to meet his eyes, she dropped in a deep curtsy.

"Mistress Lanier." He bent to kiss her hand. "How curious to receive your invitation after all this time. I see that at long last you have returned to our fair isle, and in a different state than when you left if I'm not mistaken."

So tall that his head nearly scraped the beams, Lord Hunsdon studied her with the expertise of a man whose wife had borne him no fewer than sixteen children.

"You're carrying so high and close to your heart, I'll wager it's a girl."

Aemilia burned under his scrutiny. There was no point in dissembling or trying to pass off the baby as Alfonse's, for the entire court knew Alfonse was at sea with the Earl of Essex's expedition when the child was conceived.

"Motherhood is a woman's great joy," she told Lord Hunsdon. "The solace of a woman unhappily wed."

He raised his eyebrows. "You sought solace in adultery, you mean."

Aemilia closed her eyes. The only way forward was to speak with courage. "My lord, you married me off to a dissolute fool. Alfonse returned from his voyage penniless and full of the French pox. He lies bedridden upstairs if you wish to see for yourself. You can be assured he didn't catch the disease from me."

While Lord Hunsdon stared at her, Aemilia studied him in turn. How he had aged since she'd seen him last, nearly two years ago. He had always been a vigorous man, young for his years, hunting and hawking, outriding men forty years his junior. But now she noted a vulnerability in him, a creeping frailty that hadn't been there before, the skin around his piercing eyes gone as thin and transparent as wet paper. His hair and beard, which had remained the palest red gold until the day he had ended their affair, had gone stark white. Before her she saw a seventy-year-old man who recognized the inevitability of his own death.

"No," he said decisively. "Lanier didn't catch the pox from you. I see you are in the full bloom of health. My dark rose."

His fingers, calloused from riding and archery, traced her cheek. She quivered, her belly softening.

"You left the country," he said, "taking my son with you without asking my leave."

"Fleeing the plague," she told him. "Keeping your child safe from harm. I traveled on family business with my cousin, Jasper Bassano."

"And returned an expectant mother."

"The father is an Englishman," she hastened to say. This, she knew, mattered to him.

They both turned abruptly as Tabitha entered with little Henry in her arms. Winifred followed, bearing a tray of wine and sweetmeats.

The lad froze when his natural father lifted him in his arms for the very first time. Lord Hunsdon smiled at their son, bouncing him in his arms until the child laughed and tugged at his beard. Lord Hunsdon gently tossed the boy in the air, eliciting shrieks of glee that Aemilia hadn't heard since the days when Will used to play with him. She wondered if her twenty-one-month-old son remembered Will, remembered calling him papa.

"My namesake," Lord Hunsdon murmured, stroking the lad's dark hair. "He's the very picture of his beautiful mother."

She flushed. "Look you closely, my lord. He has your jaw and brow. Your nose. And he's big for his age. I think he shall grow to be as tall as you."

Lord Hunsdon gave their son a kiss and a cuddle before returning him to Tabitha.

"You're a good mother. You've kept him in the best of health."

"Thank you, my lord." Aemilia lifted her eyes to her former lover as the servants swept out, closing the door behind them.

"So tell me why you summoned me." Lord Hunsdon sauntered around the sparsely furnished parlor. "I see your lute and virginals are gone."

"I've had to sell them, my lord." Humiliation thickened in her voice. How she hated having to grovel.

"The forty pounds a year I give you is not enough?" he asked, cold and stern.

She forced herself to hold his gaze. "The man you chose for me gambled and whored most of it away. Now I fear I must support *him,* for he is too ill to earn a living. And what, pray, will happen to me and our son when you're no longer in this world, my lord? Will your heir even permit us to remain in this house?"

Aemilia's voice shook as she spoke. Would Lord Hunsdon despise her for her boldness? Pensioned-off mistresses were meant to be supported by their husbands, but Lord Hunsdon hadn't reckoned that Alfonse would fail at every turn and contract the pox in the bargain.

To her surprise, Lord Hunsdon bowed his head and sat on the settle. "In faith, I have but a few years left, by the grace of God. I shan't live to see our son grown. But what of your new lover? Is he of no help to you?"

"My lord, he's a penniless poet." She didn't dare confess that her poet had spurned her.

Lord Hunsdon laughed. "My lovely Aemilia, I thought you had more sense than to take up with a pauper. If you are to be an adulteress, at least be more discerning. How I prized you for your wit."

"My wit, you say?" She clenched her hands. This was her chance. "Then, pray, hear my proposal, for I would use my wit and education to earn a respectable living."

"Well, speak then, my dear." He inclined his head, inviting her to sit beside him on the settle.

First, she poured him a goblet of wine, then she opened her lap desk and pulled out a stack of pages.

"Whilst in Veneto, I have written comedies, my lord. Such comedies as have never appeared on the stage in this kingdom. With your help, I might see them performed and so secure an income."

He shook his head. "The theater is no respectable place for a woman. I won't have your name sullied."

"My lord, in Italy there are women players and playwrights. The great Isabella Andreini, whose patrons are the Medicis—"

He raised his palm to cut her off. "Papist countries might breed such spectacle, but this is England. The Queen won't tolerate women on the public stage or suffer any lady tainting her reputation with the theater."

The Queen, Aemilia wondered, *or the men who claim to speak her will?*

"With the Puritans in the Privy Council," he continued, "we're fortunate to have theater permitted at all."

"If the plays were not associated with my name," she said, speaking quickly to hide her desperation. "If a man was to act as my play broker—"

She broke off when she saw the skepticism settling on Lord Hunsdon's face, as though he were about to lose patience and march out of the room. As Lord Chamberlain, he was a busy man, and she was fortunate that he'd granted her even an hour of his time.

"My lord." She grasped his hand. "Will you not read just one page? If you think it doggerel, I swear I'll never trouble you again."

She handed him the comedy, *Giulietta and Romeo,* that she had finished since leaving Verona. In the final scene, the happy lovers were united for all eternity as their warring families reconciled and laid down their enmity. Everyone must bow in the face of true love.

With a sigh, Lord Hunsdon perused the first page as if to indulge a tiresome petitioner. Aemilia's legs shook beneath her skirts while she waited. When he reached the bottom of the first page, she braced herself, expecting him to fling the play aside and declare he needed to be on his way. But he turned the page and continued reading.

The room was so utterly silent, she could hear her racing heart. She stole glances at him as the minutes passed and ran together. *Surely now he must stop and say he's seen enough.* Outside, the sky began to darken. Tabitha tiptoed in to light the lamps and draw the curtains, and still he sat there reading *Giulietta and Romeo.* Aemilia stared into her wineglass, not daring to hope. She could not breathe for her astonishment when she saw him read to the very end. Then she was so nervous of his verdict, she hardly possessed the courage to look at him.

"Aemilia, my Hypatia." Lord Hunsdon turned to her with the glistening green eyes she remembered from when he was first enamored of her, his gaze drinking her in as though she were Venus descended to earth.

"Such poetry," he murmured. "Such passion. *You* wrote this?"

"I did, along with a collaborator." She struggled to steady her voice. "A man who will stand in as its sole author to avoid any hint of scandal."

"So I suspected," he said, with a nod to her belly. "Your penniless poet whose child you carry."

She could neither move nor speak. Her entire fate hung from a thread.

"Ah, my lovely lady," he said at last, kissing her brow. "You gave me such pleasure. How can I begrudge you claiming pleasures of your own?" He took her face in his hands and stared at her so intensely, as if to commit her to his memory so that her image might burn in his mind's eye forever, a secret portrait. "I hope your poet loves you as you deserve to be loved."

Aemilia bent her burning face to kiss his hand so he wouldn't see her tears. "Henry, you are good to me."

"Does your poet have a name?"

"William Shakespeare, my lord."

Lord Hunsdon scratched his jaw. "Ah, now I recall. That fellow who wrote those history plays." He laughed under his breath before caressing her hair. "But that was before he had *you* as his sweet Muse."

His breath was as hot as a kiln as he clasped her in his arms and kissed her. She kissed him back, allowing herself this comfort. Her first lover still cherished her even if Will had deserted her, he whose career she had just secured. How easy it would be to allow Lord Hunsdon to heal her pain, yielding to him completely. But his grip on her loosened when her pregnant belly jutted between them. He released her and kissed the crown of her head.

"Your poet may stage your plays under my patronage," he said. "Let the troupe call themselves the Lord Chamberlain's Men. I shall arrange for them to put on their play at Gray's Inn during the winter," he said, referring to one of the ancient Inns of Court. "If it proves a success they may perform at the Theater in Shoreditch come spring."

"Yes, my lord." *The Shoreditch playhouse!* Her heart thrilled at the very thought of her plays being acted out at the first theater she had ever visited, stealing in with Jasper to see Papa on stage.

Lord Hunsdon's hand on her shoulder brought Aemilia back to earth. "But you must remain in the shadows, my dear. No one must know this venture has aught to do with a mistress of mine."

Aemilia kissed his lips to seal the bargain.

AFTER LORD HUNSDON HAD left, Aemilia paced the parlor, her mind turning cartwheels. Though she had the plays in her possession, she couldn't proceed without Will, but she had no clue where to find him. She presumed that he had returned to London by now, but in her condition, she could hardly comb the boardinghouses of Saint Giles-without-Cripplegate to seek him out. For this task, she needed a man. If anyone in her acquaintance knew Will's whereabouts, it would be her maternal cousin, Ben Jonson, who also haunted the playhouses.

Opening her lap desk, Aemilia sat down to write yet another imploring letter.

"Yes, dear cousin, I know where he lives," said Ben, when he visited Aemilia three days later. "Above an apothecary near Saint Helen's in Bishopsgate, if you please. But why you should wish to know is another question."

He glanced at Aemilia's belly and looked as though he were trying very hard not to smirk as he drank down his coddled ale. Her cousin was one of the few who knew Will had disappeared in Aemilia's wake the previous year.

Ben had turned up at her door drenched from the driving rain. Now he splayed on the settle before the fire. With his ruddy face and the steam rising off his sodden hair and breeches, Aemilia thought he looked like Lucifer.

Though three years younger than she was, Ben seemed older, his body bent and scarred, for his early life had been a vicious struggle. His father, a clergyman, died before Ben was born, then his mother had married a brute of a bricklayer who dragged Ben out of Westminster School, where he had been learning Latin and Greek from the great William Camden, and forced him into a backbreaking apprenticeship building walls and laying foundations. Heavy labor at so young an age had left her cousin's body bent and squat. His only escape had been to run away to the battlefields of Flanders.

Even as he sought to earn his bread with his quill, Ben remained no less a fighting man than he'd been in his soldiering days. His tongue and pen were as razor keen as his sword and rapier. Only an idiot with a death wish would pick a fight with Ben Jonson.

"Do you know that I am to marry in November?" Ben seemed infinitely pleased with himself. "I would happily invite you, dear Aemilia, but I think you wouldn't like all the Johnsons gawping at you and muttering. One day I must bring Annie so you can meet her. I reckon the pair of you shall be thick as thieves, for she's an honest shrew after your own heart."

"Felicitations." Aemilia hoped her cousin's intended wife was indeed strong enough to hold her own against the sheer force of Ben's character. "I wish you every happiness."

He was so loud and volatile, her cousin, the settle creaking beneath his weight, his wet boots squelching against the floorboards, that Aemilia decided she had better not offer him any more ale.

"Now that I have answered your most mysterious query as to the whereabouts of our Warwickshire bumpkin, would you have me do anything more?" Ben asked, his eyes sparking, as though he found her summons both scandalous and darkly amusing.

"Pray, bring Master Shakespeare to me," she said, eyes lowered. "Tomorrow if you can. I must speak to him on matters most urgent."

Her cousin barked out an irreverent laugh. "On the matter of your belly, gentle kinswoman?"

Aemilia glowered at him until he blinked. "On the matter of these." She opened her lap desk to show him the plays.

"Are those *his* works?" Ben spoke contemptuously even as he craned his neck to read the first page of *Giulietta and Romeo*. "His plays always put me to sleep. For a provincial with poor Latin and less Greek, he is far too self-important."

A great lover and praiser of himself was Ben Jonson, and a great condemner and scorner of others.

"In truth, these are *our* works," Aemilia said. "He and I wrote them together."

"When you ran off to Italy with him whilst your clodpole husband was at sea?" Ben quaked with laughter, his huge arms folded across his chest.

Aemilia cringed and raised her eyes to the ceiling. She feared that Alfonse, still ailing in the chamber above, could hear every word. Speaking quietly, she informed Ben of the agreement she and Will had made, once upon a time, when they were mere acquaintances.

"I have the patronage of the Lord Chamberlain, but I need Master Shakespeare to stand in as the sole author of our work. I also need to hold him true to our original agreement. That is, to evenly divide the profits between us."

Leaning back in the settle, Ben appeared to consider this. "And if he won't? He's already had what he wanted from you. What's to stop him from basking in the glory and hoarding every last ha'penny for himself? Sure, you can plead your belly, but hasn't he a wife and three brats already?"

"Two," she said brokenly. "His son died."

"God's blood," Ben muttered, hanging his head as though stunned.

But Ben's words had hit their mark. Would Will indeed grab everything for himself? Would this all turn ugly and vindictive?

"If he seeks to renege on our agreement, why then I must unmask him," Aemilia said. "Make it public that a woman collaborated on the plays."

"And if no one believes you?" Ben's heavy-lidded eyes flashed his cynical distrust of nearly everyone. "Who *would* believe you? What woman has ever written a play for the public stage?"

Aemilia was about to mention Isabella Andreini when a scorching heat rose from her belly. For one awful moment, she feared her waters would burst in front of Ben Jonson. But when she found her voice, it sounded cool.

"Because you, cousin, won't let him abuse me. If *you* were to announce that the plays were cowritten by a woman, you'd make him the greatest fool in London. He wouldn't be able to live down the shame."

Ben sat bolt upright. "Dear Aemilia, you make me a party to blackmail!" He sounded delighted.

She tried her best to smile. "He would not dare cross you."

"He had better not." A ferocious grin spread across her cousin's face.

Has Ben agreed to this plan out of family loyalty, she wondered, *or because it so thrills him to be holding this secret over a rival playwright's head?*

"But for now," Aemilia said, "pray just bring him to me in peace and goodwill."

"Why did you pick *him* of all people to be your secret collaborator?" Ben asked, cocking his head like a pigeon eyeing a morsel. "Why not *me*? Would it not have been more prudent to keep this sort of thing in the family? And you could have avoided your current predicament."

Now came her turn to laugh. "Because you, Ben Jonson, are far too vain to collaborate with a woman."

"Ah, you know me too well, dear cousin. But in your case, I think

I could amend my opinion." He leaned forward to take her hand. "Though a woman born, you are a manly and most learned soul."

One hand on her belly, Aemilia inclined her head. She had never felt less manly in all her life.

AFTER BEN LEFT WITH the promise to return with Will, Aemilia could not sit still. Neither could she stand. She could not seem to rest in any one position for longer than a few seconds, for the child was so un-settled, leaping like a dolphin in the briny sea of her womb. How could she face Will in her current state, an object of ridicule and shame? Her own cousin had laughed at her. She couldn't even walk with dignity—her swaying bulk forced her to waddle.

And what if Will refused to come? What need did he have of her, a brilliant poet like him? He didn't even need their plays—he could write new ones. What was to stop him from truly being rid of her? A cold forboding seized her chest. All this worry and fear could literally prove the death of her. When she tried to envision her life after giving birth, of cradling her infant in her arms, she only saw her own grave.

A knock on the front door sent Aemilia's heart banging. She froze, her ears pricked to the muffled voices in the corridor. Winifred and Tabitha entered with two packages.

"Gifts from Lord Hunsdon, mistress." Winifred sounded pleasantly surprised.

Aemilia let out a long shaky breath. Sinking onto the settle, she un-wrapped the first package with both eagerness and care, for she knew it to be a lute from its shape. A warm flush crept over her cheeks just to touch the satiny soundboard, the graceful neck, the strings of gut and wire.

The second package contained a ream of paper along with a mes-sage written in Henry Carey's own hand:

My musical lady must have music. My gentle Muse would also wish to know that I have arranged for your poet to stage his first play on Twelfth Night in the Hall at Gray's Inn for an august audience of barristers and nobility. I therefore require a comedy befitting this most auspicious date for jests, japes, and wonders. Now it is your task, my beautiful Hypatia, to choose the play and write out fair copies for the players.

Fondly, H. C.

Before Winifred's ever-watchful eyes, Aemilia kissed the letter. At least copying out the plays would provide some welcome distraction. With reverence, she leafed through the creamy paper, each leaf bearing the watermark of a swan, the most iconic symbol of the poet, the mute bird that shattered a lifetime's silence to sing most exquisitely before it died.

After tuning the lute, she began to play and sing.

> The silver Swan, who, living, had no Note,
> when Death approached, unlocked her silent throat.
> Leaning her breast upon the reedy shore,
> thus sang her first and last, and sang no more:
> "Farewell, all joys! O Death, come close mine eyes!
> More Geese than Swans now live, more Fools than Wise."

Yet even as the mournful words left her throat, a secret joy arose in her heart. She, like the swan, could yet unleash her song. Perhaps part of her must die, that tenderhearted woman who walked into the chapel in Verona, but another Aemilia would rise phoenixlike, for such were the souls of poets.

23

HEN BEN JONSON BURST into her parlor with Will in tow, Aemilia was as armed as any knight. Across her lap she held the lute. The beautiful instrument that curved and swelled like a woman's body was her shield. Her weapon was the music itself.

Serenely, she strummed as Ben flung himself on the settle in the lordliest manner possible and Will hunched on a stool as far away from Ben as he could manage. As Aemilia played on, she thought of Orpheus, whose music enchanted even the Lord of Death. Let it disarm Will. His body was rigid, as though he had been taken prisoner. She could nearly taste his resentment to be reduced to this, dragged here by his most detested rival.

"How good of you both to come," Aemilia said, her voice rendered more gracious by the trilling arpeggios she played. "I trust you have been well, Master Shakespeare?"

Though she felt like an impostor addressing him thusly, Aemilia reminded herself that she had called him here on business matters.

"I have been well indeed." The look Will shot her was bruised. He had lost weight and looked as pale as if he had never walked beneath an Italian sun. "How fares your husband, Mistress Lanier?"

She nearly struck a wrong note as the heat spread over her cheeks. But her voice remained as light as her fingering on the frets. "Master Lanier is ill if you must know. How does the Earl of Southampton?" The words flew out before she could stop herself.

Ben erupted into laughter. "Dear cousin, have you not heard the news? The Queen has banished Southampton from court and, tail between his legs, he's legged it to France."

Aemilia shook her head in bewilderment. "How, pray, did he fall from Her Majesty's favor?"

Surely Lord Burghley couldn't have forced Harry into exile for refusing to marry his granddaughter. Or was there some new scandal—had the young Earl been caught with a high-ranking man?

Ben hooted. "Why, he secretly married one of the Queen's Maids of Honor. Can you imagine the uproar?"

Harry *married*? Aemilia thought her head would spin off her neck and fly out the window.

"Full of surprises, Southampton is." Ben slapped his thighs. "Just when I had him pegged as a sodomite, he runs off with one of the Queen's own women."

Aemilia observed Will's downcast face as he stared at his clenched hands. His last source of refuge and patronage had been taken from him. *My dear man, now your only way forward is with me.* He had wanted to be free of her, yet here he was. Aemilia nearly pitied him.

"Might I ask why you summoned me, madam?" Will's voice was chilly.

"In faith, I have good news for you." She plucked a sprightly galliard.

Will's gaze was guarded, yet beneath it, she knew there was his poet's heart broken wide open for his dead son. He wore his grief like a hairshirt. *Has he been back to Stratford?* she wondered, picturing him bereft and broken at Hamnet's grave.

"With the Lord Chamberlain's patronage," she said, "the first of our plays shall be performed at Gray's Inn on Twelfth Night."

Her words seemed to knock him off guard, and he nearly lost his balance on the stool.

"And should it prove a success," she continued, "your players shall move on to the Theater at Shoreditch in the spring."

"Gray's Inn? Shoreditch?" He sounded both dubious and amazed.

"Expedient for you, is it not?" she asked him. "Seeing as you live in Bishopsgate."

Before she could say anything more, Tabitha entered with a jug of wine. Ben grinned like a demon when he accepted the goblet from her hand. Will, however, refused the cup before shooting Aemilia a dark look, as if accusing her of doctoring the wine with a love philter. Losing patience with him, Aemilia nearly snorted aloud.

"The Lord Chamberlain might wish to know I have of late written the best plays of my career." Will's injured pride shone like beaten metal. "*The Tragical History of Hamlet, Prince of Denmark.*"

Tragedy set in Denmark! As far a departure from their Italian comedy as Aemilia could imagine.

"Oh, not another of your insufferable history plays!" Ben thundered. "The Lord Chamberlain doesn't want the stage littered with dead bodies. At least not for your first performance."

"The empty vessel makes the loudest noise," said Will, seething on his stool.

Ignoring him, Ben waved his empty cup at Tabitha, who cast a covert look at her mistress. Aemilia nodded with a discreet gesture to only fill his cup half full.

"This venture, sir," Aemilia said, addressing Will, "is not meant to serve your vanity or mine. The play must absolutely regale your genteel audience at Gray's Inn and so convince the Lord Chamberlain that it shall turn a tidy profit once you begin performing in Shoreditch. Master Burbage shall want his playhouse packed to the rafters. That is why I've chosen the comedy of Viola and Sebastian, the shipwrecked twins. Given the date of its first performance, I suggest we call it *Twelfth Night.* I have already written out fair copies, which you will find upon the table there."

Ben lunged to grab one before Will could even rise to his feet. "Such clean, unblotted copies! No one will believe *you* wrote it, Shakespeare."

Aemilia winced to hear her cousin take such pleasure in mocking Will.

"I've taken the liberty of arranging music to accompany the piece," she interjected, before Will could sling some insult back at Ben. "It's to be the most musical of plays."

Closing her eyes, she began to sing.

O, mistress mine, where are you roaming?
O, stay and hear your true love's coming,
That can sing both high and low.

Trip no further, pretty sweeting,
Journeys end in lovers meeting.
Every wise man's son doth know.

What is love? 'Tis not hereafter,
Present mirth hath present laughter,
What's to come is still unsure.
In delay there lies no plenty,
Then come kiss me, sweet and twenty,
Youth's a stuff will not endure.

"By my troth, a good song," said Ben.

Aemilia turned to Will, who blinked and rubbed his eyes, for he had written those lyrics during their idyll in Verona. She had merely set his words to music.

"Now your task, Master Shakespeare, is to gather a troupe of players and begin the rehearsals," she told him. "Do you agree to this?"

"It appears I have no other choice," he said.

She remembered their last bitter quarrel in Verona. *You thought I was yours for the taking. Your creature.* Did he think she was using him even now?

"Why so dour, man?" Ben blustered. "Don't be such a churl. You've gained the patronage of none other than the Lord Chamberlain. Other men would sacrifice their firstborn sons —"

His face a mask of rage, Will sprang to his feet, knocking over his stool. For one awful moment, Aemilia feared the two men would come to blows.

Then Will fixed Ben with an icy stare. "You are not worth another word."

"Leave us, please," she told her cousin.

Ben raised an eyebrow. "As you will." Swiping the wine jug from Tabitha's tray, he sauntered out of the room. Tabitha tiptoed in his wake and closed the door behind her.

Setting aside her lute, Aemilia heaved herself out of her chair and took a step toward Will, but a sudden pain in her belly made her founder. Before she could crash to the floor, he seized her arms, raising her to her feet. They both stood paralyzed.

"You might have sent for me without using that tedious fool to strong-arm me," he said. "I never see his face but I think upon hellfire."

"Master Jonson knew where to find you, and I did not." She broke off, her eyes searching Will's. "Did you think you could just wash your hands of me?"

Her anger, bottled up for so long, commanded his attention in a way that sobbing or pleading could never have done.

"Once you wrote of the marriage of true minds," she went on. "Our intellects might still work in harmony even if we are otherwise estranged. Think of all the sweet words we wrote together. If the stars are kind, our words shall endure long after we're both dead."

"It's not our stars that hold our destiny, but ourselves," he said. "Our collaboration has reached its end. I cannot write your comedies anymore."

"Your tragedy of Hamlet," she said. "Is it named after Hamnet, your son?"

He looked away.

"I could help you even there," she said. "Peregrine Willoughby, whose sister educated me, is ambassador to Denmark and has been a guest at Elsinore Castle."

She wondered what Perry and his brittle wife would make of her predicament. If she could not contrive to restore her fortunes, she would live the rest of her life as a disgraced woman set on a path of inevitable decline.

"I have rewritten *Giulietta and Romeo* as a tragedy," Will told her.

"*That's* no surprise." Aemilia sighed and took his hand before he could pull away. "Don't be so blinkered by your bitterness now that you stand at the threshold of something better. My dear man, you may yet have your tragedy if I don't survive this birth. Then our plays and their profits shall all go to you. I only ask you to surrender my half to our child."

Will suddenly seemed unsure of himself, as though his knees might buckle. She clasped his hand to her womb.

"I think it shall be a girl. She swims like a mermaid in her watery home. Can you not feel her dance?"

He closed his eyes and bent his head as she held him there with the babe kicking against his palm.

"Shall I send word to you when she's born?" Aemilia could no longer keep her tears at bay. "I'm calling her Odilia after our chapel. Can you still remember?"

He fingered her golden ring.

"Is this the ring I gave you?" His voice had gone hoarse.

"Do you want it back?"

"Aemilia," he said, brushing away her tears.

He held her as though she might crack at any moment.

"You are far too strong and stubborn to die," he finally whispered, his hand resting on her burning cheek. "Besides, you must live to see your beauteous Olivia being played by some pimpled boy from Putney."

For the first time in weeks, she heard herself laugh. She stroked his hair, as soft as she remembered, and then his jaw, now covered in a golden-brown beard. Before he could stop her, she kissed his open mouth. Yet even so, she knew she had lost him, that she couldn't possibly hold him to her any longer. Drawing away, she picked up the fair copies of *Twelfth Night* and pressed them in his hands.

"Now go in peace," she said.

WILL EXITED THE ROOM as silently as a ghost. Behind him, the door closed with the quietest sigh. Sinking back onto her chair, Aemilia cradled her lute in her shaking hands. She couldn't see for her tears.

What if Will was right and life was but a tragedy, a cruel joke? What if all her love and suffering were for nothing, cold stars abandoning her to ill fate?

"Zounds, dear cos! Do you truly weep for that provincial poetaster?"

Aemilia looked up to see Ben. He knelt and took the lute from her hands.

"Never you worry. I'll make sure Shakescene never cheats you, at least as far as money is concerned. Don't trouble yourself about the child either. My wife and I shall stand in as godparents. If you're married to a fool of a Frenchman, I'd say even adultery is forgivable."

Merry from the wine, Ben strummed her lute and began to sing. His comically off-key voice sent her rocking in laughter.

> Sigh no more, lady, sigh no more,
> Men were deceivers ever,
> One foot in sea and one on shore

To one thing constant never.
Then sigh not so, but let him go,
And be you blithe and bonny,
Converting all your sounds of woe
Into Hey nonny, nonny.

Winifred came in to listen.

"It might be a silly ditty," the maid pronounced, "but it's the most sense I've heard all day."

THOUGH FOREVER EXILED FROM her lover, Aemilia thought of herself as an invisible player, scribing fair copies and arranging the stage music. Why should Jasper and her other Bassano cousins not benefit from her plays and earn a lucrative side income as theater musicians? She wrote a letter to Jasper in hope that this opportunity might be her means of smoothing her way back into the family fold.

When Jasper called in later that week, he looked as conflicted as when they had parted in Venice more than a year ago. At least his face betrayed no shock at the sight of her pregnancy. Indeed, he appeared resigned, as if he had suspected such an outcome all along.

"I should have never left you with that interloper," he said. "Had I only insisted that you return to England with me."

"I would have refused," Aemilia told him amiably. "When, dear Jasper, have you been able to bend me to your will? Let's hope that the theater venture might at least prove profitable for us both."

"Profits? Is that all you can speak of?" He stared at her in disbelief. "This man has humiliated you."

"Do you propose to challenge him to a duel?" She threw up her hands. "What purpose would that serve? If you would champion me, then see if you can arrange for Alfonse to join the Queen's Musicke again—should he ever rise from his sickbed."

Jasper fixed her squarely in his gaze. "Aemilia, you walk a dangerous path. You weathered one scandal with the Lord Chamberlain—"

"Fortune be praised for that," she said. "The man has been my lifeline."

With a start, she realized that she had passed beyond the realm of shame.

"And now you are pregnant by this scribbler, a married man."

Aemilia regarded her cousin in silence. No more tears flowed. No blush crept over her cheeks. Finally, it was Jasper who lowered his eyes.

"Let's hope your husband plays along and gives you cover of decency," Jasper said.

"At this point, I'd say he has little other choice."

"*Two* scandals," Jasper said, as if to drive his point home. "In God's name, you can't afford a third."

"You needn't worry. Henceforth, I am a reformed woman." She clasped her hands in a semblance of contrition. "The penitent Magdalene."

Jasper stared as if trying to determine whether she spoke in earnest. Finally, he changed the subject. "Was Bassano as grand as you thought it would be? The villa with its painted façade?"

"The villa is just a building," she said. "But Jacopo had the biggest heart of any man I've met since Papa died. He was sorry not to meet you, Jasper. Do you know that he and Papa wrote letters to each other?"

"Aemilia," her cousin said. "Can you forgive me for abandoning you in Italy?"

Her laughter surprised even herself. "I wouldn't take back my time in Italy for all the world. Not one minute of it."

"In faith, you don't sound particularly penitent to me."

"Jacopo would have said our deepest regrets are about what we didn't do," she said.

Jasper bowed his head.

"By the way," he said quietly, "I've returned something that belongs to you. I left it in your garden. You'll want to order hay and straw."

"Hay and straw?" She looked at him in confusion until suddenly it registered.

Planting a kiss on her cousin's cheek, she rushed as swiftly as her condition allowed to the kitchen and tore open the door to the garden. There, covered in shaggy winter fur and cropping winter's grass, was a chestnut mare that now threw up her head and whinnied. Bathsheba ambled toward her, inserted her pink muzzle in her mistress's arms, and blew softly on her belly.

24

EMILIA PANTED AND THRASHED, in thrall to her body. Wrenching waves surged through her, building into a tempest that swept her out to sea. Even her sweat tasted of brine.

Winifred offered her hand. "Squeeze as hard as you're able," she pleaded, as though yearning to take all of her mistress's pain onto herself.

Prudence wiped Aemilia's face with a cool cloth and told her when it was time to bear down and push.

But Aemilia's thoughts soared free from the prison of her flesh. Already in character, Will and his players rehearsed *Twelfth Night*—she could see him as clearly as if he stood before her. He had chosen the role of Feste, that mercurial poet-jester who by his wit and wordcraft could pass effortlessly between the servants' quarters and the duke's court, mingling with both high and low, and yet transcending all social stations and being no man's vassal. To think she had once aspired to such freedom, thinking it merely a matter of donning a male disguise, as though a pair of boots and breeches could erase her womanhood— and her troubles.

"Mistress, you're fading." Prudence's voice was sharp. "Stay with us. Now push."

The most overpowering force Aemilia could imagine seized her in its fist, the unstoppable might of her womb pushing new life into this world. She clenched Winifred's hand so hard that even her stalwart maid grimaced. She wailed and bellowed, unleashing noises that didn't even sound human. *Some swan song this is.*

But all pain dissolved when she felt the child slip from between her thighs. She wept and laughed and trembled as she held her slippery little mermaid. Her heart swelled until she thought it was large enough to contain the earth and starry heavens.

"She's perfect." Aemilia kissed her daughter's damp head and counted her fingers and toes.

Even covered in the blood of birth, Odilia was a marvel. Henry, as a newborn, had appeared as an ordinary healthy baby, his skin blotchy and his head a bit misshapen, although he looked fine enough when he was a few weeks old. But Odilia was a creature set apart. After Prudence washed and dried her and delivered her back into Aemilia's arms, Aemilia saw that her daughter's skin and form were completely unblemished. This baby was exquisite, as though she were more angel than flesh, her eyes as blue as the midnight sky, her crown already covered in her father's soft brown hair. Yet she seemed so tiny, even for a child who had just emerged from the womb. Odilia breathed sweetly but did not cry.

With Henry weaned, Tabitha's milk had dried up. Aemilia would have to nurse Odilia herself. Prudence showed her how to let the baby suckle on the clear fluid that came before the first milk. Cradling her daughter to her breast, Aemilia couldn't get over her wonder. To think this creature was *hers,* flesh of her flesh. Even if she had lost the man, the child redeemed everything, this rush of love that transfixed her. How could any man's love compare to that of a mother's for her newborn?

Settling back against the bolster with Odilia in her arms, Aemilia dreamt of the life she would give her. Teaching her to read, to write, and to ride. Instructing Odilia and Henry in Latin and Greek, astronomy and music. Odilia would be more learned than her father, more fortunate than her mother. This girl child would eclipse both her parents. As brilliant as the morning star, she would outshine any poem or play either of them could hope to write. Aemilia would weave garlands for her hair. She would clothe her in silk and brocade.

Her heart leapt to see Tabitha leading Henry into the chamber to meet his new sister. Not even two years old, the lad stared with enormous eyes at the baby. Shy and gentle, he rested one finger on the baby's hand. When her tiny fingers closed around his, he jumped then gazed at Odilia in amazement, as though too awed to be jealous.

Aemilia invited the boy to clamber into bed with her. One hand still cradling the baby, she cuddled him close.

"You must always protect your little sister," she told him.

How might my own story have played out, she wondered, *had I been blessed with an adoring older brother?*

"A FINE MORNING FOR a christening!" Ben said that snow-bright day, as they walked toward Saint Margaret's. "To think I shall be a godfather."

"Had you only picked a man more godly," his bride, Annie, said, with a wink to Aemilia.

Newly risen from her childbed, Aemilia had emerged from the house for the first time in more than a week. She measured each step on the icy ground and kept a careful grip on Odilia, who was bundled like a precious package in layers of blankets and quilts. The baby's breath floated up in steamy little puffs. Winifred kept hold of her mistress's elbow, prepared to catch both mother and child should Aemilia slip.

Ahead of them, Tabitha walked with Henry, and Jasper hung his head as he slunk along, as though he felt a guilty responsibility for the baby's very existence.

"Odilia." Ben leaned over to peer at the infant's face. "An exotic name."

"An Italian name," Aemilia told him. "Like my own."

Her cousin waved his hand in dismissal. "Spare me any explanation of whichever weeping saint inspired the appellation. I prefer to think you gave her a humanist name."

"Humanist?" Aemilia asked, exchanging a smile with Annie. "How do you reckon that?"

"You have ingeniously turned *ode* into a girl's name that rhymes with your own," Ben said, beaming at his own cleverness. "The name of a poet!"

Aemilia laughed in genuine happiness, warmed by the idea. It was as if Ben had unwittingly removed Will and the chapel from her daughter's story, as though she hadn't named her baby in memory of the man who had deserted them both. Instead, she had named her daughter for poetry.

"Odilia, Aemilia," Annie said. "I think they're beautiful names. Far less plain than Anne and Ben."

Aemilia felt a fondness for her cousin's new wife and hoped that she and Annie would be friends. Small and neat with nut-brown hair, Annie wasn't flashy in her looks, but her mind was as fiery as her husband's. *My honest shrew,* Ben called her. A man like him could never love a meek mouse. Aemilia could not fail to notice the way the newlyweds walked arm in arm, their paces in harmony. She saw the secret looks they shared. Truly, they adored each other. *May their love endure,* she prayed, even as her own loneliness gnawed at her.

Ben abruptly stopped in his tracks and cast a look behind him. "We had better slow down or we shall lose our Lazarus."

With a guilty start, Aemilia turned to see Alfonse struggling along, one hand gripping his walking stick, his other arm supported by Prudence. This was his first foray outside the house since Aemilia had arrived back in England to find him deathly ill. Thanks to Pru's physick, his boils and fever were gone, but he remained gaunt and weak, barely limping along. She felt a stab of pity even to look at him, though Pru had assured her that a brief spell of fresh air would do him good. His face bore an expression of dazed astonishment, as if he could not get over his shock of still being alive. *Lazarus, indeed.*

Can Alfonse and I live together in amity now? she wondered, while waiting for him to catch up. A weight settled in her chest. To think it was Will's child that chained her to this marriage that she had run away to Italy to escape. Alfonse's ring was back on her finger.

Smiling faintly at her husband, she walked the rest of the way to the church at his side. It seemed the least she could do.

When they reached the church, Aemilia observed her circle of kin gathered round the baptismal font, the one gaping absence being the baby's true father. Still, her eyes remained dry and her voice steady as she murmured the replies to the curate's prompting.

Under the cleric's keen gaze, Alfonse's eyes seemed to snap open at last. He looked from Aemilia to the baby as if finally awakening to the depths of her treachery. No longer Lazarus, he was a man betrayed, forced to wear the cuckold's horns as he posed as the father to his wife's bastard for a second time.

"Dost thou forsake the carnal desires of the flesh, so that thou wilt not follow, nor be led by them?" the minister asked of Aemilia and Alfonse.

Alfonse's eyes were like needles, but Aemilia returned his stare head-on. What right did he have to judge her considering that he nearly died of the French pox?

"I forsake them," Aemilia and Alfonse said in unison.

Jasper covered his eyes while Ben smirked. Odilia remained tranquil, not even crying when the water splashed down on her forehead.

BACK AT THE HOUSE, the Weir sisters laid out the sparse feast of pottage, mutton pie, and stewed apples. Aemilia hoped the plays would soon bring money into the household.

His face pale with exhaustion, Alfonse retreated to his bed. While her guests sat down to eat, Aemilia took the baby into the nursery to feed. In truth, it troubled her that Odilia hardly cried. What if she wasn't getting enough milk? Henry had been such a lusty baby, crying then feeding till he was content. But this infant was so quiet, Aemilia needed to be especially vigilant, offering her breast if Odilia so much as opened her mouth or turned her head toward her.

"Is she latched on properly?" she asked Tabitha. "I fear she's lost weight since the birth."

"Don't fret," said Tabby. "She'll soon gain it back. If worse comes to worst, you can always hire a wet nurse, mistress."

The girl sounded guilty, as though she blamed herself for her milk drying up after weaning Henry.

Aemilia peered at her little babe, so helpless and fragile. "I'm her mother. Pray God, I can feed her."

Even after Tabitha helped her to get the baby to latch on, Odilia suckled for only a moment before falling asleep. Aemilia tickled her feet to wake her then offered her the other breast, all the while blowing softly on her face to keep her awake.

"Try rocking her in your arms whilst you're nursing," Tabitha said.

Aemilia rocked her and tried to stop worrying, to simply surrender to the baby's sweet tug on her breast. But after a few moments, Odilia fell to sleep once more.

"Maybe she's just weary from all the fresh air," Tabitha said. "Shall we let her rest and try nursing again in another hour?"

Tabby eased the baby from her mother's arms and tucked her into the cradle.

"Henry was an easy feeder," Aemilia said. "He grew so fast."

"Every babe is different, mistress." Tabitha smiled down at Odilia while tucking the blankets around her. "Some are noisy, some are quiet. She's a cherub, she is. Don't you worry. In six months, she'll be twice as big as she is now, mark my word."

AFTER TABITHA HAD LEFT the room, Aemilia took her smallest pair of scissors and cut a brown ringlet off her slumbering daughter's head. Opening her lap desk, she selected a sheet of fine paper and put the lock of hair upon it. She plucked the gold ring Will had given her from its hiding place at the bottom of her desk and placed it on the paper, beside their daughter's hair. Dipping her quill into the ink pot, she wrote on top of the page:

Odilia Lanier baptized 2 December, 1594

After the ink had dried, she folded the paper carefully around the ring and hair then sealed it with wax she heated over a candle flame.

Writing a proper letter to Will alluding to his daughter's paternity would be far too incriminating should the missive fall into the wrong hands. All the world must see Odilia as Alfonse Lanier's child.

The missive hidden in her palm, she headed back downstairs to join her guests.

IN THE PARLOR, JASPER played Aemilia's new lute while Annie fussed over Henry. Aemilia took Ben aside.

"Please deliver this to Will," she whispered. "To his own hand. No one else's."

Her heart ached to surrender the ring. In truth, she had wanted to keep it forever as her secret treasure to prove that he had once loved her. Instead, she made herself let it go. *What's past is past.*

"Cousin, you must stop weeping for him." Ben offered her his hand-kerchief, the cleanest she'd ever seen on him, owing no doubt to An-nie's care and attention. "Sweet Aemilia, you're as soft as a lamb. In this world, lambs get devoured."

DURING HIS NEXT VISIT, Ben brought her Will's reply along with news of the rehearsals.

"The sets are nearly ready and the music fits the play quite well. I imagine it shall be a success. At least our Warwickshire pretender wasn't vain enough to cast himself as the handsome Duke Orsino. I must say he found some very pretty youths to play the female roles."

No pimpled boy from Putney then.

"I'm pleased to say I've angled an invitation to see the performance," Ben told her. "An old friend who is a barrister has invited me as his guest. A pity no ladies are allowed in that hallowed hall."

A surge of anger welled up inside her to think that she could nei-ther write plays under her own name nor even see her creation en-acted in this rarefied male enclave. Then again, going out to plays was inconceivable to her now as the nursing mother of a new baby. Per-haps in spring when Odilia was a bit older, she might see her plays in Shoreditch.

"In the meantime, dear Ben," Aemilia said, "you must be my eyes and ears."

"The pleasure," he said, with a wicked laugh, "is mine."

AFTER BEN HAD LEFT, Aemilia retreated to the nursery to read Will's letter, breaking the wax seal with her penknife. From out of the folded paper, a necklace of Murano glass beads tumbled into her palm. In an instant, she was transported. She and Will clasped hands while watch-ing the commedia dell'arte.

Surely he had purchased these beads in Venice, though she couldn't remember him doing so. Perhaps he'd bought them for one of his daughters back in Stratford only to return to find her grown too big to wear this necklace that would only fit a small child.

Accompanying the beads was his message. Even the sight of his handwriting made her ache for everything they had shared and lost.

Dear Mistress Lanier,
   Please accept this, my humble christening gift for your daughter.
With wishes for the good health of mother & child,
   W. S.

His message was both respectable and respectful, above reproach, so that even Alfonse might read it and not be offended. But it was so distant, the kind of letter one might write to a near stranger. Then again, what could he say in a letter without bringing dishonor upon her and Odilia?

Aemilia held up the beads to the cold winter light. They gleamed as blue as Odilia's eyes. She lifted the baby from her cradle, careful to support her head, and dangled the beads before her, watching her gaze follow their sparkle and flash.

Will had acknowledged his natural daughter with a necklace if nothing more. These beads her patrimony.

AEMILIA FELT AS THOUGH she had washed up on some strange and foggy island thousands of miles from the rest of the world. She hardly strayed more than twenty paces from her daughter. To think she had once traveled the world, sailing to far Italy. How she had swaggered in her breeches, as though she would never have to suffer a woman's lot again. And how improbable those adventures seemed now, as unreal as the fairy tale that Will had ever sworn his troth to her.

The vast tapestry that had been Aemilia's life shrank to a tiny point. Odilia became her entire world.

How she fretted over this baby, over each and every feeding, in her desperation to see roses in those pale cheeks, to see Odilia grow as chubby and robust as her brother. How could she have ever taken Henry's appetite for granted? Day after day Aemilia waited for proof that her daughter thrived, that she wasn't just her mama's precious angel but a girl of growing flesh and bone who would endure in this world.

Aemilia's breasts engorged with enough milk to drown them both, but Odilia remained a fickle feeder while her mother throbbed with milk fever. Yet, she kept nursing through the pain, for the only cure was to keep the milk flowing, so Tabby told her. Prudence treated Aemilia's hot swollen breasts with cabbage leaves. It seemed she spent half her waking hours coaxing Odilia to suckle, waking twice or more in the night.

Alfonse, meanwhile, convalesced. Hobbling on his stick, he staggered through the rooms, as pale and utterly wrung out as she must look. Of an evening, they sat together for pottage and bread, both of them too shattered to quarrel. What a strange truce this was.

Yet even here, news of the outside reached Aemilia with a banging on the door.

A breathless Winifred handed her the letter. "That's Lord Hunsdon's seal if I'm not mistaken. Go on, read it, mistress. I'll hold the baby."

Aemilia had to smile at the sight of her tiny daughter in Winifred's enormous arms. Her maid gazed down at Odilia with a face full of ferocious love while the baby gurgled and waved her hands. The letter, however, filled Aemilia with trepidation—what if the play had been an utter failure, an embarrassment to Lord Hunsdon? She'd heard not a word from either Ben or Jasper since *Twelfth Night's* debut performance several weeks before. Since the christening gift, she had heard nothing at all from Will.

My shining Hypatia,

I must congratulate you on your foresight, for Twelfth Night *is indeed a success. How the audience relished the rude wit of Sir Toby Belch. Whenever Malvolio the Puritan appeared, they hissed. Yet they also marveled at Viola and Olivia's poetic exchange.*

Your Master W. S. has gathered together a most accomplished troupe of players while your Bassano cousins have played fine music to accompany the drama, though they could hardly be heard at times for all the cheering and roaring. Thus the players have staged encore performances of Twelfth Night *in both the afternoon and evening. Now the goodly gentlemen of Gray's Inn clamor for more comedies.*

Pray choose another similarly convivial piece, but you need only submit one copy this time. Master W. S. himself shall then make fair copies for the players. In faith, I've heard it said that some of his actors thought the last batch of copies looked to be written in a woman's hand, which was the subject of much mockery at Master

W. S.'s expense. Surely you agree that it is best to put an end to such speculation.

May I not forget to congratulate you on the birth of your daughter. I hear you are staying home these days, which is most sensible, given this inhospitable weather. May both your children flourish and their good mother rejoice in this most felicitous turn in fortune.

Fondly, H. C.

"Whatever is the matter, mistress?" Winifred asked, her face creasing in concern. "Is it not good news?"

Aemilia blinked. "It's very good news. The play is a success."

"Then why do you look so sad?" Winifred wiped drool from Odilia's chin.

"It's only the lack of sleep."

Aemilia tried to beat down her disappointment that she had received this news from Lord Hunsdon but had not heard a word from Will. Such adulation had come his way. Could he not at least thank her for securing Lord Hunsdon's patronage? Perhaps Will was simply caught up in his newfound success. If he did return to Stratford, he would go as a man who had proved his worth in the great world. His family would honor him and take pride in his accomplishments.

Our accomplishments, she reminded herself. Yet it was a struggle to remember that she'd had a hand in this all, scribing those lines in partnership with Will, spinning her Viola and Olivia from the gossamer of her longing until at last they had taken form and flesh as the players enacted them upon the stage.

After Winifred carried Odilia up to the nursery for her nap, Aemilia reached for her lute. As she strummed and hummed beneath her breath, she felt a presence behind her.

"Henry?" She glanced over her shoulder.

Alfonse stood staring at her. Aemilia's stomach clenched. Her hands froze on the lute strings.

He opened his mouth to speak when voices erupted in the hallway.

Tabby came running. "Mistress, Master Jonson has come to visit."

Aemilia nearly wept in relief to see her cousin barge in with the bombast of a hero marching toward the Queen to receive his knighthood. He stopped in his tracks at the sight of her. She burned to think how she must appear to her cousin with her unkempt hair crammed beneath her coif, her smell of milk.

"Gentle kinswoman," he said, recovering his composure. With a flourish, he placed a heavy sack of coins in her hand. "I've kept my word and held Shakescene to his side of the bargain. This is your half of the first profits of *Twelfth Night*."

As Aemilia grasped the money, Alfonse walked out of the room.

Ben appeared bemused. "I am left with the distinct impression that Master Lanier dislikes me. Oh well. To every man his humor."

Her cousin's sheer presence made it impossible not to smile. She allowed herself a shiver of victory as she weighed the silver and gold coins in her hands.

"Thank you, Ben."

Her cousin seated himself in the most regal fashion. "I, too, hope to grow rich off my shares in the Lord Chamberlain's Men. Now could one of your servants be so good as to offer refreshment? It's a long way to travel from Billingsgate and I am *parched*."

Tabitha trotted off toward the kitchen.

"Lord Hunsdon says the play has been a success," Aemilia said.

"My dear, it's the talk of London, the closest thing to the commedia dell'arte most of those souls have ever seen. Thanks to *you*, I might add. Of course, everyone is asking how some provincial with a grammar-school education can write Italian comedies all by himself."

Aemilia bowed her head, wondering how Will had reacted when his actors ribbed him about the play being written in a woman's hand. But Lord Hunsdon had eliminated the possibility of that ever happening again. She, the coauthor of the plays who had brought Will to Italy in the first place, had become invisible, a phantom. But was that not what she had asked of Will at the very beginning of their collaboration? *I need you to be my mask.* At least the sack of coins in her hand was tangible and real.

"I must grant he's a good actor," Ben said. "He plays his part well, both on stage and off, if you know my meaning. When those gullible fools congratulate him on his natural genius, he just smiles, as though enjoying his new mystique."

Her cousin grinned when Tabitha delivered his coddled ale, but his cup froze an inch from his mouth at the sound coming from the next room.

"What in God's creation is that?" he asked.

Aemilia turned her head at the high piercing note. "A flute."

When first she married Alfonse, he was a flautist in the Queen's Musicke, but she couldn't remember the last time she'd heard him play. Indeed, she was astonished to discover that he still owned his instrument and hadn't pawned it to pay his gambling debts. Was there an inkling of possibility he might still earn his living as a minstrel?

Aemilia tiptoed into the dining chamber with Ben at her heels. Even Winifred, Pru, and Henry had come to gape at the spectacle. Alfonse had spread the sheet music on the table, but his eyes were squeezed shut as he played. Lost in his own world, he seemed. Oblivious to their presence. His first notes were halting, but as he continued, his music swelled in certainty and power. He was unpracticed, to be sure, but he had not lost his art.

Aemilia's blood froze when she saw Henry approach Alfonse, as though in a trance. She stepped forward to snatch her son away, but it was too late. Henry hugged on to Alfonse's leg. Her heart was in her throat as she prepared to charge forward. She gripped Ben's wrist.

Alfonse stopped playing and looked down at the little boy who gazed up to him in wide-eyed wonder. Something moved over her husband's face as he slowly reached down to ruffle her son's hair.

A FORTNIGHT LATER, BEN delivered another sack of coins along with the news that rehearsals for the next comedy, *Much Ado About Nothing*, had begun. Aemilia wrote copies of the three remaining comedies to deliver to Lord Hunsdon. Jasper, in gratitude for his employment at Gray's Inn, sent her a wagonload of hay and straw for Bathsheba.

But Aemilia was utterly unprepared for the sight of the new virginals delivered to her door and hefted into her parlor, courtesy of Lord Hunsdon.

Beside herself with joy, she played a *saltarello* for Henry, who laughed and danced. Then she pressed Odilia's little fingers to the wooden jacks till the baby squealed at the tune her mother had her playing. In a few years, she'd teach her daughter to play properly.

Balancing the baby in her lap, she tore open the letter that had come with the virginals.

My most musical lady,

Your plays have reaped such acclaim that I have purchased this virginals from my shares in the company. God willing, you shall never have reason to sell any of your instruments again. Once the troupe moves to the Theater at Shoreditch, they shall turn a huge profit indeed.

The most joyous news of all is that I have arranged for the Lord Chamberlain's Men to perform Twelfth Night *at Whitehall before Her Royal Majesty. Your W. S.'s fame is now assured.*

Fondly, H. C.

Aemilia had scarcely finished reading when Odilia grasped the paper and tore at it, jabbering contentedly. The ink was already running from her spittle. Only when the baby tried to suck on the letter did her mother rescue it and put it out of her daughter's reach.

Twelfth Night to be performed at Whitehall, right here in Westminster, a mere stroll from her door! So close and yet a universe away, for she had been banished from court. Tears pricked at her eyes to think of that glittering circle where she had once shone like a diamond in the Queen's necklace, that circle she might never enter again.

A royal audience—what a triumph for Will. Even Ben would never be able to dismiss him again. If nothing else, Will would have to acknowledge that she had kept the promise she had made to him that morning in his boardinghouse when he was still a pauper. By bringing him to the attention of Lord Hunsdon, she had drawn him into the sphere of the Queen. But she received no message from him. Her poet who wrote so beautifully of love had not sent her a single word.

In February, around the Feast of Saint Valentine when the wild birds began their mating flights and true lovers sent each other tokens, came the thaw. The first snowdrops appeared in her garden. Sunlight spilled through her window and cast its gold on Odilia's face as Aemilia held the Murano glass beads over her and swung them back and forth. Reaching for the necklace, her daughter grabbed it and held it in her fist.

"Carissima!" Aemilia hugged her daughter and covered her in kisses.

Odilia had survived the worst of winter. Degree by infinitesimal degree, the days grew longer and the world grew green again. Spring was on its way and her daughter thrived. Exultantly, her mother squeezed the plump muscles in Odilia's arms and legs.

Henry bounded in, waving a child's wooden flute. Standing before his mother, he blew a few notes while she watched in amazement.

"Where did you get that, love?" Aemilia asked, hugging him close, one arm around him and one around his sister.

"From Papa," the boy said, his face gleaming in pride.

A tight place inside Aemilia came unwound. She had never seen this side of her husband, the kindness that had moved him to gift Henry with this treasured toy, and Henry was calling Alfonse his papa. She wondered where Alfonse was, why he did not come to join them. Outside of mealtimes, he hardly seemed to spend any time in her presence, and yet he had clearly shown affection to her son. She supposed it was much easier for Alfonse to care for an innocent boy than an unfaithful wife.

"Oddy," Henry said to his sister. It was the closest he could come to saying her name.

He blew his flute for her then made funny faces and stuck out his tongue till the baby mimicked him and stuck out her own tongue. Helpless with giggles, Henry fell against his mother. They were already playing together, her son and daughter. Aemilia's heart overflowed.

25

INCE RETURNING FROM ITALY, Aemilia had slept in the nursery with her children, leaving the marriage bed to Alfonse. One morning in March, she awakened with the sunlight already streaming through the slats in the shutters—Odilia had slept through the night.

Her breasts heavy with milk, Aemilia reached into the cradle, but the baby didn't stir. Her daughter felt stiff in her arms, her skin cold to her touch, and her eyes wouldn't open. In a panic, Aemilia unwrapped the baby's swaddling and listened for her heartbeat, but she heard only her own ragged breathing.

She hadn't even known she cried out until the Weir sisters came running. Henry tumbled out of bed and stared, his eyes huge and frightened.

Her heart pounding in mad hope, Aemilia passed the baby to Prudence, who seemed to have every herb in existence hanging from their kitchen beams. If Pru had raised Alfonse like Lazarus when he had nearly died of the French pox, surely she could revive a little baby. Perhaps Odilia had a fit during the night or perhaps she had only fainted.

While Prudence examined Odilia, Aemilia comforted Henry.

"If it stays fine today," she told him, "I'll take you riding on Bathsheba."

Trembling, she lifted her gaze to Prudence, who wrapped Odilia back into her swaddling. Everything in the room seemed to blur and twist when she saw Prudence's tears. Her stoic Pru.

"Sweet mistress, forgive me." Prudence's hands squeezed hers. "There's nothing I can do. Your precious angel's in heaven now."

No, no, no. Pushing Prudence away, Aemilia snatched her baby off the bed. Surely there must be some way she could warm her daughter's cold flesh, breathe life back into those little lungs. Her knees buckled as the awfulness settled in her heart and sent her crashing to the floor.

Winifred knelt beside her and wrapped her arms around her. Still holding her baby, Aemilia fell against her maid with shuddering sobs. Had Will passed his curse of loss and grief onto her, destroying their daughter? *You may have your tragedy yet.* She could have borne any loss, but not this. Not her child, drowned in dead sleep. Her tears rained down on Odilia's face.

PRUDENCE BREWED HER MISTRESS a cup of valerian root steeped with lavender and hops, but Aemilia's hands shook too hard to take the cup. How could it have happened that Odilia simply died in the night just as she was beginning to grow so rosy and plump?

"You mustn't blame yourself," said Pru. "Scores of infants die in this very parish. Our own Tabby lost her babe." Prudence held the cup to her mistress's lips. "Please drink. It will do you good."

Aemilia stiffened and clenched her teeth—no brew of Prudence's could dull this pain. *Of course, I blame myself,* she wanted to scream. If only she had awakened in the night to see if Odilia needed her even if she hadn't cried. If only she'd taken better care while pregnant, but, no, she had worked herself ragged in the vineyard and then crossed the Alps on muleback. If she had hired a wet nurse, might her daughter have lived? What if her own milk hadn't been wholesome enough?

How she had loved the child, pouring out all her care and attention to make her strong. Yet she had failed. How could fate be so cruel? Anne Locke's ghostly voice whispered in her ear, *The Lord giveth and the Lord taketh away.* Anne had believed in predestination. Had Odilia been damned from her very inception, her death Aemilia's punishment for her sin? An adulteress and a bigamist, she was reviled even by God.

WINIFRED AND PRUDENCE WASHED the baby in preparation for the funeral.

"Let her be buried in her christening gown," Aemilia said, her head turned to the window, for she couldn't bear to look at that poor corpse. Instead, she watched Tabitha lead Bathsheba around the garden. Henry perched in the saddle and held on to a leather strap around the mare's neck. Her little lad looked contented, or at least distracted from the torrent of grief running through the rest of the household.

"That gown will be too small for her now," Winifred said, her voice choked.

"Then we must alter it." Aemilia watched how carefully Bathsheba trod along, as if mindful of the vulnerable young life on her back.

"But you might still need the christening gown," Winifred said. "Should you have another."

"There will be no more children," said Aemilia. *Burying another child would kill me.*

Turning from the window, she approached the kitchen table where her lifeless baby lay. The sight was enough to make her double over, but she kept her spine rigid. Wound around her hand was the necklace of Murano glass beads that she now fit around Odilia's neck. Let this, the one token of her father's regard, be buried with her. Aemilia kissed her dead daughter's brow.

SAINT MARGARET'S CHURCHYARD WAS a carpet of crocus and daffodils that March morning. Primroses, anemones, and the first violets bedecked the tiny coffin, borne by Ben and Jasper. When they set the casket beside the newly dug grave, Aemilia laid a wreath of rosemary upon it.

While the vicar spoke the last rites, she could hardly see through her tears. Each time she remembered the way Odilia used to smile and babble, Aemilia foundered. She would have collapsed without Winifred holding her arm and supporting her.

Beside her was a gaping emptiness, the absence of her child's father. So was this how Anne Shakespeare had felt, standing alone at Hamnet's grave, her husband having abandoned her to begin a new life in Italy? Aemilia thought for a moment that she and Anne had become kindred spirits in their suffering and loss. *Oh, don't be a fool. If Anne Shakespeare so much as laid eyes on you, she'd spit and curse the womb that bore you.*

Aemilia didn't dare look at her husband. She could not stomach any more contempt than what she had already reaped. *You don't have to hate me, Alfonse. I hate myself enough for both of us.*

THE FUNERAL DINNER WAS steeped in a suffocating silence. Even Ben hardly ate or drank, and Annie quietly wiped the tears from her eyes. Odilia's death had made it impossible to ignore how precarious life was, how easily Death could gain the upper hand and steal away their own future children.

Before her guests departed, Aemilia placed the folded and sealed paper in Ben's hand. "Please see that Master Shakespeare gets this." Her voice was as heavy as lead.

Her cousin nodded and pressed her hand before tucking the missive inside his doublet.

She had written two sentences.

Odilia Lanier, christened 2 December, 1594, and
buried 6 March, 1595. Rosemary for remembrance.

Folded into the paper was a sprig of rosemary from her garden.

AEMILIA FEARED HER GRIEF might pollute poor Henry. When the weather proved fair, she sent her son out with the servants so that the boy might amuse himself by watching the boats and barges sailing down the Thames. *Let him look upon something other than his mother's misery.*

Shutting herself up in the parlor, she surrendered to the sobs that broke like storm waves inside her with a violence that left her gasping. On her hands and knees, she moaned and pummeled the floor in hope of purging herself, so that when Henry returned she could at least attempt to cling to some semblance of self-possession.

At the creak of the opening door, she reeled. A man stood upon the threshold, his face in shadow. For an instant, she allowed herself the madness of believing that Will had come to mourn beside her and share this burden. They would bear the yoke between them.

When he stepped forward, she saw it was Alfonse. How could he look at her like that? Was he gloating to see her punished for her sin, to find her so helpless and undone? With the servants gone, he finally had his chance to do his worst. Her heart pounded sickly, but instead of leaping to her feet and staring him down, she covered her face, too defeated to offer resistance. Let him murder her if that was what he wanted. Let her rest beside Odilia for all eternity.

She swallowed a cry as he pulled her hands away from her face and clasped them. He knelt beside her.

"I am so sorry." He spoke with such humility, as though not simply expressing condolences for Odilia's death, but begging her pardon for every unhappiness his own words and deeds had brought upon them both.

She gaped at him, too dazed to speak.

"Is it too late to win your regard?" he asked her. "Misfortune might still be reversed, no? I will join the Earl of Essex on his next expedition. By God's grace, I shall yet be knighted and you shall be a lady."

As if such titles could mean anything to her now. But she had never heard him speak with such tenderness. She considered the many mistakes they both had made. She had abandoned him only to return with another man's bastard while his whoring had saddled him with the pox he would carry for the rest of what might prove to be a short life. Each in their own way, she and Alfonse were utterly broken. But they no longer had to be enemies.

"May you be knighted." Aemilia tried to smile, but it hurt her face. "In Henry's eyes, you're already a hero."

She thought of how Alfonse had carved the wooden flute for her son, how Henry looked up to him. Surely Alfonse offered better company to the boy than she herself had of late.

"I am teaching him to play the flute," Alfonse said. "He's a very musical child."

"Like his parents," she said gently, in a stroke making Alfonse Henry's father in love if not in blood.

IN MAY, AEMILIA DECIDED the time had come to see her comedy performed by the Lord Chamberlain's Men.

Before her daughter's death, she had harbored a secret dream of donning her breeches and riding Bathsheba to Shoreditch, where she would occupy the floor with the groundlings and elbow her way to the lip of the stage where she could gaze into the players' eyes as they delivered their lines. Their swinging garments might touch her face.

Instead, Winifred laced her into her best gown, and Aemilia pinned rosemary to her sleeves and hatband so all the world would see she was in mourning. Alfonse escorted her to the landing where they boarded a wherry to Billingsgate. Thanks to Jasper's intervention, her husband had taken up his old post in the Queen's Musicke while he bided his time until Essex's next voyage.

At Billingsgate they joined Ben and Annie. The four of them walked up Gracechurch Street toward Bishopsgate and on to Shoreditch, passing Saint Botolph-without-Bishopsgate, where Aemilia's parents and uncles lay buried. A balmy day, the hedges were frothy with blossoming hawthorn.

The Theater buzzed and throbbed, but Aemilia saw no playbill posted outside.

"A curious thing," she pointed out to Ben, as they squeezed their way through the throng. "Do you know what today's performance is to be?"

"In truth, I can't say," he replied. "Perhaps this is the debut of a new play and they didn't get the new playbill printed on time."

Aemilia hoped it would be *As You Like It*, the romance of Orlando and the spirited cross-dressing Rosalind, whose every line she relished.

Ben led the way up to the first tier gallery where he said they would have the best view. Taking her seat between her kinsman and husband, she thought how at last she had assumed the mantle of respectability, as though she were a lady with an untarnished reputation.

"Ben's writing his own new play," Annie said, stroking her husband's arm. "A comedy of the humors."

"Comedy to banish melancholy." Aemilia could feel her own humors lifting, borne up on the crowd's anticipation and excitement.

Alfonse hushed them as the minstrels on stage began to play a dirge so mournful that Aemilia gathered this was to be no comedy. An armor-clad actor marched center stage and announced the drama, *The Tragical History of Hamlet, Prince of Denmark*.

Good God, had she only known what this day's performance was to be. After so much anticipation, she would not, after all, watch the actors delivering the lines she had penned. Wrestling down her disappointment, she decided she'd best resign herself. *Let us see his tragedy then.* At least she could observe the new shape his writing had taken since their collaboration had ended. She guessed it to be a revenge play like *The Spanish Tragedy* by Thomas Kyd, with phantoms, gushing wounds, and heaps of dead bodies to regale those in the audience who would otherwise spend their leisure hours in the bear-baiting pits.

From her perch in the gallery, she viewed the proceedings with a critical distance. How incongruous for the dead king's ghost to appear, even as the May sunshine cast its benevolence upon the groundlings who bayed for blood and vengeance. But nothing prepared her for the jolt of seeing Will stride upon stage as Prince Hamlet.

"Is he not too *old* for the part?" Ben grumbled.

Clad entirely in black, Hamlet's every word and gesture conveyed his deep mourning. Aemilia's heart quickened to think that perhaps Will indeed shared her grief over their daughter's death. His poetry sent her pulse racing and yet each phrase reeked of pessimism. As Hamlet, Will muttered of suicide. Swinging his contempt like a mace, he denounced his mother's marriage to his uncle only two months after his father's funeral.

Will gazed into the audience, as if to envelop each one of them in Hamlet's brooding, when his eyes locked on Aemilia with the shock of recognition. All the crowd seemed to melt away and only the two of them existed. Pinned there in the gallery, in the full light of day, she couldn't hide from him. He seemed to falter, as though forgetting his part.

But he delivered his next line like a blow.

"Frailty, thy name is woman."

She set her jaw. *That* sentiment was hardly original. Indeed, she expected better of him, but let him say what he would. Frail she was not. Frail souls didn't cross the Alps on muleback.

Queen Gertrude, played by a boy with hair as dark as hers, seemed so insipid, as though the actor were trying to embody capricious femininity as he clung to King Claudius and simpered like a Southwark doxy. Where were the strong, spirited heroines of their comedies?

The next scene introduced the second female role, played by a boy with sensuous lips and long golden curls, so beautiful that he reminded her of a younger and more vulnerable Harry. Clad in a maiden's silk gown, this was Hamlet's beloved, Ophelia. What did Will play at, using a name so similar to that of their dead daughter? Ophelia wasn't a proper name, even in Denmark.

In the second act, Ophelia's father read a poem Hamlet had written to his beloved.

> *Doubt thou the stars are fire,*
> *Doubt that the sun doth move,*
> *Doubt truth to be a liar,*
> *But never doubt I love.*

Aemilia shivered and burned at once. Such devotion that poem promised only for the poet to rip it to shreds. Just as Hamlet made Claudius and Gertrude watch a play mimicking their crimes against the dead king, Aemilia was forced to view Hamlet abusing Ophelia with the very words Will had said to her in Verona the day he announced he was leaving.

"I did love you once."

But now he cut even deeper, raising his face to meet Aemilia's eyes again for one blinding moment.

"I loved you not."

With a tight twist of his mouth, he swung round to confront the boy Ophelia, who cowered and appeared to weep real tears as Hamlet towered over him, belting out his derision, denouncing all women as two-faced whores who deserved to be abandoned.

"God hath given you one face and you make yourselves another. You jig, you amble, and nickname God's creatures, and make your wantonness your ignorance."

No longer just a grieving father turned cynical, Will's genius had turned into something vicious and vengeful. And why? Because his players had teased him about the copies of *Twelfth Night* being written in her woman's hand? Did he seek to prove his worth by demeaning all women? But it was not just women—it seemed as though he desired to lampoon her and Harry both, destroy every last trace of any love he'd shared with either of them. He wanted to kill his old self, that tender poet, and be his own man, unfettered by the heart. Love's slave no longer, he employed the illusion of the stage to unveil his most galling truth.

Don't let him intimidate you. It's just a play, all make-believe and boys in skirts. But Aemilia felt as though she were being flayed alive until she'd no more skin left to hide her bleeding flesh.

Ophelia entered strumming a lute and singing the heartbroken songs of a ruined and cast-off lover. Seeing such a sickly distorted portrait of herself harrowed Aemilia's soul. Clearly gone mad, Ophelia sang the words "There's rosemary for remembrance."

Aemilia thought she would crack. She already predicted Ophelia's end. The hapless girl, like Will's love for her, his former mistress, had to die. It was no surprise when Ophelia drowned herself, the preferred suicide method of pregnant unmarried women. Throughout the play, Will had dropped hints that Ophelia was with child. "Conception is a blessing," Hamlet had told Ophelia's father, "but not as your daughter may conceive."

"Her clothes spread wide," Queen Gertrude said, describing Ophelia's watery death. "And mermaid-like awhile they bore her up."

Aemilia tried to push away the memory of her last meeting with Will, clasping his hand to her womb where Odilia swam and danced.

Then followed Ophelia's funeral, the girl buried with minimal ceremony on account of her suicide. With a raw heart, Aemilia looked on as, in a final act of degradation, Hamlet and Ophelia's brother wrestled and grappled upon her coffin.

Will could not have made his malice more obvious. It was as though he had written this play with the intention of driving her as insane as Ophelia. He wished to excise her from his life, exorcise her ghost, drown her in a sea of her own tears, then bury her and walk away, abandoning her to the worms and dust.

"Unblind your eyes," Ben whispered in Aemilia's ear, as they followed the tide of the departing crowd. "He wants to break your heart so that you shrink away and no longer hold him to the bargain you made. Don't think like a spurned woman, but like a man would. A man of business! No sentimentality."

Annie regarded her with anxious eyes, as though well aware how hard it was for Aemilia to shake off her utter shock and distress. Indeed, it demanded her entire resolve to hold on to her dignity as she walked on her husband's arm.

"You look ill," Alfonse said, examining her when she could hardly bear to look him in the eye after this debacle.

"Come with us to the Pye Inn for cakes and wine," Annie said.

Aemilia shook her head. All the wine in the world couldn't blur her pain. The very thought of food made her heave. Letting go of Alfonse's hand, she plodded off alone. More than anything, she yearned for her male disguise, longed to gallop across the green fields and lose herself. But here she trudged, a woman dragging her good skirts in the dust.

Will hadn't only dealt his death blow to their love but also to her aspirations as a playwright. Could she write without him as Aemilia Lanier? Who would read a woman's work? Even Anne Locke had contented herself with publishing translations of Calvin's sermons and kept her sonnets for her family and friends.

In the space behind her, Aemilia heard Alfonse telling Ben and Annie to go on without them.

"So that was your lover," her husband said, when he caught up with her.

Though Alfonse had known of the affair since she had returned to England pregnant with another man's child, seeing Will on the stage seemed to have raised all her husband's buried pain.

"How could you betray me for someone so cruel?"

So it was not her betrayal itself that hurt him as much as the one she had chosen—a man who had just treated her far worse than Alfonse ever had even in the first bitter months of their marriage. And what could she say in her own defense—there were no words. Her husband's wounded face struck her dumb. What he must have suffered sitting beside her through that endless play that had laid bare her every sin. Meanwhile, she stood before him like the condemned adulteress in Jacopo Bassano's painting. Will had certainly shown every desire to stone her, and now Alfonse turned away.

"Let us go," he said, and headed toward Bishopsgate, no doubt intent on walking back down Gracechurch Street to Billingsgate where they would board a wherry to Westminster.

But Aemilia couldn't take a single step in that direction—what if she met Will and his players in the street? Surely, like Ben and Annie, they would be heading for the Pye Inn to drink and feast and carouse. Clutching herself, she looked off into the green distance where lambs played behind blooming hedges, their bleating sounding almost like infants' cries.

"Why do you not come?" Alfonse retraced his steps and took her hand, but her flesh was so limp, there was nothing for him to grasp.

At the back of her head, she heard her father's urgent whisper. *Cara mia, instead of despairing over what you have lost, be grateful for what remains.* Was her tragedy greater than what Papa had endured? Everything had been taken from him—his home, his country, his religion—and yet he had lived on. He had been a good man and lived a good life.

"Can we not walk home over the fields?" Aemilia asked, when she had at last regained her voice.

"You wish to walk all the way to Westminster?" Alfonse gave her a doubtful look, as though fearing her senses had deserted her.

"Is it not a beautiful May?" She reached for his hand. "Will you walk with me, my husband?"

He nodded and touched her face. Together they set off across the undulating green countryside where she had once cantered Bathsheba. Passing beneath the windmills in Finsbury Fields, they headed west toward the outskirts of Saint Giles-without-Cripplegate where Aemilia had visited Will in his old boardinghouse. *What would have happened if I had not spirited him away to Italy when the plague raged through London and Westminter?* she wondered. *If I had just left him there?*

He was a player, after all. Perhaps he had been deceiving her all along. She told herself she possessed nothing of his anymore. Not the ring he had given her, not even their child. Ah, but that was not quite true—she still had the *tarocchi* cards he'd bought for her in Venice.

Blackbirds trilled and swooped over meadows thick with speedwell while Alfonse told her about his childhood in Greenwich where he and his brother used to dig in the tidal mud along the Thames in search of treasure—once they found an ancient Roman coin. Aemilia sang a madrigal to tease a smile from her husband as they crossed a bridge over Fleet Ditch, where a mad girl like Ophelia might have drowned herself.

Before long, they passed Southampton House, its mullioned windows shuttered now that Harry and his bride had fled to France. She wondered what the young Earl would have made of seeing his likeness in the boy who played Ophelia. Would Harry have laughed and brushed it off as though Will's satire were no greater concern to him than a fly or would he, like her, have felt the blade cleaving flesh and bone?

At a farmhouse near Saint Giles-in-the-Fields, she and Alfonse bought a simple supper of buttermilk, coarse country bread with soft new cheese, and strawberries and cream. Then, heading south past Saint Martin-in-the-Fields, they walked in the shadow of the Royal Mews, where, as a girl, she had first met Lord Hunsdon when he was the Queen's Master of Hawks.

She remembered the first time Lord Hunsdon set a merlin falcon on her gloved arm. How she had trembled with both awe and pity to see such a glorious creature held captive by jesses and hood. Lord Hunsdon squeezed her shoulder and told her to release the bird.

With unpracticed fingers, she uncovered that beautiful head and loosed the fetters. Her entire being had exalted to see that raptor spread her wings and shoot high into the air until Aemilia could see only a tiny speck in the endless blue sky.

A lightness now spread within her, as though she were so buoyant that the wind might sweep her aloft.

"You are smiling." Alfonse caught a tendril of her hair in his fingers.

"*Lanier*—does it not mean hunting falcon in French?"

He laughed. "You think we are birds?"

"Magnificent birds!"

Like the falcon, she had been blinded by her hood, bound by jesses. But the time had come to soar free. If Will had thought she could be so easily broken, she must disappoint him. She would endure.

Whitehall was washed pink in the evening sun and the ancient oaks in St. James's Park were lit fiery orange. She and Alfonse reached their home in Longditch as the last light faded.

WHEN THEY SLIPPED THROUGH the garden gate, Alfonse wrapped his arms around her.

"When I saw you as Cleopatra in the masque," he said, taking her back to the days when she was Lord Hunsdon's mistress, the dark jewel of Elizabeth's court, "I thought you were the most beautiful woman I had ever seen."

His eyes, as dark as her own, moved over her face, and finally Aemilia understood with a shock of clarity. Alfonse had never despised her, but he had been angry and jealous because he thought she would never love him. Her heart opened in remorse to remember the many insults and slights she had hurled his way. How she wished she had uncovered the gentle lover inside her young husband early in their marriage before they had both made their irrevocable mistakes.

"Come, love," she murmured, stroking her husband's curly hair. "Let's to bed."

Taking his hand, she led him in the door and up the stairs to their chamber. Although they couldn't make love in the usual manner lest she risk catching the pox from him, there were other ways to share tenderness. She guided his hands to the lacings of her gown and stays. In their marriage bed, in the deep cradle of night, Aemilia held him and let herself be held.

VI

The Arctic Star

26

"A LETTER FOR YOU, MISTRESS," said Winifred, entering the parlor where Aemilia played the virginals. "Is that not the Lord Hunsdon's seal?"

The maid shivered as if the missive had flown out of the man's grave. Henry Carey had died only a month ago. Aemilia's heart was still raw from the loss of him, her first paramour, her son's father. Hands frozen on the wooden keys of her virginals, she stared at the letter.

"It will be from the new Lord Hunsdon," she told her maid.

George Carey was her dead lover's son and heir, a debauched rogue who had driven his father to despair and who dosed himself daily with mercury to treat his French pox. Like it or not, the man was now her landlord and also the new patron of the Lord Chamberlain's Men.

After Winifred withdrew from the room, Aemilia counted to eleven before breaking the wax seal. As she read, her hands began to shake. The letter floated to the floor. She stared around the parlor that was no longer hers. Her numb fingers brushed the wooden keys of the virginals, Henry Carey's gift to her, which she would have to sell.

George Carey had ended her forty pounds yearly income. Simultaneously, he was evicting her from this house. *Is it that he cannot abide his dead father's former mistress living on his property*, she wondered, *or does he claim the residence for a mistress of his own?*

Now she must break the news to Alfonse and the Weir sisters.

Where would they go now that they were reduced to her husband's income and what she earned with the plays? What if Alfonse's health took a turn for the worse?

Aemilia felt a drop in her stomach. *Here begins my decline.* Her face in her hands, she remembered how swiftly Papa had sunk into poverty, how misfortune had broken him. *Henry, did you know your son would cast me out into the cold?*

ALFONSE WAS WHITE LIPPED when Aemilia read him the letter. When he finally recovered himself sufficiently to speak, she wanted to clap her hands over her ears.

"You must go live with my father and stepmother in Greenwich," he said, "whilst I am at court."

She could have spit blood, preferring John Knox's hell to going to live with her in-laws who had never once visited them in Westminster, who shunned her as the old Lord Hunsdon's whore.

"Greenwich is too far from my kin," Aemilia said.

"My stepmother is your cousin!" her husband pointed out.

Aemilia gritted her teeth. "Jasper will take me in."

BUT ALFONSE REFUSED TO demean himself by allowing his family to live off the charity of Jasper, his fellow court musician. Instead, Jasper found them a narrow, crooked house in the Liberty of Norton Folgate, not far from Aemilia's childhood home. Rents were much cheaper there. As long as Alfonse kept his income as a royal musician, they could afford to live here, albeit on diminished means.

Although Aemilia had once reaped a tidy income from her share in the Italian comedies, that revenue was reduced to a trickle now that Will had moved on to staging his own new work. He had even taken to rewriting their comedies and making them his own, excising her spirited Emelia from *The Taming of the Shrew.* If only she had been so prescient, not just desperate and pregnant, when she surrendered the fair copies of the plays to Lord Hunsdon. She was lucky she still had Ben to enforce their agreement on her receiving her share for *Twelfth Night, As You Like It,* and *Much Ado About Nothing.*

Jasper, meanwhile, showed her and Alfonse around their new home. There was a kitchen and a tiny parlor, two bedchambers upstairs, and a drafty, low-ceilinged attic where Prudence, Winifred, and Tabitha would have to make do.

"In faith, it's much smaller than your old house," her cousin told Alfonse. "But when you're away at court, Aemilia will live here alone."

"Not alone!" she interjected. "I have Henry."

Through the open doorway, she saw her son in the kitchen tugging Tabitha's skirts as she reassured him, yet again, that Bathsheba would be coming with them to the new house. Aemilia had already sold her virginals and every scrap of furniture and pewter she could spare. She had pawned the last of her jewels from her time with Henry Carey. But her lute and her old mare she would keep.

"You have the boy for only a few more years," Alfonse said, as though that was obvious to everyone but her. "At seven, he shall begin his apprenticeship."

Of course, he was right. Jasper, too, had begun his musical apprenticeship at that age. Still, the thought choked her into silence. After all she had lost, must she also lose her son?

When Jasper and Alfonse went to see the upstairs rooms, Aemilia remained below and gazed out the smudged windows into the garden of weeds. At least the downstairs windows were glazed.

The floorboards creaked like ships' masts as Winifred trundled toward her. "Don't despair, mistress. We'll scratch by. Come spring we'll plant a kitchen garden. We'll keep chickens."

Her maid's goodness left Aemilia racked with guilt, for her change in circumstance had reduced the servants' wages to a pittance.

"You don't have to stay with me, you know," she told Winifred, taking her hands. "You and your sisters are free to seek your fortunes wherever you wish."

Winifred's eyes filled. Her voice wobbled. "Mistress mine, where else have we to go?"

Aemilia and Winifred bowed their heads and stood brow to brow, hands clasped, in that cramped parlor while Alfonse and Jasper paced overhead, sending a shower of dust and plaster falling from the ceiling. Aemilia thought that fate itself was walling her in, squeezing her into a box that shrank and shrank until there would be no place left for her at all.

Her sole consolation was that the new house was only a short walk from the Shoreditch playhouse. When Alfonse was away at court, she accompanied Ben to the theater. Ben insisted on paying the tuppence for her gallery seat beside his.

"It's only fitting," he said, "that you should see our erstwhile poet's new plays. He's a wealthy man these days. Bought the second biggest house in Stratford—ten fireplaces and five gables!"

Aemilia remembered Will's old boardinghouse and then tried to envision him strolling through such a huge property. It seemed that she and Will were at opposite sides of Fortuna's turning wheel. While he seemed to ascend to ever more glorious heights, her descent seemed never ending. Yet somehow she sensed her fate was bound up with his.

For all Will's prosperity, a dark thread ran through his work. Even his new comedies had taken a bitter turn. Seated beside Ben in the gallery, she watched *The Merchant of Venice*, his cold and loveless play of a Venetian Jew and his daughter that left her shivering in rage, for she felt as though she were viewing a satire of the tales she had told Will of her father. One of his Jew-hating characters was even named Bassanio. Will played the part of Antonio, the merchant.

"Our poet apes the late Kit Marlowe," Ben whispered in her ear. "Is this not in a similar vein to *The Jew of Malta*?"

Aemilia nodded, for she, too, saw how Shylock, the Jewish moneylender, was a character not dissimilar to Marlowe's. Played by a comedian who sported a hideous red wig and a bulbous false nose, Shylock was as grotesque a parody of a Jew as she could imagine—greedy, sly, and pitiless—who elicited both hisses and savage laughter from the audience. The Christian characters denounced him as a dog, a cur, a demon. His own servant called him "the very devil incarnation," and Shylock seemed to embody this very evil when he insisted on taking a pound of flesh from Antonio to punish him for his late repayment of a loan.

"Oh, you *hypocrite*!" Forgetting herself, Aemilia spoke so loudly that the actors on stage gaped in confusion. His eyes stark, Will froze while the groundlings roared in laughter to hear the great actor and playwright heckled by a woman.

"Once he told me his own father was *twice* accused of lending money at exorbitant rates," she hissed to Ben, who rocked in hilarity.

"Marry, you are an Amazon," he wheezed, clapping her shoulder. "I think the poor man lives in terror of you."

"If I were a man, I'd give him a taste of terror." She imagined herself challenging Will to a duel. "How fortunate for him that I am only a woman."

How could Will have written something so hateful, he who should have known better? To think they had once stood side by side in the Scuola Grande Tedesca in the Venetian Ghetto and listened to the brilliant philosopher-rabbi Leone da Modena. Will had been a trusted guest in Jacopo Bassano's house. Even if her former lover had turned against her, why condemn an entire people?

Will's comedy ended with Shylock's ruin, which stripped him of his daughter, his property and wealth, and his religion. Shylock, like Aemilia's own father, was forced to convert.

I think the poor man lives in terror of you. Ben's words lingered with Aemilia. *Is it indeed fear that lies at the heart of Will's rancor?* she wondered. Did he view their secret arrangement to evenly divide the profits of the comedies they had written together as the pound of flesh he was forced to sacrifice lest she step out of the shadows?

Perhaps what irked Will most was that he simply couldn't banish her. His wife might be left behind in Stratford with their daughters, but he had no power over Aemilia, who could attend his plays whenever it pleased her and even yell out catcalls. And so he used his plays to purge himself of her, his gadfly, his dark Muse. In *Othello,* he even named one of his characters Emilia only to have her husband call her a villainous whore and stab her to death for her too-quick tongue. Aemilia imagined that if she had been one of Will's heroines, Alfonse would have murdered her ages ago. Instead, she remained stubbornly alive and well. Will had wanted to be rid of her, but that was impossible. As high as he rose on Fortuna's wheel, she carried on even in decline, carving out her life in the margins of his fame.

In 1599 Aemilia's men scattered like starlings. Will and the rest of the Lord Chamberlain's Men left Shoreditch for the Globe, their new theater in Southwark, that district packed with brothels and bathhouses that made it insalubrious for women like her. Had she been bold enough to wear her breeches and journey forth as Emilio, she might have gone whenever she desired. As Aemilia, she reserved her forays to the Globe for Ben's new plays, when she might use kinship as her excuse. Alfonse was happy enough to escort her, considering that his nephew, Nicholas Lanier, and his brother-in-law, Alfonso Ferrabosco, composed stage music for her cousin.

But Aemilia never saw another play of Will's. Ben, however, kept her abreast of the gossip.

"Our poet has tried to *buy* a coat of arms!" This appeared to amuse Ben to no end. "For his father, he says. And his motto? *Non sanz droict.*"

"Not without right," Aemilia translated drily.

Ben's latest comedy, *Every Man out of His Humour,* concerned a bumpkin who paid thirty pounds for a ridiculous coat of arms and the motto Not Without Mustard. The satire was performed by actors from Will's own company. Yet Aemilia knew that Ben and Will drank together at the Mermaid Tavern. The two rival poet-playwrights had both become too prominent and prolific not to acknowledge each other so they appeared to reach an accord. Will even acted in one of Ben's plays.

ALFONSE APPEARED HOME FROM court unexpectedly, bursting into the parlor where Henry was playing his flute while Aemilia accompanied him on her lute.

"Papa!" Six-year-old Henry carefully set down his flute before throwing his arms around Alfonse.

"What brings you home so early?" Aemilia kissed him in greeting.

"Now is my chance! All my life I have waited for this!"

Alfonse whirled her and Henry round the little room, leaping so high she feared he would crack his skull on the sagging beams.

"What good news, my husband?" The dancing left Aemilia breathless.

Alfonse's eyes shone like scimitars. "I shall sail to Ireland with the Earl of Essex."

Her hands dropped to her sides. "But what of the Queen's Musicke?"

He laughed. "*Chérie,* I shall not earn a knighthood by playing the flute." He turned to Henry. "Do you want to help me pack?"

As Henry trotted up the stairs after him, the boy whooped as though he, too, were going to war. Aemilia called Tabitha before following them into the master bedchamber, where Alfonse showed off his sword and rapier, skewering imaginary enemies while Henry cheered him on.

"Henry, go with Tabitha. I must speak to your papa alone."

Her son simmered in mutiny and clung to Alfonse's waist. She winced to see the child so close to the blades meant to kill.

"Tabby will let you ride Bathsheba," she said.

Henry gazed up at Alfonse. "Will you come out later and watch me?"

"But of course," Alfonse said, winking as the boy finally permitted Tabitha to lead him out of the room.

"Please don't go," Aemilia begged her husband. "Essex's star is no longer rising. If he falls, you fall with him."

Everyone knew of Essex's quarrel with the Queen, of his insistence on war instead of peace with Spain despite all arguments to the contrary. In her anger, Her Majesty had boxed Essex's ears in front of the entire council chamber. Then Essex had made the unforgivable move of laying his hand on his sword. Elizabeth's punishment played on the very hot-headed valor that made Essex fall from grace — she commanded him to lead her forces against the Irish rebels, a post he could not refuse and a mission from which he and his men might never return.

"You could die." Aemilia took Alfonse's hands. "Prove your loyalty to Her Majesty by staying here and serving her in court. And think of your health."

Her husband's disease still troubled him with bouts of fever, nausea, and swollen joints. He paid regular visits to Clerkenwell to drink and bathe in the water from the healing springs. But now his thoughts seemed leagues away from such considerations.

"I must go." He fairly quivered with ambition. "Do you not see? This is my chance to be the Queen's champion, and to serve a great man as well."

Aemilia read into what he did not say for fear of speaking treason. Could it be that the Queen's star, not Essex's, was falling? By taking part in this battle, Alfonse could distinguish himself in one of two ways, allying himself with the victor of this feud, whether it be the elderly Queen or Essex in all his vainglory. Essex had never had more supporters.

Her husband caressed her shoulders as if trying to instill within her the same excitement that vibrated through him. "Why, even the Earl of Southampton shall sail with us!"

Harry sharing the battlefield with her husband? Aemilia felt as though her breath had been knocked out of her lungs. She could only pray Harry would be decent and not regale Alfonse with tales of her secret forays to Southampton House in her breeches and codpiece those many years ago. It seemed a lifetime since she had last dressed as Emilio.

"You foolish man," Aemilia whispered in the darkness of their bed, the curtains drawn around them. "What if we lose you forever?"

"I will come back a knight," he said, kissing her breasts. "And make you a lady."

"Whatever you do, come back alive."

27

S THOUGH LEADING A triumphal parade, Henry sat tall in the saddle, riding Bathsheba through Bishopsgate into the City of London. His breeches, cloak, and doublet were new, cut from the cloth of the fine gowns Aemilia no longer had occasion to wear. Her son's breath floated like a banner in the January sky.

Aemilia walked at her mare's shoulder while behind them the Weir sisters carried her son's belongings. On this, Henry's seventh birthday, he was leaving home to live with Jasper and so begin his seven-year musical apprenticeship. How eager her son looked, how proud, riding toward his future, just as Alfonse was charging into battle somewhere across the Irish Sea. Henry looked only forward, not at his mother or at the shabby little house he had left behind.

When they turned into Camomile Street and reached Jasper's house with its tall gable and big windows, Aemilia tried not to feel betrayed by her son's gaze of adoration, as though this handsome residence were the home that was always meant to be his.

"Let me help you," Aemilia said, reaching for Henry, but her son sprang down from the saddle on his own, landing smartly on his feet.

Already the door opened. A servant came to take her son's things from the Weir sisters who said their good-byes to Henry before turning and leading Bathsheba back home. Tabitha was crying. Aemilia hoped the girl might soon marry and have children of her own. Lately, Tabby had been walking out with a young wainwright brave enough to face Winifred's scrutiny in order to court her beautiful sister.

Jasper and his family crowded the doorway to welcome Aemilia and her son. Last year her cousin had married Deborah, a widow with a boy Henry's age and a girl one year younger. Deborah was pink cheeked and auburn haired, her belly huge with her and Jasper's first child together.

Jasper already had four apprentices, so Henry would be the fifth. Her cousin's house was as crowded and bustling, as lively and warm, as Jacopo's villa in Bassano had been. The wainscoting gleamed with beeswax, there were real tapestries on the walls, and enough fireplaces to keep the place cosy. The air smelled of freshly baked bread and roasting meat.

Because Jasper was not ambitious like Alfonse but content to be a minstrel, he had prospered, saving his money as a court musician and stage minstrel, and earning an additional income taking on apprentices. Aemilia wished her husband could be so prudent and not waste their money on foreign expeditions and schemes to advance himself.

She exchanged kisses with Deborah, who took her into the dining room with its table set for ten. The family shared all meals with their apprentices.

"Don't you worry about your Henry," Deborah said. "He'll share the truckle bed with my Edward. They'll be like brothers. Aemilia, you're crying!"

Aemilia was about to turn away so Henry wouldn't see her tears. How could she embarrass her son on his day of days, when his childhood ended and he became an apprentice musician? But Henry was too busy chattering with Deborah's children to even notice, as though they were the longed-for siblings Aemilia had failed to give him. *Let him be part of a proper family.* He couldn't hope for a more accomplished teacher than Jasper, and Deborah was goodness itself. How could Aemilia stand in the way of her son's education and happiness? As a loving mother, she would have to let him go.

Now you are truly *alone.* Aemilia unlocked the door to her house, so empty and silent with the Weir sisters gone to the market.

The men in her life, even her seven-year-old boy, had left her to pursue their destiny. But what of her own dreams? Fetching the *tarocchi* cards down from their hiding place in her trunk, Aemilia sat at the kitchen table and shuffled those cards of fortune as though she, like Simon Forman or Doctor John Dee, could glimpse into the future. Nine cards she drew and laid in a row, both trumps and court cards, their colors and faded gilding flashing in the weak sunlight coming through the window. All nine were female figures reveling in inconceivable authority and might.

A female knight brandished her unsheathed sword. A girl danced fearlessly at a cliff's edge while cupping a star in her open palm. A queen held in her lap a golden coin as big as a shield. La Papessa, the female pope, wore a nun's habit and the papal tiara. Balanced on her leaping steed, another female knight wielded a baton as though it were a magical wand. In the trump Il Carro Triumphale, a crowned woman bearing a scepter and an imperial globe drove a chariot pulled by winged white horses. L'Imperatrice sat enthroned, her shield emblazoned with the black eagle of the Holy Roman Empire. Her fair hair flowing, La Temperanza danced with a jug in each hand, not spilling one drop. Serene and unmoving, Fortuna sat at the hub of her ever-turning wheel, while those hapless figures clinging to the wheel's rim rose and fell in a never-ending round.

Aemilia's brain revolved in circles, struggling to decipher those images that filled her with such yearning.

"Good cards indeed," a familiar voice behind her murmured.

She turned to see Prudence.

"Pray, what does it all mean?" she asked her maid.

"I'd reckon you shall encounter any number of esteemed ladies, though I can't say when or where."

Aemilia kept her own counsel. Surely those images were allegorical —apart from the Queen, precious few women in this world wielded that sort of power. But Prudence held her gaze and grinned, as if she already saw that august circle of ladies her mistress would one day meet.

I have placed all my hopes in men and where did that get me? The time had come to take refuge in the company of learned women, if only she could meet them. Her memory traveled back to her days at Grimsthorpe Castle where Susan Bertie had taught her Latin and Greek, and allowed her to dream of great things. Aemilia had thought that idyll was forever lost, yet the cards hinted that she might gain such a haven once more.

The triumph promised to her in the *tarocchi* cards, that constellation of brilliant and powerful women, seemed as distant as the farthest-flung stars. And yet she was her own mistress again. A woman of slender means, to be sure, but she had her privacy and independence. *Now I might be a poet.*

BUT WHEN AEMILIA SAT down to write, she trembled at the very cost of paper, aware that she might soon be a widow. Even if, by the grace of God, Alfonse returned unscathed, war was a costly adventure. Gentlemen volunteers such as her husband were obliged to pay their own way even while fighting the Queen's battles. What if Essex's folly left them ruined?

All the more reason to write and aspire to some sort of patronage, she told herself. This time she must write in her own name, write something that couldn't be taken from her as the plays had been taken. If she had remained in Italy, she might have penned her own comedies or poetic allegories of love and philosophy. Here in England, a woman might write only if she translated the work of a great man or if she wrote about religion — the Queen's religion.

Aemilia's quill hovered above the page and dribbled black ink, but no words came.

Soon she would be thirty, her youth well and truly spent. In a matter of months, the century would end. What new world might be born when the old one passed away? Aemilia gazed into her steel mirror, hoping to catch a shadow of a vision of what would unfold.

Despite her Latin, Greek, French, and Italian, she had no desire to be a translator; she wanted to write only her own poetry. But religious verse? Who could take that seriously, coming from a woman like her? She would have to claim some dramatic conversion, similar to Paul's being speared by lightning on the road to Damascus.

She considered her Puritan education with Susan Bertie, considered Anne Locke's pious sonnets. Mary Sidney Herbert, the Countess Dowager of Pembroke, had written a collection of poetry based on the psalms, a project her brother, Philip Sidney, had begun before his untimely death. Mary had finished where Philip had left off to create a tribute to him. Being an aristocrat, the Countess could hardly sully herself by allowing her work to be published on the printed page. Instead, she permitted her hand-scribed manuscripts to be shared in a few chosen circles. Aemilia had chanced to read the poems when Ben had shown her the pages. How they had amazed her.

Closing her eyes, she thought how Jacopo Bassano, after his forced conversion, had spent his life painting masterpieces of Christian art, yet still his soul and deep truth were present in each despite the mask he was made to wear.

Dipping her nib into the ink, Aemilia wrote four words, forming each letter slowly, deliberately, as if in a dream.

Salve Deus Rex Judaeorum

Hail, God, King of the Jews.

28

VERY SOUL IN THE realm seemed to converge on Westminster that April morning in 1603. Men, women, and children of all ranks crammed the streets and jostled for the best view. Others hung out of windows and even crowded the rooftops to watch the funeral cortege of a thousand mourners, Aemilia among them, who followed the Queen's coffin from Whitehall Palace to Westminster Abbey.

There she passes, the Virgin Queen. Aemilia strained her eyes to see to the very front of the procession, where four gray stallions draped in black velvet drew Her Majesty's hearse. The coffin was covered in royal purple and topped with an effigy so lifelike that it made the onlookers point and gasp. Six knights supported a canopy over the coffin. Behind the hearse, the Queen's Master of the Horse led Elizabeth's palfrey. As Chief Mourner, the Marchioness of Northampton led the peers of the realm, all of them arrayed in black.

Aemilia hadn't been in the presence of so many aristocrats since her days at court. Her sole reason for being allowed to walk in the procession was on account of her husband being one of the fifty-nine musicians chosen to play for the Queen's funeral. Her ten-year-old son would sing in the choir.

Aemilia nearly tripped over her hem when she sighted Mary Sidney Herbert, the great poet, and there was the Countess of Bedford, a noted patroness of arts and letters. On this somber occasion, the eminent circle of ladies Prudence promised to Aemilia in the *tarocchi* cards seemed close enough to touch. But surely these noblewomen would dismiss her as only the wife of a minor courtier.

A woman of middle years stepped into pace with Aemilia. Though the lady appeared as an aristocrat in bearing, her black brocade gown with its silver thread was faded and worn. Her heart-shaped face looked so familiar, as did her huge brown eyes.

"Forgive me, madam, but are you Aemilia Bassano?"

"I was before I married, my lady," Aemilia said, intrigued to be addressed by her maiden name for the first time in years.

"I thought so." The lady smiled. "I'd recognize you anywhere, Amy."

"My lady?" Aemilia struggled not to laugh aloud in joy. "My Lady Susan!"

More than twenty years had passed since she last laid eyes on Susan Bertie. *Is it a sin*, Aemilia wondered, *to feel this rush of felicity while marching behind the Queen's coffin?* She took Susan's hand and Susan squeezed hers in return.

Aemilia had always feared that her former mentor would have forever forsaken her after she had fallen from grace and become the late Lord Chamberlain's mistress. But looking into Susan's eyes, she saw nothing but affection. The years seemed to melt away.

"How happy we were back in Grimsthorpe," Aemilia murmured. "How I missed you when you married and left for the Netherlands. I thought I'd never see you again."

"I missed you as well," said Susan. "You were such a spirited little girl. You know, I had two sons, but I always longed for a daughter."

"My lady, I'm so sorry to hear of your brother's passing."

Susan lowered her gaze. "Poor Perry! In truth, I think that death was his only escape from his horrid wife. I am a widow now—did you know?"

Aemilia shook her head.

"The fate of being married to a soldier," Susan said. "They sow their fortunes on the battlefield and reap only debt and death."

Catching the glint of unspilled tears in Susan's eyes, Aemilia took her arm and held it tightly. "My husband sailed to Ireland with the Earl of Essex."

She couldn't hide her contempt when speaking the traitor's name, that turncoat who had led an armed rebellion against the Queen. When Elizabeth beheaded Essex, Aemilia had quietly rejoiced. Essex, the author of Alfonse's misfortune. Southampton, who had joined the rebellion, was imprisoned in the Tower.

"My husband had no part in Essex's plot," Aemilia told Susan. "Three years he fought in the Irish wars and returned only after the Spanish were defeated in Kinsale." She dropped her voice to a whisper. "We, too, are much impoverished."

Alfonse had proved his loyalty to the Crown but at great cost, depleting their entire estate. He had run up a staggering four thousand pounds in debts, yet he didn't even have a knighthood to show for his sacrifice, only the title of captain. In the early years of their marriage, he had ruined his health and wasted her income on his dissolute life. In recent years, when he had been striving so hard to be a good man in the Queen's service, he had suffered even more ill luck. Her family's future remained uncertain. Aemilia could only hope that Alfonse would find a place in the new King James's court.

War and hardship, the great levelers, Aemilia thought, as she walked arm in arm with Lady Susan as if no rank separated them.

WHEN THEY HAD TAKEN their places in Westminster Abbey, Aemilia pointed out her husband to Susan as he played with the other musicians.

"Captain Alfonse Lanier," she said, careful to mention the only title to which anyone in her household could lay claim.

The wars had left their mark on Alfonse, scarring his face and thinning his hair. But the beauty of his flute playing moved Aemilia as much as ever.

"And that's my son," she whispered, pointing to Henry in the choir.

"The child has an air of nobility about him," Susan observed, making gentle note of his parentage.

At ten, Henry was tall and solemn, with his natural father's penetrating gaze and his mother's dark eyes and hair.

The Queen's funeral service was half in English, half in Latin, as if the country's religion were again uncertain. Everything might be turned upside down, as when Elizabeth ascended to the throne after her Catholic sister Mary Tudor's death. The new King James was Catholic Mary Stuart's son, but he had been raised a Protestant. Who could say what the new order might bring—the Scottish monarch had yet to show his face in London or Westminster.

AFTER THE FUNERAL HAD ended, Aemilia walked with Susan through the throng of grandees gathered outside Westminster Abbey.

"Nothing in this world is constant," Susan whispered, her face white with indignation. "Just look at them all."

The lady's eyes darted to the noblemen who muttered behind their hands, as though already plotting how to secure their positions in the new court even though the old Queen's coffin had barely been laid to rest. Aemilia, likewise, could read the thoughts emblazoned on the courtiers' faces. They could barely contain their jubilation to have a man back on the throne after two reigning female monarchs.

"Now watch them take flight," Susan whispered. "They'll gallop to York to greet the new King, killing three horses in a day to try to get there before all the others."

Susan pointed out a man whose face bore an expression of barely concealed impatience, as though he couldn't stand to wait another minute before racing north to stake his claim. With his sweeping dark hair and black-velvet doublet, he cut a dashing figure, but his entire mien was of insufferable arrogance.

Aemilia recognized him at once—George Clifford, the Earl of Cumberland, the late Queen's champion of the tiltyard. Beside him stood his wife, Margaret Clifford, the Countess of Cumberland, who still looked much the same as Aemilia remembered from her days at court. She was a lady with the modest manner of a virtuous wife, except her husband appeared as though he couldn't stand the sight of her. Even Aemilia had heard the rumors that George Clifford had all but repudiated his wife. Margaret's face, clenched in humiliation, tore at Aemilia's heart. She knew that pain only too well.

Beside Margaret stood a slender girl whose eyes gleamed falcon bright. Aemilia noted the way the girl stood close to her mother and held her hand, as if to shield her from her father's disdain. Aemilia could not take her eyes off their clasped hands. Love seemed to radiate from mother and daughter like the glow around a lamp. *At least you have this consolation,* Aemilia longed to tell Margaret Clifford. Her own arms ached for the daughter she had lost.

The crowd began to disperse, and already George Clifford was walking away from his wife and daughter. Before they, too, could depart, Susan drew Aemilia forward and greeted Margaret Clifford and her daughter, Anne.

"This is my dear friend, Mistress Aemilia Bassano Lanier, wife of Captain Lanier, a most loyal servant of our late Queen."

Aemilia was mystified why Susan should make such a show of presenting her, but she dropped down in a curtsy just the same.

"Aemilia Bassano," the Countess of Cumberland said. "Yes, I remember you from your time at court."

Aemilia was on fire before her gaze. Margaret Clifford had witnessed her downfall, the ignomy of fainting in the masque then coming to in that room full of scandalized, gossiping women. Only Margaret had looked on her with compassion.

The Countess now regarded her with dark, serious eyes in a face that was as pale as the pearls at her throat. Aemilia could sense the intelligence pulsing inside her. This was a woman of great forbearance. *She showed me kindness that day because she knows what it is to suffer and be shamed.*

"I educated Aemilia when she was a girl," Susan told the Countess.

"And a fine education that was," Margaret Clifford said. "I remember your many accomplishments, Mistress Lanier."

"My Lady Margaret, would she not make a fine tutor for Anne?" Susan spoke smoothly with a subtle smile.

Aemilia could not believe her mentor's boldness. Meanwhile, Anne seemed to examine Aemilia with sharp, inquisitive eyes.

"Master Samuel Daniel is my tutor," the girl said grandly.

"The renowned poet!" Aemilia interjected. She couldn't help herself. "How I admire his *Complaint of Rosamond.*"

"You yourself are a poet as I recall," Margaret said. "Did you not once write a poem for Her Majesty?"

"My lady, I did." Aemilia was light-headed with elation that the Countess remembered. "Though it was but short."

Closing her eyes, she recited the poem that she had offered to the

Queen when Lord Hunsdon had first introduced her at court. Her voice wavered in grief at Her Majesty's passing. Though Aemilia had suffered the Queen's ire and banishment when she fell pregnant, Elizabeth had been the bedrock on which this realm had stood for Aemilia's entire existence. How could England go on without her courageous Queen?

> The Phoenix of her age, whose worth does bind
> All worthy minds so long as they have breath,
> In links of admiration, love, and zeal,
> To the dear Mother of our Commonweal.

The circle of women remained silent, heads bowed.

"Elizabeth was truly the phoenix of our age," Margaret said, tears in her eyes.

Aemilia saw the genuine love on Margaret Clifford's face, for had she not been one of Elizabeth's most trusted Maids of Honor? The Countess had attended Elizabeth on her deathbed.

"In faith, Mistress Lanier," Margaret said, drying her eyes, "I think your talents would impress even Master Daniel."

"She's fluent in French and Italian," Susan said. "Are not languages a marvelous accomplishment for a young lady?"

"Father won't *let* me learn languages," Anne said, with the savage bluntness of a maid of thirteen.

Aemilia couldn't hide her astonishment. "What, not even Latin?"

"My husband thinks it unbecoming of a woman," the Countess said drearily. "The new King won't even allow his daughter to learn Latin."

Aemilia wanted to wring her hands. The late Queen had mastered Latin, Greek, and many modern languages. What would James's reign hold if even the Princess Royal was forbidden a humanist education?

Anne exchanged a look with her mother, who seemed to view Aemilia more intently.

"What else can you teach, Mistress Lanier?" Margaret Clifford asked.

Aemilia's tongue froze in her open mouth.

"Music," Susan said, speaking swiftly to hide Aemilia's awkwardness.

"I could teach your daughter to play the lute and the virginals," Aemilia said, inclining her head in deference. "And to sing madrigals."

"I could *sing* in Italian, could I not?" Anne looked at her mother. "Father only said I couldn't *speak* foreign languages."

"But you are married, Mistress Lanier," the Countess said. "Would your husband permit you to live elsewhere?"

"My husband is often away at court," Aemilia told her. "He would begrudge me no honorable occupation." Alfonse, she knew, would kiss every coin she could bring to their household.

The Countess nodded. "Tomorrow my daughter and I ride north to greet Queen Anne, but when we return, I shall send for you to join us at Cookham."

For a moment, Aemilia forgot to breathe. Then she blinked and the Countess and her daughter had departed.

Susan took her hand. "You said your husband has fallen into poverty and decline. Why should you not use your learning to raise yourself back up?"

29

LIMBING OUT OF THE wherry at Cookham Village with its cottages hugging the banks of the Thames, Aemilia felt as wide-eyed and unsure of herself as when she had first made her journey to Grimsthorpe as an eight-year-old child. Though she was grateful to finally have a meaningful occupation, she had no clue what to expect from her new life as a tutor. Had the Countess of Cumberland hired her out of pity, as an act of charity to the wife of a man who had impoverished his family in service of the Crown? What if Margaret Clifford began to have second thoughts about hiring a woman of Aemilia's tarnished reputation to teach her innocent daughter? How easily Aemilia could slip up.

No such doubts seemed to cloud Winifred's mind. In her exuberance, her maid nearly capsized the boat as she scrambled out.

"*I* shall carry your lute," Winifred declared, clutching her mistress's prized instrument in her huge arms as though the boatman couldn't be trusted to lay even a finger on it.

The wherryman heaved Aemilia and Winifred's boxes onto the landing.

Before paying the fare, Aemilia gripped Winifred's arm. "It's not too late to go back. Will you not miss your sisters?"

With Alfonse at court in the King's Musicke, Aemilia now employed at Cookham, and Henry serving his apprenticeship in Jasper's home, they had given up the rented house in Norton Folgate. Tabitha had married her wainwright and was expecting their first child. Pru had stayed behind to act as midwife.

"Don't you want to be there when Tabby's baby is born?" Aemilia asked.

"Who will look after you then?" Winifred sniffed and rubbed her eyes but stood as tall as a soldier. "A gentlewoman requires a maid."

"I am now a gentlewoman *servant*," Aemilia pointed out.

"Look, mistress! Here comes the cart to take us to the manor house."

Leaving behind the village, the cart carried Aemilia and Winifred past cherry orchards and meadows of lacy flowers where cattle and sheep grazed. Though this felt like the deepest countryside, they were only twenty-five miles up the Thames from London and a short distance from Windsor and Maidenhead.

At last the ancient timber house came into view. Owned by the Crown and leased to Margaret Clifford's brother, Cookham Manor had become the Countess's refuge when the strain in her marriage had become intolerable.

Before the driver could help her down, Aemilia leapt from the cart and stood face-to-face with Margaret and Anne, her new pupil. Aemilia pitched herself forward in a curtsy, but Margaret grasped her hands and held her upright.

"Welcome, Mistress Lanier. I hope you will feel at home with us."

"*Promise* me you'll teach me to sing in Italian," said Anne, taking Aemilia's arm.

"A pity you missed Master Daniel," the Countess said. "He was called away, but his poetry books are here should you wish to read them."

Mother and daughter drew Aemilia into their realm, that masterless manor with no husbands or fathers.

A medieval hall, Cookham was nowhere near as opulent as Grimsthorpe, but it was all the more hospitable with its creaking oak floors and uneven walls with their faded tapestries of dancing goddesses.

Taking her new tutor by the hand, Anne led Aemilia through the great room and up the staircase.

"I hope you like to walk," the girl said. "In fair weather, we walk for *hours.* Mother even lets me take my lessons beneath the oak tree on Cookham Dean."

"That sounds delightful," Aemilia said, mindful that her best manners be on display.

When they reached the top of the stairs, the Countess led them down a paneled hallway. With a flourish, Anne opened the door at the very end. "Here you are, Mistress Lanier!"

Tucked under slanting eaves, the room not only contained a bed but also a writing desk with an ink pot, a goose quill, a stack of freshly cut paper, and Master Daniel's book, *The Complaint of Rosamond.* A clay jar held a bouquet of bluebells.

"This was Samuel Daniel's room, was it not?" Aemilia asked.

The air seemed to shimmer with poetry.

The Countess nodded. "I hope you find it suitable."

"My lady, it's more than suitable." Aemilia paused, unable to believe her luck. "But it seems the good poet left behind his paper and books."

On the shelf near the desk, she saw the Geneva Bible and *The Book of Common Prayer,* along with Spenser's *The Faerie Queene,* and Arthur Golding's English translation of Ovid's *Metamorphoses.*

"Mistress Lanier, they're for your use," the Countess said. "You confessed your great love of poetry. I thought you might write some verse during your stay here."

The sunlight streaming through the open window struck Aemilia blind. Then she blinked and peered through that radiance at Margaret Clifford.

"My lady, that's generous." Aemilia couldn't keep herself from smiling at the Countess as though she were the very apparition of Pallas Athena.

A WHILE LATER, WINIFRED entered the room with her mistress's lute. In her wake followed two youths lugging Aemilia's trunk. After setting down the lute and chasing the young men back out the door, Winifred hugged Aemilia hard enough to crack her ribs.

"Oh, my sweet mistress, this is what I always wanted for you! A respectable home amongst honest ladies. Surely here you'll get into no mischief at all!"

Aemilia watched as her maid, filled with the zeal of renewed purpose, hunted through her trunk in search of something presentable for her to wear.

"Such a pity you sacrificed your finest gowns to make clothes for Henry that he'll only outgrow, but *this* will do." Winifred seized a gown of light summer wool, the same hue as the bluebells in their jar. "Ah, but we need water for washing."

Beside the curtained bed was a washing stand with a pewter ewer, a cake of soap, and a white linen towel, but Winifred discovered that the ewer was empty.

"Let me go fill this," the maid said, letting herself out of the room.

Aemilia stuck her head out of the ivy-draped window and breathed in the scents of the rose garden below. She caressed the leaves of paper, blank and pure. From the pocket hidden in her skirts, she drew the fustian pouch containing her *tarocchi* cards. Sitting at the desk—Samuel Daniel's desk!—she laid out, one by one, the nine cards she had drawn three years ago. She hadn't touched her deck in all that time, keeping those nine cards at the top, waiting for their promise to be fulfilled.

Losing all sense of time, she pored over those gilded pictures of mighty women—warriors, queens, empresses, maidens who danced fearlessly at cliff's edge.

"What are they, Mistress Lanier?" a voice behind her asked.

Swallowing a yelp, Aemilia turned to see Anne Clifford. Winifred must have left the door open. Yet as flustered as Aemilia was, she discovered she couldn't lie to the girl. "They're called *tarocchi* cards."

"Marry, they're lovely! May I touch them?"

"Yes, my lady."

Without hesitation, Anne chose the card of the female knight brandishing her unsheathed sword as she charged into battle.

"This is my card." The girl leaned close as if to impart a secret. "When we rode to York to meet the new King, my father made bold to exercise his right as a peer of the realm to wear his sword in His Majesty's presence. Afterward, when he unbuckled his sword belt and handed it to his servant, *I* took it. Before Father could stop me, I belted his sword around my waist before the King."

Aemilia was staggered to picture this thirteen-year-old virago standing armed before both her father and her monarch.

"Am I not Father's heir?" The girl seemed anxious that Aemilia should understand her reasoning. "My ancestral office, it is, to bear my father's sword. One day I shall be mistress of his estates in Westmoreland and Yorkshire."

Aemilia wondered what she possibly had to teach this girl who seemed a force unto herself.

"These are fortune-telling cards, are they not?" The girl placed the female knight beside the maiden dancing with the star in her palm. "My mother can foretell the future, but she doesn't need cards. She has the gift of prophecy. Like Deborah in the Bible."

"A prophet? Truly?" Aemilia didn't know what else to say.

"Mother's an alchemist, too."

Aemilia fell silent at the sight of Margaret Clifford standing in the doorway.

"Mother, come and see Mistress Lanier's *tarocchi* cards!"

Aemilia stepped aside so that the Countess of Cumberland could inspect the nine cards that had foretold their meeting and Aemilia's very presence in this house. The Countess's eyes were riven on one card in particular, which she held up to Aemilia with a questioning look. The card of the nun wearing the papal tiara.

Petrified, Aemilia wondered what the Countess, who was by all accounts uncommonly pious, would make of this. Would Margaret Clifford accuse her of filling her daughter's head with papist perdition? Aemilia would be cast out of Cookham as unceremoniously as she had been booted from Grimsthorpe.

Just then, Winifred entered with the ewer of water. Her maid looked as though she would drop it in despair as she viewed the scene unfolding before her.

"La Papessa," Aemilia said in a small voice. "The female pope." She cleared her throat. "The cards are from Italy, my lady."

"As are you," Anne said brightly.

Up until this point, Margaret Clifford had been the portrait of solemnity and reserve, but suddenly she laughed. Her mirth filled the room like the fresh air wafting in from the garden.

"I think we shall not have a dull summer now that Mistress Lanier has come to join us," the Countess said.

Smiling, she drew her daughter out of the room.

"*That* was a close call!" Winifred huffed, when she and her mistress were alone.

"Peace, Winifred." A lightness stole over Aemilia's heart as she placed the cards, one by one, back in their fustian pouch. "I suspect the Countess is broader minded than either of us imagined."

Never in her life had she thought to meet a woman alchemist. Who was this Margaret Clifford? Though only nine years older than Aemilia's own thirty-four years, the Countess seemed so wise. Her secrets and veiled tragedy, and her fierce love for her daughter, reminded Aemilia so much of her own father. If Papa had been a magician, so was this lady.

AT CHAPEL THE FOLLOWING morning, Aemilia almost believed she had been spirited back to Italy. Though the service itself was soberly Protestant, frescoes covered the walls and the centuries-old stained-glass windows depicted miracles and saints. Carved on the baptismal font were the Instruments of the Passion. Above the altar, dominating the entire space, was the crucified Christ, an image that Anne Locke would have denounced as idolatry and replaced with a plain wooden cross. Flanking the crucifix was a statue of the Virgin Mary as the Mother of Sorrows. Though seemingly every other church and chapel in the entire kingdom had been whitewashed, its statues destroyed, this private chapel had been spared, undoubtedly because it was owned by the Crown.

"Mistress Lanier, I can see you are as thunderstruck as I first was," Margaret Clifford said, after the service had ended.

Anne and the chaplain had already gone on ahead, leaving the Countess and Aemilia alone in the chapel.

"In truth, I've come to take great comfort from these images." The Countess paused before an image of Christ, naked and bound, being scourged by the Romans. "Meditating upon this helps me endure my own sufferings as a wife."

"My lady," Aemilia said, shocked to hear a woman of her rank reveal so much of herself. Then she remembered how George Clifford's scorn of his wife had been on display for all the world to see. Perhaps the Countess had discovered that the best response was candor.

"For who inflicted such agony upon our Lord?" Margaret Clifford asked.

Aemilia felt bruised inside, thinking that the Countess expected her to reply that the Jews killed Christ. But the lady's answer to her own question took Aemilia's breath away.

"Men," the Countess of Cumberland said. "Men killed Christ. And yet they blame poor Eve, and all womankind, for our fall from grace."

Not since Aemilia was a girl and her father had whispered in her ear that hell was empty had she heard such a radical pronouncement.

Before leaving the chapel, the Countess lingered beneath a stained-glass window showing Saint Clare in her nun's habit.

"If I envy the Catholics one thing, it's that," she said, lifting her gaze as the sun pierced the warm umber tones of Clare's habit. "If only I had been able to marry God instead of George Clifford. The sole good to come of our marriage was Anne, and he despises her because she's not a son."

"Your daughter is a magnificent young lady," Aemilia said. "I trust you're very proud of her."

The Countess took Aemilia's arm as they walked out of the chapel. "Let her enjoy her girlhood. If it stays fine today, would you be so good as to give her her lessons outdoors? You shall teach her the lute, of course, and to sing madrigals in any language you please. And you'll read Ovid and Spenser with her."

"Of course, my lady." Aemilia remembered the books the Countess had left in her room. "Nothing would give me greater pleasure."

Already she anticipated long summer afternoons discussing poetry and philosophy.

The Countess gave her a wry look. "I think writing your own poetry would give you greater pleasure still."

Aemilia ducked her head, uncertain what to say.

"I was in earnest, you know, about encouraging you to write during your time with us," Margaret said. "Once I, too, attempted to write."

"You are a poet, my lady?" Aemilia thrilled at the possibility of meeting another Anne Locke.

The Countess shook her head. "No, I began writing my autobiography—for my chaplain, you understand. *The Seven Ages of Woman*, I called it. Alas, I had only reached the Fifth Age when I ran out of inspiration. Better I should provide patronage for those who are truly blessed by the Muses."

Aemilia's heart surged.

"Sometimes I think a woman's life is a dance with backward and forward movements," Margaret said. "A pilgrimage of grief." She fixed Aemilia with rueful eyes. "But enough of my melancholy. Come, let's walk beneath the sun."

"I TOLD YOU WE would walk and walk." Anne clasped Aemilia's hand as she led her along the winding path up Cookham Dean. "Wait till you see it! The tallest hill in miles!"

What a counterpoint the girl's enthusiasm sets to her mother's gravity, Aemilia thought. When she looked back at the Countess marching behind them, the lady's eyes appeared lost in contemplation. In Margaret's wake came the servants, carrying Anne's and Aemilia's lutes and books.

Their uphill progress was slowed as Anne swooped to gather white harebells, purple vetch, blue forget-me-nots, and the lacy white blooms of cow parsley. Aemilia helped her tuck the wildflowers into her hat band.

"Look!" Anne struck an allegorical pose. "I am a rustic shepherdess! And you are a dryad!"

Laughing, Aemilia fended Anne off as the girl tried to tuck a spray of new birch leaves in her hair. Instead, she carried Anne's offering in her hand.

On they wandered, through cherry and apple orchards, across pastures of sheep and curious heifers, past brooks nearly spilling their green banks. The air rang with birdsong and lambs calling to their mothers. The winds and waters sang in harmony.

When they arrived at the heights of Cookham Dean, Aemilia marveled at the view, an endless tapestry of hills and vales, towns and hamlets, groves and pastures, castle turrets and church steeples, and the Thames winding into the green distance.

"From here," the Countess said, "you can see into thirteen shires."

Margaret Clifford, Aemilia noted, was not even out of breath from the climb.

The Countess led the way to an ancient oak. In its shade, the servants laid down a cloth for pupil and tutor to sit on.

"What think you of my schoolroom, Mistress Lanier?" Anne asked. In the shade, the girl flung off her hat.

"Why, surely this is Mount Parnassus," said Aemilia. "The home of the nine Muses."

Winifred, red faced from the climb and puffing like an old donkey, handed her mistress her lute. Aemilia threw her maid an apologetic look before tuning her instrument.

"Let us begin with music," Aemilia said to Anne, "and finish with Ovid."

The Countess sat a short distance away upon a much-weathered bench built around the oak's massive trunk.

"She's reading her Psalter," Anne whispered.

Gazing off into the green hills, Aemilia understood why the Countess allowed Anne to have her lessons here. From this summit, they might see so far in the distance. Margaret Clifford longed to give her daughter the world.

WINIFRED NEEDN'T HAVE WORRIED about my clothes, Aemilia reflected. In this house of women, with no men to dazzle or appease, they dressed simply, without jewels or ostentation. The Countess wore sober dark gowns and even Anne's attire was robust, allowing her to freely rove across the grounds.

But on this glittering May morning, Anne was invited to the neighbor's estate for a fete. Aemilia stood beside the Countess and waved to Anne as she rode forth. Bedecked in pearls and brocade, the girl looked as though she were a princess on procession, accompanied by two maids, two footmen, and the stable groom.

Her mother, however, stayed behind, as though she embraced the life of a recluse.

"Let the girl amuse herself with the other young ladies," the Countess said. "I can't abide those gatherings. All the local gentry who pity me."

Aemilia longed to take Margaret's hand but feared that would be overstepping the boundary between them. *Remember your place.*

The lady regarded Aemilia with her dark eyes that radiated quiet intelligence. "Mistress Lanier, would you like to see my laboratory?"

NOT SINCE HER VISIT to Simon Forman's consulting room ten years ago had Aemilia set foot in such a place, its walls bedecked with mystical diagrams. The Countess showed her the furnace and oven, the retorts and hermetically sealed fermenting vessels, and the copper distilling body with its glass head and receiver. There was a pestle and mortar, and all manner of dishes, beakers, and tubes.

But what arrested Aemilia's attention was the oratory in the alcove. Along with the cross on the wall, there hung a piece of virgin parchment inscribed with Hebrew letters.

"The letters of the Hebrew name of God," Margaret told her. "Alas, I don't know that language—I copied it from a book. Each working begins and ends with prayer and meditation."

Here in the laboratory, the Countess's air of melancholy dropped away. Aemilia sensed that this was the place where Margaret was most comfortable in her own skin, her private sanctuary, holier to her than even the chapel because it was wholly *hers*. None could enter without her permission. She wore the key on a silk cord at her waist.

"Alchemy, you must understand, is nothing but the art that makes the impure into the pure through fire," Margaret said. "Even men and women. As it is written in the Book of Isaiah, 'When thou walkest through the fire, thou shalt not be burnt; neither shall the flame kindle upon thee.' But I don't occupy my hours attempting to transform base metals into gold. Instead, I distill healing elixirs from plants."

She opened a cupboard to reveal a row of labeled flasks and drew out a bottle of clear fluid.

"This," she said, "is my own elixir. Pure spirit of the grape. I use it for dissolving herbs when I create my medicinal remedies."

One by one, the Countess unstoppered her flasks, allowing Aemilia to smell her various perfumes and tinctures.

"In another few weeks, it will be time to start harvesting flowers and herbs," she said. "I harvest them by night according to the phase and astrological sign of the moon to preserve their moisture. Ah, here's my most secret elixir, made from nineteen different plants."

Smiling to herself, she poured a tiny glass for Aemilia to taste.

"My lady, these are potent spirits." The first sip was enough to make Aemilia's eyes water, yet the flavor was clean and subtle. "I haven't tasted its like since my visit to Bassano del Grappa, where they distill their own aqua vitae."

"Strictly medicinal, you understand." The Countess poured some for herself.

"My lady, what do these represent?" Aemilia went to examine the sigils drawn on virgin parchment.

"Salt, mercury, and sulphur," the Countess said. "All matter is composed of these three components, ranging from the gross to the subtle: salt for the physical body, mercury for the spirit, and sulphur for the soul. All alchemical operations separate a substance into these separate elements. But then the three are brought together again in a single vessel and join, this time in perfect harmony, to create a brand-new essence."

Aemilia was struck by the thought that Cookham was a crucible in which its three residents — the Countess, Anne, and her — might be utterly transformed. Transmuted into something brilliant and clear.

QUILL IN HAND, AEMILIA sat at her desk, yet she simply couldn't find her Muse or conjure a single phrase commendable enough to justify the expense of the paper she scribbled upon. The only poems that emerged were groveling odes of praise to the Countess, which Aemilia feared would only embarrass the lady, if they were worthy of her attention at all, which Aemilia was beginning to doubt.

At least the lessons with Anne seemed to be going well, with a steady rapport developing between her and her pupil, although sometimes Anne's high spirits got the better of her. One day Aemilia found her charge dashing off to the cherry orchards in the middle of a reading of Ovid. Anne soon returned, cheerful and contrite, her fingers stained, her kerchief full of ripe cherries to share with her tutor.

When they sat beneath the great oak on Cookham Rise, strumming their lutes and singing in harmony, Aemilia felt transported to a pastoral scene from Virgil's *Eclogues*. She was seized by such an overwhelming love and loss all at once, her fondness for Anne evenly matched by her grief and longing for her lost Odilia. Even as she rejoiced in these precious hours with another woman's witty and precocious daughter,

Aemilia realized with a guilty start that in the space of weeks she had grown closer to Anne Clifford than she was to her own son now that Henry was Jasper's apprentice. She sent Henry a long letter describing her life at Cookham and received a note in return saying that he had sung in a masque for the new Queen. At the age of ten, her son had already gained his entry into the new court that Aemilia would probably never see.

AEMILIA LAY IN BED with the covers thrown off and listened to the sultry July night. Outside her open window, trees trembled in the wind. The old house creaked and settled. Though all seemed exactly as it should be, something remained unsettled in her heart.

She had heard rumors of plague in London. Pray God Henry was well. She worried about what Alfonse might get up to while she was away, what new foolish and expensive scheme might take his fancy. Ever since he had returned from the Irish wars, he seemed haunted, even more desperate to distinguish himself. What if he fell into bad company?

Oh, why couldn't she put these things out of her head and simply sleep?

Rolling over, she closed her eyes and tried to envision Morpheus, the god of dreams, arriving in his chariot. Then she jerked at the sound of a drawn-out cry. *Is it some nocturnal creature?* she wondered. *A screech owl? No, it seems to be coming from within the house.* The cry rose and fell, rattling her bones.

She groped for a candle and her cloak to cover her nightshift before venturing into the hallway, which appeared as a tunnel of darkness but for another guttering candle on the far end. Her stomach pitched in fear, but she forced herself forward, bare feet clammy against the floorboards, toward that unsteady pool of light.

She found Anne huddled outside her mother's chamber door where the wailing dragged on and on, as though someone were trying to murder the Countess.

"Mother's having her nightmares," Anne whispered.

In the candlelight, the girl's face appeared as disembodied as a ghost's, her brown eyes huge in her pale face glistening with tears.

"We must go to her." Aemilia tried to open the door, but it was locked.

"She gave me the spare key." Anne pressed it into Aemilia's hand. "She dreams of my father. Once he nearly killed her. The servants had to pull him off her."

"Good God," Aemilia murmured.

As the shaking girl clung to her arm, Aemilia understood that Anne was terrified of venturing into that room and seeing her mother so undone.

"Allow me." Aemilia turned the key in the lock.

With Anne at her heels, Aemilia stumbled through the dark room until she came to the bed where the Countess thrashed in her sleep. After setting the candle and key on the bedside table, she grasped the Countess's shoulders and gave her a gentle shake.

"Peace, my lady, it's only a dream!"

With a judder, Margaret Clifford shoved herself upright. Her face was as white and rigid as a death mask.

"Mother?" Anne reached for her hand.

"Go back to bed, child," Margaret said. It seemed the Countess was mortified to have her daughter see her in this state.

Anne retreated at once.

Aemilia imagined that the Countess wanted her gone as well, but she was reluctant to leave her alone. The lady's nightdress was translucent with sweat and there was no maid in attendance.

"Are you ill, my lady? Feverish?" Aemilia dared to touch her forehead. "Shall I send for a physician?"

Margaret now appeared cross. "What need have I for a quack to apply leeches when I have physick enough of my own making? Marry, I shall take a remedy in the morning. Good night, Mistress Lanier. I'm sorry I awakened you."

Yet behind Margaret Clifford's wall of brusque authority, Aemilia sensed that the nightmare still held her in its thrall.

"Forgive me, my lady, but your nightdress is sodden. Have you a fresh one I may bring to you?"

"In the chest at the foot of the bed," the Countess said.

"You had better wash as well if you've had the night sweats." Aemilia carried an ewer of fresh water, a basin, a cake of soap, and a towel to the bedside table. "To sleep with damp skin is to invite sickness."

Aemilia then turned her back on the Countess to allow her to wash herself. After what she thought was a decent interval, she turned to face her again. Margaret shrank behind the towel. As she snatched the fresh nightgown from Aemilia's hand, Aemilia could not avoid seeing the atlas of welts on her skin.

"Oh, my sweet lady. Who could do this to you?"

Margaret crumpled and began to weep, as though she were a broken thing. Aemilia helped her into the nightdress and wrapped her in her own cloak. She held her and let her cry.

"Let it all out," she whispered. "All the melancholy and grief, my lady. If you bottle it inside, it will poison you."

"He took a horsewhip to me," Margaret said. "No God-fearing man would treat his horse as he treated me."

They sat at the edge of the bed, their hands clasped.

"At first I thought it was because he thought me plain," she said. "I thought that had I been beautiful—like you—he would have been kinder."

"My lady," Aemilia said, her cheeks burning. "In truth, I had a sister who was the loveliest creature who ever lived, but her beauty did not spare her. She suffered from such a husband as yours, only he was of meaner birth."

"Where is your sister now?" Margaret asked her.

"Dead, my lady." Aemilia's eyes filled. "Her child, too."

"I longed to die," said Margaret. "But I couldn't—I have a daughter. And your husband, Mistress Lanier—is he good to you?"

"Bless him, he tries to be a good man, but he wasted my money, and his traffic with whores infected him with the great pox. Once I was so desperate, I took a lover, but all in vain, for the man proved fickle and faithless."

Aemilia's voice shook, for she had never revealed so much of herself to any other woman besides her own servants. Would Margaret dismiss her as a wanton, unsuitable to teach her daughter?

But Margaret offered her a sad smile, as if their misfortunes as women bound them together. "I might have taken a lover, had the chance arisen. Perhaps, after a manner of speaking, I did." The lady flushed as she spoke. "By my troth, the only way I endured my marriage was by telling myself that my true husband was not George Clifford but he whose sufferings eclipsed all my own."

Now Aemilia understood why Margaret took such solace in that image of the scourged and tortured Jesus.

"Do you think me a heretic, Mistress Lanier?" As Margaret framed the question, Aemilia realized she had been entrusted with the lady's most guarded secret.

"I think you are a godly woman," she said, meaning every word. "Why, think of the women in the Bible whose grace helped them overthrow the most despicable men. Judith, Esther, Deborah, Susanna, and Jael. You are their daughter, my lady. If I held a mirror to your virtues, you would never doubt yourself again."

Aemilia blinked when she saw that her words had moved Margaret to tears.

"My lady, may I bring you a glass of your herbal elixir?" she asked.

"You'll find a flask in that cabinet," Margaret said. "Pour a measure for yourself as well. But no more 'my lady,' if you please. Not after what you've seen and heard this night."

"How so?" Aemilia asked, as she poured the aqua vitae into tiny goblets of Venetian glass. "You are still the Countess of Cumberland and I the wife of a minstrel."

"Such distinctions are but worldly vanities. Does not God make both even, the cottage and the throne?"

"Then you must call me Aemilia." She handed Margaret her goblet. "No more 'Mistress Lanier.'"

Margaret smiled. Before she even took the first sip, the color returned to her face. "To friendship."

"Friendship," Aemilia echoed.

They clinked their glasses and drank.

"I have been so lonely for friendship, Aemilia. I hope you stay with us for a very long time."

As the aqua vitae's warmth traveled from Aemilia's tongue straight into her heart, she felt lifted beyond herself, suddenly whole and complete.

THE EARLY MORNING SUN shone through the ivy curtaining Aemilia's window, casting a delicate tracery on a fresh new page. Sitting at her desk, as though she were a poet on par with any man, Aemilia dipped her quill in the ink pot and began to write.

> Sweet Cookham where I first obtained
> Grace from the Grace where perfect Grace remained,
> And where the Muses gave their full consent,
> I should have the power the virtuous to content.

Grace welled up in her heart like precious oil. Only a single drop was needed to light her inner lamp. Her very soul blazed.

This was an idyll more priceless than her time in Italy. Instead of the torch of passion, that inconstant betrayer, the quiet flame of friendship illumined her days. That lost Italian romance shrank into the cobwebs of distant memory, for this was the culmination of all her yearning. Here she had found her fountain of delight. Cookham was the alchemical vessel that burned away her dross until only her highest essence remained.

On her desk was a bouquet of roses and scented stocks, a gift from Anne, but their lessons did not begin until midmorning. Margaret had purposely given these early hours to Aemilia so that she could rise at dawn and write for hours in the sunlit stillness before resuming her duties as tutor. *Write to your heart's content, as long as your writing serves virtue.* Under her friend's patronage, Aemilia could truly dedicate herself to poetry.

She longed to give Margaret, her Muse, something in return. Let her write poetry that was powerful enough to ease the melancholy that gnawed at her friend's heart. Margaret might one day have to leave this house with its painted chapel that gave her such comfort. Yet Aemilia hoped her poetry could immortalize what they shared in this hallowed place. In secret she penned her everlasting tribute to Margaret Clifford.

At the top of the page, Aemilia wrote the title that had come to her, as if in a dream, three years before: *Salve Deus Rex Judaeorum.* Beside her stack of writing paper lay the Geneva Bible open to the Gospel of Matthew. Let her words create a tableau of the Passion, of the suffer-

ing yet victorious Christ as Margaret's true and eternal husband, as lov-
ingly rendered as Jacopo Bassano's paintings.

Jacopo's voice whispered in her ear, telling her to turn to the Canti-
cles, the book of wedding poems in the Old Testament, for inspiration.
The words flowed from her quill like paint from a brush.

> This is the Bridegroom that appears so fair.
> His lips like scarlet threads, yet much more sweet
> Than is the sweetest honey-dropping dew,
> Or honeycombs, where all the Bees do meet;
> Yea, he is constant, and his words are true,
> His cheeks are beds of spices, flowers sweet;
> His lips, like Lilies, dropping down pure myrrh,
> Whose love, before all worlds we do prefer.

SUMMER PASSED IN A round of poetry, lessons, and walks up and
down Cookham Dean. In the evening, the three of them gathered
in the great hall to sup beneath the tapestry of the dancing goddesses. Come nightfall, Aemilia followed Margaret into the moth-
haunted garden where they harvested flowers and herbs under the
rising moon.

"So much beauty," Margaret murmured, as she filled her basket
with blooming roses, their scent heavy and sweet in the cool air. "Is
this not a glimpse into paradise?"

Aemilia lifted her eyes to the waxing moon sailing high, pouring her
silver on meadow and grove. Enchanted by the night, she began to sing
as she and Margaret worked together.

> Over hill, over dale,
> Through bush, through briar,
> Over park, over pale,
> Through flood, through fire,
> I do wander everywhere,
> Swifter than the moon's sphere.
> And I serve the Faery Queen
> To dew her orbs upon the green.

Only when she had sung the last note did Aemilia remember that this was what she had sung for Harry and Will that midsummer night at Southampton House a decade ago.

"Your voice is still as lovely as when you used to sing at court," Margaret said, plunging Aemilia even further into her past.

"I was just a girl then. Barely older than your Anne."

"The dark jewel of the court," Margaret said, her skirts rustling like the wind in the leaves as she moved through her garden. "Isn't that what the Lord Chamberlain used to call you?"

In the darkness Aemilia felt herself blush. Why did Margaret speak of that now?

"If only you knew how I envied you then," Margaret said. "In those days I would have given anything for my husband—or any man—to look at me the way Henry Carey looked at you."

"He was a good man," Aemilia said. But something about the intimacy of the moonlit night demanded greater honesty. "In faith, I doubt any woman envied me when he put me aside and married me off. I envied highborn ladies like *you* who seemed so secure."

Margaret laughed. "Ah, but now you know better. Sometimes I think you are my confessor, Aemilia Lanier. You know my every secret. But to me, you still seem a mystery, like a lake hiding an entire city in its depths."

Aemilia remained silent, cutting the lavender. The night breeze touched her nape, sending a shiver through her. "You think I conceal some terrible scandal?"

"Forgive me lest you think I pry, but sometimes when we bear our secrets alone, the burden becomes so heavy. You helped lift my burden and I would help you bear yours—if you let me." She peered into Aemilia's basket. "I think that's enough lavender. Now let's take this to the still room."

Following Margaret down the flagged path, Aemilia thought how she had yearned for a true friend all her life. But to have a friend, one must be a friend. She thought how she had lost sweet Olivia by keeping so much hidden from her and telling her too many lies. Her soul's depths she had revealed to Will, who had betrayed her, but never to another woman.

In the laboratory they worked by lantern light. After stripping the lavender blooms from the stalks, Aemilia ground them with mortar and pestle.

"My entire life I have worn a mask," she told Margaret.

"So have we all," Margaret said, grinding rose petals. "Most people's masks slip from time to time. But you wear yours so well, I cannot tell where the mask ends and your true face begins."

Aemilia carried on pounding the lavender until her muscles ached. "Is it the secret of my lover? He was . . . he is a poet. Would you know his name?"

"You misunderstand me," Margaret said. "I don't believe it's a scandal you hide, but something precious and rare."

Aemilia thought how Jacopo had borne his secret regret for his forced conversion all his days, only unburdening himself to her as he lay dying. Would she go to her grave with all this heaviness in her heart? The pestle slipped from her sweat-slick hand.

"I am a Jew's daughter," she said.

Margaret touched her face, wet with tears. "Come, sit you down. You're shaking, dear."

"When I was a child," Aemilia told her, "my sister's husband tried to blackmail my father on account of his religion. What Papa suffered! He was the greatest, kindest man I ever knew."

She went on to tell Margaret of her childhood, the Hebrew singing in the cellar, the secrets Papa had kept even from her. As she made her confession, she realized that in writing of Jesus as King of the Jews, it was her own father she sought to resurrect. She told Margaret of her journey to Italy with Will, her visit to the synagogue in the Venice Ghetto, her time with Jacopo Bassano, all of this driven by her love and longing for her lost father.

"Papa told me that hell is empty," Aemilia said. "All the devils are up here in plain view."

"Did your father ever meet my husband?" Margaret asked, making Aemilia laugh in spite of herself. "You are a paradox, my dear. A Jew's daughter who writes Christian poetry that moves me to tears. Your work surpasses that of Anne Locke and her son."

Aemilia squeezed her friend's hands. "That's because I have you for my sweet Muse."

Over the coming weeks, Aemilia shared her every secret with Margaret until there was nothing left to hide. A chamber that had been dark and dank was now bathed in summer sunlight. With Margaret, she could show her true face, live in the open without a mask. Margaret embraced her as she broke down and told her, sobbing, about losing Odilia. Margaret, in turn, revealed her own heartbreak over the deaths of her two sons.

"Every day I thank God I still have Anne," Margaret said. "Now I understand why you're so fond of her, almost as if she were your own daughter."

At dawn Aemilia vaulted from bed and, still in her nightshift, began to write until she could write no more. She longed to capture the sweet magic of Margaret's moon-drenched garden.

When shining Phoebe gave so great a grace,
Presenting Paradise to your sweet sight,
Unfolding all the beauty of her face . . .

She wrote and wrote, no longer caring that her poetry was as much a celebration of her love for Margaret as it was an homage to Margaret's God. For Margaret had revealed to her that the only religion was love.

At summer's end, when rosehips and hawthorn berries bejewelled the hedges, Queen Anne summoned Anne Clifford to court. But Margaret remained resolute in her wish to remain in her rural retreat.

"Truly, I have retired from that world," she told Aemilia, as they headed up to the towering oak tree to view young Anne's progress down the Thames toward Whitehall. "In my mind, all the joy of courtly life died with our dear Elizabeth. This Scottish King is no lover of women. He and his Queen keep separate courts—his for politics and influence and hers for empty-headed amusements."

"My cousin Ben writes that the Queen is a great lover of the masque," Aemilia said. "In fact, he has written some for her."

"Did you bring Master Jonson's letter, my dear?" Margaret seated herself on the weathered bench encircling the great oak. "Pray, read it. I am a great admirer of his."

Pulling the folded letter from her pocket, Aemilia began to read aloud while Winifred unpacked the fruit, cheese, bread, and wine she had carried up in a basket.

Indeed, Fortune smiled on Ben now that he had gained the Queen's patronage, but he complained that Will had bested him, for James had become the official patron of Will's theater company—the King's Men.

"Master Shakespeare has staged a murky Scottish tragedy full of ghosts and murder, all in our Sovereign's honor," Aemilia read. *"Most curious were his three witches—the Weird Sisters. Strangely enough, they reminded me of your Weir sisters."*

With a lurch, Aemilia stopped reading.

Winifred was outraged. "Ooh, the wicked man! To insult three honest sisters from Essex!"

"Peace," said Margaret. "The court is but a shadow box filled with vanity and illusion. Pay such folly little mind. I do hope our Anne doesn't become too frivolous in such company. Back in Elizabeth's day," she said, gazing at Aemilia, "a lady of the court might aspire to learning and brilliance. Like Mary Sidney. Like *you*, my dear. Now what have you been writing?"

Aemilia reached into the basket and found the bundle of pages written in her best italic hand. "An apology in defense of Eve."

Margaret's smile was as rich as claret.

The passage was long and Aemilia read it with care, knowing that both Margaret and Winifred listened with their full attention, as if in firm belief that her words were inspired. Here on this hill, she was a poet with an audience that imbibed her words.

Her poem argued that while Eve was blamed for humanity's fall from grace the sin was actually Adam's for taking the forbidden fruit. For he, unlike Eve, was fully aware of the consequences. Out of selfishness and the desire for power, Adam let Eve take the fall.

If Eve did err, it was for knowledge sake,
The fruit being fair persuaded him to fall:

No subtle serpent's falsehood did betray him,
If he would eat it, who had the power to stay him?
Not Eve, whose fault was only too much love.

Winifred nodded. "How right you are, mistress. It's about time someone defended poor Eve."

Margaret remained in contemplative silence as the wind passed over the long waving grasses. "Pray, make fair copies of all your poems," she said at last. "So I might keep them and reread them again and again."

30

ITH THE FIRST SNOWFALL, Aemilia and Winifred boarded a wherry for London to spend Christmas with their families. Winifred clutched an overflowing sack of gifts for her sisters and Tabitha's new baby girl. Bursting in her excitement to see them again, she kept nagging the wherryman to row faster.

But Aemilia felt an emptiness spreading through her chest with each mile separating her from Margaret and Cookham. Already she longed for her room beneath the eaves and the endless supply of writing paper, the admiration in her friend's eyes when she read each new poem. Even on the wherry, new verses spun themselves in Aemilia's head, though she had nothing to write with.

JASPER AWAITED AEMILIA AT Billingsgate landing, accompanied by a tall, dark-haired youth she scarcely recognized until he called her Mother. She threw her arms around Henry and embraced him with all the force of her stored-up love.

"My darling, you must have grown three inches since I saw you last!"

In her satchel she had a brand-new cloak for him. She hoped the new garment would be big enough.

"Where's Alfonse?" she asked Jasper, when at last she released her son.

"Carry your mother's satchel," Jasper said. "There's a good lad."

While Henry walked on ahead, her cousin spoke in a low voice so the boy wouldn't overhear. "Your husband was arrested in Hackney for disturbing the peace. He and another gentleman from the Irish military campaign, I believe. I fear he shall have to spend a day in the stocks before they release him."

Aemilia gulped the cold air. "Oh, what mischief is he tangled up in? I hope at least Henry has behaved himself."

"You have every cause to be proud of your son," Jasper said in a loud voice. "Why, Henry's the most diligent of all my apprentices, well on his way to becoming a virtuoso."

Henry, his cheeks glowing as if from both embarrassment and pleasure, turned and grinned at them. Jasper then took the satchel from the boy and Aemilia reached for her son's arm, holding it tightly as they walked up Gracechurch Street.

"I *am* proud of you," she told him. "You shall make a fine court musician."

"I sang again for the Queen," Henry told her. "And I saw Lady Anne Clifford dancing with Her Highness in the masques. But I think Lady Anne has no future as a musician. Her fingers on the lute are far too clumsy, and when she sings, she sounds like a wounded goat!"

"Pray, speak no ill of my pupil," Aemilia said. "If you sang for the Queen, you must also sing for me. I shall write a song just for your voice."

Though she tried to focus her mind solely on her son, her anxieties about Alfonse kept crowding in. *Arrested?* What if he lost his good name along with everything else? Trouble and ill luck seemed to chase him at every turn.

ONCE THEY ARRIVED AT Jasper's house in Camomile Street, Aemilia found a scrap of paper and wrote the poem that had been playing in her head since she left Cookham. She would turn it into the song she had promised Henry—the melody a jewel case for his haunting soprano that so enchanted the Queen. But the lyrics she would dedicate to Margaret. She would sing the song to her friend as her New Year's gift when she returned to Cookham after Twelfth Night.

WITH JASPER'S FAMILY AND apprentices gathered round, Aemilia played the lute to accompany Henry as he sang her new composition. His every note shimmered like silver.

Sweet holy rivers, pure celestial springs,
Proceeding from the fountain of our life —

Her son's ethereal voice was lost in the great racket erupting from the front door.

"Captain Lanier," a dazed servant announced.

"Papa!" Henry cried, charging forward to hug him.

Aemilia set down her lute and sprang to her feet as Alfonse swaggered in, none too sober, looking more jubilant than she had ever seen him. Her relief to see him again, safe and whole and in such high spirits, was overshadowed by her worry.

"Jasper said you were arrested," she murmured, with a quick glance to her cousin and his wife. "How did they let you go so soon?"

Her husband twirled her in his arms. "My noble friend, he came to my rescue!"

When his companion strode in, Aemilia felt the floor drop away. She shrank behind her son, clutching his shoulders as though the boy were her shield.

The mere sight of this man stung her. His long mane, as lustrous as any maiden's, had darkened from gold to auburn. No longer a boy, he was stalwart looking, tall and muscled, but no less beautiful. Harry was the epitome of male perfection grown into maturity. Pray God, let him not recognize her. Perhaps he had forgotten about her visits to Southampton House eleven years ago. But the moment Harry laid eyes on her, his face shone in recognition.

"Ah, the lovely Mistress Lanier! Your husband has told me so much about you."

Alfonse made her son step aside so Harry could kiss her hand. He looked her up and down as though tempted to lift her skirts to see if she wore breeches beneath them.

At least Alfonse appeared oblivious to all this as he made his obsequious introduction. "We are graced by the presence of none other than my Lord Henry Wriothesley, Earl of Southampton!"

Her son frowned and folded his arms in front of his chest. "But, my lord, the late Queen locked you in the Tower!"

Alfonse looked as though he would weep.

Harry laughed and cupped her son's chin. "Ah, the monstrous regiment of women! If Elizabeth imprisoned me, our gracious Majesty James released me and restored me to court. Now I am at liberty to reward my dear Alfonse for his loyal service in Ireland." He looked at Aemilia while he spoke. "I have petitioned the King to grant your husband a patent on the weighing of hay and straw brought into London and Westminster. He shall have six shillings on every hay load and three shillings on every load of straw."

"Our worries, they are over!" Alfonse said, kissing her. "We shall have a proper home again."

"A patent," she said, turning to Harry. "Truly, my lord?"

"For past services rendered," said Harry, his eyes on her, not Alfonse.

Aemilia gripped her son so tightly that young Henry looked up at her in confusion.

As ALFONSE, JASPER, AND Deborah fussed over their aristocratic guest, Aemilia found an excuse to slip out into the garden and breathe some fresh air.

Had Harry been in earnest? Could such a patent truly meet the King's approval? Or did Harry only toy with their hopes? She conjured Margaret's quiet presence, her sober counsel. If Fortune was inconstant, Margaret was Aemilia's Polaris, her arctic star, steadfast and ever radiant, shedding light on her deepest turmoil. The Muse that guided her hand.

"This is where you hide, my old friend!"

Aemilia spun round to see Harry.

"Won't you even say thank you?" he asked her.

"It's kind of you if you're being serious and not playing games with my poor husband."

From inside the house came the sound of Alfonse's singing.

Harry laughed. "As if *you* never went behind his back and played the trickster, my dear Emilio."

"My days of wearing breeches are long past," she told him.

"Indeed, I hear you serve the most pious Countess of Cumberland," he said, his voice as light as hers was grave.

"And what is that to you, my lord?"

"My dear Aemilia-who-is-no-longer-Emilio, pray, don't be so cross! Am I not allowed to pine for my vanished youth and its lost pleasures?"

She fell into silence, recalling that midsummer night when she had witnessed Will's hopeless love for Harry.

"At least *you* still remember," he said, with a note of mournful nostalgia. "At least I can still make you blush. Unlike *him*."

"You refer to Master Shakespeare, my lord?" She turned to Harry and saw the hurt in his eyes. *So Harry loved him after all.* "He's quite rich, I hear. A gentleman with a coat of arms." She realized for the first time that there was no bitterness left in her heart. *Now I speak with the wisdom of a poet—not the anguish of a poet's spurned mistress.* "Those whom Fortune favors do as they please."

"But he's grown so very self-important," said Harry. "And *cold*, Aemilia, as though he never loved at all."

She saw that he trembled and wondered if he wept.

"Whilst I was in the Tower, I wrote letter after letter to him. Most respectable, you understand, for the guards read them before allowing them to be sent. He never answered one. I fear I was no longer useful to him. How I miss my William as he was that summer—so humble and sweet."

"Let the past rest," she said. "Let your heart be at peace."

"We were so beautiful then," he said, with such yearning that she thought his voice would break. "The three of us in that room and you playing the virginals whilst he read his poetry."

"If it's music you desire, you are in a house of musicians. Come, let's join the others. My son will sing madrigals for you." Aemilia gave Harry's arm a sisterly squeeze before leading him back inside the crowded house.

THE MORNING AFTER TWELFTH Night, Aemilia bade her farewells to her husband and son. When she cried into Henry's hair, Alfonse gently gripped her shoulders and kissed her. "Peace, our boy shall be fine."

Then Alfonse returned to court and Henry to his apprenticeship while she boarded the wherry back to Cookham. Though it always wrenched her to leave her son, a quiet joy glowed in her heart as she and Winifred traveled up the Thames. No matter what happened at court, no matter the outcome of Harry's patent, no matter what misadventures Alfonse tangled himself up in, Margaret awaited her. Her kindred spirit, her soul's harbor.

Margaret embraced her in greeting and Anne clasped her arm and chattered as they traveled by cart up to the manor house.

"As a New Year's gift, I gave the Queen a fan of lace and she gave *me* a pair of embroidered gloves!" The beaming girl held up her gloved hands for Aemilia's inspection.

"Poor Aemilia can hardly get a word in, the way you prattle, my dear," her mother said. "How fares your son, Aemilia? I hope you found him in good health."

"The best health," she said, with gratitude. "One day I must bring him here to sing for you both."

"I've heard him sing at court," Anne said. "In truth, his voice moves the Queen to tears."

"He mirrors his mother's brilliance," Margaret said, not masking her fondness.

Though it was bitterly cold, Aemilia felt radiant and warm from the roots of her hair to the tips of her toes. Likewise, Winifred, sitting in the depths of the cart with the satchels and boxes, seemed as sleek with contentment as a well-fed cat. She wore her brand-new cloak with the rabbit-skin collar, Aemilia's gift to her.

The manor house was fragrant with the smell of Yuletide evergreens burning in the great hearth to bring luck for the New Year.

"Master Daniel is returning in a fortnight," Margaret told Aemilia, as they walked up the stairs. "But we shall put him in a different room so that you might keep yours. He's to teach Anne mathematics and rhetoric while you teach her music and read with her."

"I prefer my lessons with Aemilia," Anne said. "Master Daniel is so solemn and serious. He *never* laughs."

Margaret took Aemilia's arm as they entered Aemilia's freshly aired room beneath the eaves. A pomander of roses and spices was set in a dish beside the stack of fresh paper.

"With Master Daniel teaching half of Anne's lessons, you shall have more time to write," Margaret said.

Without the least hesitation or embarrassment, Aemilia threw her arms around her friend, her patron, her savior. "My every poem I shall dedicate to you and the Lady Anne!"

"To me!" Anne cried, dancing around the room and clapping her hands as though performing in one of the Queen's masques. "Ah, but you haven't seen our surprise!"

With a flourish, the girl pulled back the curtains on the bed, revealing a brand-new gown of lilac silk trimmed with ivory brocade. Beside herself, Aemilia stroked the soft, slippery fabric. Not since her days as Henry Carey's mistress had she owned anything so fine. Margaret's belief in her raised her up to heights she had thought impossible. For a woman of her station to receive such finery not in exchange for the favors of her body but for leading a virtuous life dedicated to poetry and learning. She found she was in tears, too moved to speak. In Margaret's company, she was not an adulteress or a jilted mistress or the discontented wife of an impoverished courtier. Margaret had washed her clean.

Her friend placed a gentle hand on her shoulder. "Our New Year's gift to you."

THAT EVENING, AFTER A meal of roast pheasant with apples and chestnuts, Aemilia performed her new composition, the poem she had written for Margaret. Each word fountained up from the depths of her soul.

Sweet holy rivers, pure celestial springs,
Proceeding from the fountain of our life;
Sweet sugared currents that salvation brings,
Clear crystal streams, purging all sin and strife,
Fair floods, where souls do bathe their snow-white wings,
Before they fly to true eternal life:
Sweet Nectar and Ambrosia, food of Saints,
Which whoso tasteth, never after faints.

This honey dropping dew of holy love,
Sweet milk, wherewith we weaklings are restored.

THE MONTHS PASSED, SNOW melted to reveal new grass, and Aemilia's stack of written pages grew, improved upon day by day as she chanted the verse aloud in the privacy of her room and later read each poem to Margaret.

She gave Anne her lessons in the library until at last it was warm enough to walk up Cookham Dean and play their lutes beneath the oak.

With Master Daniel, Anne was stiff and formal. With Aemilia, she was like a younger sister, grabbing her hand and whispering secrets, showing her bird nests and the orphaned hedgehog she had adopted.

Mewed up in her laboratory, Margaret distilled perfumes for Anne and Aemilia made from flowers and herbs chosen especially for them. Anne's was light and sweet with freesia and lily while Aemilia's was darker and more mysterious with rose, lavender, and night-blooming jasmine. Margaret's own scent was a blend of rosemary, cedar, lavender, and hyssop, the purifying herb celebrated in Psalm 51.

IN SUMMER MASTER DANIEL departed to visit other noble patrons on their country estates. Aemilia taught Anne to sing new madrigals in French and Italian while Anne taught Aemilia the latest dances she had learned at court. Tutor and pupil crowned each other in floral garlands before enacting masques for Margaret. Afterward, they bowed and laid their garlands in Margaret's lap. The three of them lay in the long summer grass, their heads touching, forming a three-spoked wheel as they watched the clouds form fantastical shapes then dissolve in the infinite sky.

31

Queen and huntress, chaste and fair,
Now the sun is laid to sleep,
Seated in thy silver chair,
State in wonted manner keep;
Hesperus entreats thy light,
Goddess excellently bright.

EMILIA SAT BESIDE MARGARET on the weathered bench beneath the great oak and plucked her lute to accompany Anne as she sang the lyrics of Ben's poem, "Queen and Huntress," written in praise of departed Elizabeth. Nicholas Lanier, Alfonse's nephew, had composed the melody. Anne's voice had much improved during the two and a half years Aemilia had been teaching her. The girl wore a simple woolen gown and had woven a wreath of bloodred grape leaves about her loosened hair to better resemble a maiden of antiquity, one of Diana's retinue. The wind whipped her brown tresses as she sang.

Now fifteen, Anne was turning into a woman. Soon George Clifford would intrude on their idyll, Aemilia suspected, with talk of arranging the girl's marriage to a nobleman of his choosing. He would wrest the girl from her mother, like Hades abducting Persephone. Margaret's heart would break to be separated from her daughter, still so young. Aemilia knew that her friend wanted her daughter's days of youth and freedom to stretch on and on.

The year had passed quickly. To think it was October, the week before All Hallows' Eve, yet still balmy enough to have this performance
on Cookham Dean. *Our Mount Parnassus.* Aemilia glanced at Margaret,
who leaned back against the massive oak trunk. Her eyes were closed,
as if to better savor her daughter's singing in praise of the great Queen
Margaret had served and loved.

> Lay thy bow of pearl apart,
> And thy crystal-shining quiver;
> Give unto the flying hart
> Space to breathe, how short soever.
> Thou that mak'st a day of night,
> Goddess excellently bright.

As the final lute chord faded into silence, Aemilia saw her pupil leap
and point down the hill. The ground itself shook. The unwelcome image of Hades encroached on Aemilia's thoughts again, the earth opening to swallow the girl and sever her from her mother.

Margaret stood, her face rigid, her arms clasped before her as if to
shield her inner organs. Aemilia sprang to her feet at the sight of the
rider galloping up Cookham Dean, white foam flying from the dark
stallion's mouth.

The messenger, appearing as winded as his mount, flung himself
from the saddle and nearly collapsed at Margaret's feet.

"My Lady Margaret Clifford, Countess of Cumberland," the man
panted.

"That would be me," Margaret said, her face as pale as the clouds
passing overhead. She gripped Aemilia's arm.

Reaching into his doublet, the messenger took out a man's emerald
ring, which he handed to Margaret.

"This is my husband's," she said, holding it up to the light.

"My Lord George Clifford, Earl of Cumberland, lies dying at the
Duchy House by the Savoy and requests your ladyship's presence and
that of Lady Anne."

The rider was so exhausted, it seemed to drain his last strength to utter that long sentence.

Margaret turned to Aemilia with brimming eyes, as if in dread of facing her husband again even as he lay helpless and near death. *What will this mean for Margaret and Anne?* Aemilia wondered. Even after death, George Clifford controlled their fate by way of his last will and testament.

Anne rushed to her mother's side and clung to her. Aemilia's heart quickened, for she hadn't seen Anne so frightened since the night of Margaret's terrible dream. The girl wrenched the garland from her head and flung it to the ground.

Her husband's ring hidden in her closed fist, Margaret addressed the messenger. "We will travel to the Duchy House with all speed. Pray go to the house and take refreshment. My groom will look after your horse."

Aemilia followed as Margaret and Anne walked shakily downhill into the abyss of their uncertain future.

"THE BLACK GOWN," MARGARET said to Aemilia, who was helping her pack.

Aemilia located the black brocade Margaret had worn to Queen Elizabeth's funeral folded inside the chest of drawers, kept fresh with pomanders of lavender and orange rind.

Tears in her eyes, Margaret gazed around the room as if she would never see it again.

"Margaret," Aemilia said, fighting back her own tears. "Shall I stay with my family and wait till I hear word from you?"

Her friend embraced her. "Sweet Aemilia. Pray wait for me here at Cookham until I return."

"My lady, I will."

Margaret gave her a crooked smile. "How many times do I have to remind you? I'm not your lady. I'm your friend."

"COOKHAM JUST ISN'T THE same without the Clifford ladies," Winifred said, towering over her mistress who hunched at her desk. "Neither, dare I say, are you. The way you mope, anyone would think it was Lady Margaret dying, not her dung-heap husband. Good riddance, I say."

Aemilia allowed herself a small smile. "Peace, Winifred. Let me write."

After her maid had left the room, Aemilia arranged her written pages in rows across her desk. In the past two and a half years, she had written scores of poems for Margaret Clifford: her "Eve's Apology in Defense of Women"; her many poems praising Margaret's virtues and comparing her to the heroic women of the Old Testament; her narrative poem describing Christ's passion, based on the Gospel of Matthew; and the poem depicting Christ as Margaret's divine husband.

If Margaret's time at Cookham, this blessed refuge, might be coming to an end, how better to honor and comfort her friend than to arrange the disparate poems in a grand narrative? Aemilia already had the title, *Salve Deus Rex Judaeorum*, but how could she piece it all together, Eve's apology with Judith's defeat of Holofernes?

How would Jacopo Bassano have wedded the different images in a monumental master painting? Her love for Margaret provided the answer—by revealing her friend's sorrows and joys as a mirror to Christ's narrative. By proclaiming Margaret and, by extension, all virtuous women who suffered under the tyranny of unjust men as Christ's true imitators. These good women would share in the triumph of the resurrection and so be liberated from the bonds of men. What was more, they could even use the scriptures to state their case for liberty and justice. She recalled Margaret's argument that the weight of guilt upon men for the crucifixion far exceeded poor Eve's plucking the fruit from the tree.

Dipping her quill in the ink pot, Aemilia began to write.

Let us have our Liberty again,
And challenge to yourselves no Sovereignty,
You came not into the world without our pain,
Make that a bar against your cruelty;
Your fault being greater, why should you disdain
Our being your equals, free from tyranny?
If one weak woman simply did offend,
This sin of yours hath no excuse, nor end.

The force of her words made her tremble, scattering ink across the page. She, a Jew's daughter, was writing Christian poetry to vindicate all women, and all in honor of her beloved friend, her Muse, whose faith was vast enough to embrace the Geneva Bible, the Catholic chapel, and the Hebrew name of God.

On Cookham landing, Aemilia gazed eastward into the mist rising from the steely Thames until the vessel emerged from the November fog. She waved to the Clifford women in their stiff black cloaks.

When the craft drew up to the landing, Aemilia was quicker than any of the servants to help mother and daughter out of the boat. She had never seen Anne so wretched.

"Oh, Aemilia." The girl hugged her and quietly wept.

How fragile Anne felt in her arms, a slender girl of fifteen shaking in the late autumn wind. Gazing over Anne's shoulder at her mother, Aemilia regarded Margaret, whose face was set in tired, grim lines.

"Come, my sweeting, let's get you home," Aemilia murmured. "My Winifred had the cook prepare pheasant pie."

"Home?" Anne reeled away toward the waiting cart. "I have no home."

Again Aemilia looked at Margaret, but the lady's face was shuttered and guarded. She uttered no word of explanation until they reached the house. After Anne retreated to her room to change, Margaret ushered Aemilia into the library and locked the door behind them. Only then did Margaret's mask slip to reveal her rage. With the violence of a caged she-wolf, she paced the room, her sweeping skirts knocking down a globe.

"My friend, I beg you, what happened?" Aemilia asked, as the fear spiked in her belly. "I've never seen you like this."

"If I thought George Clifford was hateful whilst he lived, his curse endures beyond the grave." Margaret seized the back of a chair and sent it crashing to the floor. "That man has robbed Anne of her inheritance. Left everything to his brother, the new Earl of Cumberland."

"Oh, Margaret, no." Aemilia remembered the girl's own terse summary of events: *I have no home.*

"Everything, Aemilia!" Margaret shook her empty hands at the ceiling. "The estates, titles, and offices in Yorkshire and Westmoreland.

Even those which by writ of Edward II are entailed to heirs general in the Clifford line — daughters as well as sons. Even the properties and titles in *my* jointure!"

Aemilia had never heard her friend raise her voice to such a pitch. Pious, studious Margaret had become a Fury.

"Surely he can't leave her nothing." Aemilia grasped her friend's hands.

A bitter laugh ripped from between Margaret's clenched teeth. "He has granted her a monetary settlement, all of which shall go to her husband when she marries. She will indeed have *nothing* to call her own. The sole direct heir of the Clifford line!"

Margaret's pain became her own. Aemilia recalled how, on her first day at Cookham, Anne had claimed the *tarocchi* card with the female knight riding into battle. *This is my card.* The girl who had dared to wield her father's sword before the King. *My ancestral office, it is, to bear my father's sword. One day I shall be mistress of his estates.* Had the girl only known.

"What if her future husband wastes her entire fortune?" Gulping for air, Margaret looked into Aemilia's eyes. "At least when my marriage turned a living hell, I had my brother to provide this refuge for me at Cookham. But Anne? After I am dead, she will have *no one*. Nothing and no one!"

Everything seemed to drain from Margaret. She drooped in Aemilia's arms and wept.

"Sweet Margaret, what will you do?"

Her friend sighed and stepped away from her. Picking the chair off the floor, she sat down, as though conserving her strength for the ordeal that lay ahead.

"I will fight this, so I swear. I will take on his brother. I will go all the way to the King. I will contest this injustice until my last breath."

"Where will you and Anne go now?" It hurt Aemilia just to ask the question.

Margaret glanced up, her dark eyes shining with tears. "We must leave Cookham and travel with all speed to my dower estate in Westmoreland before the executors of the will find some excuse to take that away as well."

"I shall mourn to see you go." Aemilia's world shrank to a dust mote. She sank to the floor and rested her head in Margaret's lap.

"Nothing would give me greater solace than to take you with us." Margaret stroked her hair. "Now, more than I ever, I need a friend. But I fear that would be selfish of me."

"'Entreat me not to leave you or turn back from following after you,'" Aemilia said, quoting the Book of Ruth. "'For wherever you go, I will go; and wherever you lodge, I will lodge; your people shall be my people—'"

"Aemilia," Margaret said, her voice softening. "How can I take you away from your son? Have you any idea how remote Westmoreland is? A week's journey from London in the best weather. In bad weather, you cannot travel at all over those mountain passes. If you came with us, your Henry would lose his mother."

Aemilia lifted her face to Margaret, who leaned forward to wipe her tears. Of course, Margaret was right. Aemilia had stretched her liberties as a wife as far as they would go. If she went with the Clifford women to the distant north, she would effectively be abandoning her family. Alfonse, for all his foibles, had stood by her in her darkest hour after Odilia's death. How could she even consider deserting him a second time? Still, she found she couldn't speak, and Margaret held her as though she never wanted to let her go.

"My dear friend," Margaret said. "Will you write a poem about Cookham to preserve it in my memory?"

Aemilia looked at her through her tears. "Sweet Margaret, I will." She bowed her head. "Anne once told me you possessed the gift of prophecy. Can you reveal anything of my future?" *How shall my life go on without you?*

Margaret took Aemilia's face in her hands. "Yours is the soul of a true poet. Your words shall endure long after I am dead and forgotten."

THAT NIGHT AN ARCTIC cold descended. When Aemilia awakened, stiff and numb, she saw that outside her window the garden, hills, and trees glittered with frost.

In defiance of the chill, she and the Clifford women took their last walk up to the heights of Cookham Dean.

"We should have known our fleeting worldly joys couldn't last," said Margaret, her voice spectral as she marched up the path.

Anne rushed off ahead of them, reminding Aemilia of a filly fighting the bit and bolting away.

"Now I must arrange her marriage," Margaret said. "Pray God, her husband will prove kinder than her father."

Aemilia's heart weighed on her, slowing her steps as she recalled her first stroll up this hill in May 1603, when the trees were crowned in new leaves. When wildflowers spangled the grass. When the air rang with the songs of nesting birds. Now crows perched on naked branches. The weak sun gave no comfort. It was as if the world had grown old, the frozen grass brittle with age's hoary hairs. How desolate everything appeared, each arbor, bank, and bush. Everything that had once been green withered away in cold grief, making the earth its grave.

"Nothing's free from Fortune's scorn," Aemilia told Margaret.

"There's one small property from my jointure that George neglected to pass on to his brother," her friend said. "In Clerkenwell Green. In faith, I think it was too humble for them to trouble themselves over."

"I've often accompanied my husband to Clerkenwell," Aemilia told her, "so he could drink the healing waters there."

"Why, then, if you don't find it too lowering, I would offer it as a domicile for you and your family. You say Alfonse still struggles with debt and ill health."

"Sweet Margaret, how can I thank you?" Moved to tears, Aemilia took her friend's hand. "Maybe one day you will visit me there."

"God willing."

Margaret's hand enclosing hers was the only warmth on that November day.

BENEATH THE GREAT OAK tree, Anne awaited them. From the look of her red swollen eyes, the girl had been crying. When Margaret went to console her daughter, Aemilia turned to gaze out over the hills and fallow fields, the villages and valleys, the Thames mirroring the dull sky. A blast of wind swept right through her, as though she were a skeleton with no flesh to clothe her knocking bones, no heart beating inside her rib cage. But when Anne came to hug her, she held the girl and wept over her as if she were her own lost Odilia.

"I shall never forget our lessons," Anne told her. "Every time I sing a French chanson or an Italian madrigal, I shall think of my Mistress Aemilia."

"Godspeed, my brilliant girl." Her breath turning to mist in the cold air obscured her view of Anne's young face. "You shall become a great lady. As magnificent as your mother."

Aemilia and Anne turned to Margaret and caught her in the act of embracing the towering oak.

"Mother is kissing the tree," Anne whispered in wonder, as though her mother had become a pagan before her eyes.

WHEN MARGARET AND HER daughter set off downhill, Aemilia remained behind. Opening her arms as wide as they would go, she pressed her body against the riveled rind of the tree trunk, allowing the rough bark to imprint its pattern on her cheek. Her lips sought out the precise spot Margaret had chosen. Closing her eyes, she stole her friend's kiss from the tree. *Why should a mere senseless oak possess so rare a favor?*

Only then did she turn and head down the path where mother and daughter had stopped to wait for her. Anne took her hand before they continued on their way, three women cast out of Eden. Their idyll couldn't last. But Aemilia made a silent vow that her poetry for Margaret would endure.

> This last farewell to Cookham here I give,
> When I am dead thy name in this may live,
> Wherein I have perform'd her noble hest,
> Whose virtues lodge in my unworthy breast,
> And ever shall, so long as life remains,
> Tying my heart to her by those rich chains.

❧ VII ☙

A Woman's Writing of Divinest Things

32

OU MUST TELL ME all about Anne's wedding!" Aemilia could scarcely contain her excitement as she filled Margaret's goblet with claret and offered her another portion of Winifred's lamb pie with rosemary and wild garlic.

How her heart gloried to see her friend again for the first time in five years. They supped in the dining chamber of the modest house in Clerkenwell Green where Margaret had invited Aemilia and Alfonse to live rent free. Though Aemilia's pride smarted under living off her friend's largess, Margaret insisted it was only fitting to offer patronage to a gifted poet.

Without Margaret's help, she and Alfonse might have descended into squalor. Despite Harry's promise, the patent on the weighing of hay and straw had not yet come through and they remained deep in debt. At least Alfonse still drew his yearly forty-eight pounds from the King's Musicke even though he no longer played the flute, for his fingers had grown too swollen and stiff from the disease that devoured him from within like slow poison. Yet it hadn't dampened his yearning to advance himself by seeking out the company of high-ranking gentlemen who might champion him as Margaret had championed her. Aemilia sensed it was her husband's dearest wish to die a man of noble esteem rather than a debtor and a failure.

This very evening, Alfonse was out dining with Thomas Jones, the visiting Archbishop of Dublin, with whom he had served in Ireland. This left Aemilia free to direct her full attention on Margaret, who had come down from Westmoreland for her daughter's recent wedding at the Knole estate in Kent. Margaret was staying the night with Aemilia, the first station on her long journey back north.

Aemilia couldn't be happier for her former pupil, who had written a letter to her full of infatuated praise of her bridegroom, Richard Sackville, Earl of Dorset. Knole was by all accounts one of the grandest houses in the realm and boasted its own deer park. She pictured nineteen-year-old Anne riding out in the hunt, as fleet as the goddess Diana.

"To Anne, Countess of Dorset!" Aemilia lifted her goblet.

Margaret raised her glass but not her spirits from the look of it. At first, Aemilia assumed her friend was merely weary from the long ride, but now she saw that something distressed her.

"I only hope I made the right match for her," Margaret said. "Pray God Dorset proves a man of honor."

"Have you any cause to doubt his honor?" Aemilia asked, as gently as she could.

"Once I counted myself blessed," her friend said brokenly, "that God saw fit to grant me the power of prophecy. Yet, when I needed the gift most, it failed me."

This was the closest thing to sacrilege Aemilia had ever heard her friend utter. She drank in Margaret's anguish. Having suffered such a harrowing marriage, it must have been Margaret's worst fear that her daughter might endure the same fate. And Margaret must return to Westmoreland, as far away from Knole and her daughter as she could be without leaving England. Anne had married in late February. Only now, in May, had Margaret wrenched herself away to return to her northern residence.

"I fear Dorset will use every sugared word to persuade Anne to stop fighting for her inheritance and accept the monetary settlement," Margaret said. "So that *he* might spend it as he pleases."

Aemilia reached across the table to take her hand. "As if any daughter of yours would abandon the battle for justice."

With those words, a genuine happiness seemed to bloom in Margaret's face. "How good it is to see you again. If only you knew how much I've missed you."

Aemilia basked in the warmth of their friendship. "I wish you could stay longer."

But she knew without being told that every day Margaret remained away jeopardized her claim on Brougham Castle, which she had chosen as her residence rather than the dower house assigned to her. Brougham Castle, near Penrith, was one of the most ancient seats of the Clifford dynasty. By living there, she was claiming it for her daughter. The castle had fallen into disrepair, but Margaret was working to restore it.

"I wish you could ride north with me," Margaret said. "The journey seems endless. If my health takes a turn for the worse, I fear I might never see the south of England again."

Never see Anne or me again. Aemilia tried to push away her sense of forboding.

"Pray, don't speak so," she said. "You've all your alchemical remedies. You're a stalwart soul."

But Margaret was forty-nine and there was no telling how long the fight for Anne's inheritance would drag on. Aemilia saw how it wore her friend down.

"Let us speak of happier things," said Margaret. "The poem you wrote in honor of Anne's wedding was a loving tribute. I'm sure she'll treasure it always."

"It was my pleasure, truly."

What a luxury it was to write poetry. These days Aemilia spent her days teaching music, Italian, and French to the daughters of the gentry and aspiring middling classes that thronged in Clerkenwell.

"Will you never publish your poems?" Margaret asked her.

Aemilia flushed at the very notion. "Marry, they're too private." Though once she had longed more than anything to see her writing in print, now she thought it would be like opening up her innermost soul to public mockery. "I'd much rather you and Anne treasure your copies."

She had transcribed her poetry into two small quarto volumes, one for Margaret and one for Anne, with each poem penned in her finest italic handwriting. Poets, after all, published to seek patronage, but she already had her beloved patron and Muse. It seemed churlish to ask for more.

"What nobler audience could I possibly seek?" she asked Margaret.

"Your inspiration is a gift of divine grace to be shared with the world. Surely other ladies would rejoice in your verses. In 'Eve's Apology' you defend all womankind."

Margaret's praise enveloped Aemilia in a soft, sheltering cloak.

THEY SAT UP LATE and sipped from a flask of Margaret's aqua vitae. As the liquor warmed her within and without, Aemilia could nearly believe they had been transported back to Cookham. She listened to her friend describe the harsh, wild beauty of Westmoreland, so pristine and sparsely populated, a land of wind-scoured fells and icy lakes. Aemilia told her about Henry, sixteen years old and well on his way to becoming a royal musician. Then she read from the verses she had written in honor of Anne's marriage.

> That sweet Lady sprung from Clifford's race,
> Of noble Bedford's blood, fair stem of Grace;
> To honorable Dorset now espoused,
> In whose fair breast true virtue then was housed.

She recited her poetry as if it had the power to bless Anne's marriage and keep her eternally happy.

After Margaret had retired to the guest bed, Aemilia waited up for Alfonse, who finally stumbled through the door full of wine and good cheer. Shushing him so he wouldn't awaken their guest, she steered him to bed.

WHILE ALFONSE SLEPT ON, Aemilia shared an early breakfast with Margaret before walking her to the livery stables where Margaret's groom awaited with the horses.

Flinging her arms around her friend, Aemilia could not keep herself from weeping. Margaret wept as well, even as she brushed Aemilia's tears away.

"In your lap desk you'll find a small gift," her friend told her. "Your husband needn't know about it."

"Margaret," Aemilia murmured, understanding that it was money she had left. "You mustn't. I shall return it to you this instant. Wait here."

"Nonsense," Margaret said. "Every woman must have something

that is *hers* that can't be taken away. For all I know, I'll not have another chance to offer such a gift."

Aemilia held her so tightly, she could feel their hearts beating as one. What her friend was saying was that they might not see each other again. This could truly be their last farewell.

"This is what I told Anne when I left Knole: I am always with you in spirit, even when we are far apart. Remember, my dear, through every trial, the spirit remains free."

With that, they kissed and Aemilia reluctantly let her go. She helped Margaret into the saddle of her dark bay mare and walked at the mare's shoulder until they reached the edge of Clerkenwell where the northern road stretched off into the green hills with their hedges of flowering hawthorn and gorse. As she stood waving, Aemilia thought of dear Bathsheba, who had died two winters ago. *If only I had a horse, I would ride after you, my friend. Ride all the way to Brougham Castle and no one would be able to stop me.*

AEMILIA RETURNED HOME TO find the pouch heavy with coins that Margaret had hidden inside her lap desk. Her friend's generosity and her own neediness left her floundering in both humility and gratitude. Along with the improbable sum of money, Margaret had enclosed a note.

Remember, my friend, to publish is to immortalize.

COMING HOME AFTER GIVING a virginals lesson to the neighbor's daughter, Aemilia brightened to hear Ben's booming voice in her parlor. She found him sitting with Alfonse. Both men appeared grave, and her cousin's face was red and shining in sweat, as though he had galloped from London. What could the matter be? She hoped there wasn't another plague outbreak. Six years ago Ben had lost a son to the pestilence.

When she rushed forward to greet her cousin, Alfonse threw her such a look of betrayal that she hadn't seen from him since the fraught early months of their marriage. Stung, she watched her husband rear away and leave the room without a word.

"He would have found out eventually," Ben told her. "Better he hear it from me than a stranger."

"Hear what?" she asked.

Without another word, Ben handed her a quarto volume.

Shake-speares
Sonnets
Never before Imprinted

She shook her head, still not comprehending. "What has this to do with me? Why is Alfonse so vexed?"

"It has everything to do with you. Read for yourself." Ben opened to a page and placed the book in her hands.

My mistress's eyes are nothing like the sun,
Coral is far more red than her lips' red,
If snow be white, why then her breasts are dun,
If hairs be wires, black wires grow on her head.

As the shock of recognition ripped through her, Aemilia nearly dropped the volume. Her legs trembled so hard, she had to sit down.

"So he published a sonnet about me?" She seethed. This certainly explained Alfonse's reaction. Did Will fear he would lose money if a new plague outbreak closed the theaters? Maybe publishing these verses was his way of insuring his continued wealth.

"Not just one, alas. Read on, dear cousin. *Ipsa scientia potestas est.* To be fair to Will, they were published without his permission by one Thomas Thorpe, and this book might give our erstwhile poet as much grief as it does you. Imagine if his wife should lay her hands on a copy!"

"His wife can't *read*," Aemilia said thinly, as she pored over each sonnet of lust and guilt, of disgust and blame, of bitterness and rejection, those barbed verses ripping into her flesh.

And beauty slandered with a bastard shame.

She blinked and turned the page.

When my love swears that she is made of truth,
I do believe her, though I know she lies.

"This is defamation," she said, gazing at Ben through the red mist of her rage. She turned the page again and found no respite.

The better angel is a man right fair,
The worser spirit a woman colored ill
To win me soon to hell, my female evil.

He compares me with Harry! She wanted to hurl the book across the room and yet she could not tear her eyes away from the page.

For I have sworn thee fair, and thought thee bright,
Who art as black as hell, as dark as night.

And here he unmasked her as an adulteress.

In loving thee thou know'st I am forsworn,
But thou art twice forsworn, to me love swearing,
In act thy bed-vow broke, and new faith torn,
In vowing new hate after new love bearing.

But only when she paged backward did she find the poem that cut deepest of all, the very sonnet he had written for her during their time in Bassano, before they had become lovers. His poetry of impassioned longing, gazing at her while she played the virginals for Jacopo.

How oft, when thou, my music, music play'st
Upon that blessed wood whose motion sounds
With thy sweet fingers, when thou gently sway'st.

Unable to read another word, she attempted to give the volume back to Ben.
"Keep it," he said. "In faith, you have earned it."
"This is my ruin." Her tears scalded her.
Unlike the plays, this attack on her was not veiled, but direct and

personal. Will had painted a hideous but unmistakable caricature of her, Aemilia Bassano Lanier, a dark woman with musical accomplishments, a woman of bastard birth, unfaithful to her husband, who had tempted Will into adultery. A woman who had aroused the poet's desire, driving him into a sickened frenzy. Anyone reading might guess her identity. Will's sonnets had stripped her bare for all the world. How could she live this down? Alfonse and Henry would never forgive her for heaping such shame upon them.

Abruptly, she charged out of the room.

"Where are you going?" Ben asked, his voice rising in alarm.

"To Brougham Castle in Westmoreland."

She wondered if she still had her breeches. She'd ride forth as Emilio, gallop on until she caught up with Margaret, and never look back. But when she tried to open the bedchamber door, she discovered that Alfonse had bolted it from within.

"Come, don't be so hasty." Ben took her hand and led her back into the parlor, where he poured her a glass of Margaret's aqua vitae. "A woman of your years can't just run away."

"A woman *of my years*?"

Hadn't she once said something similar to Will many summers ago at Southampton House? *A man of your years has no business leaping out of windows.* Unable to contain herself, she tore open the book of sonnets again and read the love poems at the beginning of the book that were filled with the most idealized love and admiration, written not for her but for a golden-haired youth.

> Shall I compare thee to a summer's day?
> Thou art more lovely and more temperate.

"Thy eternal summer shall not fade," she read aloud. "I shall give this book to the Earl of Southampton."

Harry, here you have your proof that he truly loved you and never forgot you.

Knocking back Margaret's aqua vitae, she remembered her friend's secret message to her. *To publish is to immortalize.* Slowly an idea formed, taking shape with each breath. Her patron and friend would not want her to run away like an outcast. No, Margaret would urge her to stand her ground, defend her own honor. And Margaret had given her enough money to print her own quarto volume.

Aemilia briskly dried her eyes and faced Ben. "I have written a long narrative poem, *Salve Deus Rex Judaeorum*. Now I would see it printed."

Ladies will rejoice in your work, Margaret had told her. *In 'Eve's Apology' you defend all womankind.* Instead of allowing Will's slanderous sonnets to define her, she would retaliate by publishing her own poetry that championed womanhood itself.

Her sudden change of tack seemed to bewilder Ben. "An anonymous work, I take it."

"No." She fixed her eyes beyond his head at the painted wall cloth depicting Pallas Athena with her helmet and spear. "I wish to write as Aemilia Lanier."

"Is that wise, especially in the wake of *this*?" Ben held up Will's book of sonnets.

"Not just wise, but necessary."

In the face of Will's defamation of her character, she must step out of the shadows and reveal her own truth. Until this moment, she had been terrified to expose her soul to the public, but with the betrayal of his sonnets, Will had ripped away her every mask. She had nothing left to hide.

"What will Alfonse think?" Ben asked her.

Aemilia quailed when she thought of her husband locked up in their bedchamber. But she lifted her chin as she gave Ben her reply. "If I write of godly things, no man may hold it against me." Her throat was so dry, she had to swallow.

"ALFONSE?" AEMILIA PLEADED WITH him until he unbolted the bedchamber door. Entering the dim, shuttered room, she let out a shriek to see her husband gripping his sword.

"What are you doing?" she cried.

A tremor shot through Alfonse's swollen fingers. With an ugly clang, the sword fell to the floor. The look he gave her left her devastated. "I should challenge this man to a duel, but I can't even hold my own sword."

She sobbed aloud at the thought of her husband fighting Will to defend her reputation.

"But Henry," Alfonse said. "Henry could challenge him."

"Henry shall do no such thing, and neither shall you." With shaking hands, she picked the sword off the floor and guided it back into its scabbard. "If you lose, you are slain. If you win, you are hanged. Remember what nearly happened to Ben?"

Her cousin had once killed a rival actor in a duel. Ben had escaped the hangman's noose only by his knowledge of an ancient law pardoning those who could read Psalm 51.

"But your honor," Alfonse said.

Aemilia laid the sheathed sword in his trunk then sat on the lid. "What pride hath lost, humility repairs," she said, quoting from her own poetry. She would challenge Will herself with the quill, not the sword.

When her husband sat beside her on the trunk, she shrank before his wounded eyes. Cupping his crippled hands in hers, she kissed them then cradled his head against her breast.

ALL MY LIFE *I have waited just for this.* At the age of forty, Aemilia would at last become a published woman of letters. She would do what even Papa had never dared—show her true face to the world. No more masks. She would trumpet her truth in the face of infamy.

Let this, her *Salve Deus Rex Judaeorum,* be her riposte against Will's cruel caricature of her, her reply couched not in drama or satire but in the only thing an Englishwoman might hope to write without condemnation—devotional Protestant verse. But as a woman writing in defense of Eve, Aemilia needed a circle of lady patrons to endorse her.

One by one she laid out the *tarocchi* cards that spelled out her destiny, those nine heroic women driving chariots and brandishing swords, holding stars and imperial scepters. That august circle of women would not just materialize out of the ether. She must seek them out. Margaret and Anne Clifford had already graced her with their support. What if she called upon seven other distinguished ladies, such as Mary Sidney Herbert, the Countess of Pembroke, whose poetry she so admired, and Lucy Russell, Countess of Bedford, one of

Ben's most generous patrons? This was no simple thing, seeing as Aemilia had no title or distinction and had been exiled from court more than sixteen years ago.

Ben had employed the language of courtly love to woo the patronage of Lucy Russell and the late Queen, a thing Aemilia herself could hardly do. Nor could she, as a woman, lay claim to the same kind of professional and public persona Ben had styled for himself as a poet-dramatist. In all England she had no female model to follow. She would have to forge her own way, soliciting the favor of lady patrons by praising their wit and virtue, comparing them to the biblical heroines of her poetry. She would call upon these ladies to support her so that she, in turn, could laud them and all women.

As well as paying tribute to Margaret and Anne Clifford, *Salve Deus* would offer Aemilia's heartfelt praise to Susan Bertie, who had educated her, and to the other ladies she most admired. And if she, being banished from court, couldn't access her icons face-to-face, she would woo them with her poetry, inviting them to her feast of words. *Saints like swans about the silver brook.* She would preface *Salve Deus* with poems in honor of each noble lady whose blessing she sought.

Aemilia's swan-feather quill, a gift from Ben, quaked in her hand as she began to write her first dedicatory poem, shocking herself with her own audacity as she addressed it to none other than Queen Anne.

> Renown Empress and Great Britain's Queen,
> Most gracious Mother of succeeding Kings,
> Vouchsafe to view that which is seldom seen,
> A Woman's writing of divinest things.

AEMILIA WROTE AND WROTE until her stack of pages doubled in height. Her manuscript now opened with nine dedications addressed to the aristocratic women whose patronage she most desired, beginning with three royal women: Queen Anne; Princess Elizabeth; and Arabella Stuart, the King's first cousin. Next came her loving homage to Susan Bertie, a poem of pure praise as Aemilia knew she could not expect any material support from her mentor who, like her, had fallen into decline. Then came her adulation of the poet Mary Sidney Herbert, the verses enthroning the lady as a goddess encircled by Muses. Following this was a poem to the Countess of Bedford; a prose dedication to her beloved Margaret; a poem to the Countess of Suffolk; and finally a poem for dear Anne, her former pupil. So that none would feel excluded, Aemilia had also penned a dedication to all virtuous women in general and to the reader of her book, whosoever he or she might be.

ALFONSE'S HEALTH KEPT DETERIORATING, and Aemilia devoted much of her time to nursing him.

"Me, I do not fear the plague," he told her, as he lay fevered in bed. "I am halfway to death's door already."

"Don't say such things," she said.

Though her husband was three years younger than she was, something in his eyes reminded her of Lord Hunsdon the last time she saw him before he passed away. Alfonse seemed filled with the stark recognition of the frailty of his own existence.

"Read to me from your *Salve Deus,*" he said. "Your voice when you read your poetry, it is like music."

And so she read aloud from her verses until she saw the solace that illumined his face.

WITH THE THEATERS CLOSED because of the plague, Will's sonnets seemed to be all that educated folk could talk about—at least those who remained in the environs of London instead of fleeing to the provinces. Aemilia struggled just to hold up her head as she walked through Clerkenwell and endured the stares and surmisings of those who connected the scheming dark temptress of the sonnets with her own tarnished history. She lost more than a few pupils.

Far worse were the sullen looks her son threw her way when he came home to visit. When they sat at the table and she anxiously inquired about his health in this time of pestilence, he hardly seemed capable of looking her in the eye. Aemilia thought she could have withstood any slight but this, her only surviving child's throbbing contempt of her.

Later, Aemilia overheard Henry speaking to Alfonse in his sickbed when the two of them were alone, no doubt believing themselves out of her earshot.

"I can't show my face anywhere without hearing murmurs that I'm the bastard son of a foreign whore."

"How dare you?" The anger in Alfonse's reply shook Aemilia to the marrow. "*Nom de Dieu,* she is your mother! Show some respect."

Aemilia crumpled to hear him, her much-betrayed husband, defending her to her own son.

And Margaret wrote in her next letter:

My dear, be bold and strong. The only humility we owe is to God, not to outraged men, even if they be our offspring. Write and publish your beautiful verses. Let your fountain never be diminished.

AEMILIA LEAFED THROUGH HER dedication poems, her long narrative of Christ's passion, and finally her elegiac poem, "The Description of Cookham," and her postscript to the doubtful reader that described how the title of her work had come to her. She read and reread every page, fretting over each line, until finally Ben wrested the manuscript from her hands.

In October 1610, a little more than a year after the publication of Will's sonnets, *Salve Deus Rex Judaeorum* was entered into the Stationers' Register and printed in January 1611.

WHAT A MIRACLE TO hold the small quarto volume bound in vellum. Aemilia couldn't keep herself from kissing it, the flowering of her life's work. Instead of silencing her, Will's denunciation of her had transformed her into a published poet. Here was her vindication of women, dedicated to the greatest women in the realm.

SALVE DEUS
REX JUDAEORUM
Containing,

1. The Passion of Christ.
2. Eves Apologie in defence of Women.

3. The Teares of the Daughters of Jerusalem.
4. The Salutation and Sorrow of the Virgine Marie.

With divers other things not unfit to be read.
Written by Mistris Aemilia Lanyer, Wife to Captaine
Alfonso Lanyer, Servant to the
Kings Majestie

"*Lanyer?*" Alfonse said, as he studied his copy. "This printer could not even spell our name?"

"Peace," said Ben. "It makes you both seem less foreign."

"Lanyer," Aemilia said, taking the measure of her new nom de plume. It was not unlike Peregrine Willoughby's renaming her when she first arrived at Grimsthorpe as an eight-year-old. *Aemilia is far too long and cumbersome a name for a child. Instead I shall call you Amy.* The printer's error had given her a brand-new identity.

Henry took the volume from Aemilia's hand and paged through each poem. Her son seemed staggered, for no other Englishwoman had ever published a printed volume of her own verse. This was something so astonishing and monumental, it would eclipse everything else Aemilia had done, even committing adultery and bearing two bastard children. She trembled to see her son gaze at her with such pride.

"I shall show my copy to everyone at court," Henry said.

"I shall ask Nicholas, my nephew, to give a copy to the Prince," Alfonse said.

Nicholas Lanier was Crown Prince Henry's music tutor.

With brimming eyes, Aemilia kissed her husband. "The Queen must have one, too. After all, the first poem is dedicated to her."

"I shall distribute your poetry in the highest circles," Ben said. "Will you walk me to the gate, dear cousin?"

When Aemilia and Ben were alone together, he whispered in her ear, "I shall even give a copy to You-Know-Who."

With a knowing wink, Ben placed the ten volumes he had purchased in his saddle bag and mounted up. His horse pulled a face as Ben settled his massive weight in the saddle.

After waving her farewells, Aemilia sat a spell in silence. She felt both triumphant and terrified to imagine Will reading her naked verses. *But no matter. He can no longer dismiss me or cast me into the shadows.* For now she, too, stood in the public eye as a poet with her name on her own book.

"MISTRESS, COME AND SEE the parcel that arrived!"

When Winifred thrust the package into her arms. Aemilia couldn't keep herself from squealing like a child.

"By my troth, that's the Countess of Pembroke's own seal!"

Before Winifred's inquisitive gaze, Aemilia opened the sacking-wrapped box to find a volume bound in calfskin. On its hand-scribed pages were Mary and Philip Sidney's poetic meditations on the Psalms. What a treasure, this book that was not formally published but only of-fered as a gift to a chosen few.

Accompanying the book was a letter, which Winifred insisted Ae-milia read aloud as she peered over her shoulder.

> *To Mistress Aemilia Lanyer,*
>
> *How I rejoice in your praise of women's virtue. Please accept this gift of the Sidney Psalter, the fruit of my collaboration with my great, departed brother. When you praise my poems over his, I fear you flatter me too much. Nonetheless, your words of admiration have touched my heart.*
>
> *I have ordered ten copies of* Salve Deus Rex Judaeorum. *God keep you and all the Muses crown you in laurels, good mistress.*
>
> *With many felicitations,*
> *Mary Sidney Herbert*

"Oh, Winifred, the great lady has read my poems!" The letter still clutched in her hand, Aemilia threw her arms around her maid.

THE LETTERS ARRIVED LIKE answered prayers. Susan sent her warm-est praise.

> *My dear, how brilliant you are! The greatest reward for a tutor is to see her protégée shine as radiantly as you, sweet Aemilia. I only wish I could afford to buy a copy of your book, so it is with much gratitude that I accept this, your gift.*

The Queen conveyed her best wishes on behalf of herself and her daughter and son. The Countess of Bedford commended Aemilia's work and ordered five copies. The Archbishop of Dublin gave Aemilia and Alfonse a gift of ten pounds. But Arabella Stuart had fallen out of favor and was imprisoned by order of the King. And the Countess of Suffolk was evidently too busy overseeing the building of Audley End House to respond.

But steadfast Margaret ordered a staggering twenty-five copies.

My dearest friend,

I cannot describe my joy to finally hold your published book in my hands. Likewise, I know that Anne finds much comfort in your verses. Alas, these are trying times for my daughter. Her husband has proved himself a brute. He has all but abandoned her at Knole whilst he swans about London with his mistresses. Neither will he grant her an income to maintain herself. He hopes to break her spirit so that she abandons the fight for her inheritance and signs over the monetary settlement to him.

Even the King seems pitted against Anne and me, yet whilst I have breath in my body, I shall battle on. My poor Anne says I am the only one left who takes her side. But I have witnessed with the gift of vision that victory shall indeed be hers if she only perseveres.

Thus I have urged her to reread your verses celebrating the women warriors of Scythia defeating the King of Persia.

The Scythian women by their power alone
Put King Darius unto shameful flight:
All Asia yielded to their conq'ring hand,
Great Alexander could not their power withstand.

If women in ancient times could take up arms, so must my daughter gird herself and keep her courage.

You, too, my friend, must hold fast to your mettle in the face of those slanderous sonnets. Your divine poetry shall restore your reputation and bring you the accolades you so deserve. If I had even a small hand in encouraging your art, I shall die a happy woman.

Your loving Margaret

Aemilia's eyes filled to learn that her former pupil was trapped in a marriage that sounded all too similar to the hell Angela had suffered—save for the fact that Anne had a strong mother who fought for her at every turn. But it tore at Aemilia that Margaret had closed her letter by alluding to her own death. With her prophetic gifts, did her friend see her demise glimmering on the horizon? Margaret's voice whispered comfort from afar. *I am always with you in spirit.*

WITH MARGARET'S CHERISHING WORDS, Fortune seemed to smile upon Aemilia and her household. Prudence came to join them in Clerkenwell Green, and under her care, Alfonse's health rallied. He rose from his sickbed to walk with Aemilia through the winding summer lanes. Their neighbors nodded to them, as if in deference to Aemilia's literary fame. Some of the music pupils she had lost in the wake of the scandal of Will's sonnets returned, their parents clamoring for Aemilia to teach their daughters Latin along with the virginals.

But if *Salve Deus* restored her good name, it did little to bring Aemilia more than a trickle of income. Books were expensive luxuries, and for all the novelty of *Salve Deus,* its intended audience of literate women was small. Religious poetry written by a female hand could not reap the same profits as a stage play that even the unlettered might enjoy or, indeed, garner the same attention as saucier verses such as Will's sonnets or his *Venus and Adonis.*

Aemilia tried to convince herself it didn't matter, for in 1612, a year after her book's publication, Alfonse finally received his promised patent on the weighing of hay and straw entering the cities of London and Westminster. It seemed that now her husband might finally make headway paying off his debts. Aemilia told herself that she had every reason to be content, that a good woman couldn't ask for anything more.

Yet it haunted Aemilia that one recipient of *Salve Deus* who still hadn't responded to its publication was Will, though Ben assured her he had placed a copy directly in Will's hand. For many months, she had braced herself for some stinging repartee or satire on his part ridiculing her poetic pretensions. But there was only silence. Did Will think this, her reply to his sonnets, unworthy of his notice? Courtesy demanded that he should at least send her a note of acknowledgment, however perfunctory.

AEMILIA BIDED HER TIME until Ben's next visit.

Her cousin was lately returned from a sojourn in Paris, where he had traveled as a tutor with his nineteen-year-old protégé, Wat Raleigh, whose father, Sir Walter Raleigh, had been locked in the Tower since Elizabeth's reign.

While Aemilia served Ben wine and sweetmeats, he regaled her with his adventures. "Dear cousin, had you only seen me. Young Wat contrived to get me dead drunk then laid me out in a cart, which he wheeled about the whole of Paris, telling its fair denizens that this was a livelier image of the crucifix than any they had."

Aemilia shuddered to imagine how much liquor her cousin had imbibed to leave him so inebriated. But when she could think of no reply and failed to even smile, her cousin leaned forward with a look of concern.

"Something troubles you," he said.

She forced herself to say the words. "Have you heard anything at all from Master Shakespeare?"

Ben clasped her hand. "Did you truly not hear the news? He's stopped writing plays and returned to Stratford."

Aemilia waited for Ben to burst out laughing at his own joke. But it appeared he was in earnest.

"He no longer writes?"

Impossible, she thought, remembering him shut up in their bedchamber in Verona, covering page after page as if in thrall to the poetry coursing through him. Now that she had become a published woman of letters, Will had ceased to write at all?

Ben shrugged. "In truth, he may of late have scribbled a play or two with some collaborator from the King's Men. But I fear we've seen the end of Shakespeare as we've come to know him."

EPILOGUE

So Come My Soul to Bliss as I Speak True

33

Stratford-upon-Avon, 1616

EMILIA TROTTED HER BORROWED mare down a road tunneled in arching leaves. She breathed in the air, redolent with blossoming elderflower. Whitethorn and blackthorn wove their branches in a living web, and at their feet sprang foxglove and greater Solomon's seal, everything glittering from the rain that had just ceased. From her perch in the saddle, her eyes sought out gaps in the hedge, hoping to catch a glimpse of the fabled Forest of Arden. Instead, she saw fields of wheat and barley, and pastures adrift in buttercups, until at last she reached the outskirts of Stratford.

"It seems an unremarkable place," said Henry, riding beside her, as they passed a row of cottages with unglazed windows.

At twenty-three, her son was only a year younger than Aemilia had been when she absconded to Italy with him as a babe in her arms. Tall and broad shouldered, Henry was armed with the sword and rapier Alfonse had wielded in the Irish wars.

"So hard to believe your father is already three years dead," she said.

Alfonse lay buried in Saint James's churchyard in Clerkenwell. He had left her with the straw and hay patent and thousands of pounds of debts. The thought of her late husband's unfulfilled life washed her in sorrow. If only she'd had the power to grant him his knighthood, his portion of glory.

"He wasn't my father." Henry stared straight ahead, his reproach of her hanging in the air between them.

Aemilia felt her temper flare. *Be thankful you're a man,* she wanted to tell him. *You will never have to make the same choices I was forced to make.* But when she replied, she kept her voice mild. "He was your father in every way that mattered."

She watched her son rub his wet eyes.

"He truly loved you," Henry said, glancing sideways at her. "He would hear no ill spoken of you."

Now it was her turn to blink back tears. She had begun to think that grief was her constant companion, for she was a woman twice bereaved. Not only had she lost her husband, but just a month ago Margaret had gone to her eternal rest. *How shall I live without you, my arctic star, my refuge?* On a silken cord around Aemilia's neck hung the golden ring Margaret had bequeathed to her, the precious metal warm against her heart.

If losing her dearest friend had left Aemilia anguished, Margaret's daughter was truly at sea, for Anne had lost her one champion in the battle for her inheritance. Her husband threatened to take her children away if she didn't submit. Aemilia carried her former pupil's letter in her saddle bag.

> *Oh, Aemilia, if you could only see me now. I am like an owl in the desert, so broken and hopeless. Every day I read your Cookham poem. My memories of our time there are one of my few remaining consolations.*

Wrenching her thoughts from Anne, Aemilia turned to her son. "It was good of you to make the journey with me."

They had been traveling for four days, covering about a hundred miles. Winifred had offered to accompany her as well, but her maid hadn't sat in a saddle for more than two decades. Aemilia had deemed it best to spare her the ordeal of the long-distance ride.

"I could hardly have you come all this way on your own, Mother." Henry spoke with an air of dutiful propriety that reminded her of Jasper.

Her son was as circumspect as she had been reckless at his age, as frugal as Alfonse had been spendthrift. Though Henry was a devastatingly handsome young man, with his natural father's aristocratic cheekbones and her own dark coloring, her son had vowed not to marry until they managed to pay off Alfonse's debts. She hoped her son wasn't condemning himself to a life of loneliness. To complicate matters, Alfonse's brother Innocent was badgering her to sign over the hay and straw patent to him as he had eight children to feed. He promised to have the patent renewed and divide the proceeds, but she didn't know if she could trust her brother-in-law to keep his word.

One thing remained certain—she needed to find a reliable source of income in her widowhood. After years of giving private lessons to young girls, she longed to have her own establishment where she could teach not just music but also Latin and Greek, offering the same kind of humanist education Susan Bertie had given her. After all, girls weren't welcome in the grammar schools and not every family, even among the gentry, could afford a private tutor. However, a day school for girls might be just within their reach.

Aemilia was negotiating to rent a property in Drury Lane near Saint Giles-in-the-Fields, where many wealthy families lived. If Fortune proved kind, the school would not only allow her to pay off Alfonse's debts but also widen the circle of learned young women. Then again, so many of her dreams had been dashed. Did she dare believe in this one?

She and Henry rode through Rother Market, where the houses grew more substantial as befitting a thriving town of two thousand souls. Still, it seemed such a small place, as though its burghers were resigned to live their lives in miniature far away from the great stage of power and influence. She could still not grasp why Will at the very height of his success had retired to this backwater never to write another play.

Townspeople gaped at her and her son. It seemed they were unused to the sight of strangers, especially one as fetching as Henry. When he stopped to ask one of the market wives where they could find respectable lodgings, Aemilia observed how the young woman gazed at him as though he were Adonis fallen to earth. But Henry seemed oblivious to her adoration.

"The Swan Inn in Bridge Street, sir." The woman pointed out the direction they must go.

Aemilia murmured her thanks and pressed a silver penny in the woman's hand.

ONCE THEY HAD SECURED rooms at the Swan and Aemilia had washed and changed into her good gown, she asked the innkeeper the way to New Place.

The man snapped to attention. "Good mistress, what business have you at New Place?"

She hesitated, knowing that whatever she replied would be spread across town, giving the gossips something to chew on.

"I'll hazard it's Master Shakespeare you've come all this way to see," the innkeeper said. "I fear you're too late. He died in April."

"I've heard the sad tidings," she said, lowering her head in respect for the deceased.

A fortnight ago Aemilia had received a letter from Will's eldest daughter summoning her to Stratford on account of a secret bequest he had left to her, one that did not involve money. *Should you venture here for lucre's sake,* the letter had sternly informed her, *you shall be sorely disappointed.*

"In faith, it's Mistress Susanna Hall I've come to see." Aemilia regarded the innkeeper without shame, as befitting a woman of forty-seven years clad in the sober attire of a widow. She told herself that no stranger could even guess at her past.

The innkeeper nodded, his curiosity apparently sated, for surely a widow calling on a matron was hardly a matter worthy of further speculation.

"Doctor Hall is away in Warwick," he said, "but you'll find Mistress Hall at home. It's not ten minutes' walk from here, New Place is. I suspect even a Londoner like you will find it impressive. Left it all to his daughter and son-in-law, Master Shakespeare did. Shamefully neglected his own wife in the will, though. That's what everyone round here says."

Aemilia's heart pricked to think of poor Anne Shakespeare and all she had endured.

"You speak as if Master Shakespeare was not the most popular man in Stratford," she said.

The innkeeper nodded, as though he harbored strong opinions on the subject. "First he runs away, a young father leaving behind three little children. His wife never complained, mind you. She just carried on with her brewing and did as best she could. Then he returns, as rich as a lord and as arrogant, too, hoarding grain in his barn during the famine a few years back when we'd hunger riots in the streets."

Aemilia struggled to connect the landlord's description of this avaricious man to the Will she had known, that hungry poet who had devoured the lamb pie she brought to him at his boardinghouse.

"But he stood by his daughter," the innkeeper said. "I'll grant him that. Terrible scandal three years ago. A scoundrel and drunkard accused Mistress Hall of adultery."

Aemilia felt a welling of sympathy for Susanna Hall. What she herself had suffered from her damaged reputation was one thing, but in a provincial town like this, even the rumor of adultery could destroy a woman. Perhaps if Mistress Hall had been forced to withstand such defamation, she would be more merciful to someone like Aemilia.

"Doctor Hall took the accuser to court and had him sentenced for slander," the innkeeper said. "For slander it truly was. I'll speak no ill of Mistress Hall. Her sister, Judith, is another matter. She was foolish enough to marry Thomas Quiney, the wretched fornicator—"

The innkeeper stopped short, as if suddenly remembering he was speaking to a lady.

HENRY INSISTED ON ESCORTING Aemilia to New Place.

"Are you sure this is prudent?" he asked. "You know nothing about this Mistress Hall. Why would she call on you to arrive precisely when her husband is away?"

Aemilia could think of a reason or two but kept them to herself.

When she turned the corner of Chapel Street, the sight of New Place was enough to stop her breath. Built of brick and timber, the house boasted five gables, ten chimneys, and many glass windows. She could scarcely imagine Will, the luckless poet she had once loved, living in this palatial dwelling set among its gardens lush with topiary and roses. The grounds were huge. Off to the far side, she noted an orchard, and over the treetops, the roofs of two barns.

"You said he was a glover's son?" Henry asked, disbelief and envy twining in his voice.

She wondered if somewhere in the furthest reaches of her son's memory, he recalled their idyll in Italy when Will had carried him on his shoulders and held him with such tenderness, as if he were his own.

At the front gate Aemilia nodded farewell to her son before continuing alone up the path to the massive oak door, engraved with the Shakespeare coat of arms and motto, *Non sanz droict*.

A maid, brawny and brisk, answered the door. "Mistress Lannery? Mistress Hall is expecting you." She ushered Aemilia into a vast parlor. "Wait here, if you please. Mistress Hall shall join you shortly."

Wealth gleamed in every nook and corner, from the carved and painted beams to the silver candlesticks and Dutch oil paintings. In one short life, Will had amassed a fortune. A tapestry of a hunting party riding through a forest covered most of one wall. So much was on display, it was almost vulgar. But Aemilia felt not the faintest sense of Will as she had known him. Nothing of his essence.

Her eyes then lit on the most exquisite virginals she had seen since her days at court. The body of the instrument was inlaid with ivory, mother-of-pearl, and alabaster, and the soundboard was painted with a pastoral scene of shepherdesses and their swains sporting in an eternal Arcadia. Beneath the scene, engraved in gilded letters, were the words she found herself speaking aloud.

"*Sic transit gloria mundi.*" Thus passes the glory of the world.

"You read Latin, Mistress Lanier," a voice behind her said.

When Aemilia turned to face Susanna Hall, it was like seeing her lost love brought back to life in the guise of a woman. She kept blinking to keep from losing herself in those clouded hazel eyes. A few soft brown curls escaped Mistress Hall's coif to soften her high, intelligent brow. Her gown was of dove-gray silk, edged in black brocade. She wore pearls at her throat and gold rings on her fingers. A fine-looking matron of thirty-three years.

"Mistress Hall," Aemilia said.

She dropped into a curtsy though, in truth, it wasn't necessary. Despite their gaping differences in fortune, Susanna Hall was not of higher birth. As gentlemen's daughters, they were of fairly equal standing, though Aemilia's family was older. Battista Bassano had not needed to *buy* his coat of arms. Then Aemilia abandoned such petty thoughts and spoke from her heart, as one grieving woman to another.

"May I offer my condolences for your father's passing."

Susanna Hall seemed at a loss to know what to say or how to treat her. Aemilia could only wonder what Will had told his daughter about her. Did the woman have any inkling that she had invited her late father's former mistress into the family home?

"You must be so proud of your father," Aemilia said, when she could no longer bear the silence between them. "Do you have a favorite amongst his plays?"

"Sometimes he read to me various speeches and scenes," Mistress Hall said, her eyes guarded, her voice tepid. "But all I know of the theater is hearsay."

Aemilia nodded, for it made sense that Mistress Hall had never visited the Globe. What gentleman would wish to expose his sheltered provincial daughter to Southwark with its bawdy houses and gambling dens?

"But I trust you've read his poetry," Aemilia said, hoping to kindle even the tiniest spark of warmth in her hostess.

Mistress Hall looked pained. "Madam, I cannot read."

This revelation left Aemilia incredulous. Though she knew Will's wife was illiterate, she had thought that the daughters of such a great man of letters would at least be able to read and write. Even in his poorer days, he had managed to send his son to grammar school. Surely when wealth came his way, he could have hired a private tutor for his girls.

Yet Will must have cherished Susanna — had he not left most of his vast estate to her and her husband? Of all the women in his life, it seemed he'd loved his firstborn above all others. Perhaps he had hoped that his tenderness to Susanna might redeem his every slight to other women, including Susanna's mother.

"Then who wrote the letter inviting me here?" Aemilia asked. It had indeed looked to be written in a woman's hand.

"My friend. She's a curate's daughter, uncommonly educated. But even *she* can't read Latin."

Aemilia didn't know what to say. At least it was a relief to learn that Mistress Hall hadn't read the sonnets.

"I forget my manners," her hostess said. "Please, sit you down. You must be weary from your journey."

She offered Aemilia a glass of Madeira.

As Aemilia took her first sip of the sweet wine, she noticed a little girl peeking around the chamber door. She looked to be about eight, with dark gold locks and merry mischief in her eyes as she gawped at the mysterious guest.

"Your daughter, Mistress Hall?" Aemilia said, alerting her to the child's presence.

Her hostess sprang to her feet. "Elizabeth, you naughty girl. You're meant to be helping your grandmother."

Her grandmother. With a stab of remorse, Aemilia wondered if Anne Shakespeare was privy to who she was and why she had come. *To have your revenge of me, all you need do is poison the Madeira.*

"Mother, who is that lady?" the child demanded, refusing to abandon her sentinel post.

To cover her mother's embarrassed silence, Aemilia spoke up. "My late husband was a stage minstrel for your grandfather. I've come to pay my respects to your good mother."

As lies went, it was close enough to fact to ring true.

The girl's eyes sparked. It seemed the word *minstrel* was the one that intrigued her most. "Can you play the virginals?"

"The virginals and the lute," Aemilia told her.

"Can you play the virginals *now*?"

"Elizabeth, that's enough," said her mother. "Off you go."

"Pleased to meet you, madam." The girl displayed a most impressive curtsy.

"And you, Elizabeth," Aemilia said.

Before her mother could scold her again, the girl pranced away.

"What a lovely child," Aemilia said, grateful to have a reason to smile. "I had a daughter—" Her eyes stinging, she caught herself and said no more.

Mistress Hall met her gaze. "I know."

Aemilia's hand shook so hard, she spilled the Madeira on her lap.

Will had not only told Susanna about their affair but also about Odilia? If their child had lived, she would have been twenty-one this year. Susanna's half sister. To her horror, Aemilia found she was in tears.

"I had better take my leave." Her hips stiff from the long ride, Aemilia levered herself up from the chair.

"Not just yet, if you please." Mistress Hall stood in her path. "First let's finish this business, shall we?"

Aemilia thought her hostess looked as miserable as she herself felt.

Mistress Hall turned her head and waited while Aemilia dried her tears then led her up a flight of stairs. From the chatelaine at her waist, she selected a key and unlocked a door. A wave of musty air struck Aemilia's face as they entered a dim room. Mistress Hall flung open the windows and shutters, allowing the early evening sunlight and breeze to sweep away the staleness.

"Father's study," she said.

Aemila gazed at the desk with its ink pot and quills, its foolscap and blotter, everything laid out in orderly fashion as though Will would return at any moment and sit down to write. She studied an oil painting of the Globe, which had burned to the ground three years ago, and then she shivered at the sight of a human skull. Will's ghostly presence seemed to fill the room. She almost felt his breath stirring at her nape. With a rush of blood behind her eyes, she saw her own *Salve Deus* on his bookshelf, resting beside his Ovid. So had he read her work after all? Had he treasured her book enough to keep it here, in his *sanctum sanctorum*?

So as not to betray her emotions, she turned to examine the map of Bermuda hanging on the wall. Beside it was an etching of a denizen of that isle arrayed in feathers and shells.

"In his last years, Father became fascinated with the New World," Mistress Hall said. "Had he been younger, I think he would have sailed to the West Indies."

Susanna's face seemed flushed with memories of her father. But then, as if reminding herself of the task at hand, she unlocked a cabinet and hefted from it a scarred wooden box with its own lock. As she grappled with its weight, Aemilia leaned forward to help her. Together they laid it on the desk. Mistress Hall then removed the smallest key from her chatelaine and handed it to Aemilia.

"Father wanted you to have this," she said, looking at the box. "I was to give it directly to you in person. He swore me to the strictest secrecy, forbade me to tell even my husband." Only now did she lift her eyes, bright with tears. "I ask you to be discreet as not to bring any dishonor on my poor mother."

"Mistress Hall, you have my word." Aemilia longed to take her hand but didn't dare. "In faith, I'm astonished you even went through with this. You could have refused."

Susanna Hall shook her head. "He made me promise. I think he feared he would wander forever in purgatory if he didn't do right by you. He was so given to popish superstitions, that man."

Aemilia imagined Will on his deathbed entrusting his beloved daughter with his soul's turmoil. "You were his confessor," she said gently.

"To listen to my father, only your pardon could wash him clean."

"By my troth," Aemilia said, her own tears welling up again. "I forgave him years ago."

For to forgive someone is to set that person's highest essence free. Now, in her heart, Aemilia absolved Will. *Let his noblest self shine through all eternity.* Not the miser who hoarded grain or the callous husband, but the poet whose tears she had touched upon a midsummer night twenty-three years ago.

Will's daughter, his female image, gave her a searching look. "Mistress Lanier, I wanted to hate you, but you confound me. He said he'd written poetry about you, but he wouldn't read a word of it to me. Beyond being his mistress, I never knew who or what you were."

"Would you know truly?" Aemilia gazed into those hazel eyes. "I am a poet."

She was tempted to take her own book from the shelf and place it in Susanna Hall's hands. But that would be taking too great a liberty. Besides, Mistress Hall seemed stunned enough as it was. In her silence, Aemilia could not keep herself from stroking one of the quills that lay on her dead lover's desk. *He held this in his hand.*

"Pray, keep it," his daughter said, when Aemilia laid the quill back down. "I think he would have wanted it so."

MISTRESS HALL'S STRAPPING MAIDSERVANT agreed to haul the heavy box back to the Swan Inn. As Aemilia descended the stairs with mistress and maid, she caught a whiff of yeast and hops. Through walls and closed doors came the muffled sound of an older woman singing and her granddaughter laughing. *With Doctor Hall away, Will's house has become a house of women,* Aemilia thought, *almost like Cookham in the old days, with the Widow Shakespeare as its beer-brewing matriarch.*

The key to the box in her hand, Aemilia followed the maid out a rear door and through the back gardens, past the sheds and barns, and out the back gate. They proceeded down a narrow alley shadowed in over-grown hedges, cut through a snicket, and finally crossed Bridge Street to reach the Swan Inn, all the while trying to attract as little attention as possible.

Aemilia found Henry waiting for her. He raised his eyebrows as she led the maid up to her chamber, where the girl plunked the box on a table as though it were an exceptionally heavy crate of onions.

"My thanks to you and your good mistress." Aemilia pressed a tuppence in the girl's palm.

"WE RODE A HUNDRED miles so you could claim a shabby old box," Henry said, as he and his mother ate their supper. "Pray, what's inside?"

"Hush," Aemilia murmured, aware of the others eating and drinking in the Swan Inn, no doubt eager for anything to gab about. "I haven't opened it yet. Tomorrow, before we depart, I shall go to Holy Trinity Church and visit his grave."

Her son nodded as though he couldn't wait to return to London and put this strange pilgrimage into his mother's past behind him.

AFTER BIDDING HENRY GOODNIGHT, Aemilia shut herself in her chamber. With the midsummer sun still blazing in the western sky, she'd no need to light a candle. Breathless, she unlocked the box and opened the lid to see a letter resting on a sheet of foolscap, which hid what lay beneath. *Yet one more secret concealed inside another.* When she broke the letter's seal, she couldn't say what she hoped to find. An apology? An explanation for his cold shunning of her? Poetry even? What message did Will have for her after these twenty-one years of separation?

Though she still recognized his handwriting, she could tell it was a weak and ailing man who had gripped the quill. His missive consisted of four words.

For my eternal Muse

From the folded paper, a gold ring tumbled into her palm. She held it aloft in the shaft of sunlight streaming through the open window until her tears blurred her vision. This was the ring he had given her in Verona those many years ago and that she had returned to him after Odilia's christening. She clasped it in both hands before setting it carefully aside, then she lifted the foolscap to see what was underneath.

Despite the bright daylight illuminating the chamber, she did not trust her senses. The stack of papers was high and densely packed, all in Will's handwriting. She had to take them from the box and leaf through them from top to bottom before she believed what her eyes saw. His plays, the oldest at the top and the newest toward the bottom. His histories, comedies, and tragedies. Some were flawless or near-flawless fair copies while others appeared to be working drafts with scribbled corrections and crossed-out lines. She found the early comedies that they had written together and that he had gone on to revise and make wholly his own, as if to erase her.

Yet, as she scanned his plays and their lists of characters, she saw variations of her name in three other pieces she'd had no hand in. Here, in *A Comedy of Errors,* was Aemilia, the long-lost wife of Aegeon. Husband and wife had been severed from each other in a shipwreck. In the end, Aegeon finally found his Aemilia, who had been living as an abbess.

When the midsummer sun finally sank into the whispering trees, she lit a candle to read on. She remembered *Othello's* Emilia, wife of the villainous Iago who slew her for her loose tongue. Yet as she began to reread Emilia's lines, she discovered that Will had rewritten them since she had seen the play performed at Shoreditch those many years ago. Emilia was much more eloquent than she remembered, lamenting the injustices that women suffered:

'Tis not a year or two shows us a man.
They are all but stomachs and we all but food.
They eat us hungerly, and when they are full,
They belch us.

Lines that cut so close to what she had endured after Will cast her off, she might have written them herself. Had he allowed her, his banished mistress, to speak through his own heroine? This Emilia even spoke in defense of women who commit adultery.

I do think it is their husbands' faults
If wives do fall . . .
Their wives have sense like them. They see and smell
And have their palates both for sweet and sour
. . . And have not we affections,
Desires for sport, and frailty, as men have?
. . . let them know
The ills we do, their ills instruct us so.

But it was Emilia's devotion to her lady, Desdemona, that moved Aemilia most, for it reminded her of what she and Margaret shared. When Emilia learned the full breadth of her husband's evil plot against Desdemona, she proclaimed his culpability to all. As Emilia declared her truth, her husband murdered her.

I will speak as liberal as the north,
Let heaven and men and devils, let them all,
All, all cry shame against me, yet I'll speak.

So come my soul to bliss as I speak true.
So speaking as I think, alas, I die.

Lines so passionate, they might have come from her own *Salve Deus.* Aemilia cradled the pages to her heart. Emilia's speech read as though she were Will's immortalized memory of *her,* Aemilia, as she truly was. Not the lascivious tigress of the sonnets but a woman who was passionate, free-spoken, intelligent, and brave. His lost love. Her own best self.

Taking the gold ring he had returned to her, she threaded it on the silk cord around her neck so it would rest there beside Margaret's ring.

By candlelight, she nestled in bed and read *The Winter's Tale*, probably one of his later works since she'd found it near the bottom of the stack. Here Emilia was a minor character with only a few lines, maid to the much-wronged Hermione. Leontes, Hermione's husband, spent sixteen years repenting his cruelty to his deceased wife. He had falsely accused her of adultery, imprisoned her, even wrenched her newborn daughter from her arms and ordered the infant to be abandoned. Everything was poised for irredeemable tragedy and yet, in the final act, the lost daughter, Perdita, returned. Reunited, father and daughter stood before a statue of the dead Hermione. Faced by their grief and love, the effigy revealed itself as the living woman, Hermione restored.

> If this be magic, let it be an art
> Lawful as eating.

Aemilia wept to imagine that *The Winter's Tale*, written in the winter of Will's life, resurrected both their love and their lost daughter. *Let Odilia live again in Perdita.* Had he spent the past twenty-one years rueing their estrangement?

Before the candle burned itself out, she set to read *The Tempest*, which she had discovered at the very bottom of the stack—presumably the last play he had written. She expected tragedy or tragicomedy, but, no, this was an Italian comedy concerning a magician and his only daughter. Here she saw her father brought back to life with none of the viciousness of *The Merchant of Venice*. Ariel, his spirit-servant, even uttered the line Papa had once whispered in her ear, "Hell is empty." All the devils roved here on earth, in plain sight, which explained the many enchantments Prospero wove to protect his treasured Miranda on their island stronghold before he set her free to explore her brave new world.

Will's poetry sent her heart brimming with a lifetime's yearnings.

Full fathom five thy father lies,
Of his bones are coral made,
Those are pearls that were his eyes.
Nothing of him that doth fade
But doth suffer a sea-change
Into something rich and strange.
Sea-nymphs hourly ring his knell.

"Rest you gentle, my love," she whispered to Will, who slumbered now with the rest of her beloved dead: Papa, Odilia, Henry Carey, Margaret, and Alfonse.

We are such stuff
As dreams are made on, and our little life
Is rounded with a sleep.

In the last minutes before the candle guttered out, Aemilia found Will's letter, that single line: *For my eternal Muse.* Finally, she understood. He hadn't needed to say more — the plays said it for him. Those four words were his dedication, his revelation that she had been his inspiration even after their love had turned to pain, even when he hated her and had written his tortured tragedies. This was his confession that his plays were written to her and for her long after they had ceased to be lovers.

Let us not burden our remembrance with
A heaviness that's gone.

In the depths of his heart, he had never stopped loving her, and this had been his most anguished secret, which he hadn't been able to admit even to himself until the very last. All those years, he had held on to her ring. In death, he entrusted his life's work to her.

Like his plays, their intertwined lives had moved from comedy to tragedy to tragicomedy and back to comedy once more. Reconciliation transformed the tragedies of human existence into a divine comedy — what life, at its core, truly was — as she had tried to tell him in

Verona all those years ago. *What could touch the spirit more deeply than the triumph of love and goodness?*

To insure Will's posterity, she must see these plays published. But she would have to keep her hand in it secret in respect to the promise she had made to Susanna Hall. If Will's work were to be published under the auspices of the King's Men, it would seem both natural and fitting. Ben would write the preface, his immortal tribute to his rival and friend. Once more, men would be her mask and she would be erased. Yet she was the indelible thread woven into Will's great tapestry. Long after she was buried, future generations might read of questing girls who dressed as boys, of a Jew's daughter, of Emilia who died speaking her truth.

In her last letter before her death, Margaret had predicted that Aemilia would survive to a venerable age and remain in robust health until her black hair turned as white as a swan's feathers. The ghosts of her past laid to rest, Aemilia could embrace her future with courage.

"So speaking as I think," she whispered to the wheeling stars outside her window, "I live, I live, I live."

To the Virtuous Reader:

Historical Afterword

THIS IS A WORK OF FICTION. There is no historical evidence to prove that Aemilia Bassano Lanier was the Dark Lady of Shakespeare's sonnets. The late A. L. Rowse was the first to identify Lanier as the Dark Lady; however, most academics have dismissed his theory. Lanier scholars in particular find the Dark Lady question an unwelcome detraction from Lanier's own literary achievements. Aemilia Bassano Lanier has earned her place in history not by any alleged love affair but by becoming the first Englishwoman to aspire to earn her living as a professional, published poet, one who actively sought a community of women patrons to support her writing.

Having established these facts, I must confess that as a *novelist* I could not resist the allure of the Dark Lady mythos. As Kate Chedgzoy points out in her essay "Remembering Aemilia Lanyer" in the *Journal of the Northern Renaissance,* this myth draws on "our continuing cultural investment in a fantasy of a female Shakespeare and reveals some of the anxieties about difference that haunt canonical Renaissance literature." My intention was to write a novel that married the playful comedy of Marc Norman and Tom Stoppard's *Shakespeare in Love* to the gravitas of Virginia Woolf's discussion of Shakespeare's "sister" in her extended essay *A Room of One's Own.* How many more obstacles would an educated and gifted Renaissance woman poet face compared to her ambitious male counterparts?

I am deeply indebted to the scholarship of Susanne Woods whose books *Lanyer: A Renaissance Woman Poet* and *The Poems of Aemilia Lanyer: Salve Deus Rex Judaeorum* proved indispensable, both for my research into the documented facts of Lanier's life and my appreciation of her poetry. I was also hugely inspired by the work of Lanier scholars Barbara K. Lewalski and Lynette McGrath.

Readers may wish to know that Lanier did indeed go on to run her own school in Saint Giles-in-the-Fields from 1617 to 1619. However, she faced difficulties with her landlord in a dispute over rent and repairs, and this appears to have put a premature end to her venture. Financial problems followed Lanier for the rest of her life. Her son died in 1633, leaving behind two small children. Lanier then litigated against Innocent Lanier, her brother-in-law, to whom she signed over her late husband's hay and straw patent with the understanding that Innocent would get it extended and share the proceeds. It appears her brother-in-law did not honor his side of the bargain. Lanier presented herself as petitioning on behalf of her orphaned grandchildren, so it appears that she was supporting them.

But when Lanier died in Clerkenwell in 1645 at the age of seventy-six, she was listed as a pensioner, indicating some source of regular income. Though I have no proof, I would like to believe that her former pupil Anne Clifford supported her in her old age. By this time, Clifford had weathered two stormy marriages and outlived the uncle who had usurped her inheritance. After decades of adversity, the widowed Clifford triumphed to become one of the wealthiest and most powerful landowners in northern England. Readers may wish to visit the Countess Pillar near Penrith, Cumbria, which Anne built as a memorial to her beloved mother, Margaret.

While there is no evidence that Aemilia Bassano Lanier ever cross-dressed, some of her female contemporaries did so with gusto and aplomb, most notably the notorious Mary Frith, the real-life inspiration for Thomas Middleton and Thomas Dekker's comedy, *The Roaring Girl*. Female cross-dressing was a popular motif not just in English comedy but also across Europe. In his 1615 comedy *Don Gil of the Green Breeches*, Spanish playwright Tirso de Molina takes his cross-dressing heroine even further than Shakespeare did in *Twelfth Night* — de Molina's Donna Juana constantly switches gender identities while pursuing her absconding lover.

I have taken some liberties with dates and chronology. Robert Greene, whose pamphlet satirized Shakespeare as an "upstart crow," died in 1592 and thus would not have been present at Southampton's party. Shakespeare's son, Hamnet, was buried in August 1596 and Lanier's daughter, listed as "Odillya" in the church registry, was baptized in December 1598 and buried in September 1599. The premiere of *Twelfth Night* did not take place until 1602.

Most sources name Aemilia's husband as Alfonso Lanier, not Alfonse. He may have been Lucrezia Bassano Lanier's son rather than her stepson, making him Franco-Italian rather than French. His voyage to the Azores with Essex took place in 1597 and his arrest for disturbing the peace in Hackney took place in 1609. While there is no evidence that Alfonso ever contracted the French pox (syphilis), Henry Carey's son George, the second Lord Hunsdon, died prematurely of the disease, which was commonplace in this era.

It is possible, though not provable, that Ben Jonson was related to Lanier on her mother's side of the family. Even if they were not related, they almost certainly knew each other as Alfonso's nephew, Nicholas Lanier, and his brother-in-law, Alfonso Ferrabosco, composed stage music for Jonson's plays and masques.

However, there is no evidence that the painter Jacopo Bassano was related to Battista Bassano and his brothers, or that Lanier's relations ever resided in the Casa dal Corno in Bassano del Grappa. Historians remain divided over the veracity of Battista Bassano's Jewish origins — some suggest Battista and his brothers emigrated to England because they were Protestant. Riccardo Calimani's *The Ghetto of Venice* was essential reading in my attempt to portray Battista Bassano's history as a Marrano, a secret Jew. Not being Jewish myself, I am immensely grateful to my friend and colleague Sue Stern and my agent, Jennifer Weltz, who critiqued the manuscript from a Jewish perspective. Any mistakes are my own.

My portrayal of Anne Shakespeare as a brewer and businesswoman is drawn from Germaine Greer's book, *Shakespeare's Wife*.

Undoubtedly, the biggest controversy this novel is likely to generate will be over my fictional portrait of William Shakespeare, not least because of my depiction of his sexuality and his writing some of his early comedies with a — female! — collaborator.

Mainstream scholars have been speculating about Shakespeare's apparent attraction to other men for quite some time. Stephen Greenblatt's *Will in the World: How Shakespeare Became Shakespeare* was a huge influence on me, especially in regard to Greenblatt's reflections on Shakespeare's Catholic loyalties, his possible Lancashire connections, and his sexuality. Michael Wood has suggested that Shakespeare was probably bisexual. In his book and BBC series *In Search of Shakespeare,* Wood points out that the most beautiful and tender of Shakespeare's sonnets, including the iconic "Shall I Compare Thee to a Summer's Day?" are addressed not to a woman but to a fair youth, who may or may not be Henry Wriothesley, the Earl of Southampton, a fair youth if ever there was one. Why modern readers, in our age of gay pride and marriage equality, would find the idea of Shakespeare's love for other men offensive or disturbing is another question.

Moving on to the most contentious issue, the authorship debate: I am in no way stating that Shakespeare did not write his own work. However, most academics acknowledge that some of Shakespeare's plays were collaborations with other playwrights and that Shakespeare's plays were altered over time. Some earlier versions of his plays originally published in quarto form underwent significant revision before they were published in the First Folio of 1623. Perhaps it isn't so far-fetched to suggest Shakespeare worked with a collaborator on some of his early comedies then later reworked these same plays, editing out the collaborator's contributions to reflect his own individual voice and vision. As the late G. B. Harrison revealed in his edition of *Shakespeare: The Complete Works,* there was indeed an early version of *The Taming of the Shrew* in which Emelia undermines Kate's homily of wifely obedience by stating that she would rather be a shrew than a sheep.

As James Shapiro's *Contested Will: Who Wrote Shakespeare?* attests, the authorship debate has ceased to be a far-left-field conspiracy theory and has entered the academic mainstream. The discussion is unlikely to be resolved any time soon.

Any fictional treatment of Shakespeare that addresses his actual humanity and human foibles risks running the gauntlet of an army of ferocious Bardolators willing to fight to the death to defend their icon. But it is in no way a detraction from Shakespeare's undisputed genius to place him in context. He was no isolated monolith but instead a denizen of a richly interconnected, interwoven world of Renaissance poetry and drama. I believe readers will glean an even richer appreciation for Shakespeare if they read his work alongside the writings of his contemporaries — Aemilia Bassano Lanier, Ben Jonson, Mary Sidney Herbert, Samuel Daniel, and the delightful Isabella Andreini.

ACCOLADES AND PRAISE POEMS for Jennifer Weltz, my agent, and for Nicole Angeloro, my editor, who studied Aemilia Bassano Lanier's *Salve Deus Rex Judaeorum* at Brown University. My deep appreciation goes out to the entire team at Houghton Mifflin Harcourt. I am also deeply indebted to David Hough, a most thorough and wise copy editor and fact-checker.

My heartfelt gratitude goes out to the kind people at the Jewish Museum in Venice, which was indispensable for my research. *Grazie mille* to the wonderful staff at the City Library and Museum in Bassano del Grappa, where I was introduced to Jacopo Bassano's monumental paintings. Shakespeare's Globe in London is a fantastic resource, not just for Shakespeare's plays but his entire world. The British Museum's 2012 exhibition "Shakespeare: Staging the World" was absolutely riveting; it was here I discovered the novelty painting of the Venetian courtesan sporting breeches and a codpiece beneath her skirts. The Shakespeare Birthplace Trust does a fine job of stewarding the Stratford properties associated with Shakespeare's life. I particularly enjoyed my visit to New Place Gardens and Nash's House.

Endless love and thanks to my husband, Jos Van Loo, who read *The Dark Lady's Mask* in manuscript and accompanied me on my many research trips, museum jaunts, and theater visits. A wreath of laurels for my writers' group, that circle of enthroned Muses: Cath Staincliffe, Sue Stern, Catherine Robinson, Olivia Roberts, and Anjum Malik. The Historical Novel Society continues to be a nurturing community and font of inspiration. Lastly, I wish to lay a garland of carrots at the hooves of Mistress Boo, my equine Muse, who appears in the novel as Aemilia's beloved Bathsheba.